THE MEMORY BOX

Sarah Webb worked as a children's bookseller for many years before becoming a full-time writer. She has written eleven novels including *The Shoestring Club*, the first novel about the Schuster sisters, Julia and Pandora.

She also writes a young teenage series, Ask Amy Green, and her books have been published in many different countries, including Poland, Italy, Indonesia and the United States.

Find out more and read Sarah's Yours in Writing blog at
www.sarahwebb.ie

Or connect with Sarah on Facebook:
www.facebook.com/sarahwebbwriter

Or Twitter: @sarahwebbishere

The
MEMORY BOX

Sarah Webb

PAN BOOKS

First published 2013 by Macmillan

This edition published 2013 by Pan Books
an imprint of Pan Macmillan, a division of Macmillan Publishers Limited
Pan Macmillan, 20 New Wharf Road, London N1 9RR
Basingstoke and Oxford
Associated companies throughout the world
www.panmacmillan.com

ISBN 978-0-330-51945-8

1 3 5 7 9 8 6 4 2

A CIP catalogue record for this book is available from the British Library.

Typeset by Ellipsis Digital, Glasgow
Printed and bound by CPI Group (UK) Ltd, Croydon, CR0 4YY

Visit **www.panmacmillan.com** to read more about all our books
and to buy them. You will also find features, author interviews and
news of any author events, and you can sign up for e-newsletters
so that you're always first to hear about our new releases.

This book is dedicated to my mum,
Melissa Webb,
with love and respect

We are all in the gutter, but some of us are looking at the stars.

OSCAR WILDE

Chapter 1

Meltdowns are a funny old thing. You can be as together as you like, and then one day – BOOM – out of the blue, something throws you into a messy tailspin. Your hands shake, your breath shunts in and out like an engine piston and you freefall into full panic mode.

For some people it can be triggered by something as simple as turning thirty. For others – me, for example – meltdowns are a little more complicated. I'm self-combusting on the inside and it's slow, ever so slow, like sparks flying off a piece of flint and never quite catching; but when they do, watch out for the furnace. For me the trigger is something rather more serious than a birthday.

Right now I'm sitting behind the till at Shoestring, the second-hand designer clothes shop I run, peering at the computer screen, when my sister, Jules, wanders in the door pushing her road bike in front of her with one hand, ten minutes late. My mind's all over the place this morning; I'm supposed to be updating our website before the shop floor starts to get too busy – adding new stock and taking down anything we've sold – but I'm finding it desperately hard to concentrate, so I'm glad for the distraction.

'Hey, Pandora, have you thought any more about your birthday present?' she says without preamble, propping her bike against the desk, swinging her bag off her shoulder and

1

dumping it on the floor, and then leaning over and plonking her elbows down on the desk, making the bracelets on her wrist jangle down her arm. She's wearing a very odd-looking outfit today – nothing new for Jules – red knitted leggings, yellow cut-off denim shorts and a purple bat-winged top.

'I had an idea on the way over,' she continues, oblivious to either my stares at her get-up or the fact that she's late for work yet again. Jules is always late; her timekeeping is appalling. But even though I know this, it still irritates me. 'How about handmade leather gloves? There's a little place in town that makes them to measure and you can choose the leather and the lining. I know you like practical presents and it's something a bit different. I'm not giving you a voucher again, not for your thirtieth.'

I've been mulling over how to work my birthday – which is in just over two weeks, on 12 May – into a conversation for days, and now that Jules has given me the opening, I may as well get it out there. Trying to sound as breezy as possible, I say, 'I'd much prefer a weekend away than a present, Jules. A city break, maybe? I'd like to be out of the country when I turn thirty. That way I can pretend it isn't really happening. Thirty's so bloody ancient. I can feel the crow's feet coming on already.' I start to rotate the skin at the corner of my eyes gently under my fingertips. 'You have to massage your face several times a day, apparently,' I add, trying to make my ageing-concern believable. 'And do special exercises.'

I take my hands away and stretch my face, jaw almost touching my chest, eye balls strained towards the heavens, which also has the effect of making me yawn deeply.

She laughs. 'Pandora, stop! You'll scare off the customers. Says who exactly?'

I relax my face, which is still tingling from the workout and the yawn. 'Some magazine article or other.'

Jules straightens up and looks at me with concern. 'It's not like you to be so wrinkle-scared. Is hitting the big three-o really bothering you all that much?'

'Yes!' I say firmly. 'It's all downhill on roller skates from here. I have a nine-year-old daughter and I'm not even married. None of this was in my life plan.' I scowl, then stop abruptly and rub my forehead, remembering something. 'The article said you should try not to frown.'

'What about smiling?' she says archly. 'Is that allowed? And do you really have a life plan?'

'*Mais oui*. I'm a master planner; you should know that by now!'

Jules smiles. 'I think the expression's "control freak".'

'That's hardly fair.'

She's having none of it. 'Do you or do you not have a uniform for work?'

'It's not a uniform exactly.'

She snorts and looks me up and down. 'Smart black trousers, check. Neat black top, check. Leopard-print ballet pumps, check.'

She has me there. 'OK, OK, I have a work uniform of sorts. Big deal! The mornings would be impossible if I had to decide what I was going to wear on top of everything else. But I do have several variations, I'll have you know.'

She's smiling at me broadly. 'And did you or did you not try to impose toilet breaks a few weeks ago?'

I can feel my cheeks redden. OK, so it wasn't one of my most inspired ideas, but it made sense at the time, until Bird, our eighty-year-old granny and part-time Shoestring assistant (who in her Chanel jackets and jeans is the least granny-ish person I know) pointed out the error of my ways.

'Darling,' she'd said in her cut-glass accent, straight out of a Jane Austen adaptation, 'I can see why it makes sense, but at my age one's bladder has a mind of its own.'

I ignore Jules's question and continue, my voice wistful even to my ears.

'I was hoping to be married by twenty-eight,' I explain, 'twenty-nine at the very latest. Two children, one boy, one girl. Nice house with a sea view somewhere in Dalkey or Sandycove; a room of my own to design in; a husband obviously—' I stop abruptly, aware that Jules is staring at me, the corners of her mouth flickering.

'What?' I demand.

She's blatantly grinning at me now. 'I like the way the husband came last on your list. But it all sounds so uncomplicated and so . . . so . . .' She's struggling to find the right word. 'Safe. Life's not like that, Pandora. It's bloody messy. You know that as well as I do. You already have a lovely boyfriend, Declan. Remember him? Not to mention Iris, your very smart and very beautiful daughter, and you do live in Dalkey. All right, so you have to share your living space with me, Bird and Dad, but let's face it, there's no way either of us would be able to afford Dalkey otherwise. So you see, you have little to complain about.'

I sigh. She's right about Iris, and the house, but Declan? The man who spends every Wednesday night if he's in town with his ex-wife, Jessica? He claims he's just keeping her sweet so she won't make trouble over the divorce, which he's hoping will come through within the next few months, but it still sticks in my throat. At least they were able to file in England, on account of Jessica being English and still owning a house in London, speeding up the whole process. Irish family law requires a 'cooling off' period of four years. They've been separated less than a year now and there's no way I'd cope with three more years of 'keeping Jessica sweet'.

I wouldn't mind, but their regular meeting takes place in what used to be 'their' restaurant, The Rosewood, all flickering candles and intimate snugs – her idea, not his. I'm convinced she wants him back, however much he protests to the contrary. But I haven't voiced my concerns to anyone, especially not to Declan. It took me long enough to find a decent man who's as good to Iris as he is to me. Besides, I need Declan. He's sensible, stable, a proper grown-up. The last thing I want is to come over all paranoid and bunny boiler and to lose him.

'I know,' I tell Jules. 'Declan's great. It's just this turning thirty thing, it's making me question my choices. I wanted to be a fashion designer, Jules. Instead I peddle secondhand clothes to stupid people who don't understand why a vintage Chanel cashmere twinset costs more than a boring new jumper from Mexos or another of those hideous chain stores. I feel like screeching, "Yes, go ahead and buy a boring polyester jumper, be a sheep. If you don't appreciate quality fabric and years of design excellence, then just go feck yourself." It makes me so goddamn angry.'

I look around quickly. I make a habit of never swearing on the shop floor, it's so undignified and it's not like me to get so riled up. Luckily it's early and there are no customers yet.

Jules certainly looks a little taken aback by my outburst. She pats my arm. 'OK, sis, take it easy. Would you like a coffee?'

I look at her intently. 'I'm all over the place these days. I keep forgetting things. I couldn't remember where I put the scissors yesterday. I spent hours looking for them before Bird pointed out that they were hanging on the ribbon around my neck. Do you think I'm going insane?'

She smiles again. 'Don't be daft, you're far too sensible. I'm the mad one in this family, remember? It must be the birthday thing. I never thought it would freak you out this much. Just goes to show, there's no calling people, is there? Look, thirty is only a number. If it makes you feel any better, you can knock off a few years, tell everyone you're in your late twenties. We'll all play along.'

'Thanks, Jules. But it's not as simple as that. *I'll* know I'm thirty. When you're about to hit your own best before date, you'll understand.' The first customers come in the door and make for the coffee shop. Jules is going to have to move her bike, so it's now or never.

'Now back to the city break,' I say quickly. 'I was thinking Paris. May is the perfect month to visit.'

Her face is a picture. 'Paris? *Paris?* Are you deranged?'

She has every right to be shocked. I spent five months studying at the Paris Institute of Fashion and Design in Montmartre in my early twenties and I came home with rather more than notebooks jammed with dress ideas and conversational French.

'Pandora, are you sure you want to go back to Paris? You haven't been back since, well, you know. Why now?' Her eyes widen. 'Hang on, am I missing something? Is there another reason you want to go to Paris? Triggered by the whole getting old thing, perhaps?' She tilts her head and looks at me intently.

I was waiting for this. 'I know what you're all going to think, that I have things to take care of over there, but honestly it couldn't be further from the truth. I just want to banish my Parisian demons and move on. If I don't do it now, I'll probably put it off for another ten years and spend the whole decade chastising myself for being such a chicken. No, it's time. A new start and all that.'

I pray that she'll believe me, and manage to persuade Bird and Dad that it's a good idea too. I desperately need her on my side but she still looks unconvinced.

'I've always adored Paris,' I add earnestly. 'And it's the perfect place to celebrate turning thirty. I know it must sound crazy, as I was only there for a few months, but I miss the place. I used to have a noticeboard full of pictures of the Eiffel Tower and stuff, remember? I was obsessed.'

'I'd forgotten that.' She gives a short laugh. 'It was really neat too, wasn't it? Rows and rows of pictures pinned up carefully in straight lines. My walls were plastered with Johnny Depp posters.'

I lift my eyebrows. 'Were? They still are, Jules.'

She laughs again. 'Only one or two. He's still a god. His ex-partner's French, isn't she? Vanessa Paradis.'

'Yep, he's clearly a man of taste. I've made my decision. Paris is my favourite city and it's time to go back, and I'd like you, Rowie and Arietty to come too. Rowie's birthday is the day before mine, remember? We can celebrate together. She's already said she'd be interested. She's a bit depressed about the big three-o too, doesn't want a party or anything, says being out of the country for it suits her perfectly. What do you think? We can do a Thelma and Louise, without the death obviously, or the violence. Girls on tour. Please, Jules? It would really mean a lot to me.'

'Rowie and Arietty, cool, now you're talking!' My sister's eyes are sparkling. She seems far more animated about the whole trip now that I've suggested that the girls join us. Rowie's an old friend of mine from fashion college (Dublin, not Paris), and Arietty is Jules's friend, an elephant keeper in Dublin Zoo no less. Jules and Arietty only met last year, but they're already as thick as thieves. I feel slightly put out, to be honest. But I try not to let it show. If I'm going to win over Dad and Bird, I need her firmly on my side. Besides, I'm well aware that she thinks I'm a bit boring sometimes, but it's hardly my fault. I have to be sensible, people depend on me. I have a shop to manage and Iris for starters. Bird may technically be the owner and Jules is a great help with things like the windows and running the customer styling service, but when it comes to the day-to-day running of the place, I'm very much in charge. I'm lucky to have family backup when it comes to Iris, but being a single mum does have its challenges. I spend most of the time exhausted. Sad, I know, but true.

'That sounds like a plan, Batman,' she says. 'So, when do we leave?'

From the child-at-the-circus look on Jules's face, I can tell I finally have her convinced. She has fallen for the freaking out over the big three-o act and, as much as I hate to deceive her, it means I now have a cover story for going to Paris and the real reasons behind my meltdown are still under wraps. Which is exactly where I intend to keep them.

Chapter 2

Later that evening I brace myself to tell Bird and Dad about our city break. Since Mum died from breast cancer (when I was fourteen and Jules was only nine) we've all lived together in Sorrento House, a rambling old Georgian pile in Dalkey – me, Iris, Jules, Bird and Dad. It's hardly conventional, but it seems to work. It's actually Bird's place – Mum grew up here and the shelves of her old room (now Iris's room) are still full of the books she loved as a child and her favourite toys. After Mum died the house was renovated and Bird moved into a specially created apartment in the basement, but she spends most of her time 'upstairs'. She's sociable, Bird. We all are, and we're used to the chatter and share of communal living.

I can feel my breath quicken as soon as I open my mouth. 'So you know I have a birthday coming up?' I say hesitantly. 'I've decided I'd like to celebrate it in style, get away. Paris, maybe . . . what do you think?'

Bird and Dad have a similar reaction to Jules's initial one. Shock. For a second there's utter silence.

'Paris?' Bird's eyes move nervously towards Dad, who appears equally worried. They exchange a loaded look.

She turns back to me. 'Are you sure, darling?'

'Positive,' I say. 'I've already talked it through with Jules and she thinks it's the ideal place to celebrate my thirtieth and to put the past behind me. Don't you, Jules? End of an era, start of a new decade and all that stuff.'

'Yes,' she says, nodding in agreement. 'We're going to ask Rowie and Arietty to join us. So we can have a proper party to celebrate.'

I think Jules still has doubts about my motivation, but is now so keen on the idea of holidaying with Rowie and Arietty that she's managing to hide them brilliantly.

From the dark expression on his face, Dad has serious reservations. He checks the door is firmly shut and that Iris can't hear, and then clears his throat. I try to stop myself wincing. I can tell what's coming.

'Pandora, I know you don't like talking about it, but does this have anything to do with Iris's father? You haven't been back since she was born.' Dad shifts around awkwardly in his chair. He's not particularly fond of emotional scenes and I know he wouldn't have asked the question unless he felt he had to.

I can feel everyone's eyes fixed on my face and irritation starts prickling under my skin. As I told them all years ago, the identity of Iris's father is none of their business. So I say nothing. I just push my chair back strongly with my feet, making the wood screech against the tiles, and stand up.

'I'm sorry,' I say, 'but that's not up for discussion, Dad, you know that. I just need a holiday, that's all, and I rather fancied Paris. End of story.'

'Do sit down, darling,' Bird says. 'Stop being so touchy, after all you're the one who mentioned Paris! Your father isn't trying to upset you, but Iris is nine now and she will start asking questions about him soon. In fact I'm surprised she hasn't already. You do need to consider what exactly you're going to tell her.'

There's another deathly silence. Maybe I did overreact. I need to say something, quick, or this trip might not happen. After all, I'm counting on Dad and Bird to look after Iris while I'm away. I sit back down.

'She's already asked,' I say, trying to keep my voice under control and my anger in check. 'I've told her that he lives in

France and when she's sixteen she can decide whether or not she wants to meet him in person.'

They are all staring at me agog. It's the most I've ever told them about Iris's dad.

'So he is from Paris, darling?' Bird says tentatively.

There's a long pause while I weigh up my options.

'No,' I say eventually. 'Not Paris. He is French, but please don't ask me any more questions about the past. I don't mean to be rude, but I won't answer them. And if any of you mention a word of this to Iris, I'll never forgive you. I can read her like a book, and I'll know if you've said anything, believe me. I'll tell her I'm visiting Paris, but not to see her father, just for a holiday. She's smart enough to understand. And I'd be very grateful if you'd look after her while I'm away. If it's a problem I can make other arrangements. Now, I'm going to put Iris to bed, so you can all discuss me to your heart's content.'

I stand up again and make my way towards the door. I know I've been a bit short with Dad and Bird, but I do wish they'd stop digging for information. They know only too well that the subject of Iris's father is taboo. I'll talk about anything else, but not that. I've got so much on my mind at the moment that I'm finding it hard to cope or act 'normal'. Right now I just want to focus on getting to Paris.

'Pandora,' Jules calls. 'Do you want some company?'

I turn and give her a gentle smile. 'No, I'm OK, I'll go on up with Iris. But thanks for asking and thanks for dinner, Bird. Sorry if I snapped at you or Dad, I didn't mean to. I'm just tired.'

'You're welcome, darling,' Bird says. 'An early night will do you good and if there's anything you want to talk about, you know where to find me.'

I nod silently, then walk out of the door, closing it firmly behind me, happy that I got through the conversation without breaking down. By the time I reach the end of the stairs, I'm having second thoughts about fetching Iris from the living room where she's watching one final nature programme before bedtime, and am itching to know what's going on in the kitchen in my absence. I pause for a moment before slipping off my shoes and creeping back towards the door, making sure not to step on the creaky floorboard. I know eavesdropping is low, but I can't help myself – I need to find out what they're saying. I press my ear against the crack between the door and the doorframe.

I can hear someone, probably Dad, give a low whistle.

Then Bird says, 'You were right all along, Jules, about Iris's dad being French. Do you think he was a fashion student?'

'Seems likely,' Dad says.

'No way,' Jules pipes up. 'Pandora's always liked older men. Declan's nearly forty. I bet he was her lecturer or something.'

I press my hand over my mouth to stop myself laughing manically. If only she knew.

'Iris's skin is much darker than Pandora's, almost olive,' Bird says then. 'I wonder where he's from? Somewhere sunny perhaps?'

'Nice?' Dad suggests. 'Or Marseille?'

'What about Avignon or Monaco?' Bird mulls.

'Where's Audrey Tautou from?' Dad again. 'Iris looks a bit like her, doesn't she? The dark hair and the serious little face.'

'You're right!' Bird this time. 'Or what about Julie Delpy or that Jolie girl?'

None of their ruminations make much sense. Angelina Jolie was born in LA and Iris looks nothing like Julie Delpy.

'Or Vanessa Paradis?' Jules says. She obviously feels a bit left out and Vanessa's probably the only French actress she can think of. Unlike me and Bird, she's not much of a film buff.

I block out their pointless chatter for a while – Vanessa Paradis is blonde, for heaven's sake, and Iris's hair is rich chocolate brown – until Dad says, 'What do you think, Boolie? Should we try to dissuade her from going?' Boolie was Mum's pet name for Jules – short for Julia Boolia. For a second Mum's face floats in front of my eyes. She's been slipping into my thoughts a lot recently. I wish she was here now; I've never needed her more.

'No,' she says to my relief. 'It seems to be something she needs to do. I think she just wants to go back, see the city again. She did spend five months there and she was Paris obsessed even before she went. I'm sure she misses it and just wants to put the whole Paris thing behind her before she moves into her thirties. I think she's a bit freaked out by getting old, to be honest.'

I smile to myself. Good old Jules, sticking up for me as usual, even if she did just call me old. We haven't always been close but lately that has changed.

'But you will keep an eye on her, darling?' Bird asks, and her voice sounds anxious. 'Make sure she's all right. Emotionally, I mean. She seems a little tense these days. Are you sure she's strong enough? It will bring back an awful lot of memories. We don't know much about what happened with Iris's father, but it can't have been pleasant, surely? Being abandoned like that.'

'Pandora?' Jules says. 'She'll be fine. Nothing knocks her, you know that. Tough isn't the word.'

'We all have a soft side, Boolie,' Bird says gently. 'Even your sister.' She pauses for a second. 'Maybe I should have a little word with Rowie.'

Poor Jules. OK, she may have had some rather wobbly moments in the past, but Bird's inference is a little unfair. It's no wonder Jules sounds a little spiky when she says, 'You don't need to bother Rowie. I'll look after Pandora and I guess you guys will be on Iris duty for a few days. Now stop worrying, both of you. It's a weekend in Paris, not Beirut. What can possibly go wrong?'

I creep away and sit on the end of the stairs, lost in thought. It looks like this trip is actually going to happen. A wave of relief hits me so strongly that I almost start to cry. Paris. I'm going to Paris to find Olivier Huppert, Iris's dad. I dread seeing him, but I have to, it's as simple as that. For Iris's sake. For Iris's future. It's the first thing on my monumental to-do list. Number two is a little more complicated and it's out of my hands this time, which is agonizingly frustrating.

Last Wednesday I opened an official-looking typed envelope. It was from a Dr Ruth Oxenbury, Head of the Medical Genetics Department at Monkstown Clinic, and her letter said that Mum had contacted her fifteen years ago. Mum had read about the pioneering work the department were doing into hereditary cancer genes and she asked to be tested. So they tested her blood as requested and found that Mum had the BRCA1 gene, short for Breast Cancer Gene 1. I didn't have to read any further to know where this was leading. Dr Oxenbury was asking if I too wanted to be tested.

When Iris and the rest of the family were in bed I Googled the gene and there it was, the information I was looking for, starkly laid out in front of me:

> Women with the BRCA1 gene have an 85 per cent chance of getting breast cancer.

I sat there for ages, just staring at the screen. An 85 per cent chance of getting breast cancer. I couldn't believe it. I read further down the screen, scaring myself more and more. There was also a 50 per cent chance of getting ovarian cancer.

I sat back in the chair. I was too shocked to do anything other than put my head in my hands and just sit there. I could hear my blood pounding in my ears, my heart pumping hard. My eyes started welling up and I swore under my breath. This just wasn't fair. I'd always eaten well, I'd never smoked and I only had the odd glass of wine.

After a few minutes I pulled the letter out of my pocket and re-read the last paragraph. As I'd suspected, Dr Oxenbury was inviting me to find out if I had the gene, telling me it was a big decision and to ring her if I had any questions, or to arrange an appointment to discuss it further with her or talk to a counsellor. She explained that normally the gene information she'd just divulged would be given at a consultation following counselling, but that due to the unusual nature of Mum's request she had taken the liberty of writing to me instead. She suggested that I should bring someone with me to the appointment for support. I took a few deep breaths, wiped my tears away and put the letter carefully back in my pocket.

I couldn't sleep a wink that night for thinking about it. Should I have the test? And if I had the bloody gene, then what? How would knowing be of any benefit? Did I have to wait around and see if I was in the lucky 15 per cent or the unlucky 85 per cent, or what? And should I tell Jules? After all, there's as much chance that she's a carrier too. If I'm gene-free but she has it, then what? Jules isn't emotionally equipped for that kind of pressure.

When Jules was nine, she watched Mum's demise from a vibrant, larger-than-life woman who could take on the world, to a fragile, physically weak shadow of herself. Mum never lost her spirit, but towards the end the pain was too much and she had to allow herself to stop fighting and slip away. She died on the morning of Jules's ninth birthday. Jules had been in the room, chatting to her, and then, as Mum lost the ability to do anything other than breathe, watched as Mum passed out of this life and into another. It's not something that Jules will ever forget.

For many years Jules blamed herself for wearing Mum out that morning, snatching precious time away from me, Dad and Bird. But we'd all been so relieved that Mum hadn't died alone, Dad especially. For years he'd blamed himself for not being there at the end. But the whole experience has had a lasting effect on poor old Jules. She's been terrified of hospitals or of any kind of illness for years now and she can be a bit emotionally fragile sometimes. I have no idea what this might do to her.

So you see, meltdown isn't the word. I can't stop thinking about Dr Oxenbury's letter and what it means. Will I have the test or not? If I do, what will I tell Jules? Or Iris? What about Bird and Dad? And what happens if I'm gene positive? Talk about monumental questions.

On Thursday morning, a day after I had received the letter, I went into work as usual, trying not to think about its contents, but it was so damn hard. I spent most of the day in a daze and by the time the shop closed I still hadn't decided what I was going to do about it.

That evening the whole family was in the sitting room after dinner, apart from Iris who was tucked up in bed. Bird was engrossed in her crossword, Dad's head was buried in his newspaper, and Jules was sitting at the round table in front of the bay window, sketching out some ideas for the next Shoestring window, biting the end of her pen dreamily. Bird was chuckling away to herself triumphantly. She loves figuring out difficult crossword clues; she's the only person I know who can finish the Crosaire in the *Irish Times*, apart from Mum, who had been a crossword genius.

I had a sudden pang of longing and a wave of sadness – I wished Mum was there to complete the picture. For a split second I could see her standing right in front of me, her huge cornflower-blue eyes strong and determined. Even towards the very end, her gaze never wavered. I blinked and her image disappeared.

Then I had a thought. You know she *is* still with us. She's in me and Jules and even Iris. Her genes are still running through every one of us. The same genes that killed her in the end. Dr Oxenbury's letter popped into my head and I remembered the decision I had to make. Before I even had a chance to start considering it properly, it was as if the mist had cleared and I had a moment of clarity. For the first time since the letter arrived I felt calm and certain.

Mum wanted Jules and me to have the test. She was trying to take care of us, even towards the end. That was why she contacted Dr Oxenbury and got herself tested, even though she must have known it was too late to do anything about her own cancer by then. Mum has given us all a chance to control our futures, to determine our destinies in some small way. It suddenly became blindingly obvious – of course I was having the test.

Chapter 3

After I made my decision, I rang what I presumed was Dr Oxenbury's office first thing the following morning. It was only eight o'clock and I didn't expect to catch anyone in, so I was all ready to leave a message when a woman answered.

'Hello?' Her voice was slightly clippy, as if I'd interrupted her in the middle of something.

'Oh, hi. This is Pandora Schuster. Dr Oxenbury wrote to me, about having a blood test.'

'This is Dr Oxenbury, Pandora. I gave you my personal number. So, what have you decided to do? Counselling is probably best, yes?'

I was taken aback for a second. I wasn't expecting to speak to the doctor herself, or to be asked the question so directly.

'Sorry, sorry,' she added before I'd had the chance to gather my thoughts, her voice softer. 'I think my head is still in the report I'm writing. I don't mean to sound abrupt. Would you like to talk to someone about the test, Pandora? Find out more about it. I can set up some counselling for you to talk about your options. It's a big decision, Pandora, not to be taken lightly. We have very good people in here, trained people who can help you make up your mind.'

I gulped before blurting out, 'I'd like to have the test.'

'There's no rush, Pandora. Are you sure you don't need more time? It's a big decision.'

'No, honestly. I've thought about it carefully and I want to go ahead. I've read up about the gene and I'd like know if I have it as soon as possible. I think it's what Mum would have wanted.'

'Yes, it is,' she says, her voice softer. 'It's the right thing to do, Pandora.'

'You knew Mum?'

'Yes. We were friends in college. That's why I wrote to you directly. Kirsten asked me to look after you, Pandora.'

'Oh, I see.' I'm completely taken aback by this.

'I'll tell you more about it when you come to see me.' Her tone becomes more businesslike again. 'Now, let's see if we can get the ball rolling as quickly as possible. Give me a second.' There's silence for a moment. Then she says, 'How does next Thursday morning suit? Is 7.40 a.m. any good? Sorry it's so early but the diary's jammed and it's the only time I can squeeze you in at short notice.'

'That's perfect. Where do I go exactly?'

'My office first, then I'll send you down to the Phlebotomy Department where they'll take your bloods.'

'How long will it take to get the results?'

'We'll do it as quickly as we can but it's a complicated procedure and it could take six to eight weeks.'

'That's OK, I understand.'

'So I'll see you on Thursday? We're in the bowels,' she added cheerily. 'But it means we have plenty of space. Ask for directions at reception. I look forward to meeting you, Pandora. Your mother was a wonderful woman. We shared the same boyfriend, in fact – not simultaneously, obviously!' I could hear the smile in her voice.

I gave a small laugh. 'I look forward to meeting you too. Thanks for squeezing me in.' I clicked off my phone. My fingers started to shake, a jittery feeling that slowly seeped through my whole body. I took a few deep breaths, trying to calm myself down. Booking the test is the first step, I told myself. Just hang in there, Pandora, and try not to think about six weeks down the line – the results. In the meantime focus on something that you can control – getting to Paris and finding Olivier.

Thursday morning is D-Day. On Wednesday evening I ask Dad to get Iris up and drop her to school, telling him that I have to get to Shoestring ultra early to sort out some outstanding customer orders, and, as this isn't an unusual request, he happily agrees. I manage to shower, dress and make it out of the house without waking anyone, which is a relief. I haven't been myself since getting Dr Oxenbury's letter and I know Bird suspects that something is up. She keeps asking things like, 'Are you all right, darling? You're looking rather peaky.' Luckily the impending Paris trip seems to have put her off the scent. And Jules is usually too caught up in her own world to notice if someone's off colour. I love her to bits but she can be rather self-obsessed.

Driving towards Monkstown Clinic my skin is crawling with nerves. I park the car and walk up the pathway towards the large modern building, wondering what's going on right this second behind its curved tinted windows. Is there someone else sitting inside, waiting to have a test done or a diagnosis, feeling like jelly on the inside just like me?

I get directions to Dr Oxenbury's office, and I make my way towards the lift at the far end of the atrium, past a pool fed by a small spluttering waterfall. I pass a busy café and try not to stare at a woman in her mid-thirties sitting at a table just inside the doorway, head bent over a newspaper. Her headscarf has slipped a little and underneath she's completely bald. My blood pumps quicker and I try to concentrate on the soothing noise of the splashing water instead of my racing thoughts. The lift delivers me to the basement and as soon as I step into the corridor my nostrils tingle with the smell of bleach.

The door to Dr Oxenbury's basement office is open and there's a woman inside, her fingers flying over a keyboard, her eyes concentrated on the screen. A vase of red tulips sits on the low filing cabinet beside her and behind her is a second door.

I stand in front of her, not knowing whether to interrupt or not. After a moment she stops typing and looks up at me.

'Pandora, yes?' She smiles. She's in her fifties, and has the kind of open, friendly face you immediately warm to. She's so different to most doctor's receptionists I've encountered, I'm slightly taken aback.

'That's right.'

'I'm Cecily, Dr Oxenbury's secretary. She's in the lab but she asked me to call her as soon as you got here. I'll give her a ring and then I'll take your details. Is there anyone joining you?'

'No, it's just me.'

'No problem, just take a seat.' She waves at the neat buttoned leather sofa. I sit down and look around the office while she contacts the doctor, my eyes lingering on the picture above the desk, a realistic oil painting of a vase of wild flowers, teacup and three books stacked with their spines showing, all painted in warm cheerful colours. One of the books is Jane Austen's *Emma*, which makes me smile; it's one of my favourites. There are white colonial blinds on the high, long windows, and a cherry-red rug on the wooden floor. Two old-fashioned brass hinged floor lamps add brightness to the dim natural lighting. It's not like any doctor's office I've ever been in; it looks more like someone's sitting room.

After talking on the phone in a low voice, Cecily takes my details efficiently and a few minutes later another woman bustles into the room and stands in front of me. She has dark cropped hair the colour of blackberries and the boyish, wiry figure of someone who never sits down. 'Pandora.' She gives me a bright smile and shakes her head. 'Such a look of your mother. And you've already met Cecily.' She nods at the receptionist. 'She runs my life. I wouldn't know what day it was if it weren't for Cecily.'

'Don't you believe her, Pandora.' Cecily smiles again, clearly pleased, and then gets back to her typing.

Dr Oxenbury opens the door behind Cecily. 'Come in, come in and take a seat. You're alone I take it?'

'Yes.' From the way Cecily and Dr Oxenbury have both asked, most people must bring someone with them. I can understand that; the hospital is pretty intimidating and it would be nice to have someone with me to ask questions in case I forget something, but for the moment I want to keep all this to myself.

I sit down opposite her pale wooden desk. It's as neat as a pin, with a stack of in- and out-boxes to the right, and a pen holder to the left, beside the white-backed computer screen. There are two more oil paintings behind the desk, clearly by the same artist, and two of the walls have floor-to-ceiling book-shelves, crammed with medical tomes and chunky stand-up folders. There are also two large filing cabinets the red of English postboxes and I can't take my eyes off them.

'Office equipment comes in all shades these days,' she says, noticing my gaze. 'And grey is such a depressing colour, isn't it? Nothing like a bit of brightness to cheer up your day. I meant to pull out your file earlier.' She pulls open one of the drawers, takes out a file and places it on the desk. 'Here we are.' Then she sits down behind it, puts her elbows on the wood and temples her fingers. 'So, you've decided to take the test?'

I nod, the lump in my throat preventing me from saying anything else.

'I am glad,' she continues. 'I know it's what Kirsten wanted. Your mum was a very special woman and I'm extremely sorry you lost her so young.' She opens the folder and studies the top left-hand corner of three envelopes carefully, then hands me one. 'She wanted you to have this on the day of your test.'

My heart pounds again as I stare at it, my name written across the front in Mum's sweeping, old-fashioned handwriting. She was very proud of her handwriting, won prizes for it at school as a girl.

To My Darling Pandora

There's also a small 'T' in the top right-hand corner. 'T' for test maybe? Seeing a tiny piece of her out of the blue like that gives me such a jolt that tears immediately prick my eyes. 'And the other letters?' I ask.

'Are for later,' Dr Oxenbury says gently. 'I think Kirsten saw this whole testing business as something she could control, unlike her cancer. She gave me very strict instructions about the letters, and I promised to comply. She could be quite bossy when she wanted to, as I'm sure you know.' She gives a tiny laugh.

I smile back. That sounds just like Mum. 'Yes. Yes, she could.' I put it carefully in my handbag and blink my tears away.

'In fact, I would have liked to have tested you sooner, but your Mum insisted I wait until your thirtieth birthday to contact you, against my advice, I should add; I suggested eighteen or twenty-one. But she didn't want your twenties to be marred by all this.'

'What about Jules, my sister? She's twenty-five now. Should she be tested?'

'Kirsten said she'd cover that in the letter. She'd thought of everything, your mum.'

'How did you know each other? You said something about college.'

She smiles again, her eyes sparking in remembrance. 'We used to run the Hist together, the debating society in Trinity, that's where we met, discussing what guests to invite to our debates. We had the odd difference of opinion but we worked well together. She liked to get her own way, but never sulked if she didn't. I moved to the States after college for many years

SARAH WEBB

and we lost touch. I was sad that we only found each other again through her damn illness.' She sighs, then pauses for a second, noticing my bleary eyes and my slight sniff. 'Sorry, I don't mean to upset you.'

I'm finding it hard to stem the tears. 'That's OK.'

'And you're sure you're ready to take the test, Pandora? There's a fifty–fifty chance of a negative result – which of course is the result we want. But if you do have the breast cancer gene your mother carried – the BRCA1 – I think I explained that in the letter . . .'

I nod silently, not wanting to interrupt her.

'Good, good,' she continues. 'If you do have the gene, then the odds of getting breast cancer do increase quite dramatically.'

'I'd have an 85 per cent chance of getting breast cancer and a 50 per cent chance of getting ovarian, is that right?'

She looks impressed. 'You've been doing your homework. Yes, that's correct.'

'And if that's the case, if I test positive, what then?'

She sits back in her chair a little. 'You'd be closely monitored by one of the team in the cancer clinic. Very closely. There are various scans and examinations, but let's not dwell on that today.'

'What about preventative surgery?' I ask quickly, wanting to get what I've read on the cancer sites and Internet forums out in the open, needing some reassurance that there is more that can be done to beat the odds.

She leans forward, her brow slightly wrinkled. 'Are you talking about a double mastectomy?'

'Yes. And maybe getting my ovaries removed,' I add firmly.

She looks at me for a long moment, then finally says, 'These are all things we can discuss later on, Pandora, if we have to. And risk-reducing surgery is a possibility, yes.' She pauses, gives me a gentle smile. 'I understand how powerless all this makes you feel, believe me. But let's just take things one step at a time, yes?'

'Sorry. I already have a daughter, you see, Iris, and she's my life. I need to be there for her no matter what. And Mum went so quickly. One minute she was perfectly fine, the next minute she was . . .' I stop, unable to say it, not now. Not when Mum perhaps sat in this very same seat, two children of her own at home.

'What age is your daughter?' she asks, her eyes soft.

'Nine.' I don't add, 'The age Jules was when Mum died,' but from the flicker of recognition that passes across Dr Oxenbury's face, she's well aware of it.

'I do understand,' she says gently. 'Believe me, Pandora. I've lost people too, family and close friends. And I deal with this every single day, remember? I'll do my very best for you, I promise. But please try not to worry about things until you have to. There's every chance you don't have the gene and if you do, as I said, we'll deal with it. I'll be with you the whole way, yes?'

I nod, tears spilling down my cheeks. 'Thank you, Doctor.'

She hands me a tissue. 'Ruth. Please call me Ruth. Now, let's get your bloods done. I'll walk you down myself.'

I follow Ruth down the corridor towards the Phlebotomy Department, one hand in my bag, resting on Mum's letter. I desperately want to find out what it says, but I know I can't, not yet. I need to read it alone.

Sitting in the car after the test, a small glass tube of my blood containing my DNA winging its way towards the lab that will tell me my future, my arm throbs but it's nothing to how I feel inside: partly numb, partly awash with waves of emotion I can't seem to control. I take Mum's letter out of my bag and carefully open the envelope with a pen, not wanting to rip it.

I take out the sheet of notepaper inside, unfold it and gulp, my eyes filling up so much I can't make out Mum's loops and curls. I put the letter on the dashboard, wipe my tears away with my fingers and take a few deep breaths.

Dearest Pandora,

Don't be sad. Wipe those tears away, my darling. You've been given a wonderful gift, the chance to control your destiny. It was too late for me, but it's not too late for you. Ruth assures me that by the time you get this letter, cancer research will have come on leaps and bounds and they may be close to preventing or curing the bloody disease, or at the very least, diagnosing it very early, which is most reassuring. Knowledge is power, Pandora, it will help you to be vigilant and it will also help you fight back when and if the need arises, which I hope to God it doesn't.

Isn't Ruth fab? A bit stroppy mind, we used to have right humdingers in college, but that's probably a good thing in a doctor, especially a female one. I bet she's one of the most respected medics in the country by now.

My goodness, can she fight her corner. If she'd had her way it would have been boring old farts at the Hist debates every week – scientists and doctors and yawn-inducing people like that. I wanted artists and business sorts, people with a bit of jazz. One thing we did agree on was this – there had to be at least one woman panellist at every debate. Too bloody right! Women have to support each other, that's what I say. Anyway, tell her I'm so grateful for her help with all of this and that I miss her and that I'm sorry we didn't have much time to renew our friendship.

So, to the test. By now your blood will be on its way to the lab, and you just have to sit back and wait,

I'm afraid. I know it's difficult, my love, I know you want to speed everything up, but you can't. You're just like me, darling, hideously impatient, but you'll just have to bide your time. Don't think the worst. Don't spend the next few weeks in a dark place. Plaster a smile on your face and get out there and do whatever it is that you love to do the best. (I do hope it's something interesting. You were always so good at art – all those adorable dresses you used to draw. Please tell me that you're using your talent.) And you'll get another letter when you get the test results back. Until then, chin up, darling, promise?

Now to Boolie. My sweet poppet. You two were always so adorable to each other (most of the time!), I do hope that you are still close. I asked Ruth to leave the decision on when to tell Jules in your hands. I only know her as a slightly dreamy but headstrong nine year old. I don't know how she will react to all this cancer gene business as an adult. But I'm hoping that you will. If you think she should know – now – then please tell her. If you think thirty is time enough, wait. I'm sorry to do this to you, Pandora, but I know you'll make the right decision and that you'll understand. I only want what's best for both of you.

Do you have a daughter, my darling? Oh, I do hope so. I am so blessed to have not one, but two daughters. You and your sister make my heart sing. I love you now and I will always love you. Remember that.

Be happy, my darling. Savour every day on this wonderful earth and know that I will carry you and Boolie with me, always and for ever.

All my love,
Mum xxx

I drop the letter on my lap, grip the steering wheel and stare out the windscreen. Tears start rolling down my cheeks and I blink them out of my eyes. I feel distraught, yes, but also hideously angry. My vibrant, glorious mum should never have been taken like that, not so young, not by cancer. It isn't fair.

'You took Mum,' I whisper. 'But you're not getting me. If I am positive, you have one hell of a battle on your hands. I'm going to fight you with everything I've got. You are not going to win this time.'

Then and there I decide not to mention the test to anyone; what's the point of worrying everyone unnecessarily? I can deal with this on my own. I jut out my chin and grit my teeth. I am not going to have the gene. I refuse to. It's a simple as that.

Chapter 4

I know Mum said to try and get on with things and not to think the worst, but for all my earlier bluster it's impossible. I can't escape; it's like having one of those hideous human monkeys from *The Wizard of Oz* sitting on my shoulder, whispering in my ear, 'Cancer gene, cancer gene, positive, positive, positive.'

I manage to drive home safely, despite the hot, angry tears that keep flooding down my cheeks. I'm not expected in Shoestring until after eleven – I wasn't sure how long the appointment would take so I told Dad to tell Bird and Jules that I was visiting a client this morning after doing the orders. I often do it, so they won't suspect that anything's up. So I let myself in to Sorrento House, the hall empty and still, shut the front door behind me and collapse on the end stair, my head bowed towards my knees. There I stay, trying to breathe deeply and calmly, the air smelling of furniture polish from the banisters. Bird has a heavy hand with the Pledge.

'Pull yourself together,' I whisper into the air. I force myself to sit up. I stare in front of me, my eyes still a little blurry. One of Iris's pink runners lies abandoned against the wall, along with Jules's spare bicycle pump and an open cardboard box of screws belonging to Dad. I rub my eyes again and try to focus on the normal domesticity of it all, letting it soothe my mind.

When I start to feel a little more like myself I stand up again, check my eyes in the hall mirror, congratulating myself for at least having the wit not to wear mascara this morning. Then I walk into the kitchen to fix myself a strong coffee.

'Get anything good this morning?' Jules asks me as I walk into Shoestring later that morning. She's standing behind the till, Bird to her right. There's a small pile of clothes on the desk. They must be checking the date on stock, ready to return unsold items to clients.

I shake my head. 'It was all Marks & Spencer and Next. There was a bag that she swore was Chanel but from the cheap lining it was definitely a fake.' I give a big sigh. 'Disappointing, really. Bit of a waste of time.'

'Where were you before that, darling?' Bird asks, her eyes bright. 'Greg said he was dropping Iris to school but you left the house at seven. Bit early for a client visit, seven in the morning.' Bird never misses a thing.

I can feel my cheeks redden so I look towards the shop window, full of eye-catching yellow and orange clothes, before saying, 'Had to check some orders in the shop first and the house was in Meath so I had to leave extra time. Took me ages to get there. Jules, are you putting in a new window this week? The spring chick theme worked well but I think a change might be nice. Any ideas for a new theme? What about a Victorian seaside scene – old-fashioned metal buckets and spades, shrimping nets, that kind of thing. It's nearly summer after all, not that you'd know it from the weather. Might cheer people up a bit.'

Jules perks up. 'Great idea. I could make a donkey out of papier mâché.'

I laugh. Last year she made two huge two elephants for a window to celebrate the visit of a famous Indian writer who was attending a local book festival. They were rather impressive. We kept them until Christmas, then Jules donated them to a children's arts centre. 'Don't get too carried away, sis.'

Her face falls. She loved making those elephants, she even persuaded Arietty to help her plaster the frames with soggy paper. She's such a child at heart.

Bird claps her hands together. 'I think a donkey would be fabulous.'

Jules smiles at her gratefully and then looks back at me. 'Please, Pandora?'

I give in. 'Oh, go on, a donkey it is, then.'

She beams at me. I'm glad I've made someone happy.

'Think of all the gorgeous navy and white stripes we could put on the mannequins,' Bird adds. 'And what about that white Prada suit that just came in, teamed with . . .' They're off, my lost morning forgotten. I smile to myself, relieved, and walk towards the staff room to dump my bag.

After work, I finally pluck up the courage to call in to Declan's apartment to break the news about Paris. It's a miracle that he's actually in Dublin. He travels a lot for work at the moment – architects aren't exactly all that in demand in Ireland these days after the collapse of the building industry, so he's often away during the week. It's not ideal, but we manage.

As soon as he opens the door I get a waft of curry.

'Have you eaten?' he asks me, leaning forward to kiss me on the cheek.

'Hi, Declan, nice to see you too.'

He smiles, his warm hazel eyes twinkling. It's one of the things that first attracted me to him, his eyes. 'Sorry, I'm starving.'

'And from the smell, you've already collected the food.'

'Correct.'

'Come on, let's eat then.' I wait until he's almost finished his takeaway before saying anything about Paris, making small talk instead, talking about the shop and his work. He's like a bear if he hasn't eaten and I know he's not going to be thrilled by the idea as it is.

Finally I say, 'Declan, Jules wants to take me on a city break for my birthday. Paris, I think.' I sense telling him that it was my idea would be a step too far.

'Paris?' He looks up from his plate. 'Why Paris?'

'Have you been?'

'Yes. Several times. On business and also with Jessica. She spent most of the time shopping, but I left her to it after the second day and went sightseeing on my own.'

'So I don't have to tell you how beautiful it is.'

'No. But so is Rome. Or Prague. Or Budapest. Does it have to be Paris?'

'What have you got against Paris?'

He clatters his fork onto his plate. 'Pandora, do you really want to go into it?'

I shake my head and stare down at my curry, moving grains of rice around the edge of the plate with my knife. This evening isn't going as planned. Declan's wiped out after a drive to Belfast and back for work, and Jessica has been on his case about extra maintenance for the second time this month (she wants him to replace the washing machine; previously it was something to do with the roof), which always puts him in a foul mood. Jessica lives with their daughter, Rachel, in their swishly renovated four-bedroom family home in Glenageary, which Declan lovingly designed himself, a subject which it's best to shy well away from if I want a quiet night. He's shown me photographs of the place – many photographs – and it does look amazing, all white walls and glass.

'Are you going to see *him*?' he asks.

'Who?'

'Pandora, please. Iris's dad. You met him in Paris, right?'

'I've told you before, we're not in touch and I have no idea where he is now,' I say, trying not to sound defensive. It's not a lie exactly – I'm not one hundred per cent sure where Olivier lives now. However, I do know exactly where his mum lives, and unless she has moved, which is unlikely, she's bound to know where her son is, as they're very close; but I have a strong feeling that she won't exactly be overjoyed to see me and I don't want to involve her in the whole business unless I have to. I tried Facebooking him, but although I found an Oliver Huppert and an Olivier Huppertz, there are no Olivier Hupperts registered at all. Luckily I did manage to find the website of an atelier run by an Olivier Huppert on Google. It can't be a coincidence; it's a very unusual name, the clothes on the site are pure Olivier and he was already on the road to becoming a brilliant designer when I knew him. That's going to be my first port of call.

'I'll be going with Jules and Rowie and Arietty,' I say breezily. 'We'll probably drink too much wine, dance bad cancan in the middle of the road, spend far too much time in the shops, manage not to see half the sights we'd planned to, and stagger back to Dublin exhausted after way too many late nights.'

'And you're not going to see Iris's dad, even though he just happens to live in Paris?'

'I'm not answering that.'

He sits back in his chair and crosses his arms. 'So you are going to see him?'

'Declan, what is your problem? You go for dinner with your ex-wife all the time and I rarely complain.'

'Because I'm trying to keep her sweet so I can see my daughter whenever I want to and not just when it suits her. You know that, Pandora. We've talked about it often enough.'

'How is me talking to Iris's dad any different then?'

'So you *are* going to see him?' he says again, a little triumphantly.

'Stop, OK! I never said that. I just meant in theory. Why are you getting so hot and bothered about me going to Paris?'

He sits back in his chair and takes a moment before saying, 'Because I think you're still in love with him.'

I laugh. 'That's ridiculous. I haven't seen the man in years.'

'But you still think about him, am I right?'

'Absolutely not!'

Declan's looking at me intently and I can feel my cheeks redden so I look away.

Yes, I think about Olivier from time to time, wondering what he's up to, how his mum is doing, hoping he's happy. But that's normal, isn't it? We were close, very close, and I haven't exactly had a colourful relationship history. Olivier was the first guy I ever really loved and you don't forget that kind of thing. I don't, anyway. But with the mood Declan is in, I am hardly going to admit all this and make things even more difficult.

'Does Iris look like him?' he asks.

'What's that got to do with anything?'

'Well, does she?'

I shrug. 'I guess. A little.' He has no idea. Apart from her straight hair, Iris is the mirror image of Olivier.

'I see.' He bites the edge of his lip.

'What do you see exactly? Declan, you're not making any sense.'

'You're reminded of him every day, that's what.'

'So? Don't you think of Jessica when you look at Rachel sometimes?'

'Not really, no. She looks more like me than her mother. And that's different.'

'Why is it different?'

'As you know only too well, I hate the bloody woman. And I don't want to talk about her any more tonight, OK? She's causing me enough grief at the moment as it is.' He picks up his wine glass, drains it and pours himself more. 'Do you want a top-up?' He offers me the bottle to fill up my empty glass.

'No, I'm driving, remember?'

'You can stay over if you like.'

'Declan, I thought you said you were leaving for the airport at 5 a.m.'

'Yeah, yeah, I suppose. Bloody Birmingham too.'

'But you must have loved Jessica once,' I say, not willing to drop the topic yet. 'You married her. And you manage to talk to her for several hours practically every Wednesday night.'

He rubs his hand over his five o'clock shadowed chin. 'Jesus, woman. I wish you'd stop going on about the damn dinner thing. I know it annoys you that Jessica gets some of my time. I understand, honestly, but there's feck all I can do about it at the moment. Can we please not have this conversation yet again?'

'Declan, I gave up choir so that we could spend more time together. But what with your work and Jessica I never get to see you during the week, and when we do see each other we're both too tired to enjoy it.'

'Maybe you should go back to choir. I know you miss it.'

I sigh, exasperated. Typical man, always trying to fix things the easy way. 'I can't go back mid-season. Anyway, this isn't about choir, it's about us not spending enough time together.' I pick up my empty water glass and start playing with it.

He takes it off me, puts it back on the table and then takes my hand in his. 'I'm sorry things are so hectic at work at the moment but it won't be for ever, just until the economy starts to settle down a bit, which I hope to God will be soon. Until then my firm has to take whatever work we're offered, even if it is out of the country. Once the divorce comes through I'll never speak to Jessica again if it makes you happy. Look, we're getting sidetracked here. I'd feel a lot better if you were just straight with me. Do you have any feelings for Iris's dad?'

I pull my hand away. 'No! Is that plain and simple enough for you?'

'What if I don't believe you?'

'Then that's your choice, Declan.'

He's quiet for a moment, then starts picking grains of rice off the table and dropping them on the sweaty lid of the curry carton.

'There's something I don't understand,' he says eventually. 'How can anyone abandon their child like that? I spend the whole time fighting to see Rachel more.' He shakes his head. 'I just don't get it. Kids need their dads.'

'It wasn't like that.'

'What was it like, then? Talk to me.'

Now my own head is bowed, staring at the whorls in the pine table, tracing over them with my finger. Why don't I just tell Declan the truth right now, about what happened in Paris and why I lost touch with Olivier years ago? I could come clean about the blood test, my cancer gene worries and why I want to contact Olivier after all this time – to talk to him about Iris's future before it's too late. That he's right, that sometimes kids do need their dads. Is it because I'm ashamed of what I did to Olivier and worried that Declan won't understand? Or is it something else? Something I'm not willing to admit even to myself, that Declan's right, that I do still have feelings for Olivier?

'Tell me, Pandora,' Declan presses. 'Was he married? Is that it?'

I give a short laugh. 'Absolutely not. Declan, I . . . It's just . . .' I shake my head. I can't do it. I can't find the words. 'I promise I'll tell you the whole story in my own time,' I manage instead. 'But not right now. I just need some time, OK?'

He goes silent for a moment and I can feel his eyes on me but I refuse to lift my head.

'Fine,' he says eventually, sounding defeated, which makes me feel even more guilty. But not guilty enough to come clean.

'Are we still on for Saturday?' he asks after a moment.

'Saturday?'

'Taking the girls out together. Rachel's really looking forward to it. You haven't forgotten, have you?'

'Of course not. I've just had a busy week, that's all.' I'd love to back out, but Iris has been banging on about the outing for months. She's mad about Declan and seems to think that she and Rachel will be instant soulmates.

'You don't sound very excited about it,' he says.

'I'm sorry, I am, really. Iris is dying to meet Rachel. Please, let's not argue any more.' I smile at him gently. 'I'm going to Paris for my birthday and I'd like you to be good with that. All right?'

He sighs. 'It's not just Paris, I may as well tell you now. I had something else organized, OK? A surprise dinner, just the two of us. In Chapter One.' Chapter One is one of the best restaurants in Dublin.

Of course – Declan's nothing if not organized. Damn. I should have thought of that. But it can't be helped. I have to stay focused. I have to get to Paris, talk to Olivier.

'I'm sorry, that's really sweet,' I say. 'I've always wanted to eat there; we'll definitely go when I get back. So what will we do with the girls on Saturday?' I say, trying to change the subject.

'I was thinking of the zoo but Jessica said that Rachel's grown out of it. So how about pizza and a movie?'

'That sounds practically perfect in every way.' I smile at him.

He just nods, the *Mary Poppins* reference clearly lost on him. 'Good. It was actually Jessica's idea.'

I try not to frown. I do wish he'd stop discussing our every move with his ex, it's unnerving and very annoying, but as his mood seems to be brightening I don't want to tip him back to the dark side.

As he starts to make arrangements, looking up the cinema times and ringing Milano's in Dun Laoghaire, my mind drifts. Olivier practically lived on pizza the whole time I knew him, not that you'd know it. Despite all the junk food and the smoking, he always looked annoyingly healthy. I wonder what he looks like now? Will I even recognize him?

'Pandora? What do you think?' Declan is staring at me.

I gulp. 'Um, definitely,' I say, banishing all thoughts of Olivier and hoping that it's the right answer.

He pats my hand. 'I thought so too. Double sleepover it is. Rachel and Iris will have so much fun. We'll be like a proper family, me, you and the two girls, all together. Good practice for the future, don't you think?' He smiles at me warmly.

'Future?' I say, my voice practically a whisper. My stomach clenches involuntarily and acid rises into the back of my throat. I cough. 'Excuse me for a second,' I murmur, before getting up and walking quickly to the bathroom. I lock the door behind me, sit down on the closed loo seat and take several long, deep breaths. This is what I wanted for so long, to find a decent man for a change, someone who treats me with kindness and respect; for Iris to have a father figure, a proper family, and then I react like this when he talks about the future? What is wrong with me?

I sit up and take some long, deep breaths. Calm down, Pandora, I tell myself. Stop with the drama. You're mad about Declan. He's a good man and Iris adores him. Go back out there and act normally. Once you've talked to Olivier, everything will fall into place, you'll see. All the ghosts will be banished, Iris will finally get to meet her dad, and you'll be able to move forward and finally tell Declan and your family why you've been acting like a kook – Dr Oxenbury's letter.

There's a knock on the door. 'You all right in there, Pandora?'

I stand up and turn on one of the taps. 'Fine. The curry was a bit hot for me I think, I just came over a bit funny for a second. Just splashing some water on my face. I'll be out in a minute.' If only it were that simple.

Chapter 5

By Saturday I'm starting to feel a little more like myself. I'm determined to overlook my double-sleepover wobble and enjoy the day with Declan and his daughter. Unfortunately Iris is determined to eat into my equilibrium.

She appears in my room, her little face anxious. 'Mummy, can you help me?'

'What is it, pet? Do you need help with your plaits?'

She shakes her head. 'I'm going to leave it down today. It makes me look more grown-up.'

I nod, trying not to laugh. 'At least ten.' Then I take in what she's wearing – black-and-white striped leggings that Jules bought for her which she's never worn before, a black T-shirt with a glittery skull and crossbones across the front (Jules again), and purple sparkly high-top runners with frilly white socks peeping out from the top. As she tends to be a conservative dresser, much to Jules's despair, and normally wouldn't be seen dead in leggings, let alone striped ones, I'm starting to get a little worried.

'You might need a cardigan,' I say, trying to keep the concern out of my voice. 'What about the nice dotty pink one that you like?'

'Cardigans aren't very cool. Jules only wears cardigans with her pyjamas.'

'Do you want to look cool at school, is that it?'

She scowls at me. 'Mum! You're not funny. Rachel is eleven. If I wear a dress she'll think I'm a baby.'

'I see. What about your white top with the dog on it? It's got long sleeves so you won't need a cardigan and Rachel has a dog so I'm sure she'll like it. Speaking of pets, don't forget to feed Fluffy before we go.' Fluffy is Iris's rabbit, a sweet little black-and-white pile of, well, fluff, hence the name. It was that or Nibbles.

'Fine!' She sighs huffily and marches out of the room. I stare after her. It's not like Iris to be so moody. Some of the other mothers at school claim that their nine year olds are already hormonal, but I haven't seen any evidence of it in Iris, until now. I guess it's all ahead of me.

In the car on the way to Declan's apartment, where we've arranged to meet, Iris seems to have calmed down a little. She's delighted with the concept of a sleepover and, to my relief, hasn't questioned or commented on the fact that I'll be staying over too, with Declan.

'When we all live together, will I share a room with Rachel or will I have my own room?' she asks brightly.

'I've never really thought about it,' I say. And I genuinely haven't. I've thought about living with Declan, in his apartment; I've considered Declan moving into Sorrento House with the rest of us (although that thought didn't last long; I'm not sure Declan would cope with communal living), but I've never considered Rachel in the equation, which I see now was a bit short-sighted of me. She does have her own room at Declan's, after all.

'When you and Declan get married, can I be a bridesmaid? I'm a bit old to be a flower girl, and Rachel's definitely too old. You can have two bridesmaids, can't you, Mummy?'

I hum noncommittally. I'm uncomfortable with the way this conversation is going.

'Will I call Declan "Dad"?' she continues, unperturbed by my lack of enthusiasm. 'After you're married, I mean. Maybe I should start doing it now, to practice. That way me and Rachel will both call him the same thing. Otherwise people might think we're not a proper family.'

It's just as well I'm stopped at a red light or I might have crashed the car.

'Iris, love, it's probably best to call him Declan for the moment. We don't have any plans to get married.'

'Why not?'

'It's a big step and we haven't known each other all that long. Let's just concentrate on having fun today, OK?'

'OK,' she says quietly. I glance in the rear-view mirror. She's slumped down on the seat, looking very disappointed.

'Mummy?' she says after a few minutes. 'What if Rachel asks where my own daddy is?'

'Why would she ask you that?'

'The kids in school do.'

'Really?' I can feel my stomach tighten. Poor Iris, I honestly had no idea that they'd even noticed, although thinking about it, of course they have, kids aren't stupid. In fact if Iris is anything to go by, they can be a lot more observant that most adults. 'What do you tell them, pet?'

'That he lives in France and that I'm going to see him when I'm a bit older. That's true, isn't it?'

'Yes.' I toy with the idea of telling her that I'm hoping to talk to Olivier when I'm Paris, but I don't want to raise her hopes just in case it doesn't work out. The trip is booked now, Bird and Dad have agreed to look after Iris and Declan has accepted the fact that I'm going, whether he likes it or not. I'm trying to take things day by day until then, and attempting not to obsess about what I'm going to say to Olivier. Yes, I'd much prefer to be able to control the situation, to plan ahead, but how Olivier reacts to seeing me is out of my hands, and even though it's a struggle, I have to accept that. If I try contacting him beforehand, there's a good chance that he'll either refuse to see me or simply disappear; no, surprising him is the only way.

'If I do my daddy some pictures, will you send them to him?' Iris asks after a moment. 'Sally-Anne does pictures for her daddy all the time. He lives in Hollywood.' Sally-Anne is one of the girls in her class who comes over to play sometimes, a bit of a madam, although Iris seems not to notice. Unless my geography is hopelessly out of date, Islington, where her dad lives now, with an English holiday rep he met on a family vacation in Porto Santo (I got the whole story one afternoon from Sally-Anne's mum, Clarinda, who likes to talk), is a long way from Hollywood. I say nothing. Poor child, I know the split can't have been easy on Sally-Anne; it's probably just her way of coping.

'Of course,' I say instead.

'Do you think he'll write back to me?'

'I'm not sure, but he might.'

'Does he like animals?'

'Yes.' This one's easier to answer. 'He's a dog person. And like you, he loves drawing.'

'I'll draw him some dogs, then.'

I smile to myself. Everything's so simple for Iris, it must be lovely to be nine. Even if Olivier doesn't want to come to Ireland to meet her yet, at the very least he might write to her. That would be something. And it would be nice to be able to talk about him to someone. Once I've spoken to him, sorted everything out, I'll tell Iris all the old stories, I decide suddenly. It's time for her to get to know her father properly.

Iris was right to up her style game. In a black Jean-Paul Gautier Junior tu-tu skirt that I spotted in a magazine recently, shiny black leather boots and a white-and-tan Burberry top, Rachel is quite the mini-fashionista. If it wasn't for the expensive labels

– which she has an allergic reaction to, unless they're vintage – Jules would be most impressed.

When Declan shows us into the sitting room, Rachel is parked on the edge of the sofa, flicking through the telly channels with the remote.

'You don't have the proper Sky package,' she says, looking up at Declan, ignoring us. 'This is just the cheap one.'

'I don't watch much television,' Declan says. 'It would be a waste of money.'

'But I do. You can't expect me to stay here for the whole weekend if you only have crap stations.' She flings the remote onto the sofa beside her and the back falls off.

'Rachel, don't throw the remote around like that, you're going to break it.' Declan picks up the pieces, fixes it, switches off the television and places it on the coffee table. 'And watch the language.'

'Hey!' she protests. 'I was watching that.'

'Well you're not any more,' he says. 'Now say hello to our guests, please.'

'Hi,' she says, then grabs for the remote again.

He takes it out of her hand. 'Rachel, we're going out now. Please say a proper hello to Iris and Pandora.'

Finally she looks at us. Her eyes are darker than Declan's, dark brown like Iris's, and with her high cheekbones and heart-shaped face, she looks the split of her mother, although her mum's hair is cut into a sensible shoulder-length bob and Rachel's falls in a feathery, layered wave down her back. Funny, I could have sworn that Declan said Rachel looked like him. There are still a few photographs of Jessica on the walls in Rachel's room – Jessica with baby Rachel on her knee, Jessica splashing in a resort swimming pool with a tanned toddler Rachel – and Declan is loath to take them down for his daughter's sake, even though he claims to hate looking at them. I've never met the woman, and from what Declan has told me of her, I'm in no rush to either.

'Hi,' Rachel says again, her eyes flat and barely focusing on us.

'This is Pandora,' Declan says, gesturing towards me. 'And this is Iris, Pandora's daughter, and this is my beautiful daughter, Rachel. Rach for short.' He puts his arm around Rachel, but she shrugs it off.

'Only my friends call me that,' she says, taking a couple of steps away from him. 'Rachel is fine.'

'OK, good,' he says. 'Rachel it is.'

I stare at him, wondering if Rachel is just acting up for Iris's benefit, or if she's always this rude. But he seems not to have noticed.

'Let's get going, then,' he says, rubbing his hands together, all fake joviality. 'It's only up the road so we're going to walk. That all right with everyone?'

'Can't we drive?' Rachel says. 'I hate walking. So boring.' She draws out the last word and rolls her eyes.

Iris giggles. 'I hate walking too.'

I can tell Declan's wavering. 'If you really don't . . .'

'Declan's right,' I cut in. 'We should definitely walk. It's a lovely day and there's nothing wrong with your legs, girls. Come on.'

It's only a ten-minute stroll to the cinema, but Rachel makes it seem like a marathon.

'Are we nearly there, Dad?' she whines a few minutes later. 'I can't believe you're making me walk. Mum never makes me walk.'

Ten steps later. 'Come on, this is ridiculous. Can't you go back and get the car? I'm tired.'

Another few steps. 'My shoes are rubbing, Dad. Do we have to walk all the way? Can't we get a taxi or something?'

I'm itching to ask her to man up a little and to stop moaning but I know it's not my place. I look at Declan but again he seems oblivious. Iris is walking along beside me quietly. I think that she's a bit intimidated by Rachel and I don't blame her.

Finally we reach the cinema and Declan queues up to buy tickets and popcorn, while I wait at the side of the foyer with the girls.

Rachel is standing with her back to the wall, arms crossed, one leg cocked up, and is pretty much ignoring us.

'You all right, Rachel?' I ask her.

'Yeah, why wouldn't I be?' She tosses her hair, and then starts watching the crowds milling past us, a scowl on her face.

'You don't look very happy.'

She snorts. 'Figures.'

'Sorry?'

'Hello? Earth calling woman with the weird name.' She rolls her eyes and pulls a whatever face.

'Are you referring to me?'

'Uh, yeah. Don't see anyone else around here with a weirdo name, *Pandora*.'

Iris is staring at Rachel, eyes wide open.

'What exactly is your problem with my name?' I say. 'You're being very impolite.' I've had about enough of her attitude and I don't want Iris thinking she can go around speaking to adults rudely too.

'Like I care.' Rachel glances towards Declan, to check he's out of earshot presumably, then looks back at me. 'Look, Mum said I had to come today or Dad wouldn't cough up money. But I'm not interested in being friends with you or your freakoid daughter, understand? Mum says that you're too young for him, that it won't last and that you're just after his money.'

Now my blood is boiling. What kind of woman would say such nasty things to an eleven year old? And does Jessica seriously believe that I'm after Declan's money?

'Your mother is mistaken,' I say, keeping my voice even and

trying not to retaliate, reminding myself that it's not the girl's fault she's like this, not if her mother has been feeding her such poison.

'I don't want to hear any more nonsense from you, Rachel, understand?' I add. 'Your Dad—'

'Is crap.'

'Rachel! You're upsetting Iris.' Iris's lip is wobbling and she looks like she's about to cry.

Rachel shrugs. 'Like I care about the big baby in her doggie T-shirt.'

Now Iris really is crying. 'Can we go home, Mummy?' she asks me, her eyes swimming with tears. 'Please?'

Just then Declan appears, waving the tickets in one hand, the other holding a tray loaded with snacks and drinks. 'So are we all set?'

'Sure,' Rachel says, as if nothing has happened. She takes one of the cinema tickets out of Declan's hand, pops the giant bucket of popcorn under her arm and strides towards the ticket desk.

'Everything all right?' Declan asks me, his eyes on Rachel's back.

'Not really,' I murmur. 'But not here.' I nod a little at Iris, who is still sniffing, although her tears have dried up.

'Are you sick, Iris?' he asks her.

She shakes her head wordlessly.

'What is it, then?'

'Rachel upset her,' I say, stepping in.

Declan frowns. 'What did she say exactly?'

'We can talk about it later,' I say firmly.

'It was probably just a misunderstanding,' he says. 'Iris taking something the wrong way. Rachel's great with kids.'

I keep my lips buttoned, and I crouch down in front of Iris. 'Do you still want to go home, pet, or would you like to see the film? Declan has already bought the tickets.'

'If we stay can I sit beside you, Mum? And Declan. Not Rachel.'

'Of course.' I stand up again. 'OK, film it is.'

Declan looks relieved. 'I'm sure the girls will bond over pizza,' he says, leading the way towards the screen.

The film is good, if a little old for Iris – about a high-school talent competition – but I can't concentrate, not after Rachel's outburst. At one stage during the film Declan tries to take my hand, but I'm not in the mood for holding it and besides, I don't think Rachel would appreciate it.

Afterwards, as we walk out of the cinema without waiting for the end credits, Declan says, 'So, who's looking forward to their pizza, then?'

Iris is holding my hand and she squeezes it, hard. Rachel doesn't say a word, just walks on ahead and out the main doors, paying no attention to Declan's request for her to slow down.

'What's up with Rachel?' he asks. 'What exactly happened earlier, Pandora?'

'Iris, I need to talk to Declan,' I tell her. 'Could you wait over there beside the teddy bear game?'

'Can I have a go?' she asks eagerly.

Usually I don't let her play, it's a waste of money – she never manages to catch a teddy in the machine's claw and it always upsets her, but today it's a welcome distraction.

'Sure.' I hand her some coins.

Rachel is loitering just outside the glass doors, playing something on her mobile, so we can finally talk.

'I think you'd better tell me what's going on,' Declan says.

I take a deep breath. 'I know Rachel's going through a difficult time what with the separation and everything, but she was out of line with Iris earlier. She called her a big baby and made her cry.'

Declan sucks his teeth. 'Iris can be a little sensitive some-times. Are you sure she didn't take it the wrong way? I'm sure Rachel was only joking.'

'Declan, she wasn't joking. She was really rude to me too. Said I had a weird name.'

He smiles a little. 'She does have a point.'

'Declan! Why are you sticking up for her? I wasn't going to tell you this bit but she also said that she was only here today because her mum made her. Jessica told her that you wouldn't give them any extra money otherwise. Jessica also told Rachel that I was much too young for you and that it wouldn't last.'

His face clouds over. 'Pandora, I find that very hard to believe. Jessica wouldn't say something like that. She may be bad, but she's not a monster.'

'What, you think I'm lying? Why would I make something like that up?'

He shrugs. 'I don't know. To get back at me for calling Iris sensitive?'

Now I'm spitting mad. 'Why don't you ask your darling daughter what her mother said, then? Go on. And there's noth-ing wrong with being sensitive, it's a hell of a lot better than being a spoilt brat.'

'Are you calling my daughter spoilt?'

I snort. 'Declan, she's wearing a Burberry coat. The kids' ones cost about three hundred quid, we get them into the shop from time to time. No wonder Jessica needs more maintenance.'

'Don't bring Jessica into this.'

'Why not? The bloody woman said I was after your money. As if!'

'Pandora, this has gone far enough. People are staring at us. Lower your voice.'

'No, I won't lower my voice. Your daughter was rude to me and horrible to Iris, and you refuse to believe me or do anything about it. So you can stuff your pizza and your stupid sleepover. We're leaving.'

Iris is very quiet on the way home and I wonder how much of the conversation with Declan she overheard.

'Are you all right, pet?' I ask as I drive slowly back along the coast road. I'm hoping proximity to the sea might help soothe my jangling nerves. I'm still so angry with Declan, on all kinds of levels.

'Yes,' she says, but from her tiny voice, I know she's disappointed.

'There'll be other sleepovers, I promise. And I'm sorry that Rachel teased you about your top. I'm sure she didn't mean it.'

She says nothing. I glance in the rear-view mirror and she's staring out the window, watching the water. I leave her be. I don't really know what to say to her. The whole Declan/Rachel episode has been such a mess.

Iris is quiet again the following morning but that's nothing unusual. Bird and Jules are covering the shop and Dad's out hill walking, so after a bit of a lie-in I settle in front of the computer to catch up on some customer emails, while Iris pulls out her art box and spreads the contents carefully out on the round table in the bay window.

'What are you going to draw, Iris?'

'Dogs,' she says firmly. 'For my daddy. My real daddy. I miss him.'

I swear I can feel my heart squeeze in my chest. She can't possibly miss Olivier, she's never even met him, but I know she longs for a dad more and more as she gets older, and from what she said yesterday about the questions in school, she is clearly starting to feel different for not having a father. Her grampa is around a lot, but I know it's not the same.

'I'm sure he'll love your picture,' I say.

'Pictures, I'm going to do loads and loads.'

And she does, she spends all morning drawing and painting different breeds, using her animal encyclopedia to get the details right – elegant long-legged lurchers, puffy white bichon frises, shaggy golden retrievers, and my favourite, seven chocolate-brown Labrador puppies rolling around and jumping in the air. She doesn't mention Declan or Rachel all day, and by teatime I'm wondering if I should say something. But Jules beats me to it.

Bustling into the kitchen where I'm stirring gravy to go with the roast chicken, Jules dumps her bag over the back of a chair and flops down at the kitchen table beside Iris, who has been reading her Jacqueline Wilson book whilst I've been cooking.

'God, I'm wrecked.' She brushes her curly hair back off her face and rolls her shoulders a couple of times. 'I was out really late last night and the shop was hopping today for some reason. We had to pull Lenka onto the floor after the lunch rush.' Lenka normally works in the Shoestring Café with her sister and her mum. They make a great team and the food is amazing.

'You should have rung me,' I say.

'Don't worry, we managed. You deserved a day off, sis. How was your sleepover last night? Did you both have fun?' She grins at me and then at Iris.

Iris colours a little and stares down at her book.

'It didn't work out in the end,' I say, trying to keep my voice even. 'So Iris and I had pizza in front of the telly last night, didn't we, pet? And then a lie-in and a yummy brunch together.' Iris nods wordlessly, then goes back to her book.

'Everything OK?' Jules mouths over Iris's head.

'Later,' I mouth back and then give the gravy a good stir.

We're all sitting around the table having dessert – Bird, Dad, Iris, Jules and I – when the doorbell rings.

Jules jumps up. 'I'll go. It's probably Jamie.' Jamie, her

boyfriend, conveniently lives next door. They were friends for years before finally getting together towards the end of last year.

But Jules comes back into the kitchen, a peculiar expression on her face. She looks at me. 'It's Declan, Pandora. He's waiting for you in the living room.'

'Tell him to come in here,' Bird trills, waving her hand in the air. 'Join us for coffee.'

'I did ask,' Jules says. 'He says he'd like to talk to Pandora in private.'

Bird looks taken aback. 'Oh, right, I see.'

I can feel Bird's stare boring into me.

'Everything all right, darling?' she asks me. 'You haven't broken up with the poor man, have you? Oh, Pandora. Such a nice chap too.'

'Bird!' I gesture towards Iris with my eyes. 'No, I haven't, actually. Not that it's anyone's business.'

Dad stands up. 'Anyone for coffee? Another bowl of ice cream, Iris?' He's clearly anxious to distract Iris, who is staring at me, her face dappled with interest at hearing about her mum's love life over the dinner table.

'Yes, please,' Iris says eagerly. I've already told her that she's had enough but it's a welcome distraction.

'You run along, Pandora,' Dad says. 'Give our regards to Declan.'

I give him a grateful smile. 'Thanks, Dad.'

I close the kitchen door behind me and stand there for a few seconds, collecting my thoughts. I'm still so angry with Declan that my hands are balled and I almost feel like screaming. If he expects an apology, then he has another thing coming. I take a deep breath, then walk towards the sitting room and through the open door. Declan is perched on the edge of the sofa, his hands clasped in his lap. As I walk in, he looks over and goes to get up.

'Stay where you are,' I say, closing the door behind me, and settling myself in the armchair. For a few seconds I find it hard to meet his gaze, and my heart is racing with adrenaline; clearly my system is expecting a confrontation, but finally I look at him and say, 'What is it, Declan? If you're expecting me to say sorry for anything to do with yesterday's debacle, you can forget it.'

He winces, having the good grace to look contrite. 'It was a bit of a mess, wasn't it? I'm sorry, truly sorry. I was out of line. I spoke to Jessica at length today and it seems that she has been saying things to Rachel that she shouldn't have. I had no idea the woman harboured so much bitterness towards me. I knew she was after more maintenance on top of all the extra bits I've been paying out, but now she's said that unless I cough up, I can forget about spending time with Rachel.'

'But that's appalling, not to mention illegal. You have every right to see your daughter.'

He shrugs. 'I can't force Rachel to stay with me if she doesn't want to. After the cinema yesterday she said you'd upset her and that she wanted to go straight home.'

I stare at him. '*What? I'd* upset *her*? Little—' I stop myself saying brat, but that's exactly what she is.

Declan puts his hands in the air. 'I know, I know. I'm just telling you what happened, Pandora. Please don't jump down my throat. I've spent the whole day being shouted at by Jessica and I really don't think I can take much more.' He drops his head and I can see he's genuinely upset. I soften and move to sit beside him on the sofa.

'You were right,' he adds. 'I was thinking about what you said last night and I guess I have been spoiling Rachel, but only because of all this separation mess. I know giving her money and letting her mum buy her expensive clothes isn't the answer, but I just want her to be happy.'

'That's understandable,' I say. 'She's obviously hurting a lot, and being fed a whole lot of lies by her mother isn't helping.'

'I agree. But I don't know what to do. Rachel says she hates me, doesn't want to see me ever again. My own daughter. How can she even say things like that?' He sighs and shakes his head.

'She doesn't mean it. She's just lashing out at you.' I pause, considering the situation. 'It might help if she talked to someone, a trained counsellor.'

He shakes his head. 'Jessica won't hear of it. Seems to think it might stigmatize Rachel if any of her friends in school found out.'

I blow out my breath. 'Then I don't know what to say. Look, I'm sure Rachel will come around. She's lucky to have a dad who cares about her so much and in time she'll see that. But for the moment, I guess you just have to respect her wishes.'

He bites his lip for a second. 'I'm going to give Jessica the extra money. It might make things easier in the long run and hopefully she might encourage Rachel to stay with me again. I know that she has a couple of tennis weekends planned in the next few months, at the very least she'll want to get away to those.'

'Can you afford it?'

He shrugs. 'Just about, if I take on some extra work. But it'll be tight.'

'What happens if she comes back in a few months looking for yet more money?'

'I'll have to move in with you, I guess.' He smiles at me gently and I'm ashamed to say, even though I had considered it briefly before rejecting the idea, right now the mere thought of it makes me tense.

'Don't look so anxious,' he adds. 'I'm only joking. I guess I'll worry about that if it actually happens. Right now I just want my little girl back.' He takes my hand, his palm warm against mine. 'Pandora, I'm so sorry about yesterday. Can we put it behind us and move on?'

'Yes,' I say simply. He's a good man and I know he's only trying to do the right thing. He moves towards me and I let him kiss me. Wrapped in his arms, his lips on mine, for a brief moment I stop worrying about the past or the future, and concentrate on the present.

Chapter 6
Paris

'That's complete bullshit and you know it,' Jules says, pointing her teaspoon towards Rowie. 'Of course men still fancy women in their thirties. And in their forties and fifties and even older. Look at Helen Mirren, she's ancient and loads of guys fancy her. Rowie, you're in your prime.'

Rowie sighs and pokes at the remains of her tarte Tatin with her dessert fork. 'I just feel such a failure, you know. I thought I'd have a whole chain of shops by now, plus my own label, not to mention a husband and two kids.'

Jules laughs. 'Rowie, are you crazy? You're managing to keep Baroque open, which is a bloody miracle if you ask me. No one's buying new clothes any more, they don't have the spare cash. Plus you have a boyfriend who adores you. You're doing pretty damn well if you ask me.'

'Jules is right,' Arietty pipes up. 'Stop feeling sorry for yourself and have another drink.' Arietty is always deliciously direct.

While Arietty tops up everyone's glasses, I look around the bistro, tucked away off a side street in Montmartre, and I smile to myself. This place hasn't changed a bit. Olivier and I spent many evenings here, curled up on the battered brown leather seats, eating the wonderfully rich, butter-laden food, flicking through their vast collection of old books and pouring our hearts out to each other. It even smells the same: a mix of garlic, wine, old leather and musty books. Even the sounds are familiar: the babble of conversation, the hiss of the coffee machine, the tinkling of glasses.

When the girls asked me to recommend somewhere in Paris to celebrate our birthdays – Rowie turned thirty today and I'll turn thirty at midnight (or, strictly speaking, at 5 a.m. when I was born) – I hesitated for a second, wondering if returning without Olivier would upset me. But in fact it has had the opposite effect; it has made me giddy, almost lightheaded, and I keep imagining that he's going to walk in the door at any minute, give me one of his melting smiles and say, '*Salut*, Dora. Miss me?' like he always did.

'Pandora,' Jules says. 'Did you hear what I just said?'

I look at her and shake my head. 'Sorry, I was miles away.'

'Are you on for doing shots?'

'No, but you guys go ahead. One of us needs to stay sober or else we'll never get home.'

Jules smiles. 'Always the sensible one, my sister.'

'Rowie, what's wrong? Talk to me.' I'm standing over Rowie, wondering what the hell to do. She's starred across the hotel bed, hammering her fists into the duvet and sobbing uncontrollably, her breathing ragged and broken. After dinner we went dancing in a small local club and then walked (or in Rowie's case, staggered) back to where we're all staying, a small boutique hotel in Montmartre, only five minutes from the Sacré Coeur. Rowie has been bawling uncontrollably since we got back to our shared room, over an hour ago.

I sit down on the edge of the bed and stroke her hair. The electric-blue streaks in the otherwise bleached mane feel a little coarse and straw-like under my fingers. Rowie loves changing her hair; she gets bored easily. Until a few weeks ago her whole head was a violent shade of pink – it's all going to fall out soon if she's not careful.

She gives a heaving sob. 'I'm going . . . to end up . . . something, something . . . cats,' she mumbles.

'Cats? What are you talking about? You don't like cats.'

'You don't understand. No one understands.'

'Understand what?'

She wails loudly. 'Leave me alone.' She presses her face into her pillow and says something else that I can't make out but from the tone sounds rather rude.

OK, I'm out of my depth here, I need help. Jules! Jules will know what to do. Emotional outbursts are her speciality and at the very least she might be able to work out what's wrong with Rowie. I try her mobile but it's either on silent or she isn't answering it. I try her room instead. The phone rings several times and finally there's a groggy, 'Yello? This had better be important.'

'Jules, thank God. Rowie's freaking out. Can you come up? I don't know what to do.'

'Up where?' she asks, sounding confused.

'To our room. Please?'

'Now? It's the middle of the night.'

'It's . . . not . . . fair . . .' Rowie lifts her head and wails. 'Jules has years ahead of her.'

'Is that Rowie screeching in the background?' Jules asks. 'What's she saying?'

'I have no idea. She's not making any sense. Something about cats.'

'Rowie hates cats. Thinks they're the spawn of the devil.'

'I know. And she won't stop crying.'

Jules sighs theatrically. 'OK, I'll be up in a minute.'

I sit there, watching Rowie howling and stroking her hair ineffectually until she whips it away.

'Stop . . . touching . . . me,' she howls. 'It's . . . annoy . . . ing.'

Ten minutes later, there's still no sign of Jules so I pick up the receiver and ring her again.

'Yeah?' she grunts.

'Did you go back to sleep?' I demand. 'I need you, Jules.'

She groans. 'Sorry, sorry, I'm coming, honestly.'

A few minutes later there's a knock on the door. I yank it open. Jules is standing there in her pyjamas, one arm propped against the wall, her curly hair sticking out wildly. She's brought Arietty with her. I'm not sure how Rowie will feel about that, as she doesn't know Arietty all that well, but I'm in no position to quibble. Even at this hour of the morning, in an old Dublin Zoo T-shirt and baggy cotton shorts, jet-black hair held back off her face with a towelling band, Arietty still looks stunning.

'Is she having a panic attack?' Arietty says, looking through the door with interest. 'From the way she's breathing it looks like a panic attack. Mum used to have them.'

'I'm not sure.' I usher them both in quickly and close the door behind us. 'I was considering ringing a doctor to give her some sort of shot. Don't suppose you carry animal tranquillizers in your handbag, Arietty?'

'We rarely use them,' Arietty says. 'Only if the animals escape or get themselves caught in fencing or something. Anyway, you couldn't use one on Rowie, the dose might kill her.'

Jules and I exchange a small smile. Arietty often takes things literally.

'Whyyy meeee?' Rowie wails from the bed. We all look over.

'I'm not good at all this emotional stuff, Jules,' I say in a low voice. 'And I can't get any sense out of her.'

'How long has she been crying for?' she asks.

'At least an hour. I hope the walls are thick.' I rub my eyes. 'Maybe she'll talk to you, Jules. I'm wrecked. I could really do with some sleep.' Tomorrow is the day I've set aside to track down Olivier, and I'm finding it hard enough to sleep as it is.

'I'll do my best.' She walks towards the bed and stands over it, staring down at Rowie.

Rowie is still sprawled belly-down on the duvet, the strange orange nappy pants she wears as pyjamas ruched up her legs into crumpled shorts. She's still sobbing and breathing wildly, her shoulders heaving up and down.

'Yep, she's hyperventilating,' Arietty says calmly. 'It's a panic attack all right. And I'm sure the drink isn't helping. Do you have a paper bag? Or a plastic one will do at a push.'

I look around the room. In the small stack of shopping bags I've already collected, mostly presents for Iris, there's a paper one from a bookstore. I slide the books out and hand it over.

Arietty takes it off me. 'Rowie, you need to sit up,' she says firmly. 'Jules, help her, please.'

Once Rowie's legs are over the side of the bed, Arietty crouches down in front of her. 'Now, I'm going to hold this bag over your mouth, Rowie,' she says firmly, 'you need to breathe into it. Try to make the breaths as long and as deep as you can, all right?'

Rowie nods. She's still crying and her face is horribly red and blotchy but she does as instructed.

'That's it,' Arietty says. 'You're doing great.'

Within a few minutes Rowie's breath goes almost back to normal and the tears have stopped flooding down her cheeks.

Jules sits down beside her and starts rubbing her back.

'Come on, Rowie,' she says gently. 'What's wrong?'

Rowie grabs a pillow and hugs it against her stomach. 'I'm not ready for this.' Her eyes well up again.

'Ready for what?' Jules asks.

'This!' she wails, throwing one of her arms out in an arc. 'I need more time.' Then she puts the pillow over her face and sobs into it again.

Jules prises it away. 'You're not making any sense. Talk to me. What has you so upset? Is it something to do with Olaf?' Olaf is Rowie's Norwegian boyfriend.

'Noooo!' she wails. 'I'm thirty. Thirty! How did I get so old? Pandora's thirty now too, and she's so bloody calm about it.'

Mainly because I have other things to worry about. But I keep my thoughts to myself.

'I understand, Rowie,' I say instead. 'Honestly. That's partly why I wanted to be out of the country this weekend. No one likes getting older.'

'It's all right for you, Pandora,' Rowie says. 'At least you have a kid. I haven't sprogged yet. The truth is, I want a baby. A baaaaby.' Her face crumples again.

'Everyone ages, Rowie,' Arietty says in a no-nonsense manner. 'We talked about this over dinner, remember? Count yourself lucky you're not a mayfly. They only live a day. Realistically you probably have another forty or fifty years ahead of you. The average life span for an Irish woman these days is—'

'None of this is helping,' Rowie cuts Arietty off. 'My life is over.'

'Technically it's not,' Arietty begins, but Jules throws her a look.

'I know it must feel that way, Rowie,' I say gently. 'But Arietty is right. You have a long way to go yet. Your life's only just starting.'

'But what if I end up alone?' Rowie's eyes go big and scared. 'In a horrible little flat with hundreds of cats.'

Ah, OK, now we're getting to the cats. 'You won't be alone,' I say. 'I'll be there – and Jules and Arietty. Won't we, girls?'

'Yes, of course,' they chorus after I glare at them to join in.

'Olaf adores you,' I add.

'But he refuses to get married. Says it's too bourgeois for words. Wants to have some kind of New Age binding ceremony instead.' She sniffs at this loudly. 'I wanted to be married *now*, before I turned, you know. I don't want to end up like Anna Winson.'

Now she's lost me again. 'Anna Winson?' Anna Winson is a

remarkably pretty, curvy, dark-haired Hollywood actress in her early forties who has starred in all kinds of big romcoms.

'Over forty and alone. A big joke, someone everyone secretly feels sorry for. She has this great Hollywood career and everything, but we all know what she really wants is someone to love her. Her husband running off with a Victoria's Secret model like that when she was in her twenties must have broken her heart.'

I go quiet. She has a point.

'Personally I think it's all a show,' Arietty says. 'I think that Winson woman has had a devoted husband for years, hidden away somewhere in the Hollywood hills. I bet he's her manager or accountant or something. She just pretends to be single so she'll get all the sad single girl parts in lame movies about love. Smart career move if you ask me.'

Rowie has stopped crying and is looking at Arietty with interest. 'Do you really think Anna has a secret husband?'

Arietty nods. 'Yes.'

This seems to perk Rowie up a little. She sits up, wipes her tears away with the back of her hand and smoothes down her pyjama top. 'Do you think I'm overreacting? To the whole birthday thing?'

I glare at Arietty and give a tiny shake of my head. She has a habit of saying just what's on her mind. No filter, Jules says.

'Not at all,' Arietty says mechanically, clearly lying.

Jules sounds a lot more convincing. 'Of course not. Lots of people hate birthdays.'

'Perfectly normal,' I add. 'Please don't let it put a dampener on your holiday.'

Rowie gives a shaky smile. 'You're right. Do you think the minibar has any chocolate? What do they charge exactly? Is it extortionate?'

Jules stares at her. 'Course it does. It's the first thing I looked for.' She looks at Rowie and then me. 'Bet you guys checked for an iron, didn't you?'

'No,' I say, but it's a fib. I can't wear creased clothes, I just can't, and Rowie's exactly the same.

Jules jumps up, pulls open the door of the mini-fridge and takes out a handful of bars of chocolate and a miniature bottle of brandy. She passes them around. 'Feck the cost. This is an emergency. A brandy will help you sleep, Rowie.'

An hour later, Rowie's equilibrium is restored and we're all in bed again. The stiff drink obviously did the trick, as she's lying comatose on her back, snoring away. But it's not just the noise that's keeping me awake; it's the thought of coming face to face with Olivier tomorrow. Ten years is a long time. A lot can happen in ten years.

I think back to the first time we met. He was sitting on the edge of the fountain in the courtyard outside the Institute and I was standing just in front of him, waiting to meet one of the American girls from my class to go for food.

My eyes were drawn to him immediately. Not because of his face – he was bent over a notebook and his floppy chestnut hair was hiding it; no, because of his shirt. It was the palest blue with a tiny, stylized floral print in pink and green, and I remember thinking an Irish man wouldn't be seen dead in that. He'd looked up and smiled at me, his dark brown eyes warm and inviting. I'd blushed, cursing myself for staring at him, thinking how rude he must think me and feeling I had to explain myself.

'I like your shirt,' I said in my best French.

'Thanks,' he said, answering me in English. 'American?'

I shook my head and smiled. 'Irish.'

'There are many American girls in this college, yes? Not so many Irish.'

'I think I'm the only one. Are you a student too?'

'No. But sometimes I sit at the back of your classes, eavesdrop you call it, yes?'

I smile at him. 'That's right. Odd word, isn't it? I think it comes from the Middle Ages when people used to lurk under the eaves of roofs, trying to overhear secrets.'

My mobile pinged. 'Excuse me,' I said and checked the message.

I must have frowned because when I lifted my head he asked, 'Something wrong?'

He seemed to be genuinely interested so I shrugged.

'I was supposed to be meeting my friend but she's not coming,' I explained. 'No biggie. Bye, I'll see you around.' I turned to walk away.

'Wait,' he said. 'You 'ungry? There's a good café around the corner. Please, come with me.'

In fact I hadn't eaten all day and I was starving, so because I liked his shirt, not to mention his eyes and his smile, and because I was curious, I said yes. Little did I know where it would lead. Olivier, my darling Olivier . . .

Eventually, as light peeps around the edges of the curtains, I drift asleep thinking about Olivier and the way the skin at the edges of his eyes crinkled when he smiled and the way he used to look at me as if I were the most beautiful girl in the world. Olivier made falling in love with him so ridiculously easy. And boy did I fall. Hard and fast.

Chapter 7

The following morning the girls and I are sharing a very late breakfast of hot, sticky croissants, pains au chocolat and plenty of strong coffee outside a café in Montmartre. It's a beautiful day, the sun is shining and we're all hiding our tired, baggy eyes behind sunglasses.

Rowie is quiet. I think she's a little embarrassed after last night's melodrama.

Jules leans back in her wicker chair, making it creak a little. 'So what's the plan for today? Will we hit the markets? Apparently the Saint-Ouen flea market is amazing for vintage clothes and shoes.'

'I'm not trailing around any more shops,' Arietty says firmly. 'My feet are still throbbing from yesterday. I was thinking of checking out the zoo, they have some interesting breeding programmes there.'

'The zoo?' Rowie says. She and Jules exchange horrified glances and I stare down at the table, trying not to smile at their reactions.

'But I'm happy to go on my own,' Arietty adds.

'I'd love to spend the day at the Louvre,' I put in.

Jules looks at me in surprise. 'Really? I thought you'd want to check out as many secondhand clothes shops as humanly possible. You took reams of photos and notes yesterday.'

I arch my eyebrows at her. 'Are you implying I'm a workaholic?'

She grins. 'Are you denying it?'

I smile back at her. 'I thought I'd like to have a bit of a culture-vulture day if you don't mind, Miss Snark. Louvre, Pompidou Centre, the Musée D'Orsay. Like Arietty, I'm happy to fly solo, there'll be quite a bit of walking involved.' I aim this at Arietty, but I'm hoping it will put all three of them off.

'Are you sure you wouldn't like some company?' Rowie says kindly. 'I wouldn't mind seeing the *Mona Lisa* again.'

'It's fine, honestly,' I say quickly. 'We can meet back in the hotel lobby at, say, seven? I've booked somewhere for tonight. It's posh, so dress up.'

Rowie nods. 'If you're sure.'

'Positive.'

I walk as far as the metro station with the others, then take a right, onto Boulevard de Clichy. Visiting this city again is bringing back so many memories. Everything looks so familiar. My apartment was just off this street, on Rue Blanche. It was small, just one bedroom, a long, narrow living room with a kitchen-ette, and a tiny bathroom with a wonky shower, but as the fashion college was on Avenue de Clichy, a ten-minute walk away, the location was perfect. Plus it was clean and bright, with large floor-to-ceiling shuttered windows that opened onto a small cobbled courtyard.

I shared it with two German girls, TEFL teachers, who largely kept to themselves. They didn't seem to like Paris much, to my utter bewilderment (what's not to like about Paris?), and never stopped moaning about how much cleaner/quieter/more effi-cient things were back home. I usually just smiled at them and let it all wash over me. One of them was a good cook though, that I do remember, and they were both anally tidy, worked so much overtime they were barely there and (a big plus) they were happy to share a futon in the living room for reduced rent, leaving me the bedroom, so not bad room-mates overall.

I guess I was hoping for friends as well as roomies, but as they hardly ever went out, and didn't seem all that responsive to my invitations, it wasn't to be. I think that's why I fell into a relationship with Olivier so quickly, although I'd promised myself I wouldn't get involved with anyone while I was here, that my studies were far too important, that I'd never be given an opportunity like this again. But I was lonely, plain and simple, that overwhelming loneliness that tugs at your gut and clouds everything grey. I was grateful when Olivier invited me into his life and unlocked the secrets of his beloved city. He brought my stay in Paris into technicolour. From the day we met, the city became more than simply a place I was visiting; it became a second home.

A girl is waiting to cross the road and I immediately notice her pregnant stomach, straining against her T-shirt, her belly-button protruding like the tied end of a balloon.

She looks young, in her late teens, and I wonder how her family reacted to the news. Suddenly my mind conjures up some of the teary conversations, the slammed doors, the shouting matches that I'd had with Bird.

'It's my life, Bird. I can wreck it if I want to.'

'Can't you see sense, darling? You have your whole life ahead of you and you haven't even finished college. Don't let one foolish mistake destroy everything.'

Dad was more sanguine. He told me that it was my call, that whatever I decided to do he'd back me. But I know it broke his heart to see me so distraught, so confused.

In the end, after a lot of soul-searching, I decided to keep the baby. I'd thought about it long and hard, and abortion didn't seem the right choice for me. I believed I was strong enough to see the pregnancy through and to give the child as good a life as I could. I knew I couldn't go through nine months of carrying a child only to give her or him away.

The last month of the pregnancy went achingly slowly, and

by the time I was full term I was fed up with being fat and uncomfortable. I went into labour in the early hours of the morning, and waited it out by myself, puffing and panting through the contractions until the dot of 6 a.m., when I woke Bird.

Dad drove us to Holles Street Maternity Hospital – looking back, I'm amazed he didn't crash; by that stage the contractions were coming so thick and fast he was in a blind panic about having to deliver the baby in the back seat of the car. On arrival to Holles Street I was almost fully dilated so I was whisked straight into a delivery room. Bird gripped my hand while I pushed Iris out, encouraging me using salty language that I think rather shocked the attending obstetrician.

Miraculously, from the moment Iris was born, Bird and I stopped sniping at each other. It was 'all hands on deck' as she succinctly put it, and my whole family threw themselves into nappy changing, washing Iris's never-ending supply of soiled Babygros and vests, and walking a teething Iris around the block so I could get some sleep. Soon we all wondered what we actually did with our time BI – before Iris.

I think about my daughter's thick, dark brown hair. Recently she'd insisted on a fringe, as Sally-Anne has one. It suits Sally-Anne, frames her deceptively angelic-looking pink cheeks. On Iris it looks rather severe and makes her brown eyes look even darker and more intense. She's generally a happy child, but I've noticed that she doesn't smile as easily as some of her school friends, especially the pearly-toothed Sally-Anne. It used to worry me until I realized that it was just her way. Feeling a little tug of longing for my daughter, I pull my thoughts away from home and concentrate on walking.

I know where I'm heading, across the road, down Rue Blanche for old time's sake, and then crossing onto Rue de la Chaussée-d'Antin towards the Opera House. Halfway down this street I'll find Atelier Ollie and hopefully one Mr Olivier Huppert. I'm already hideously nervous.

I head down Rue Blanche, stopping outside my old apartment block. It looks exactly as I remembered it – high-arched doorway with solid wooden doors that are permanently open, cobbled courtyard with four navy-blue doors off it, concierge's office to the left, with the television bubbling away in the background, the smell of damp washing mixed with garlic wafting out of the open doorway.

I walk into the courtyard, memories floating in front of my eyes like ghosts – Olivier dragging a huge bale of cotton up the stairs so that I could practise making toiles for college. We found a bale of it for a song in the Marché Saint-Pierre. Olivier insisted on carrying it home for me but stumbled with it on the stairs and managed to pull me down with him, tumbling down several stone steps. We ended up on the landing, bruised but laughing. There we stayed, kissing and giggling until an elderly neighbour shooed us along. Olivier cooking me a chicken dish with so much garlic that the whole block reeked of it for weeks. He claimed the recipe, one of his mum's favourites, was called Chicken with Forty Cloves of Garlic, but it sounded such a ridiculous name for a dish I refused to believe him. I looked it up afterwards and he was right.

Tears prick at the back of my eyes and I blink them away and then quickly leave the courtyard. I walk out the doorway, power down the street, past the *boulangerie*, the small Montessori school, the *tabac*, all so achingly familiar. On Rue de la Chaussée-d'Antin I slow down, my stomach taut, my palms tingling with nerves. I can feel my heart hammering in my chest, but I make myself walk on. Number six, number eight, number ten.

Finally number sixteen, Atelier Ollie. A simple white shopfront, with two plate-glass windows. But what windows. On the left, birds swoop down, like something from a Hitchcock film, each crafted from a blue-black man's silk tie; to the right, flowers grow up from the green felt 'floor', this time created from bright floral ties. My breath catches at the back of my throat when I spot Olivier's signature print on one of them – tiny stylized pink and green flowers on the palest blue background.

I stand there, tears streaming down my face. I can't do this. I just can't. I turn to walk away but I stop myself, wipe my tears away with the back of my hand and take a few deep breaths. I have to, for Iris's sake. Before I change my mind again, I put my shoulder against the door and gently push. An old-fashioned bell on a spring rings above me and I smile to myself. Olivier always loved simple, functional things; hated the buzz of electronic door bells. His mobile ring was the theme tune from *Sesame Street*, because it made him smile. He always sang along, his accent making 'Sunny Days' sound ridiculously sexy.

'Can I help you?' A woman is staring at me. She's about twenty-five, tall, willowy and impossibly elegant-looking, with a sharp black bob and a slash of pillar-box red lipstick. Coco Chanel reincarnated. Her English is tinged with a slight American accent.

'Yes,' I say, my voice shaking. 'I'm looking for Olivier Huppert.'

She looks at me for a second, long and hard, her grey eyes flinty, and my stomach lurches. How much does this woman know? Or am I being paranoid?

'Is he around?' I add.

She considers this for a second, saying nothing. I get the feeling that she does know something.

'I run a shop in Dublin and I'm interested in stocking his ties,' I continue, glad that I've come up with something that sounds feasible. 'And shirts. Irish men don't tend to wear hats, but if he could design some for women . . .'

She cuts me off. 'Ollie doesn't do women. Says they are too

70

fussy. Too concerned with disposable fashion.' She says the last word with a sneer.

I find myself laughing. 'I know exactly what you mean. Some people have no concept of real quality. They want cheap, mass-produced tat when they'd be much better off buying pieces that will last.'

I smile at her but she doesn't smile back, which is unnerving and rather unfriendly. 'My shop's all about quality,' I add quickly. 'It started off as a vintage designer shop but we're starting to experiment with some new stock and so far it's been going well.'

'Experiment?' Her nose wrinkles.

Oops, maybe experiment was the wrong word. 'Only exclusive labels of course,' I say. 'Have you heard of the Irish designer Maeve Fabien? We were the first shop to stock her knitwear.'

She looks vaguely impressed. 'I have a pair of Fabien leggings.' She pauses, looks me up and down once more, then says, 'OK, I will talk to him and we can set up a meeting, yes? I am Ollie's partner.'

For some reason this almost makes me cry. This hard, brittle woman can't be with Olivier, surely? I want to ask, 'Business partner or life partner?' but I don't dare. Despite everything, I feel a prick of jealousy.

I look around, my eyes sweeping the white walls, the only colour the shirts and ties hanging from functional brushed-metal rails. To the right is a workbench with two gunmetal industrial sewing machines, bales of cotton are stacked under the desk and above is a shelf of Perspex boxes, each filled with buttons and trim. It's all extraordinarily neat, not a pin out of place. I swear I can smell Olivier's favourite aftershave, Creed Orange Spice, a tingly scent that never fails to reminds me of the clementine I always got at the end of my stocking at Christmas. Olivier even *smelt* original. The skin on the back of my hands prickles. I've been thinking about this day for months, and now that it's finally arrived, I'm terrified.

'Is Olivier here?' I say, summoning up all my courage. 'Could we talk now, in person? I'm going back to Ireland tomorrow.'

She shakes her head. 'Ollie is at a photographic exhibition. In some Irish Academy place in fact.' She shrugs and gives a very French *pah*. 'How he will find inspiration looking at old pictures I have no idea. I am not expecting him back until about four. You come back then, yes?'

'OK,' I say. I have no intention of coming anywhere near this intimidating woman again if I can help it, but at least she's told me what I need to know.

'*Merci beaucoup*,' I add politely.

'You are welcome. See you at four. And your name is?'

The first thing that pops into my head is 'Arietty. Arietty Pilgrim.'

She tilts her head. 'Unusual name. Gaelic name, yes?'

'Yes,' I say firmly, although it's nothing of the sort. Arietty's originally from the Caribbean. I leave the shop smiling to myself at my tiny victory.

Luckily I know exactly where the Irish Academy is, beside the Irish College and the Centre Culturel Irlandais, near the Panthéon. I walk towards the nearest metro station and work out the most direct way to get there. It's on the far side of the river but it's an easy enough journey. Sitting on the train, I think about my last visit to the Academy. Olivier dragged me there on our second date, claiming I needed a bit of culture to perk me up. I'd had a bad day, I couldn't come up with any fresh design ideas and was starting to think I had signed up for the wrong course altogether.

'You just need inspiration,' he'd said after I'd moaned at him about my mistaken belief that I could ever be a proper designer. 'There's a furniture exhibition on in the Irish Academy. Come on. It's open until seven.' He'd grabbed my arm and pulled me along.

'Olivier, I'm in Paris. Paris! Why would I want to be reminded of home? And furniture? It doesn't sound all that exciting.'

He'd just smiled. 'You'll like it. I promise.'

He was right. It was an Eileen Gray exhibition, and we'd spent two hours examining her exquisitely designed Art Deco furniture, studying her notebooks, reading letters she'd sent home to friends and family in Dublin. Gray had lived and worked in Paris and, like me, adored the city. If you've ever seen a simple round side table made of chromed steel, with glass inlay, perfect for holding a cocktail glass, that's an Eileen Gray table. She was a pioneer and Olivier was right, her clean lines, her use of top-grade materials and her work ethic did inspire me. I made lots of sketches and left with a happy heart and several starter ideas for 1920s-inspired column dresses, reassured that I hadn't lost my design mojo.

I get off the metro at Cardinal Lemoine and make my way towards Rue des Irlandais, getting more and more nervous as I approach the Academy, an effortlessly elegant white stone building with a neoclassical façade. There's a glass-fronted notice board on the railings and the poster inside reads, 'The Irish Big House in the Early Twentieth Century. Photographs from the archives of the National Museum of Ireland'.

I smile to myself. That's right up Olivier's street. He's obsessed by historical dress, especially menswear, and used to pore over old photography books for hours, looking for tiny details – buttons, buttonholes, buckles, belts. Even had a special magnifying glass for the task. I used to tease him, call him 'Mr Professor'. But he never minded.

'Menswear is all about detail, Dora,' he'd say with a grin. He was the only person in the world I'd allow to call me that. I've always insisted on Pandora, even to my family, but to Olivier I was Dora from the very first day we met.

'Pandora?' He'd tilted his head in the café and smiled. 'Non. Too long. You are Dora.'

'I most certainly am not!' I'd protested, trying not to laugh, as I didn't really mind; from Olivier's lips anything sounded sexy, even Dora, and from that moment it had stuck. It never occurred to me to call him Ollie. I liked the Frenchness of Olivier.

I walk up the stone steps, push open the heavy, dark green door and walk inside. The hallway is cool and airy and smells of old wood and furniture polish. I nod at the uniformed security man who's sitting behind a large mahogany desk.

'The photography exhibition?' I ask him.

'Yes, through the door to the right,' he answers and waves his hand towards a doorway.

'*Merci.*'

I take a deep breath and walk through before I change my mind. But I needn't have worried; the room is empty apart from dozens of eyes staring down at me from the old black-and-white photographs hanging from the gold picture rail, stark against the pale blue walls. I feel hollow. After all the apprehension, Olivier isn't even here. The girl in the shop was obviously playing some sort of trick on me. Maybe he was in the workshop all along, hiding in a back room, not wanting to see me, let alone speak to me.

I study one of the photographs, a group shot of the staff of Moyross House, the men in black suits made from dark tweed, the women in dark, scratchy-looking wool dresses, some wearing starched white aprons, with frilly white caps plonked on their tied-back hair. No one is smiling.

'Severe-looking bunch, aren't they?' An attractive red-haired woman in her forties is standing beside me. I look over at her and smile. She's Irish, Cork from her accent.

'They are rather.'

She says, 'Have you seen the gamekeepers upstairs? They're a much livelier bunch.'

My heart skips a beat. 'There's another room?'

She nods. 'Up the stairs and to the right.'

'Thanks,' I say, already walking towards the doorway. I almost run up the stairs. I don't know why I'm rushing; I know this is going to be difficult. But I guess at this stage I just want to find Olivier, talk to him and get it over with so I can actually sleep at night.

I pause on the landing, catching my breath. This is it, I tell myself as I walk into the second exhibition room. Hold it together. Then I see the back of someone's head and I walk closer. A man is sitting on a green buttoned bench in the middle of the room, bending over a small sketchbook, his hand moving quickly over the page, recording something. I suck in my breath. The dark wavy hair, the way that he's absorbed in his work, as if nothing else matters, his foot tapping the floor as he sketches, the leather sole beating out a rhythmic noise on the wooden floor. It's definitely Olivier.

I stand and watch him for a moment. My blood is surging through my veins and I feel lightheaded. He hasn't changed a bit. Same slim, muscular frame, same mop of hair, same sense of contained, wiry energy, like a wound-up jack-in-the-box, just waiting to pop out. A wave of regret and, yes, desire rushes over me. He's wearing one of his own shirts – white with a pattern of tiny red hearts – old Levi's and the same scuffed black biker books I remember him buying all those years ago (which had cost a fortune at the time – he was always obsessive about quality); he looks effortlessly cool and very sexy.

After a moment he stops drawing and looks over his shoulder. Our eyes lock and for a second I hold my breath.

'Dora?' he says softly. 'Is it really you?'

I nod, unable to speak, tears springing to my eyes. God, I've missed him so much. But right before my eyes a look of shock, followed by pure anguish and pain washes over his face. Right at that second I realize just how much he loved me and how much damage I've caused him.

He looks away, and hesitates for a moment, before tucking his black Moleskine notebook and propelling pencil into the back pocket of his jeans, then stands up and faces me. I'd forgotten he was so tall. I'm five foot eight and he towers over me.

'What are you doing here?' he demands. His slightly spiky tone makes me uneasy.

'Looking for you,' I say honestly. 'The girl in your shop said you'd be at this exhibition.'

'Mimi. *Zut!*' He runs his hands through his hair. 'Look, I'm sorry but we have nothing to talk about. I think it best if you go, yes?' His dark eyes are now flat and hard to read. He's obviously trying to protect himself but if I can just get through to him . . .

'Olivier, I've come all this way, I really need to talk to you.'

He shrugs. 'I'm sorry, Dora, I can't, I just can't.' His voice catches. 'We have nothing to talk about.' He turns, his soles making a squeaking noise on the polished floor, and walks quickly towards the doorway.

'But, Olivier—'

He swings around, his eyes now full of fire. He puts both hands in the air and gesticulates wildly. 'What? What do you want from me? You broke my heart, Dora. One day you say you love me, the next day poof, you disappear. Drop out of college and run back to Ireland. Without a word! No explanation, nothing! You just disappeared. How could you do that to me? I thought you loved me. Clearly, I was mistaken.'

'I did love you. But I had to go home. I left—'

'A letter. Yes I know. But after all our months together, one fucking letter? For weeks I could not eat. If it was not for Bibi I would have failed my exams. She made me see sense, said it was obviously just a holiday romance for you, a fling, that there would be other girls in the future. That I shouldn't throw away my whole life because of one stupid, selfish Irish girl.'

I wince when he says this. Is that really what he thinks of me?

'It wasn't like that,' I protest. 'Your mum was wrong. It wasn't just a holiday romance.'

'Really? So why did you run away, then, eh?'

'Olivier, you told me you were nineteen. You lied to me.'

He shrugs again. 'Seventeen, nineteen, what's the difference? I thought a college girl wouldn't be interested in a school kid, but did it really matter in the end?'

'Yes! Of course it did. I was older than you. It was wrong.'

'Did it feel wrong, Dora? You look me in the eye and tell me the truth. Did it *feel* wrong?'

I stare down at the floor. My cheeks are hot, burning up. I found out the truth after idly going though his wallet while he was getting changed one day and reading the birth date on his student travel card. At first I didn't believe it; I thought he'd knocked two years off his age to get cheaper fares. When I confronted him about it, he'd just shrugged and admitted that he'd been lying to me. I was deeply shocked and upset. But by then it was too late, I was already in love with him. As he was almost eighteen, and certainly acted a lot older than any boy I'd ever met, I managed to brush my misgivings to one side.

But then I got pregnant and everything changed. How could I land a baby on a teenager who hadn't even finished school yet? It wasn't right or fair. So I ran. Leaving a letter behind saying I was sorry and that it wasn't meant to be. Wishing him all the best in his future life. Writing it nearly broke me and I had to copy it out again as the first attempt was so sodden with tears that it was unreadable. I sobbed all the way home to Dublin. I'm sure the man beside me on the plane thought I was having some sort of nervous breakdown, so he studiously avoided my gaze, sticking his head in his book the entire way home. Don't blame him, I was a mess.

'No,' I whisper. 'It didn't feel wrong. But, Olivier, you have to understand. I was under a lot of pressure—'

He gives a wry laugh. 'Pressure? Dora, I was about to do my final exams. I nearly failed because of you. If it wasn't for Bibi making me study, sitting beside me every night, helping me cram, I certainly would have.'

'How is your mum?' I ask. When I knew her, Bibi was an amazing woman, if a little formidable. Her husband had died in his late thirties, leaving her a very young widow with a tiny son to raise alone and no life assurance or pension to fall back on. A trained artist, she moved from Perpignon to Paris to work as an art teacher, and Olivier was her life.

He just looks at me. 'None of your business. What do you care anyway?'

'Olivier.' I feel desperately hurt. Olivier could be sharp sometimes, but he was never cruel.

He sighs and softens a little. 'She is fine, no thanks to you. She liked you, Dora. God knows why, but she did.'

I stare at him. 'Olivier, she hated me. Told me that I wasn't good enough for her precious son, remember? She said I should find a boy my own age and leave you alone.' Bibi was nothing if not direct. I was terrified of having dinner at their house, but pushed myself to accept when invited, longing to be fully installed in all areas of Olivier's life.

He smiles a little. 'She didn't put it quite like that. I think your memory is playing tricks on you. Underneath it all she thought you were smart and hard-working. Every girl I've brought home since, she compares to you. Not as clever as Dora, she'll say. Not as funny as Dora.'

I look at him. 'Really?'

'You seem surprised. You are quite addictive, Dora. Unfortunately, you get under the skin. But I'm over you now and that is why this conversation is also over. I have no desire to get sucked back in. Why are you in Paris anyway, some sort of

nostalgia thing? Trip down memory lane?' Then he pauses and
snorts. 'Ha! I know, it's your birthday, isn't it? Must be the *grand*
three-zero, yes? Whatever it is, I'm sorry, but I'm not interested.'

'But I really need to talk to you. Can we just sit down for a
minute, please? Or go for coffee or something.'

'No,' he says simply. 'Enough, Dora, please.' He starts walking towards the door again. I run after him and put my hand on
his arm. He shakes it off.

'Please, leave me be, Dora. It took a long time to get over you.
I loved you once, but you clearly did not feel the same way, let's
leave it at that. Like the movie says, "We'll always have Paris."'
He gives a short, dry laugh then strides out the door and
powers down the stairs.

'Olivier, please.' I run after him, down the stairs, past the
security man who is staring at me with interest, and out the
door. Olivier is marching down the street.

'Olivier!' I call after him. He breaks into a run.

'Olivier!' I say, sprinting to catch up with him. It's my last
chance. 'You have a daughter. Iris. She's nine.'

He stops for a second and his head drops. Finally he turns
around and faces me. 'Dora, please, don't do this to me. I don't
know why you would say such a thing. It is cruel, too cruel. I
beg you, leave me alone.' He looks on the verge of tears.

'Please listen to me,' I begin, but he spins around and starts
to walk away again.

'Olivier!' I shout at his disappearing back. 'Olivier.' But it's
no use. He ignores me, then disappears around a corner.

I feel completely wretched. It wasn't supposed to be like this.
Why didn't I bloody well think? I shouldn't have surprised
him, appeared out of the blue like that, it wasn't fair. I guess
in my heart of hearts I was hoping for, oh, I don't know, some
sort of grand Disney-style reunion. That after a few minutes of
awkwardness we'd be able to talk about our time together,
despite everything that happened. But I see now I was being

stupid and naïve. Olivier was always so passionate about everything, so intense. I should have guessed that he'd react like this. But maybe I just wanted to believe that he'd changed, grown up, that he'd listen to me calmly, understand why I'd run away all those years ago, even though it was cruel, I know that now. Then I hoped that he would consider what he wanted to do about meeting his daughter. But people don't change, do they? I certainly haven't. I'm still a delusional fool. Olivier doesn't want anything to do with me, and he thinks I'm lying about Iris. As if I'd do such a thing! By my actions now and my actions all those years ago, I've deprived Iris of her father. Plus her paternal grandmother. Two people who could have played an important role in her life now and in her future. And what if I have this bloody cancer gene. What then? No! I block it out of my mind. I do not have the gene; I will not die and leave Iris without a parent. I will not. But I know I've failed Iris, which leaves me feeling utterly distraught and powerless. I collapse against a doorway and sob into my hands.

Chapter 8

'You've been very quiet all day, Pandora,' Jules says as we settle into our seats on the plane back to Dublin. 'Is everything all right?'

'I'm desperately hungover,' I tell her, instantly feeling bad. Last year Jules gave up drinking for good. She'd been binge-drinking for a few years but it had only come to a crisis last summer when she started having blackouts and accidents. We were all very relieved when she decided to knock it on the head. I try not to drink in her company, but last night, after the whole episode with Olivier, I felt like getting utterly obliterated.

'The little men with pickaxes still chipping away at your brain?' She smiles at me gently.

'Something like that. Which is why I don't normally drink much. I don't know how you coped in work the day after a bender, Jules.'

She shrugs. 'I was just used to it, I guess.' She looks at me, her eyes kind. 'Are you sure there's nothing else bothering you?'

I hesitate. On the far side of Jules, Arietty has her DJ-style headphones on and is bopping her head to an old Nirvana track. It's turned up so loud that even I can hear it. Beside her, Rowie's fast asleep already, snoring gently, her head supported by a sensible grey blow-up cushion, pink eye-mask over her eyes. She hates flying so threw a Valium and a sleeping tablet down her throat as soon as she was in her seat. I don't even know if that's safe, but she refuses to fly without self-medicating. Wish she'd told us about the Valium the other night.

'It's been a strange kind of trip for me,' I begin. 'Just being in Paris brought back so many memories.' Olivier's face flashes in front of my eyes and I wince. I've been trying not to think about him all day but it's been difficult.

'I understand.' She squeezes my arm, then pauses for a moment before asking, 'Pandora, where were you yesterday afternoon?'

'In the Louvre. I told you all about it last night.'

'But you didn't take any photos or buy any postcards. I've never known you to visit a gallery and not come back with something.'

'I took my sketchbook instead,' I say. Then I stop. Why am I covering up? I ask myself. Why can't I just tell Jules what happened with Olivier? I guess it's still so raw and I know I'd be in danger of starting to cry and being unable to stop.

But Jules just smiles and the moment is lost. 'I'm so glad you're sketching again. The dresses you made in college were amazing. Do you still have any of them?'

I nod. 'The ones I did for my finals.'

'Why did you stop designing? I've never really asked you. You got your degree then went straight into Brown Thomas instead.'

I shrug. 'Iris. You have to be pretty bloody-minded to be a designer and work incredibly hard for next to nothing. I couldn't spend years penniless, as a struggling designer trying to make a name for myself. I couldn't live in London or Paris or New York or Milan and work as a pattern cutter for one of the big designers. Just wasn't practical. It was a miracle that I got my degree at all. Iris was born four months before my finals. Then I took the summer off to mind her, and in October I landed the job in BT's.'

'But being a designer was your dream. It's all you ever

wanted, even when you were little. You used to talk about nothing else.'

'It wasn't to be,' I say, trying not to sound wistful. It's one of my greatest regrets and most of the time I try not to think about it. But Jules isn't to know that.

'I know, you should design a range for Shoestring,' Jules says, her eyes animated. 'Those cotton shift dresses you made were amazing. You remember the ones – they were like fitted T-shirts. So simple.'

'Maybe,' I say noncommittally, hoping she'll forget about it once we get to Dublin. Right at this moment I have no idea what I'll be doing in the future and it terrifies me.

Jules looks at me. 'Is that what you were doing yesterday? Finding inspiration for a collection?'

I decide to humour her. 'Something like that. But please don't tell Bird or Dad. It's early days yet. It might not come to anything.'

She grins. 'Pandora, when have you not seen something through? You've always had such amazing sticking power. And you're so not a quitter. That's fantastic news. I can't wait to see your sketches. Have you anything to show me yet?'

'No.' Which is the truth, of course.

'Take your time. But it really is brilliant. Good for you, Pandora. I knew you'd go back to designing, it would be such a waste if you didn't.'

'Thanks. I'm going to try to get some sleep now if you don't mind. I'm wrecked.' I press my head against the head rest and close my eyes. Now Jules is expecting to see sketches. This is all getting too complicated for words. I should have opened up about Olivier while I had the chance, got it over with, but I don't have the energy or the will. I really am exhausted, mentally and physically, and I'd love to sleep, but my mind is all over the place.

*

Jules is right, I'm not a quitter. I've always seen things through to the bitter end. Damn Olivier anyway. I grit my teeth, my eyes still jammed shut. OK, maybe Olivier doesn't want anything to do with me, but like it or not, he does have a daughter and Iris deserves to know something about him. But if anything happens to me before I get a chance to tell her – at the moment I'm not sure she's quite old enough to understand a lot of it, and I don't want to confuse her – she'll know absolutely nothing unless I leave something behind for her, a record of who Olivier was and why I loved him.

A lone tear rolls down my cheek, and I open my eyes and wipe it away with my finger, hoping Jules hasn't noticed. That's what I'll do, I decide, I'll collect my memories for Iris, a record of the time I spent in Paris. The happy, exciting, joyful parts of my brief time with Olivier. He can deny me, and deny Iris, but he can't take away that. It will be my Parisian memory box.

I smile to myself, remembering the old Greek legend of Pandora's box, the story I was named after. Dad wanted to call me Hope, but Mum was far more prosaic. In the legend, Pandora's box was full of all the sorrows of the world, but it also contained Hope, and my box for Iris would too. If I wish and pray for it enough, maybe Iris will never need her box.

Chapter 9

On Wednesday morning, although still wrecked after a sleepless night, tossing and turning – worrying about the mess I've made of the whole Olivier business and trying not to think about the test results – I throw myself into work, trying to keep my mind off things. Luckily it's not hard; as usual there are oceans of jobs to keep me occupied, including a backlog of unsold clothes to return to clients, and an even larger amount to label up and add to the rails. Every day the shop is getting busier and busier. With the way the economy is going, women just don't have the money to spend on brand-new designer clothes, but they still love shopping and still love the thrill of finding nice pieces for a good price. Which is where Shoestring comes in.

One of the benefits of running the shop is that Jules, Bird and I get first dibs on all the pieces that come in. Unfortunately we often can't afford many of the more expensive labels, even at our knock-down prices. Last year Jules had her heart set on becoming the new owner of a stunning pink silk chiffon Faith Farenze dress, but at twelve hundred euro, it was way beyond her budget. So she came up with a clever way of buying the dress – time-sharing it! That's how she met Arietty in the first place. Arietty came into the shop, also fell in love with the dress and agreed to share it with my enterprising sister and become the very first member of Jules's dress share 'Shoestring Club'. I'm also in the club, along with Alex, who Jules found after putting an ad up on the Internet. We strongly suspect that Alex may actually be a man, but as we haven't met her yet, that hasn't been proven. It's a long story, but basically Jamie found an image using Google Earth or something showing a tall man collecting a package from the Wicklow post office. Jamie's a genius with computers and says spying on people is really easy these days if you know how to hack into the right places, which is rather frightening. Jules thinks it's brilliant, but she would! Anyway, we'll soon find out. We're having a Shoestring Club dress handover dinner soon, and meeting this 'Alex' in person should be rather interesting! Everyone in the Club has worn the Farenze now, except Alex, who has it at the moment. I wore it first, to a charity ball, one of my first big nights out with Declan. Then came Arietty who wowed everyone in it at her school reunion; and finally Jules, who out of all of us probably needed it the most. Her best friend, Lainey (ex-best friend, I should say) married Jules's long-term boyfriend, Ed, last year which, as you can imagine, was no picnic for my poor old sister. She was determined to hold her head up high and to attend the wedding, which she did. In fact the Farenze gave her the confidence to consider going in the first place and played an important role in getting her through the day.

Once we get the dress back from Alex at the dinner, if everyone agrees, we're hoping to put it up for sale in Shoestring. It will be sad to see it go, but exciting to buy and wear another stunning piece of couture with the proceeds. Everyone should have the chance to wear an extraordinary dress once in their lives; it really does make you feel like a princess.

Today I'm visiting a client called Poppy Holland. Poppy lives in a huge restored Georgian red-brick pile in Ballsbridge. She does very little as far as I can see, other than shop and lunch. She has a rich businessman husband, Robert (never Rob), a full time au pair (they downgraded from a nanny at the beginning of the year as both the kids are in school now – oh, I hear all about Poppy's staffing dilemmas, believe me), a huge shiny black jeep and two blonde, angelic children, straight out of a Ralph Lauren ad. Fleur and Sasha. A chocolate-brown Labrador called Turtle completes the picture. Yes, it's all as nauseating as it sounds.

On the plus side, she does have a well-honed shopping habit and she likes to clear out her wardrobe regularly to make space on the rails for new purchases. Surprisingly, she has rather good taste. Plus she knows her labels.

To be honest, today I could do without out her wittering on about whether or not she should get train tracks (all the rage with the ladies who still lunch, apparently), or if Antibes has lost its cachet (as if I'd know anything about ski resorts, if it even is a ski resort).

'Pandora, wait up.'

As I'm about to run out the door, Jules catches me. She's waving something in her hand. Looks like a printout.

'Is it important? I'm late for Poppy.'

'Very. It's a letter from one Markham Cinnamon.'

I look at her blankly.

'He's married to Alex Cinnamon,' she says. 'Otherwise known as Alexandra.'

I smile. 'So Alex *is* a girl. That's a relief.'

Jules hands me the printout.

Dear Shoestring Club,

My name is Markham Cinnamon and I'm married to Alex, who is the proud part-owner of the lovely pink dress. For the first few days she used to put it on every evening and parade around the house, swishing the skirt around like a movie star at the Oscars.

I decided I'd take her out so she had something to wear it to. Booked tickets to this charity black-tie thing – *Swan Lake* in the Grand Canal Theatre (and I hate ballet) – but she wouldn't go. She has a problem with going outside the door, you see, makes her nervous. And it's been getting worse lately.

The day the dress arrived she was so happy, but now seeing it hanging on the back of the bedroom door, knowing she'll never get to wear it to anything, is starting to really get to her.

So I had a thought. If she won't go out, maybe I could have a special dinner for her in the house. Unfortunately she's lost touch with a lot of her friends so I was wondering, if it wasn't too much of an imposition, would you have a Shoestring Club dinner at our place? I've read your blog and I know you have special dinners where you hand over the dress to the next person. I'll cook and everything. You wouldn't have to do anything other than just turn up. And maybe we could make it black tie. I'll stay in the background, so it can be a proper girls' night.

What do you think? It would mean an awful lot to Alex and to me.

Kind regards,
Markham Cinnamon

I look up. 'What a sweet man. Booking tickets for the ballet like that. Such a shame Alex wouldn't go.'

'Do you think she has agoraphobia?' Jules asks.

'Sounds like it. So what do you think? Are you on for going?'

'Definitely. I'm sure Arietty will come along too. As long as they're not some sort of catfish weirdos and this is all an elaborate ruse to get us to Wicklow. Not that it's all that far.'

'Jules! Hardly. This is Dublin, not the wilds of America.'

'You never know. Until this morning we all thought Alex was a transvestite.'

I smile. 'True. So you'll email him back, say it's a yes? And let Arietty know. What about this Saturday? Declan is out with the she-devil and it would help take my mind off things.' Last week Jessica cajoled Declan into dinner, ostensibly to talk about Rachel and access, but I'm convinced she only did it to aggravate me. Little does she know that it's actually a relief to have a weekend off. The way I'm feeling at the moment – basically all over the place – he's bound to sense that something's up. No, it's best just to avoid him.

'She-devil?' Jules looks puzzled.

'His ex.'

'Ah, of course. Cool, then it's a date.'

'Now I really must fly or else Poppy will do her nut,' I say. 'You know what she's like.'

Jules rolls her eyes. 'Good luck. Think of the Prada dresses.'

As I crunch slowly up Poppy's sweeping drive, I notice that the large stone cherub in the fountain isn't spurting water out of his mouth today. In fact the pond water is green and full of algae threads. Usually it's clear. There are weeds sprouting from the gravel, and the patch of grass in front of the house looks wild. It's usually as short and manicured as a putting green. Poppy's gardener must be on holiday.

There's a red Ford Fiesta parked where the jeep usually sits. I park beside it, walk up the large granite steps and ring the brass doorbell. Nothing for a moment, then the door sweeps open. I'm surprised to see Poppy herself behind it. Answering the door is usually the housekeeper's job.

I try not to stare at Poppy. She's wearing jeans and a plain and slightly crumpled white shirt, sleeves rolled back. Her hair is pulled into a loose ponytail and her lips are pink and glossy, but apart from that her face is make-up free. Her cheeks are slightly flushed and I've never seen her look so fresh and so normal. Usually she's groomed to within an inch of her life.

Poppy smiles at me. 'Come on in, but watch the bikes. I knocked one on top of me the other day and bruised my shin.'

I follow her into the hall and try not to gasp. Gone are the oriental rugs, the tasteful oil paintings, the mahogany sideboard with two matching antique vases. The huge Waterford crystal chandelier is still dripping from the ceiling, but without all the other trappings it looks out of place, like a glitter ball in a convent. Three adult-sized bikes rest against the right-hand wall, and the striped wallpaper is scuffed where their handlebars and pedals have met it once too often.

'They belong to my students,' Poppy says easily. 'I've rented the shed out to one of my neighbours for his classic car.'

I look at her, baffled. 'Students?'

'I have five of them. Four Chinese and one American. Medics. Got them from the College of Surgeons. The Chinese lads are a bit quiet but Tallulah, that's the Texan girl, she's a hoot. Brilliant babysitter too. I'd never get to my course if it wasn't for Tallulah. The price of babysitters these days.' She wrinkles her nose. 'Scandalous.'

'Doesn't your au pair babysit?' I ask.

She waves her hand in front of her face. 'Got rid of her weeks ago. And the rest of the staff. Gardener, the works. Can't afford them you see. Bank owns the house as it is. There's a whole lot of legal stuff going on, and we can stay here until it's all tied up. Me and the kids wouldn't be eating if it wasn't for the students.' She says this in such a cheery manner that I almost don't believe what I'm hearing.

She must see it in my face because she continues, 'Came as a shock to me too, I can tell you. Losing your house is a really frightening prospect. But don't worry, my family won't see us out on the street.' She gives a bright smile. 'I'm a bit tight on time today, so let's grab a quick coffee and then get stuck in downstairs. You'll love me today, Pandora. I'm clearing out most of my wardrobe. Tallulah is in the master bedroom so all my clothes are sitting in piles downstairs. Hope they aren't too creased. All I need at the moment are jeans and tops. Oh, and maybe a few work suits. That's the next thing on my list when I've finished the course, finding a part-time job.' She leads me into the kitchen.

A job? I've known Poppy for several years now and she's never worked. I look at her in concern. She's losing her house and she's had to take in students to feed her kids; why on earth is she still smiling? Maybe she's on the verge of a nervous breakdown. She has every right to be. Maybe this is all manic energy.

'I'm so sorry, Poppy,' I say gently. 'I don't know how you're coping with all this. Are you sure you're all right?'

She sweeps some stray hair back off her face. 'Never been better, honestly. Sit down for a second and I'll tell you the whole story. The condensed version. You don't need the details, the legal stuff is very tedious.'

She flicks on the kettle and pulls out a jar of instant coffee. I've never been in Poppy's kitchen before, the housekeeper usually brings a tray to the living room, and as Poppy makes the coffee I look around. It's like something from a show house – gleaming white units with horizontal chrome fittings that look like slender towel rails, huge high-tech cooker, central island with funky white leather-and-chrome stools pulled up to it and a long chrome panel overhead with multicoloured bulbs that looks more like a modern art installation than a light fitting. I sit down on one of the stools.

'Milk?' she asks.

I nod. 'Please. No sugar.'

She pulls open one side of the enormous American larder fridge. Inside the shelves are carefully arranged and I spot packets of meats and cheeses from Lidl and several large Tupperware boxes.

'I cook for the students in the mornings when the kids are in school,' she says, noticing me looking at the boxes. 'They all get full room and board, hot evening meal and a packed lunch. It's a lot of work but I can charge them more that way. Luckily they're not too fussy about their food. The Chinese lads won't eat dairy though.' She shrugs and laughs. 'Never thought I'd be running a boarding house, but there you go. Life throws you curve balls sometimes, doesn't it?'

'It certainly does,' I say, thinking instantly of Olivier.

She puts my coffee in front of me and joins me at the counter. 'But needs must. In a nutshell, darling, Robert pissed away all our money. Got greedy, overextended, borrowed too much from the banks, and built too many fancy apartments that no one wants to live in. Half of them aren't even finished, they're just sitting there, concrete shells. As for his ghost estate in Wicklow, don't get me started. I have no idea how he got planning permission in the first place. Anyway, during the good years he'd thrown a whole load of our money into offshore accounts in my name, faked my signature. When his company went belly-up, he tried to make me up sticks to Portugal with him and the kids. As if. All my family are here and I wasn't raised to run away when things get tough.'

Her eyes go hard. 'He owes everyone money, several different banks, builders, suppliers, interior designers, it's endless. Some of them have gone out of business because of him. He refused to pay any of it back from the money he'd stashed away over the years, said that was my money and nothing to do with his business. Well, I wasn't having it. So I sold everything I could – furniture, the jeep, the paintings, the works. Then I got a lawyer and instructed her to withdraw all the money from the offshore accounts and to pay back Robert's suppliers. Not the banks, mind. That would just be a drop in the ocean. But the small guys, the ones who had been loyal to him at the start, when he was building up his business. The ones who came to all our parties, whose wives were my friends, or my ex-friends, I should say. Once Robert absconded, no one wanted anything to do with either of us in case they were tainted by it all too. I don't blame them really, I suppose, but it was a bit of a kick in the teeth. I hadn't done anything wrong.' She sighs. 'Anyway, it didn't make much difference, a lot of the companies still went belly-up regardless, but at least I could hold my head up again. Down the line I'll be able to tell my kids I did my best to sort the whole mess out.'

'And your husband?' I ask.

'Is in Portugal. I gave him a lump sum, enough to keep him for a few months, but he'll have to find a job soon. The kids can visit him during their school holidays, but other than that I want nothing more to do with him. I can't be with a man who screws people over, I just can't. He was lying to me for years about what he was up to. I know this country is in a mess, but it's my home and I want to stay here. To be honest, for the first few months I felt like my whole life was tumbling down around me. The worst bit was when I was trying to pretend everything was OK, terrified that someone would find out that we were broke. But you know something, it's only money. I know that may sound flippant, but seriously. I have clothes on my back, the kids are enjoying their new national school and everything's going to be OK. My sister has said we can stay with her for a while if the worst comes to the worst and we're kicked out of this place. I'm trying to get back on my feet work-wise. I got halfway through a dental hygienist course years ago, then met Robert and within a few months we were engaged and he didn't see the point in me continuing it. So I've gone back to college in the evenings to finally finish it. I'm actually quite enjoying using my brain again.'

'Good for you. I'm sorry about Robert and everything. I know how tough parenting on your own can be.'

She shrugs. 'He was never here and I think it's good for the kids to see their mum working hard.'

'You look happy, Poppy. In fact I don't think I've ever seen you looking so well.'

She grins. 'I know, ironic, isn't it? Poor as a church mouse and I don't give a damn. As long as the kids are happy and healthy, that's the main thing.'

'Can I ask you something?'

'Sure.'

'Don't you miss the shopping?'

She laughs. 'Honestly? Yes, of course. But I don't have time to browse in BT's anymore. I can't afford all the charity lunches and balls I used to go to, which is quite a relief, to be honest – some of them were very tedious – so I don't need half the clothes I used to. I do miss having time to myself and I do miss my jeep; it was lovely to drive. But the Fiesta gets me around just fine. Hopefully I'll be earning soon, fingers crossed.'

She glances at her watch. 'Sorry, we'd better get moving. Have to get to the supermarket before the kids get home.'

'No problem.' I drain my coffee and rinse the mug out in the sink.

'Oh, don't worry about that, I'll do it later. Now, let's get stuck in.'

Poppy's room is in the basement, where the au pair used to sleep. From the bunkbeds against the wall, it looks like Fleur and Sasha are also sharing the space. Under the window sit three large piles of clothes, some still in their designer bags, others in clear plastic dry-cleaners' sheaths. My heart starts to beat a little faster. Poppy has been collecting designer pieces for years; if she really is doing a complete clear-out, this could be quite the hoard for Shoestring.

Usually I don't take everything a client offers us. I go through what they have picked out to sell and check if it's suitable. The items have to be clean (you'd be surprised what some people try to pass off as 'clean'), in good nick – no loose threads or missing buttons, the right season – no woollens in summer, no linens in winter, and they have to have a designer label.

For a naturally curious person like me, going through clients' wardrobes is a fascinating process. First you find the pieces that have literally never been worn, price tag still intact. In most cases these are hastily bought sale items that are a size too big or small but that linger in the wardrobe, waiting for the woman to lose a few pounds or take them to the local alterations shop so that they will actually fit.

Second you find the real gems, classic pieces that the client has just grown tired of but that still have plenty of wear in them. Chanel suits, Burberry trenches, Mulberry satchels, Jimmy Choos worn to one too many parties. This is why people come to Shoestring in the first place, to find heritage pieces at knock-down prices. It's what we're best known for.

Third you have the high-fashion mistakes. The silk jumpsuits that look amazing on twenty-year-old models, but ridiculous on fifty-somethings, especially in leopard skin or any animal print. Nappy pants, peg legs, or any kind of fashion trousers, ditto. Unless they are worn with the right heel, they can look disastrous.

Poppy waves her hand at the piles. 'I've divided them up into dresses, separates, and then tops and knitwear. I've left the shoes in their boxes. Will we start with them first?'

'Good idea.'

She opens the first box, brown with 'Christian Louboutin, Paris' written across it in white cursive script, and pulls out one beautifully made black patent court shoe, with its signature red sole. Even reading the word Paris makes my heart tug. I try to block Olivier out of my mind and concentrate.

'Wore these at the Tallaght Children's Lunch,' she says, putting it back in the box. 'I'm going to keep my favourite pair of Loubes, so these can go. Along with the three other pairs of practically identical courts. I mean honestly, who needs so many shoes? These days I spend all my time in runners and flats. Far more comfortable.'

I look at her quizzically. Poppy used to spend days getting ready for charity balls. 'It is nice to dress up once in a while though.'

'I'm sick of dressing up,' she says. 'Such a palaver. But one day I'll feel differently, I'm sure.'

We move on to her extensive Pedro García and Armani sandal collection – I take every pair for the shop, as they're barely worn and will make lots of our customers very happy indeed; in fact I'm itching to put Poppy's whole collection on the website. Then we move on to her dresses, the bit I'm most looking forward to.

She holds up a perfectly cut silk dress in midnight blue.

'Issa,' she says. 'I bought the same dress in three different colours. This one, red and black. What was I thinking?'

I smile. 'One of Princess Kate's favourite labels. Hugely popular with the yummy mummy brigade. They'll be snapped up in an instant.'

'This one I will miss,' she says. 'My Jonathan Saunders colour block dress. Always reminds me of a Mark Rothko painting.'

'You're a Rothko fan?'

'Sure am. Can't stand the insipid landscapes Robert was so fond of, even if they were worth a fortune. I'm much more of an Abstract Expressionist girl myself.'

Poppy really is full of surprises. She holds up a stiff black fitted dress with a silk chiffon panel at the top, hand-coloured in shades of blue, yellow, green and pink that all merge into each other, like a Turner sunset. It's simple yet stunning.

'How many Saunders do you have?' I ask her.

'Three. This one's my favourite. I wore it at Sasha's first Holy Communion party.'

'Keep it,' I say gently. 'It'll never date. Especially if it has good memories attached.'

She nods. 'You're right. Maybe I'm being too brutal. Thanks, Pandora.'

We go through the rest of her dresses – African-inspired Temperley pieces, colourful zigzag Missoni knits, and lots of sweeping silk ballgowns – and then move on to the other piles. At the end of it all, I've accepted practically everything for Shoestring, in season or not. Yes, knowing she needs the money does have something to do with it, but I have no doubt it will all sell.

'Thank you for thinking of Shoestring,' I say. 'You're going to make a lot of women very happy.'

'Good,' she says. 'You're most welcome. You've always been very kind to me, Pandora. Sometimes if I'm having a really off day I go into your shop and have a quick coffee and a look around; it never fails to perk me up. It's like my Tiffany's. Nothing bad ever happens in Shoestring. That should be your shop's motto.'

For a second we smile at each other and I almost reach out and hug her. But instead I say, 'I think that's the nicest thing anyone's ever said about the shop. Thanks, Poppy.'

Driving back to Shoestring, the back seat of my car piled high with clothes, front seat and footwell awash with shoeboxes, I think about how appearances can be deceptive, and how her husband's bad business practices might just be the making of Poppy Holland. All in all, it's been a strange but satisfying morning. But then I spot the brown Louboutin box on the passenger seat and my heart sinks. Try as I might to shake him out of my mind, he's still there, lingering like perfume on a shirt or lipstick on a collar. Olivier. Always Olivier.

Chapter 10

'Pandora?'

I look up. Declan is standing in front of the Shoestring cash desk, his jaw set, a serious look on his face. He's wearing his customary blue shirt and chinos, and for some reason the lack of sartorial imagination niggles today.

His presence isn't exactly a surprise; I've been avoiding his calls for days now. My burning cheeks betray my guilt. I will them to cool down.

'Declan,' I say and give him what I hope is an easy smile. 'What are you doing here? Shouldn't you be at work?'

He ignores my question. 'Your mobile's been off all week. I've tried ringing the shop but you're never here. Haven't you been getting my messages?'

I shrug. 'I'm sorry, it's all been a bit manic since I got back. I've been all over the place visiting clients' houses. It's typical; everyone wants to clear out their wardrobe at the same time. I'm sorry; I did mean to ring you.'

'It's not like you to go incommunicado like that. I haven't seen you since you got home. I just, well, I was worried.' From the faint purple shadows under his eyes, he's clearly been sleeping as well as I have. I feel even guiltier.

I give him my best reassuring smile. 'As you can see, I'm grand.'

He nods. 'You're sure nothing's wrong?'

'Positive. Look, I'm a bit busy right now, but I'll give you a bell later, I promise.' I shuffle some customer printouts on the desk, trying to look as if I'm swamped.

He looks around the annoyingly quiet shop and his eyebrows lift. He's not buying it.

'How about a quick coffee?' he says. 'I'm sure Bird would hold the fort.'

If I protest, he'll know there really is something up. He has me cornered.

'Sure,' I say. 'I'll just go and fetch her, back in a second.'

As I walk towards the office, my mind begins to go into over-drive. Right now, talking to Declan is the last thing I want to do. Things are just too confusing and I need some space to figure everything out.

I'm so glad I never told him about my plan to find Olivier while I was in Paris; it makes everything far less complicated. At this stage I've pretty much decided to keep the disastrous Olivier experience completely to myself, to try and wipe it out of my mind. Unfortunately Iris is still drawing dog pictures for her 'daddy', but I'll just have to pretend to post them to him and then, when she doesn't get a 'reply', tell her that I'm so sorry, he's obviously moved away. And that maybe he'll get in contact when she's a little older. Pathetic, I know, but what can I do? I will only make matters worse if I really do send them to him.

To be honest, I'm not sure how I feel about Declan at the moment. Everything was clear-cut before I saw Olivier again (OK, I was having a few doubts, but nothing like I am now) and I realized how he still made me feel – as if my blood was on fire. Because with Declan, it's different. Yes, he's a good man, he's kind and decent and reliable and I love spending time with him. But my heart doesn't sing every time I see him. Also he comes with the added complication of a manipulative ex-wife and Rachel, who I haven't exactly connected with.

I open the door of the office and peek in. Bird is tapping away on the computer. She looks up.

'Everything all right, darling?'

'Declan's here. Would you mind covering the floor for a few minutes?'

'I'd be delighted to.' She beams at me. 'So glad you two are getting along so well. Any plans to make things—'

'Stop right there,' I snap, cutting her off. 'I mean it.'

She frowns. 'No need to be so sharp, Pandora. You're not teenagers and you have been together for a while. I just think it may be time—'

'Bird!'

'You are a grumpy boots this morning,' she says, following me out. As soon as she spots Declan she walks briskly towards him, crying 'Declan!' as if he's the Great White Hope. She gives him a kiss, leaving a pink lipstick stain on his cheek, then wipes it away with her fingertips.

'Hello, Bird,' he says with a smile. 'I swear you look younger every time I see you.'

She smoothes down her shell-pink Chanel jacket and preens her white hair, swept back into a neat chignon. 'Thank you. Isn't he a darling man, Pandora?' Her eyes twinkle. She loves a compliment, the more extravagant the better. 'Now, you two lovebirds toddle off and make cow eyes at each other. Go on, shoo.' She pushes me away. For her tiny size, she's always been remarkably strong, and I lurch forwards a little.

'Bird!' I protest again, but she just gives a chuckle. God, the woman is incorrigible.

Sitting opposite Declan in my favourite booth in the café within our shop – a lovely bright open space that occupies the left-hand side of the building and brings in lots of business of its own – mugs of coffee in front of us, I start to relax a little, until he leans forward and takes one of my hands over the table. I resist the urge to pull it away.

'Pandora, I know there's something wrong,' he says in a low voice. 'Please talk to me.'

He looks at me intently and I pull my eyes away from his face and stare down at the table.

'There's nothing wrong, honestly.' I flounder around for an excuse, and then remember Rowie's meltdown. 'I'm just finding the whole turning thirty thing difficult. I know it's pathetic.' I raise my head and give him a wan smile.

'Sorry, just need my hand back for a second.' I pull it away and tuck my hair behind my ears with my fingers. Then I cup my hands in my lap.

He sighs happily and sits back a little in his seat. 'Phew! You really had me going there. I thought you'd met some sort of French hunk in Paris or something. I know women find significant birthdays hard. Jessica was depressed for months after turning thirty-five, in fact that's what started all that yoga thing. But let's not go there today.' His ex-wife had a bit of a mid-thirties crisis after reading *Eat, Pray, Love* and took up yoga and, after a few months, she took up her yoga teacher too – it was sun salutations and downward dogs all the way. Didn't last long, though; the man must have come to his senses quickly.

After a moment Declan smiles at me. 'Pandora, honestly, you look amazing. And thirty is so young. Wait till you get to my age. Your knees will start to go and you'll begin to lose your hair.' He gives a laugh. 'Sorry, sorry, that's just me. But speaking of dodgy knees, what about a walk on Sunday morning? And maybe some lunch afterwards?'

'Yes, of course. I have a Shoestring dinner on Saturday night, so a late start would be great. Iris is sleeping over at her friend's house so it'll be just me.'

'Sounds good. About twelve?'

'Yes, perfect.' He grins back at me, looking so relieved I can't possibly tell him what's truly in my heart. Anyway, it doesn't make sense to me yet, so it's going to sound even more odd and confused if I confess it out loud. As he chatters on about his plans for Sunday my gaze dances around his face, not settling on his eyes. How can you be happily in love with someone one week and barely able to look at them the next?

I know what my heart is telling me – that I'm still in love with Olivier. I've been daydreaming about him all week, replaying all the time that we spent together, wrapped in each other's arms. It's been torture. I've tried to push his handsome face from my mind, but I can't. Olivier is embedded in my psyche, and every time I look at Iris it's him that I see. I know he soundly rejected me in Paris, but I can't help myself. And how can I be with Declan when I know that my heart lies elsewhere? He deserves better.

But I know that my feelings for Olivier are not real, it's infatuation, hormones, wanting something I can't have. I was only with Olivier for five months, not long enough to form a proper, adult relationship. And we were young, so young. No, I must forget Paris, forget Olivier and concentrate on the here and now, on rekindling my grown-up, sensible relationship with Declan. I need all the support I can get right now, and even if he does come with a bucketful of complications, I know his heart is in the right place and that he genuinely cares about me.

So I sit there, trying to concentrate on what Declan is saying and look interested. But when Jules approaches our table, I'm very relieved to see her.

'Hey, guys,' she says. 'Bird said you were over here dodging work. Mind if I steal Pandora away, Declan? I'm having a problem with the window display and I need her advice.'

Declan smiles. 'Sure. I have to get moving anyway.'

I'm out of my seat in a second. Declan follows me and stands beside me, so close we're touching shoulders.

'What are you up to this evening?' he asks.

I stop myself moving away from him. 'Promised Iris a girls' night in.' Which is true.

'I could always babysit,' Jules offers.

I try not to scowl at her. 'Thanks, Jules, but I need to spend some time with Iris. I know she missed me a lot when I was in Paris.'

'OK, I'll see you on Sunday then,' Declan says. 'I'll try not to miss you too much.'

He holds my shoulders and gives me a kiss, his mouth firm against my lips. It feels warm, comforting, and I throw my arms around his neck and pull him in closer, kissing him hard.

I hear Jules giving a wolf-whistle and I pull away.

'Now that's my girl,' Declan says with a wink. 'I'll have more of that on Sunday.'

As soon as Declan's gone Jules studies my face. 'What was that Hollywood kiss all about? Before that you looked so bored I thought I'd better come over and rescue you. And you look positively relieved to see the back of the poor man. Come on, what is it? What's he done?' She puts her hand on my arm.

I swallow. I know if I tell her the truth, that it's not just Declan, that my life is unravelling in front of my eyes, the flood-gates will open and I'll cry so much that I won't be able to stop, and I can't allow that to happen, not on the shop floor. I need to hold it together.

'Nothing,' I say. 'Everything's fine, honestly.'

She opens her mouth to say something, and then stops. Finally after a long pause she says, 'If you need someone to listen, I'm here. I know there's something up, sis. You've been acting odd for weeks now. When you're ready to talk, you come and find me. Promise?'

I bite my lip and blink quickly, willing the tears away. I have a lump in my throat so I just nod and give her a half-smile.

'You're a terrible one for bottling things up,' she says. 'But we'll talk later, yes?'

I nod again, grateful that she's letting it slide.

'Now, let's get stuck into that window,' I say, dying to change the subject.

She smiles at me gently. 'There's nothing wrong with the window, I did a fantastic job if I say so myself.'

'What's the theme this time? The seaside window worked really well, lots of people commented on it. You seem to be on a bit of a roll.' Jules ran out of time to create a donkey, but found some fantastic old fishing nets and metal and wood buckets and spades. I drew the line at putting real sand on the floor. It would have been a nightmare to clean up, even with the plastic floor liner that Jules suggested. Sometimes I have to rein her in a bit!

'Thanks, sis. This time it's flowers and bees. Even made sure to highlight the clothes – the Prada dress with the tulip print is the centrepiece. I know you hate the arty-farty windows.'

'Not at all,' I protest, but she's right. She does get rather carried away sometimes and forgets to put any actual stock in the window. Recently we've had New York skyscrapers made from copies of the *New York Times* as well as the papier-mâché elephants.

'I saw you there with Declan and your eyes were glazing over,' she continues. 'I could see you twisting your hands together under the table and I figured you didn't really want to talk to him, so I came over to rescue you.'

'Thanks, Jules.'

She bumps me gently with her shoulder. 'Any time, sis. I know you'd do it for me if I wanted to get away from Jamie. Not that I would, of course, although he does have his moments. I have just the dress to take your mind off things. This way, m'dear.' She puts her hand under my elbow and leads me gently towards the staff room.

*

I stare at Jules. She's wearing a red dress with a full, just-below-the-knee skirt. The bodice is cleverly draped to flatter even fried-egg chesters like me, and the neat cap sleeves over the arms are very flattering. But it's the skirt that stuns, a riot of poppy red that hangs in delicious swathes from the gently gathered waist. Jules has tied a black leather belt around her waist, and teamed the dress with glittery black shoe-boots. I can't take my eyes off her.

She does a twirl, the skirt of the dress puffing up like a hot-air balloon. I grin. 'That's not a dress, Jules, that's a theatrical event. And the colour – so dense. What on earth is it made of?'

I take the skirt in my hand and study it, rubbing the stiff material gently between my fingers.

'Seems to be satin that's been treated to make it matt,' I say. 'The colour is straight out of "Little Red Riding Hood".' I stand back and look at Jules again. I give a deep, happy sigh. 'You're right, it's utterly swoony. Who brought it in?'

'Kathleen Ireland. She wore it to a Moulin Rouge Ball last year but it's been sitting in her wardrobe ever since. It's by a young Irish designer called Maisie Hersh, who works in London. Trained with Carven.'

'How much?'

'It was two thousand new, but she's happy to sell it for eight hundred.'

My eyes light up. 'Eight hundred? We'll easily get that for the Farenze. Do you think Arietty and Alex will agree to let us sell it and buy this one with the proceeds? It's a great way of getting a new dress without spending a cent.'

She nods and flicks the skirt with her hand. 'Once they see this beauty, absolutely. Apart from Alex, we've all worn the Farenze now and fingers crossed Jamie will win some sort of animation award for his *Bold Tales* and I'll actually have something to wear it to. Imagine if he won an Oscar or something. It's such an Oscars dress.'

I smile at her. Jules has a habit of getting carried away, although Jamie is a very talented animator. 'Let's bring it with us to Alex's dinner, see what the others think.'

'Fab idea. Want to try it on, sis?'

I shake my head. 'Not right now. But well spotted, Jules. As always you have an amazing eye for the most dramatic dresses.'

She gives a curtsy. 'Thank you, sister dear. Now, for the Oscars, I'd have to get some new shoes, obviously. Louboutins would be amazing, wouldn't they? The red soles would match the dress and . . .' While she loses herself in fashion daydreams I zone out, picturing me wearing it and running into Olivier's arms. He always loved me in red, said it brought out the copper highlights in my hair and made my eyes . . .

Jules is looking at me. 'Pandora? I asked you a question. Are you all right?'

'Yes, sorry, I was miles away.' I smile at her. 'What was it?'

'I was just saying that everything is confirmed with Markham Cinnamon for Saturday night. I asked you how long it takes to get to Wicklow by car? Arietty has offered to drive.'

'That's kind of her. About forty minutes, I guess.'

Jules is still staring at me. 'Want to talk yet?' she asks, her eyes soft.

I shake my head. 'Not right now. Later, I promise.'

'You're starting to scare me, Pandora. It's nothing bad, is it?'

I shake my head, determined not to concern her. Because there's so much I've been keeping from her and from myself. There's the whole Olivier thing and there's also the test result, which I'm trying not to think about, but failing miserably. So no, nothing on my mind at all, no siree!

Chapter 11

The shop is hopping all afternoon and I'm glad of the distraction. Lately we've had to start making appointments for our sell-in clients as the Shoestring word has started to spread far and wide. It's extraordinary; women travel from all over Ireland to give us their clothes to sell, thanks largely to regular mentions on Sissy Arbuckle's *Style on a Shoestring* show on RTÉ. Every week she features ways of saving money while still looking great.

At first Jules was raging that Sissy had stolen our name – Shoestring – until Bird pointed out that every time the programme is mentioned on RTÉ it's a subliminal ad for our shop.

'You can't pay for that kind of advertising, darling,' she'd said. 'You must admit, Sissy's show has been good for the shop, whatever you think of her personally.'

Jules thinks that the show is complete rubbish and that Sissy's sense of 'style' is too *Footballers' Wives* for words. Jules runs a service for customers called Shoestring Style Snap – taking photographs of clients in suggested outfits and making up a bespoke scrapbook using the images, a personal style bible – and it's very popular. Sissy has had several sessions, not to mention stern lectures from Jules about showing too much cleavage and leg together, but after a few days Sissy still regresses to low-cut tops, teamed with short skirts, leaving Jules exasperated. The joke is that Sissy worships Jules, largely because Jules has no time for the woman. Sissy keeps begging her to do a styling slot on the show but so far Jules has refused.

'Why on earth would I want to do that?' she demanded last week when I brought it up yet again after being harassed by Sissy to persuade her. 'I have no interest in being on the telly, unlike that pathetic Sissy creature who seems to think she'll dissolve away like the Wicked Witch of the West if she's not on the box or in a glossy magazine every week.'

I'd smiled. Sissy was fame-obsessed all right. 'Come on, Jules,' I cajoled. 'It wouldn't kill you and it would be great for the shop. You might even enjoy it.'

She glared at me. 'No, and tell Sissy to stop annoying me about it or there'll be no more style advice, end of story.'

By six o'clock I'm exhausted, so tired my eyes feel scratchy, my neck aches and I can't stop yawning. I haven't slept properly for weeks and it's starting to catch up with me. I collect Iris from the Magic Roundabout, her after-school club, and grab a curry from the takeaway. There's no way I'd have to the energy to cook more than beans on toast tonight, and besides, Iris is a curry freak.

She's in a talkative mood as always, and as she chatters away about school, and funny things that happened in after-school club – a boy called Douglas putting popcorn up his nose and blowing it out again seems to have been the highlight – I try to resist the urge to ask her to keep it down.

'Lovely, darling,' I say every now and then so she thinks that I'm listening. As we pull into Sorrento House, I'm pathetically grateful to see that Dad's car isn't there. The fewer people I have to talk to this evening, the better. I just want to eat and then fall into bed. Bird is out at her friend Daphne's for dinner, so it looks like I'll have the place to myself.

As I walk into the hallway I hear music from the kitchen and wince. The *Glee* chorus murdering a song from *Wicked*, one of my favourite musicals. It must be Jules. She and Iris are huge *Glee* fans. I pretend to disapprove of their *Glee* fests, but I'm secretly delighted that they have so much fun together. Jules is an amazing aunt and Iris dotes on her.

I walk into the kitchen and plonk the takeaway bags down on the table.

'Thought you were going out with Jamie tonight,' I say loudly over the music.

Jules plays with her iPhone, which is wired up to the stereo, turning the noise down. 'Thought I'll hang with my favourite sister instead. Hey, is that curry I smell? Can I rob some? I'm starving.'

'You can share mine, Auntie Jules,' Iris says sweetly.

'There's plenty to go around,' I say. 'I always order too much when I'm tired. You set the table and clear up afterwards and it's a deal. Iris can give you a hand. I'm so wrecked I can barely speak.'

Jules sticks her tongue out at me. 'You're a right slave driver, sis.'

I flop down at the kitchen table and hinge my body over until my chest is flat against the wood. I put my hands under my head and pretend to snore.

'Mummy!' Iris squeals. 'Stop being such a banana head.'

Jules smiles. 'Banana head? Is that the latest insult at the Magic Roundabout?'

'Douglas made it up,' Iris says.

'Is Douglas your new boyfriend?' Jules teases.

Iris colours. 'No!'

My stomach rumbles loudly. 'Feed me,' I say in a deep, monster voice. 'Feed me, now!'

Jules and Iris laugh.

'I think your mother's gone a bit fruit loop, Iris,' Jules says. 'So we'd better get our skates on.'

After dinner I start to feel a little better. As Jules puts the plates in the dishwasher, I help Iris get ready for bed. She's old enough to do it by herself, but I like to spend as much time with her as possible in the evenings. Working mother's guilt.

'Will you read me some more Judy Blume tonight?' she asks, jiggling her legs into her pyjama bottoms. I found some of my old *Superfudge* books and she's flying through them.

'Quick then, into bed. Unless I do it right now, I'll probably fall asleep in the middle of a page.'

She hops under her duvet, rearranges her pillows behind her slight body and snuggles back against the headboard.

I kick off my shoes, climb in next to her and read Fudge's antics out loud for a few minutes, before my eyelids start to droop and I begin to drift off.

'Mum.' Iris digs me in the side.

'Sorry.' I try to read a little more, but it's no use, I just can't stay awake.

'You were snoring a bit,' Iris says, shaking my shoulder. 'I think you should go to bed now.'

I sit up a little and smile at her. 'I think so too.'

I just about manage to take my make-up off and stagger into bed. I've just started dozing off when I hear the door open.

'Pandora? You all right?' It's Jules.

'I'm wiped out,' I say through a yawn.

'You're going to sleep? It's not even eight yet. I thought you wanted to talk.'

'Sorry. Another time, yes?'

'I know there's something bothering you, sis. I'm here when you want to tell me. Don't leave it too long, OK? Pinkie promise?' Pinkie promise is one of Mum's old expressions. She used to hook her little finger around mine and say it.

I smile to myself. 'Pinkie promise.'

She leaves, closing the door behind her, and within seconds I'm out like a light. The next thing I know I'm chasing a tall, shadowy male figure down an alleyway, falling over old-fashioned metal dustbins, running past an old dumpster full of cardboard boxes, stray cats sitting on them, meowing forlornly at me.

'Stop!' I yell, but he doesn't slow down. There's a dead end and he halts and slowly turns around. It's Declan. Then his stomach erupts and something eels its way out like a scene from *Alien*. It's Olivier's head, his face dripping with blood and bile. I wake up in a cold sweat, my heart racing uncontrollably, my skin creeping from the revolting image. Jules used to get appalling nightmares and now I understand why they bothered her so much.

I lie there for what seems like hours, waiting for my heart rate to slow down before finally drifting back to sleep. Just before 6 a.m. I wake up. Finding it impossible to doze off again, I switch on my bedside light, get up and throw a cardigan over my pyjamas. I open my curtains and then my shutters, carefully, trying not to make any noise, and I stand at the window for a second, staring out. The sky is grey and heavy, threatening rain.

I have an hour to fill until seven, when I can feasibly take a shower without waking the household too early. I look around the room for ideas – the off-white walls, the framed movie poster of *The Wizard of Oz* that Jules gave me one Christmas, the chest of drawers I'd painted eggshell blue and brightened up with jewel-coloured glass handles, the small antique glass chandelier Declan had found me recently at a flea market in Temple Bar. My eyes rest on the book on my bedside table, a surprisingly interesting biography of Emily Dickinson that Dad had recommended, but my mind is too agitated to read. Then I notice that the door to my small walk-in wardrobe is open and I spot some shoeboxes out of place. Iris must have been at my sandals again. She loves trying them on but never puts the boxes away properly. I start tidying up, stacking them neatly with their labels outwards, so I can see where every pair is. If it wasn't for Shoestring I'd never own such beautiful shoes. I treat myself to one amazing pair every year – classic Louboutin courts, soft Chloe ballet pumps, striking YSL wedges, spiky Balmain boots. I know wearing secondhand shoes bothers some people, but I always give them an extra-thorough clean before putting them near my feet. For these beauties, other peoples' cooties are worth it!

As I put the Louboutin box back in its place, the red Paris lettering makes me think of Olivier and I remember my plan to make a memory box for Iris. I'm far too awake to sleep now, so instead I rummage at the back of my coats and find the plastic Au Printemps bag I hid there many years ago.

As I start pulling out photographs, museum flyers, exhibition programmes, riverboat ticket stubs, cards from bars and cafés, even an old Air France boarding pass, the memories come flooding back. I'd forgotten how many places Olivier and I visited over the months. He was determined to show me all the sights, to give me both the tourist version of Paris and the local insight. My fingers rest on a postcard. An elegant stiff-necked ballerina in a white tutu, the net skirt built up with layers of real net sewn onto the front of the card and beaded with tiny silver sequins. I know Iris will adore it. I run my fingers over the stiff netting.

Then I have an idea. I take the Louboutin courts out of the brown shoebox, place them in their soft red shoe bag instead and put them on a shelf. Then I put the postcard in the box, walk back into my room, take out one of my sketchpads and a pen, and sit on my bed staring into space.

In the event of me not being around to tell her, I want Iris to know how wonderful Olivier *was*. Not *is*. I will also make it clear, however much it will hurt her at first, that meeting him in person is out of the question. I can't bear the thought of Olivier rejecting Iris. Yes, of course he could be made to take a paternity test, there is no doubt whatsoever that he's her father so it would certainly be positive. But what if he rejected her even then? Wouldn't that be worse? No, I want to paint a picture of my time in Paris, and my time spent with Olivier, nothing more. I want her to know about Olivier so that if anyone asks in the future she can tell them all about him with confidence. I want her to feel complete, not like a part of her history is missing. Knowledge is power, as Mum always said.

I want to give it to her soon – I've been thinking about her tenth birthday. Nine months' time feels about right. Not now, not with all the Declan/Rachel business still so raw in her mind. But soon enough. The box will be a way of sharing some of my memories, and leaving her with something tangible in the future, for her to look at and read when she likes. Yes, it will probably trigger questions – oceans of them, knowing Iris – but I can deal with that when it happens. Right now I need to concentrate on what I'd like her to know, on bringing Olivier to life on paper. I tap my pen against my teeth for a few more seconds before starting to write.

Dear Iris,
    Happy Birthday! This box is for you. It's a record of my time in Paris with your dad.

Then I stop abruptly, finally allowing the paralysing thought that's been playing in my mind since I first thought of the box to surface. What if I'm not around in nine months' time to give it to her? Mum went so quickly. I gulp. This box is about Olivier, not about you, I tell myself. Try to focus on the present. Tell Iris about Paris, about her dad.

I know you are curious about your Dad, which is only natural. I'm truly sorry that he's not present in your life, Iris. I'm sorry that you will never meet him. Unfortunately he moved from Paris a while back, leaving no forwarding address and there is no way of contacting him.

I loved your dad very much. He was tall, with brown eyes just like yours, and a mop of wavy dark hair. He was very artistic, like you he loved to draw and paint and he went to college in Paris, which is where I met him.

I've picked out some things that mean a lot to me, cards and photos and bits and pieces that I think you'll like. I'll write something to go with each item. I hope this will give you some idea of what your Dad was like, Iris. He was one of a kind, I want you to know that. And like him, you are also one of a kind. A very special, talented person with such a bright future ahead of you.

This was your dad's favourite quote, Iris: 'We are all in the gutter, but some of us are looking at the stars.' It's by Oscar Wilde. Keep reaching for those stars, Iris.

I love you.
Mum XXX

I stop and read back over last few sentences. I'd forgotten all about that Wilde quote and I'm surprised I still remember it. I'm feeling a little teary now, but I pick up the ballet postcard and turn it over.

Dora Schuster
You are invited to Swan Lake
in Opéra National de Paris Garnier
on Thursday 23 March
Wear your red dress - I love you in red!
Always yours,
Olivier XXX

I start writing the memory to go with the card.

Unusual for a boy, I know, Iris, but Olivier was a big ballet fan. He was brought up by his mum, who was also a fan, and she took him from when he was very young. She was a strong woman, an artist and an art teacher, and she always spoke her mind. She was never much bothered by what other people said or thought. A lot like Bird, I guess!

We had such a wonderful night at the ballet. Olivier collected me from my apartment and he looked so handsome in a dark suit with a sky-blue tie with tiny darker blue birds on it that he'd made himself. He took my arm and we walked to the Opera House. It's such a beautiful building, Iris, I'll take you there one day, like a giant wedding cake, with lots of columns and sculptures outside, and a huge white marble staircase inside. Walking up towards the auditorium I felt like Cinderella.

The ballet was magnificent, and every time a dancer did a special leap or pirouette, Olivier would squeeze my hand and sigh happily. Afterwards, Olivier walked me home and at every lamp post he stopped and gave me a kiss. It took a long time to get there!

A tear plops down onto the page and I soak it up with the edge of my sleeve before it has a chance to blot my writing. I blow out a breath. This isn't going to be as easy as I thought. I carefully tear the pages out of my sketchbook and attach the ballet memory to the back of the postcard with a paperclip. Then I place the card and sheets in the shoebox and gather the rest of the Paris paraphernalia back into the Au Printemps bag, promising myself that I'll add to it every week. However much it breaks my heart to remember, Iris will have her memory box.

Chapter 12

'What's in the body bag?' Arietty asks as she pulls away from Sorrento House. Jules is squished in the back of Arietty's old but surprisingly clean Mini, with a zip-up dress carrier laid carefully over her legs.

'It's a Maisie Hersh dress,' I explain from the passenger seat. Jules has kindly let me sit in the front as I get carsick in the back. 'Jules spotted it the other day and we've been keeping it on hold. It would make the perfect second Shoestring Club dress. But only if everyone likes it as much as we do, of course.'

'Wait till you see it,' Jules adds. 'Sex on legs. It'll look stunning on you.'

'Don't say anything to Alex about it yet, OK, Arietty?' I say. 'I'm not sure if she'll want to stay in the club with things the way they are.'

'What do you mean?' Arietty asks.

'According to her husband, Markham, she never leaves the house,' I say. 'If she doesn't go out, she'd hardly have anywhere to wear it to. I don't want to put her under any pressure to stay in the club either.' I stop and give a short laugh. 'Look, we haven't even met her yet. Maybe she'll be appalling or a real psycho, or even worse, really boring and we'll all be happy to see the back of her.'

Jules hoots with laughter. 'Pandora Schuster! That sounds like the kind of thing me or Arietty would say. It's not like you to be so cutting.'

117

I sigh. 'Sorry, it's a just been a long week. Ignore me.'

I stare out the window as Jules tells Arietty more about the dress. Jules is right; it's not like me to be so unkind. But my whole body feels practically rigid with stress and I can't seem to relax. I take a few deep breaths and tell myself to calm down. I've found myself slipping back into over-organizing things in the last few days, folding and re-folding the towels in the airing cupboard until they sit just right, making sure the book on my beside table is exactly parallel to my bed; I even took a spirit level to the paintings on the wall running up the hall stairs, convinced that they weren't hanging perfectly correctly. I'm aware that I have to watch it – I became a compulsive hand-washer after Mum died and Bird had to take me to someone to talk about it, and I can be slightly obsessive about things. I know it can be triggered by anxiety and lack of sleep, and being aware of this helps a little, but not completely. I resist the urge to clean Arietty's grubby windscreen with a tissue and try to concentrate on what Jules is saying instead.

Twenty-five minutes later we turn off the N11 and drive through Kilcoole as per Markham's emailed instructions.

'What does it say next?' Arietty asks me. I'm on navigation duty.

I read out, 'Take a left directly after the pink farmhouse with the tractor graveyard outside it.' Then lift my head. 'Anyone see a pink farmhouse?'

We drive for several minutes, past several white and yellow farmhouses, and a lot of trees and open fields, before Arietty says, 'Could that be it?'

She nods at a low-lying building surrounded by rusty old farm machinery. It's lurid, Barbie pink.

'Must be,' I say. 'There's the left turn. He says it's quite bumpy and to take it slowly.'

Arietty swings the car off the main road, onto a rutted lane-way with grass growing up the middle .

'You'd definitely need a four-wheel drive if you lived up here,' she says, her voice jiggling like her car. 'How far up is the house?'

'He says there'll be a sign for it. Summer Cottage. There it is.' A hand-painted wooden sign peeks out of the bushes. Beside it is a long, low wooden gate.

'I'll get the gate,' I say.

As soon as I get out of the car I'm greeted by noisy barking, and three large black Labradors come bounding towards me – to be accurate, two bound, and one fellow with greying jowls lumbers as if he's had a hip replacement. I'm not great with dogs; Iris is the animal lover in our family and if it wasn't for their enthusiastically wagging tails I'd be nervous. A tall, well-built man is following them down the short muddy drive. Behind him, on the crest of a small hill, must be Summer Cottage, a pretty two-storey house with white and pink clematis around the wooden porch. There's a large wooden shed to the right of the house painted eggshell blue, and, as Arietty suspected, a chunky navy Land Rover that looks well able to cope with the bumpy lane. To the far right of the shed is what looks like a covered-up sand pit in the shape of a boat and a toddler's swing seat hangs from one of the trees. It really is idyllic.

I hesitate at the gate, not sure whether to open it because of the dogs.

'Don't worry about that, I'll get the gate,' the man says, reaching me. He has navy-blue eyes, tightly cropped dark hair and a wide smile, and I'm instantly impressed by his smart grey pinstripe trousers and a beautifully cut white shirt. Irish men often have a problem with smart casual, hence Declan's semi-permanent blue shirt and chinos combo.

'Sorry about the boys,' he adds. 'They can be a bit noisy but it's all bluster. They're not used to many visitors. I'm Markham.' He sticks his hand over the gate and shakes mine warmly. 'Thanks so much for coming. Alex is dead excited to be finally meeting you all. She's just inside putting the final touches to the table.'

'I'm Pandora,' I say. 'And Jules and Arietty are in the car.'

'Good. You can drive on in,' he says, opening the gate and then leading the dogs away from it. 'I'll deal with these messers. Don't worry if they run out, they can't go far, there's an electronic fence around the land. Alex would be distraught if one of them went wandering. The gate's mainly to keep stray cattle or deer out. Park anywhere you like, plenty of room as you can see.'

'Thanks.'

As I climb back into the car Jules says, 'Yum, is that Markham?'

'Shush!' I say. 'Arietty, he said to drive on up and park wherever you like.'

Arietty parks beside the jeep and we all pour out, taking care not to dirty our shoes on the muddy drive. As requested, we've dressed for dinner. Markham leads us towards the small porch at the side of the house.

'Come on inside,' he says, opening the bottom part of the split wooden door and standing back politely. The top is already open. 'Alex is in the kitchen, waiting for you. You're all looking fantastic, I might add. Thanks for making the effort.'

Inside is a slightly dark utility area, with a huge dog basket taking up most of the tiled floor space. Markham makes sure the dogs stay outside by shifting them back gently with his booted foot. Arietty bends down and starts rubbing their backs and talking to them and, distracted, they stop trying to force their way inside.

'Sorry, it's the back entrance really, but we rarely use the front,' Markham says, leading us over the chunky grey-slate threshold. 'It's a bit smelly from the dogs.' He's right. There's a strong whiff of damp dogs in the small room, mixed with lavender fabric conditioner.

'Who are you calling smelly? Not my boys, I hope.' A small blonde woman appears in the doorway to our right. When she realizes that Markham has company she blushes deeply.

'Are we early?' Jules whispers in my ear. She nods at the woman, who is wearing a sky-blue apron over cropped jeans and flip-flops.

'Don't think so,' I whisper back.

The woman gives us all a nervous smile and says, 'Come in, come in,' ushering us into the kitchen. 'Apologies, I'm running a tad late.' This must be Alex.

'Arietty,' Jules says, calling her away from the dogs. Arietty gives them one final rub and reluctantly joins us.

As we pile into the kitchen, a lovely cosy room with a low ceiling and traditional cream wooden cabinets with small hearts cut out of the doors, the woman scuttles away from us and props her bum against the cream Aga. She brushes her hair back off her flushed face and I notice her hands are shaking a little. She looks at Markham, as if willing him to say something.

He says, 'Alex has been hard at work all day, cooking for this evening.'

'I'm afraid it's only a stew thing,' Alex says, her voice shaky, her eyes flitting around the room and not resting on anyone. 'I hope you all eat meat.' Arietty is about to open her mouth until Alex adds, 'But I made a vegetarian tart just in case. I'm mortified not to be dressed yet. The time just ran away with me.'

'When you see what Alex has done in the dining room, you'll understand why,' Markham says. 'Sorry, Alex, this is Pandora here,' he says gesturing at me. I give her a warm smile.

'And this is Arietty and Jules, Alex,' he continues. 'Which is which, girls?'

'I'm Arietty,' Arietty says firmly. 'And that's Jules,' she points at Jules.

'I like your dogs,' Arietty adds. 'What are their names?' She looks at Alex.

'Mo, Digby and Ryle,' Alex says, her face coming alive. 'Three boys. Ryle is Digby's dad.'

Arietty smiles her ultra-broad smile, which is like the sun coming out, changing her face from closed and a little severe to gloriously open in one swift movement. 'Beautiful coats,' she says. 'So glossy. Do you give them supplements?'

Alex nods eagerly. 'Cod liver oil. And I brush them every day. They love their food but they can get a bit overweight sometimes, especially Ryle. They should probably get more exercise.'

Markham laughs. 'Nothing to do with spoiling them rotten, Alex, no? Listen, you run upstairs, love, and get changed. I'll fix the girls a drink. What can I get you all? There's white wine in the fridge and beer, or there's red if you prefer. Or I have plenty of fizzy grape stuff in the fridge; Alex isn't much of a drinker. But what about a glass of cava to start off with? It's pink to match your lovely dress.'

Once he's taken our drink order, Markham gestures towards the seating area to the far end of the kitchen, overlooking the garden, and we settle ourselves, me and Jules on the squashy sofa, Arietty in one of the olive-green wicker armchairs, her long legs stretched out in front of her.

I take a good look around. It's still bright outside and through the French doors I can see a freshly mown lawn at the far side of the house, with several large raised vegetable beds to the right, against a dry-stone wall. The dogs are rolling around on the grass in front of the beds, nipping each other playfully.

There's a wooden dresser against the wall in front of the sofa, the shelves packed with jauntily painted pottery plates and mugs, and several framed photographs of Markham and Alex. I spot a baby feet plaque tucked behind the mugs. Beside it are two small pink leather baby shoes.

'How old is your baby, Markham?' I ask him.

Markham swings around. 'Sorry?'

'The baby shoes are so cute,' I say, nodding at them, but his face has suddenly turned grey. He puts the bottle of cava he's holding in his hand down on the kitchen table. He seems to need to take a minute before replying.

'They belonged to Adela,' he says eventually. 'Our baby daughter. She died eighteen months ago.'

'God, I'm so sorry,' I say. 'I shouldn't have been so nosy.'

'It's OK,' he says. 'We should probably put the shoes away. I keep meaning to move them but . . .' he tails off. 'And Alex . . . Anyway, if you don't mind, probably best not to bring it up tonight. Alex is a bit fragile about it all still.'

'Of course,' I say quickly, utterly mortified for saying anything in the first place. I can feel my face blushing.

I think Markham senses my discomfort. 'It's not a problem at all; honestly, it's just not something Alex is comfortable talking about.'

He goes back to preparing the drinks. Moments later he walks towards us and hands me a glass of sparkling cava. He goes back, fetches Jules and Arietty's soft drinks and a beer for himself, then sits down on the other wicker armchair and leans towards me. 'She blames herself, you see. We were out hill walking and Addie was in the backpack. Halfway up the Sugar Loaf her breathing started to go funny. We couldn't get any mobile reception, so we ran back down to the car park and rang an ambulance. When it finally got to us it was too late, we'd lost her.'

'That's so sad,' I murmur.

'The doctors said there was nothing we could have done. She had this congenital heart thing and it was a miracle that she lasted as long as she did.'

'What age was she?' Jules asks gently.

'Eight months,' Markham says. 'Just starting to pull herself onto her feet and coast around the furniture. She was such a sweet little thing, so good-natured.' He blows his breath out in a rush, and blinks rapidly, his eyes tearing up. 'Sorry, it still gets to me. But she was part of our lives and I like talking about her.'

'Who do you like talking about?' Alex appears in the Farenze and she looks a different woman. She has pinned her hair back in a simple bun, added a slash of dark pink lipstick, and her platform shoes give her a good two extra inches. She looks stunning. Then I notice her eyes, blue like Markham's, but a delicate pale china blue, like a summer's sky, though unlike her husband's they're flat, dead almost. But it's no wonder, after what she's been through.

'You look beautiful,' Markham tells her, standing up. 'Let me get you a drink. You take my seat, love.'

She sits down and holds her hands in her lap.

'Have you enjoyed sharing the dress?' Jules asks. 'Amazing to get the chance to part-own and wear something so beautiful, isn't it?'

Alex nods. 'Yes. Yes, it is.'

'Here you go, love.' Markham passes Alex a glass of cava and then stands beside her, his hand sitting on her shoulder. Alex moves a little, away from his touch, and he removes his hand and then takes a step back, standing behind her instead, his hand now resting on the back of the chair.

'And we're buying another dress,' Arietty says baldly. 'The girls decided as long as you weren't boring you could share that one too. But you seem pretty cool to me so I'm sure it's a goer. The dress is in the car. Pandora's going to show us all after dinner, isn't that right, Pandora?'

'Correct,' I say, trying not to laugh.

Jules is staring rather crossly at Arietty, who really is irrepressible. When I'd told Arietty the dress plan in the car, I didn't expect her to blurt it out like that. Clearly neither did Jules.

'What?' Arietty looks at Jules. 'Was it something I said? Alex is normal, not a looper at all, so what's the problem?'

Now I really do laugh. 'There's no problem, Arietty.'

Jules is just rolling her eyes in exasperation; both Alex and Markham seem to think it's funny too, thank goodness.

I turn back to Alex. 'You're going to love the new dress, Alex.' The poor woman clearly needs a bit of cheering up and if our new dress helps in any way, then good.

'Where's that one from, Pandora?' Alex asks me. 'The dress you're wearing, I mean. Is it from your shop? It's very unusual.'

I smile, looking down at the black knitted mini-dress with its green, white and blue zigzag pattern. 'Thanks. It's Missoni. Definitely from Shoestring. There's no way I'd be able to afford it new.'

'Pandora wears a lot of black,' Jules adds. 'It suits her dark personality.' She grins at me.

I chuckle. 'Thanks a lot, sis. What does your dress sense say about you then, exactly, eh?' Today Jules is in a rather eccentric green-and-pink Miu Miu dress with a large swan head painted down the front.

'That I have impeccable taste,' Jules says.

'And that you mate for life,' Arietty adds. 'Like a swan. You should see her and Jamie together, Alex. That's Jules's boyfriend. They're completely inseparable. He's the boy next door too, honest to God. They grew up together.' She pretends to put a finger down her throat. 'Sickening sweet.'

Jules punches Arietty playfully on the arm. 'Lies, the whole lot of it. Pandora and Declan are far worse. You're just jealous, Arietty, you'd love a boyfriend like Jamie.'

'Yeah, right. He'd fit under my arm like a handbag. I'd look like a giant beside him.' Arietty gives one of her wonderfully fruity, rumbling laughs. 'I'd like to point out that Jules dressed me this evening,' she says. 'I don't normally go around in this kind of get-up; it says absolutely nothing about who I am. I spend my life in work overalls or jeans, in fact. I think the animal print amused her. I work at the zoo, you see.' Arietty's pale yellow House of Holland dress with a grey rhino print is rather zany, but looks wonderful against her dark skin.

'With the elephants,' Alex says, nodding. 'I've read all about you on the Shoestring blog. You're so lucky. I'd love to work with animals again.'

'Again?' Arietty asks. 'Were you a vet or something? Why did you stop?'

Alex twists to look up at Markham, slight panic on her face.

Markham picks up the thread. 'We used to run a pet shop together, but Alex finds it difficult to leave the house at the moment,' he explains in a gentle voice. 'Don't you, love?'

Alex nods. 'Yes,' she says softly. 'I know it's stupid, but—' She shrugs. 'I just do. I'm happy here. With all my boys. I don't need to go anywhere else.'

'By boys she means me as well as the dogs, I hope,' Markham says. He squeezes Alex's shoulder. 'Right, sweetheart, why don't we show our guests into the dining room?'

We follow them both down a short white corridor and into a room with warm terracotta red walls and a large, rustic-looking wooden fireplace.

I gasp. 'Alex! Did you do all this?' I say. I look around, trying to take it all in. The long table is dressed with a starched white linen table cloth. Ivy winds its way down the middle and spills over both ends, entwined around chunky white church candles. There's bunting criss-crossing the ceiling, and peering at it I realize that each triangle is embroidered with a different coloured evening shoe. A white napkin is sitting on the dinner plate at each setting; our names have been hand-stitched onto them in swirling raspberry-pink script.

'Did you make the napkins yourself?' Jules asks, picking one up and examining it. 'Holy moly, that must have taken you hours.'

'You've even spelt my name right.' Arietty looks most impressed.

Alex smiles shyly, but I can tell she's delighted. 'Do you like them?'

'They're fantastic,' I say. 'You shouldn't have gone to so much trouble.'

'Alex is a dab hand with the sewing machine,' Markham says proudly. 'Makes some of her own clothes and everything. She loves making things, don't you, love?'

Alex blushes and starts to look a little embarrassed. 'I'm sorry, I probably went a bit over the top with the table, but we don't have many people over. I just wanted it to look special. I hope it's not too much.'

'No, no, it's perfect,' I assure her. 'Our new dress is definitely worth celebrating in style.' We all stand there for a second slightly awkwardly before I say, 'Shall we sit down?'

Alex looks flustered. 'Yes, yes, of course. Sorry, please take your seats. Markham will pull out the chairs for you. Be careful, they're heavy. He's my waiter this evening, aren't you, hon?'

He smiles at her. 'Certainly am. I know my place. I'll be eating in the kitchen with the boys.'

'You're welcome to join us,' Jules puts in. 'I'm sure no one would mind.'

'Not at all,' he says. 'This is Alex's special night with the Shoestring girls. Much as I love shoes and stuff, I'm happy to watch the match in the kitchen. But thanks for the offer.'

As soon as we've all taken our places I raise my glass.

'I have a good feeling about tonight, girls,' I say. 'To the Shoe-string Club. To new friends and fabulous dresses.'

Markham's as good as his word. He brings in the baked pear and stilton starter and then disappears.

'How long have you been living here?' I ask Alex as soon as he's gone. 'It's a gorgeous place.'

'About six years,' she says. 'Markham built it himself.'

Jules drops her fork with a clatter. 'No way, José! Seriously?'

Alex laughs and it's lovely to hear her light, girlish chuckles. She seems to be less fraught now that we're all sitting down and eating.

'He had a lot of help with the plumbing and the electrics,' she explains. 'But he did most of it on his own. He's really practical. Made that fireplace from old railway sleepers and the slates on the floor are roof slates from the old cottage that was on the land previously. It was falling down so it had to be demolished.'

'I'd love a man like that,' Arietty says with a sigh. 'Practical, good with his hands. They don't make them like that any more, not often anyway, and he likes animals too? How lucky are you, Alex?'

Alex's cheeks go pink and she gives another happy laugh. 'I know. He's amazing; he's my rock.'

Normally the 'rock' description, along with 'soulmate', makes me wince, but from Alex it sounds, well, honest.

'Where did you meet?' I ask, genuinely interested.

'In first year at college,' Alex says. 'We were both doing English at Trinity and bonded over our mutual bafflement at *Ulysses*. After college we spent a year in New Zealand together, then came back home and drifted around for a bit. Lived in a couple of really dingy flats in town, worked in mobile phone companies, that kind of thing. Markie did a stint in Google, which paid well but it was pretty full-on and we never got to see each other during the week. Every weekend we'd drive into the mountains, try and get a bit of head space, you know? We used to do a lot of hill walking . . .' her voice trails off, then she shakes herself and continues. 'Anyway to cut a long story short, eventually we decided we'd like to live nearer the mountains, but not too far from our families and friends. So we rented a house in Wicklow for a while and commuted to Dublin to work. Then we found this place, which was going for a song as it was completely rickety and the roof had caved in, so we decided to buy.'

'What about the pet shop?' Arietty says. 'Markham said something about a pet shop.'

I watch Alex's face but she seems OK with the question.

'That's right,' Alex says. 'Markie's mum and dad ran one for years in Wicklow Town. He used to work there every summer during college. Then his dad died a few years back and closing the shop would have broken his mum's heart so we took over the lease. Unfortunately his mum's health isn't great, she had a stroke last year, and he and his sister take turns looking after her. So the shop's not open at the moment. But the Internet site is still up and running. It's called Pet Planet and sells pet supplies and accessories for cats and dogs and things like that. But the site's a bit slow at the moment what with the recession and everything. People are cutting back on luxuries, especially for their pets. Tesco's sell pet food now, which doesn't help; people just grab it with their shopping.'

'Did you manage to sell on the lease?' I ask. From Bird's experience with the Shoestring lease, I know these things can be tricky.

Alex stares down at the table. 'No. The shop's empty at the moment, and unless we find a sub-tenant, we'll have to pay the full rent for five more years.'

'I'm sorry to hear that,' I say. 'That must be tough.'

She gives me a brave smile. 'We'll manage.' She slugs back her cava just as Markham reappears to clear the plates.

'Who'd like some wine now?' he asks. 'Red or white, ladies? I have Alex's favourite in the fridge, a nice New Zealand Sauv Blanc.'

'Sounds perfect,' I say.

'Just a small glass for me, please, then I'll move on to sparkling water or that nice grape juice,' Jules says.

I throw her a sympathetic look and she smiles back at me. She's progressed to the stage where she can have a glass over dinner and is then able to stop, and I'm proud of her. It hasn't been easy, especially not in Ireland where people tend to look at you funny if you order a soft drink. But Markham doesn't flinch.

'Excellent,' he says. 'Coming right up.'

During the main course, we talk about the new dress for a little while and Jules and I tell Alex all about Shoestring and its customers. Arietty has a few elephant stories to keep us amused and before we know it, two hours have flown by. Alex and I are well stuck into the second bottle of wine when Markham brings the dessert through, a tray of sundae glasses heaped with smashed meringue, cream and strawberries.

'Eton mess,' Alex says, as Markham places one in front of each of us.

He serves Alex before me and she tut-tuts at him and says, 'Markie, visitors first,' before passing the tall glass across to my setting. Her hand is unsteady and the glass wobbles a little precariously before I right it. I think the wine has gone to Alex's head.

'Most people seem to like it and the strawberries are from the garden,' Alex continues. 'We planted them when I got pregnant with Addie.' She stops for a moment, picks up her dessert spoon and starts turning it over in her hands. Her voice drops as she adds, 'Every time I got pregnant we planted something different, didn't we, Markie?'

He's standing perfectly still, looking at her, the empty tray frozen in his hands. 'Yes, love, we did.'

She continues, her voice wistful. 'We started with fruit trees – cherry trees, apple trees, pear trees. But by the time we got to Addie, things weren't going so well so we decided perhaps we should be less ambitious. Looking at the blossom every spring started to make us feel a bit sad. So we thought, strawberries, nice and simple, nothing splashy, no blossom to remind us of . . . everything. But it didn't make any difference. We still lost Addie.' She gulps and a single tear runs down her cheek. 'We should never have gone up that mountain. It was so stupid. She was only a baby . . .' Her eyes spill over and she dabs at them with her napkin. 'I'm sorry; I don't know where that all came from. I think it's the wine. Please excuse me for a second . . .' She stands up and runs out of the room, past Markham who just gazes after her.

'Are you all right, Markham?' I ask him gently after a moment.

'That's the first she's talked about Addie to anyone, ever,' he says, still looking rattled. 'She pretty much shut down after the accident, which is understandable, but it's been nearly two years now, we have to move on. She can't spend the rest of her life inside, it's a waste, she's only twenty-nine. The doctors say to give her more time, but it seems to be getting worse, not better. All she ever wanted was to be a mum, to have a baby of her own to look after. But it doesn't look like it's ever going to happen. We're on the adoption list, but unless her condition changes, I think it will scupper our chances, to be honest. Unless she can show the adoption people that she can care for a child, drive him or her to school, do all the normal things, we don't have a hope. She has to want to get better. I thought all this dress stuff might help, having you guys here, wanting to go to another dinner in the future, outside the house . . .' He sighs deeply, clearly distressed and overwhelmed. 'I really am doing my best. I can't believe I'm telling you all this. You must think we're a pair of weirdos, telling complete strangers our whole life story.'

'Markham, it's absolutely fine,' I say. 'And we do know Alex, from the blog, so we're not complete strangers. You've clearly been through a lot over the past few years, and it's understandable that Alex is, um . . . that Alex is . . .' I'm stuck for words.

I look at Jules, hoping she'll help me out by jumping in as I have no idea how to safely finish my sentence without offending him. I can hardly say 'a bit odd', now, can I? But it's Arietty who saves me.

'I think you're both doing brilliantly in the circumstances, Markham,' Arietty says. 'We were saying earlier how lucky Alex is to have you, weren't we, girls? A man who can build his own house and who likes animals, now that's rare. And she's clearly devoted to you. I know I was teasing Jules earlier about being joined to Jamie by the hip, but I have to come clean and admit that she was right – I'm dead jealous of couples that obviously love each other as much as you and Alex do. And working in a pet shop together, that sounds idyllic.'

'Hear, hear,' Jules says firmly.

'Thanks,' he says, smiling at us all gratefully. 'Actually, I really miss working together. The ironic thing is I know Alex misses the pet shop too. She loved working there, she had all these fantastic ideas about how we could build it up, with pet owner evenings, talks for children, petting days in schools, dog and owner drop-in sessions, a book club based on novels featuring animals, *Watership Down*, *Animal Farm*; she even found one called *The Accidental Tourist* which is about a dog trainer. We had an event space all designed too, at the back of the shop, but it's all come to nothing. Once I found good homes for the last of the rabbits and guinea pigs, I had to shut the place down. It was too much to run on my own plus look after Mum and Alex.'

'You have to be fully committed to a shop all right,' I say. 'It's a bit of a vocation. But does Alex know what's at stake, Markham, that unless she tries to go out, you may get turned down for adoption?'

He shrugs. 'I'm not sure. Sometimes I think she lives in a bit of a bubble. As long as I don't mention going outside, she's absolutely fine. As soon as I suggest it, it's a different story.'

'Maybe you're being too nice to her,' Arietty suggests. 'Maybe she needs a firm hand, like those dogs of yours.'

'Arietty!' Jules hisses.

'I'm just saying.' Arietty looks unrepentant. 'Those Labs are a bit spoilt. Going to fat too.'

Markham just laughs. 'She's right, you know. Alex lets them lick the plates in the dishwasher and polish off all the scraps. Maybe Arietty's right, I could try being stronger with her. One of the doctors did suggest it, in fact. I'm just not good at being firm.'

'Pandora's very good at being firm,' Jules says. 'She could help. Give you some advice on how to boss people around.'

'Thanks a lot,' I tell her, a little miffed.

'It's a joke, sis,' she says. 'Just trying to lighten the mood.'

'But you know, Jules, you're actually right,' I say. 'We could help, if you'd let us, Markham. We could plan a special Shoestring trip, and insist that Alex comes along. Prove that leaving the house is actually possible. When she's done it once, it might make it easier the next time. I presume it's all about slowly building up her confidence again.'

'And I'm well used to panic attacks,' Arietty says breezily. 'If Alex gets really bad we can feed her some Valium or something. Pandora's friend Rowie has loads.'

Markham looks a little alarmed at this statement and I don't blame him. He probably thinks Rowie is some sort of drug dealer. Which reminds me that I haven't heard from her since Paris.

'Rowie's scared of flying,' I explain quickly, eager to clear things up. 'She takes Valium to calm her nerves in the air. But I'm sure it wouldn't come to that. What do you think, Markham? It must be worth a shot.' I pause for a second. 'Do you know what? I might have an idea for something to take Alex to, something that she'd love. Somewhere she could wear the new Shoestring Club dress to as well. How are your carpentry skills?'

Chapter 13

I wake up with a throbbing headache on Sunday morning, which isn't surprising. It was a late night in the end and I didn't get to bed until after two. Alex came back downstairs during coffee and apologized profusely for running off like that.

'Don't be daft,' I said. 'We're all friends here. No need to apologize.'

'Are we?' she asked, her expression lifting. 'Friends, I mean?'

'Of course,' I said. 'Friends in fashion.'

'And in animals,' Arietty adds. 'Anyone who's as nutty about dogs as you are can't be all bad.'

Alex smiled. 'That's what I think too. Animal lovers are generally good people.' She looked at Arietty for a second. 'I hope you don't mind me asking, but are you adopted?'

Arietty usually gets quite shirty about questions like that, but she didn't seem to mind Alex asking. 'No, my mum's from Trinidad, but my stepdad's Irish. I was born in Trinidad but I grew up here.'

'Sorry,' Alex said. 'That was crass of me. I didn't mean anything by it. I really shouldn't drink. Things pop out that shouldn't.'

'It's fine, really,' Arietty said. 'Don't worry about it.' But it was clear the whole adoption thing was on Alex's mind.

'It wouldn't bother me if I was adopted,' Arietty added thoughtfully. 'My stepsisters are white but funnily enough, apart from the obvious, we look quite alike. Must be the old nature versus nurture thing.'

At that stage I kicked Arietty under the table, willing her to stop before Alex realized that Markham had been filling us in about their plans to adopt. But Arietty had already moved on to tell Alex about this gorilla that had adopted her sister's gorilla baby in one of the American zoos.

It had been quite the night all in all. Alex promised to write the whole evening up for the Shoestring Club blog and post it later today and I can't wait to read her take on everything. From the warm hugs and kisses we got on the doorstep, she seemed to have enjoyed the evening. The more I think about it, the more convinced I am that my plan to get her out of the house will work.

Declan texts me at twelve on the dot.

Are you on your way over? Will I come and collect you?

I sigh. I wish I hadn't promised to meet Declan today. I really can't face a pre-lunch walk, so text him back to say that I'm running late and I'll meet him at one at his apartment instead.

I drag myself through the shower, throw on some jeans and try to dress them up a bit with a white shirt and a beautifully cut black Burberry jacket that one of Poppy's friends brought into Shoestring last week, along with a suitcase of other designer pieces, most of them barely worn. Poppy's clearly not the only one downshifting.

I drive over to Declan's apartment and reverse into a parking space. I can't see his car, but all the spaces directly outside his block are taken, so sometimes he has to park it around the back. I climb out of my Golf, lock up, walk up the short pathway to his block and ring the buzzer. There's no answer, so I ring again. Still nothing. I fish around in my bag and find my mobile.

It takes a few seconds for him to answer. 'Hello?'

'Declan, I'm outside your apartment block, where are you?'

'Sorry, sorry. I'll be back in five minutes. Rachel wanted a bagel so we nipped into Dun Laoghaire. Will you wait?'

My heart sinks. He never said anything about having Rachel this weekend, it must have been a last-minute thing. I could do without her amateur dramatics today.

'Sure. But if you've already eaten . . .'

'No, no. I've booked a table at The Rosewood. I know you like it.'

'Declan! I'm not really dressed for The Rosewood—' But he's gone.

Then I notice a woman staring at me though the open window of a navy BMW. She's wearing heavy tan make-up, bubblegum-pink lipstick and a lot of mascara, making her eyelashes look like two hairy spiders. Her black hair is long and sleek, held back off her face by large white-and-gold framed Versace sunglasses. I recognize her from somewhere – she must be a Shoestring customer, so not wanting to be rude, I give her a cheery wave and say, 'Hello. Nice day, isn't it?'

She scowls at me. 'You've got a bloody nerve.' Her voice has a slight accent, London maybe, or Home Counties.

'Excuse me?' I say, confused. What did I just say?

She climbs out of the car and totters towards me, nearly coming a cropper on the edge of the path but righting herself just in time. She's wearing head-to-toe Versace: skintight white jeans, red and white striped top, red peep-toe sandals.

'I know exactly who you are. Pandora Schuster. You know that's a married man you're playing around with, don't you? Or doesn't that bother you?' Her eyes narrow to slits.

The penny drops. Now I recognize her. It's Jessica, Declan's ex, minus the neat bob and wrap dresses from the photographs in Rachel's room. She's clearly gone from Boden to Beckham in one large fashion leap. My stomach lurches. This is not good, not good at all.

'Look, I don't think this is the time or the place—' I begin.

'Women like you should be locked up. Husband stealer!' She walks towards me and stands inches away from my face, her lips pressed firmly together.

I take a few steps backwards, my heartbeat starting to quicken. 'I'm going to wait for Declan in the car,' I say as calmly as I can. There's no way she's dragging me into a catfight; the woman's clearly deranged.

'That's right, run away,' she says. 'Do you have any idea what it's like being me? I know I made a stupid mistake, I know I hurt him, badly, but I thought that he'd forgive me eventually if I waited long enough. But then *you* came along. Although I must admit you're not what I expected. I imagined tight dresses and swishy hair.' She looks me up and down. 'If I'd known I wouldn't have bothered with the bloody hair extensions.'

Charming! 'I'm sorry, I'm really not comfortable talking about this with you,' I say, edging away from her. I start walking towards my car. She stays on the path. I can feel her eyes scorching into my back. Luckily she's decided not to follow me.

But she clearly hasn't finished. 'Why are you being so high and mighty?' she says loudly to my back. 'Have you ever stopped to consider how I must be feeling? How much I miss him? We were good together, you know, he was my life.' Emotion shakes her voice.

'If it wasn't for you our marriage might have a chance. I can't believe you won't even talk to me. Coward!'

I still have no idea what to say to her and she's starting to sound angry as well as upset, so I climb into my car and start the engine. Thankfully she starts walking away from the car. I'm about to pull out when someone knocks at my driver's window. I jump a little, but it's Declan, not Jessica. Rachel is standing behind him looking bored and resentful, her bum resting against a parked car. I buzz open the window.

He bends down and peers in at me, looking confused. 'Pandora, where are you going?'

'I just bumped into your ex,' I say in a low voice, so that Rachel can't hear. 'She was here a second ago and she's a bit upset. It's probably best if I just go home. I'll ring you later.'

'Don't go anywhere,' he says. 'What did she say? Are you all right?'

I sigh. 'We can talk about it later, OK. Right now I just want to—'

'Declan!' Jessica screeches. 'Stop looking at her like that in front of me. I can't bear it. Stop!'

I look over. She's running towards us barefoot, her sandals in her hand. She swings her arm back and one of them hits the windscreen; the other, the side of Declan's head.

He rubs his skull. 'Jesus, Jess, that hurt. Are you crazy? What's Rachel going to think?'

'That her mum's devastated.' Jessica's nostrils are flaring. 'Seeing you with someone else.'

'We're separated, remember?' Declan reminds her. 'Come on, Jess, stop this. You're making a complete fool of yourself. Rachel, go upstairs and get your bag, please. I need to talk to your mother.' He hands Rachel his keys.

'Fine,' Rachel says huffily. 'And Mum, would you put on your shoes. Dad's right, you look a state. Your new hair's stupid and what's with those jeans?' She wrinkles up her nose. 'You're too old for them and they're too tight, everyone can see your—'

'That's enough, Rachel,' Declan says firmly. 'That's unfair, your mum looks very nice. Go and get your things from the house.' He hands her his keys.

As soon as Rachel's gone Jessica asks him, 'Do you really think I look nice?'

He ignores her question. 'You can't say things like that in front of Rachel. It's not right. I want you to apologize to Pandora. None of this is her fault.'

Jessica says nothing for a moment. I know she believes that I'm partly to blame for her marital problems, but she surprises me when she says, 'Declan's right, I'm sorry, Pandora. I'm just finding this incredibly difficult. I'm sure you understand. It's just . . . I . . .' And then her face crumples and she starts to cry.

Declan immediately puts his arm around her and she buries her head in his jumper. 'It'll be OK, Jess. Please, don't cry.'

'But it won't,' she says, her voice muffled. 'I still love you, Declan. I can't help it.'

He strokes her hair. 'Shush, Jess, it'll be all right.'

I watch them, feeling more and more uncomfortable. I really, really shouldn't be here. Eventually Jessica draws away, sniffs and rubs her fingers under her eyes, leaving long, dark mascara streaks.

'Sorry,' she murmurs. 'I have to go.' She walks towards her car.

'I'll send Rachel down to you,' Declan calls after her. 'Stay there, will you, Pandora?'

Before I have a chance to protest, he jogs towards his apartment block, presses the buzzer and disappears. I sit there anxiously for five long minutes, not daring to look towards Jessica's car in case she takes it as encouragement to come over and talk to me. Her anger I can deal with, but not her tears. I'd like to say that they were put on, conjured up to soften Declan's mood, but from the anguished look on her face and the pain in her eyes they clearly weren't. And yes, I do feel guilty. But Declan's marriage was over long before we got together; I was not responsible for their break-up. He was in a dark place when I first met him and I like to think that I helped him get back on an even keel.

Declan appears again, opens Jessica's car door and says something to her, then walks towards my car, puts his hands on the edge of my open window and smiles in at me. 'Sorry about all that. Rachel's on her way back down. Are we still on for lunch?'

Is he crazy? Men! I ignore his inane question. 'Declan, this is all very bizarre. Your ex-wife is still sitting over there in her car. And you have to stop arguing in front of Rachel, do you understand me? You'll scar her for life.'

'I know, I know. But Jess started it.'

'Declan, that's pathetic. You have to take equal responsibility. And I'm not sure you're doing her any favours by being so nice to her. She's clearly still holding a torch for you. I think you need to talk to her, tell her that it's completely over. And you both need to start thinking about your daughter for a change and not yourselves.'

There's silence for a moment. 'You're right. You're completely right. I'm so sorry. Jess and I urgently need to talk. I know it's a huge ask, but would you mind if we skipped lunch? And maybe you'd take Rachel for a couple of hours so that we can discuss things? Sort it all out today.'

I stare at him. 'Declan, are you crazy? Rachel hates me.'

'No, she doesn't. Maybe you could take her shopping or something? Please? It's important. I can't go on like this. I want us to be together, properly, me and you. I need to convince Jess that our marriage is one hundred per cent over and that it's serious between us. We're practically divorced, and you're right, she needs to start thinking about a future without me.' He looks sad at the thought, which is understandable; they must have had a lot of happy times together before the rot set in.

I sigh. 'Why right now? Can't you arrange to meet her next week or something?'

There's a long pause. 'OK, I'll come clean, it's Rachel too. She just admitted that she's fed up with me and her mum upsetting each other and unless we can find a way to stop, she wants to go to boarding school.'

I smile to myself. Clever, manipulating little madam. But I'm livid with Declan now. How dare he pretend talking to Jessica was his idea, when it clearly wasn't?

'Rachel's the one who suggested she could spend the afternoon with you while we talk,' he adds.

'Really?' I'm genuinely surprised and I start to feel sorry for the girl. I'd hate Iris to be in the same position. 'OK, fine, I'll take Rachel.'

'Thank you. Things will get easier soon, I promise. And Pandora? I love you. You're amazing.'

That has me completely flummoxed. It's not something he's ever said to me, not like that, except during or after sex. It bothered me for a while, but I've got used to it as he's affectionate in other ways.

'Uh, thanks,' I manage. I can't believe he just came out with it, seconds after we've been discussing his ex. Men really are a different species.

Chapter 14

'What do you think of my mum's hair extensions?' It's the first full sentence Rachel has said to me since she got into my car. I've decided to take her to Shoestring for hot chocolate. Iris isn't being dropped back from her friend's house until five, and it's all I can think of. Rachel suggested Dundrum, but its half an hour's drive and I can't face a busy shopping centre today, so I managed to talk her around. I've parked the car and now we're walking towards the shop.

'She's had Botox too, you know. Can't frown any more. Sad, really. I think she's trying to look young like you.'

My heart sinks. I think she's probably right, but it saddens me that Rachel has come to the same conclusion. 'I'm sorry they were talking like that in front of you. Are you OK?'

She shrugs. 'I'm used to it.'

'You shouldn't be. Hopefully after their chat today it will all stop. But you need to tell them if things upset you. If they're arguing, you should go into another room or something.'

'Yeah, yeah, whatever.' She starts to look all pouty.

Back to the old Rachel. But this time I'm not having it. 'I'm trying to help, Rachel. Less of the attitude, please.' I pause outside the door of Shoestring. 'And this is a nearly new designer shop, I run it with my sister and my gran. So I'd appreciate it if you didn't make any snarky comments about smelly old secondhand clothes, got it?'

Her eyes light up a little. 'Secondhand? Is it, like, vintage?'

'Some of the pieces are, yes.'

'Cool. Mum won't let me wear vintage stuff, says it's un-hygienic. Can I have some stuff for free?'

'No,' I say simply. 'But if you see something you like, I can let your Dad know. Or, here's a novel idea, you could always pay for it yourself.'

She wrinkles up her nose. 'As if. There have to be some advantages of being stuck in the middle of domestic World War Three.'

I give a laugh. 'You're pretty smart, Rachel. Do you read a lot?'

'What's that got to do with anything?'

'Iris is a big reader and she's pretty smart too.'

Rachel pauses for a second. 'I was a bit mean to her, wasn't I? When we went to the cinema.'

'Yes, you were.'

'Sorry. She's not so bad for a kid. Does she like Jacqueline Wilson?'

I nod. 'Loves her.'

'I could give her some of my old books. I've grown out of them.'

'She'd like that. Now, let's go inside.'

'Hey, Pandora, what are you doing here on your day off, are you mad?' Jules walks towards us. She looks quizzically at Rachel.

'I'm showing Rachel around,' I say. 'Rachel is Declan's daughter.'

'Nice to meet you, Rachel,' Jules says easily, smiling at her. 'Love the dress. It's not Miu Miu, is it?'

Rachel nods eagerly. 'Got it for my birthday.' It's a white dress dotted with a random pattern of lime-green hearts and dark pink heart-shaped pockets. I thought it looked familiar.

Jules and I exchange a look.

'Lucky you,' Jules says, and I'm grateful she leaves it at that.

She knows exactly how expensive the label is new. 'I think there's a Miu Miu jacket on the rails somewhere that would look amazing with jeans. Similar pattern, in fact. It's small, an eight, I think, so it might just fit you. Would you like to have a look?'

Rachel smiles for the first time all day. 'Yes, please.'

'You go and grab a coffee, sis,' Jules tells me. 'You look a bit stressed.'

'You have no idea,' I say softly, behind Rachel's back.

While Rachel potters off with Jules, I order a coffee and a sandwich from the counter, and settle in my favourite seat in the café, a wooden booth Dad made from old church pews. Someone's left the 'Style' magazine from the *Sunday Times* behind them, so I dip into it eagerly. I'm still reading when Rachel appears twenty minutes later.

'I've ordered myself a latte,' she says. 'Is that OK?'

'Of course. As long as your mum doesn't mind you drinking coffee.'

She rolls her eyes. 'She's the coffee queen of Dublin. She's addicted to skinny frappy lappy something or other. Dad says she keeps Starbucks in business.'

I smile. 'So, did the jacket suit you?'

She shakes her head. 'Too big on the shoulders. But Jules found me two really cool vintage dresses instead. A blue silk one with yellow splashes on it, and a black cotton one with big red flowers. She showed me how to wear them too. With coloured tights and boots. She's really cool.'

I smile again. 'She is. So, what do you want to do next? Are you hungry?'

'I had a bagel earlier.' She nods at the magazine. 'If you want to read I could go and get my book. It's in my bag in the car.'

'Are you sure?'

'Yeah. Mum hates me reading or watching telly during the day. She says it's a waste of time.'

'What does she like doing instead?'

Rachel shrugs. 'Shopping. Starbucks. Getting stuff for the house. She used to do a lot of things for Dad, collecting his suits from the dry cleaners and ironing and things like that; and cooking, she used to be big into cooking and having dinner parties, but not so much any more.'

'No yoga these days?' It's out before I can stop it.

Rachel looks at me for second, then says, 'She doesn't do yoga any more. I never met him or anything, that yoga guy. It wasn't serious.' Poor Rachel, another fact that she shouldn't have to know.

Desperate to change the subject and feeling horribly guilty that I brought the whole yoga affair up – it was childish of me, thoughtless – I remember something that Declan said earlier. 'Did you mean it, about boarding school?' I ask her.

She looks a bit sheepish. 'Actually I really would love to go to boarding school. Have you read the Malory Towers books?'

I nod. 'Years ago. I used to love Enid Blyton and I read *The O'Sullivan Twins* to Iris recently. It does make boarding sound fun, all right.'

'Yeah, really cool. But I couldn't do that to Mum. She wouldn't cope on her own. She'd have no one to look after or anything. Nothing to do.'

My heart skips a beat. Poor girl, she has a lot on her plate. 'It's not your job to worry about your mum, Rachel,' I say gently.

'Yeah, it is,' she says. 'She doesn't have anyone else, and she's not the worst. We have fun together sometimes. And Dad's all right for an oldie.'

'You do give him a bit of a hard time, though.'

'Yeah, yeah, I know. I just get fed up sometimes.'

'That's understandable.'

She looks at me, and then stares down at the table again. 'Pandora?'

'Yes?'

'Sorry for being rude to you at the cinema.'

'It's fine, honestly. Forget about it.'

'Will you tell Iris she can have all my old books? I'll bring them to Dad's with me when I see him next.'

'I will.'

'Cool.' Then her latte arrives and she starts to drink it using her teaspoon.

'Pandora?' she says again after a few minutes.

I look at her. There's a serious expression on her face.

'This is probably a bit of a weird question, you being Dad's girlfriend and all, but how serious are you and Dad? Do you think they could ever get back together? Mum and Dad, I mean. Before all that yoga stuff happened they seemed happy enough. It's all I want, really. Is there any chance . . .' she tails off and stares down into her latte.

'Honestly? I don't know, pet. But you're right, I'm really not the best person to ask about all this.' I avoid a direct answer and I don't mention the impending divorce. I'm still feeling guilty about my yoga comment earlier and I don't want to make Rachel feel any worse. Declan seems serious about me, but he's not the most demonstrative of boyfriends and frankly I don't know the answer to Rachel's question. Maybe he does still love Jessica; he certainly cares about her. I've always tried not to think about it too much.

'Oh, OK.' She sounds completely flattened. 'No one will tell me, you see. Mum says they might and Dad won't talk about it.'

I know Jessica still has feelings for Declan, thinks their marriage still has a chance, I've known that all along. Declan swears that Jessica's delusional, but even so my stomach tightens when I hear it from Rachel's mouth. 'Things will work out for the best, Rachel, you'll see,' I add quickly. 'It'll all get a lot easier soon, I promise. Families come in all shapes and sizes, it doesn't mean your mum and dad love you any less.'

She scowls at me. 'You sound like a teacher or someone on a

kids' show on the telly.' She puts on a sing-song voice. 'Families come in all colours of the rainbow. That's such crap.'

I wince. 'I'm sorry, I forget that you're a lot older than Iris.' Only two years, in fact, but two years is a long time in any child's life, especially when, like Rachel, you've had a lot to deal with.

'Do you say that kind of stuff to Iris too?' She twists her face up. 'You don't have a daddy, Iris, but it's OK 'cos families come in all shapes and sizes.'

I must look a little shocked because she immediately adds, 'Sorry. Dad told me. But it is total crap. Look, I know they both love me, OK? I just want them to love me together, in the same house, not like this. I hate all the packing and unpacking. And the fights over who gets me at Christmas and all the stupid hassle about presents. Dad bought me a new Nintendo at Christmas, and then Mum had a fit 'cos he hadn't told her and she'd got me one too, a pink one. Then she got cross with me 'cos I'd told Dad I wanted one in the first place. So she made Dad take his one back, even though it was black, and I wanted a black one, not a pink one. So I got a black marker and I coloured in the pink one, and Mum had an epi with me, started screaming and crying, saying I'd wrecked it. Then she rang Dad and started screaming at him, saying he must have put me up to it and calling him all kinds of horrible names. But he didn't. It was my idea, the marker thing, but she wouldn't believe me. She wouldn't let him see me for three whole weeks. It wasn't fair.' Her eyes start to well up and she blinks and rubs the tears away with her knuckles.

I remember it only too well; Declan was so angry at the time he could barely speak about it. I slide my hand over and touch hers with my fingertips. 'I'm so sorry, Rachel.'

'It's not your fault,' she says.

'Look, things can't go on like this. You're completely right, it isn't fair on you. I'll have a word with your dad, your mum too, if I have to. In the meantime, if you want to talk about anything, anything at all, I'm here, OK?'

She nods. 'Thanks. Can I go and hang out with Jules now? I might be able to help her or something.'

'Sure. Don't leave the shop, though, OK?'

'Thanks, Pandora, you're the best.' She gives me a happy grin and bounces off, the tears of only seconds ago already forgotten.

I order another coffee, then sit there for a while, mulling things over. Why is everything always so complicated? Why does every decent, single man seem to come with a whole Louis Vuitton suite of luggage? At least Rachel seems to have defrosted a little towards me, that's something. She seems pretty resilient despite everything, and, regardless of the arguments, at least she has a dad. But what if Jessica's correct, what if their marriage does stand a chance? I know Jessica's still in love with Declan and wants nothing more than to make a go of things again, but he won't even consider it. She hurt him and betrayed him, too deeply to forgive, and that's that in his book.

It's not like stepping away from the relationship is going to make any difference. Declan met me after he broke up with Jessica; I have no reason to feel guilty. But despite everything, I do.

At least he's devoted to Rachel, and that's something I can encourage. He's a good dad; he does his best to be there for her when he's allowed. She's lucky to have a father who knows her and loves her, not like Iris. Poor Iris. I think about Olivier for a second, resolving to add another memory to Iris's box as soon as I get home. I can't conjure up the real, flesh-and-blood Olivier, but I can create an image of him, a collage of memories. At least that's something.

When I drop Rachel back to his apartment at four, Declan and Jessica are standing outside the lobby, waiting for me.

'Jess has something to say to you, Pandora,' Declan says, his tone grave. He sounds like a headmaster whose pupil has been found misbehaving and is being made to apologize.

Jessica is shifting from foot to foot, and from the hollow in the left side of her face, I can tell she's chewing severely on the inside of her cheek.

'Maybe Rachel would like to wait inside,' I suggest.

'She needs to hear this too,' Declan says. 'Jess?'

Jessica's gaze meets mine. She looks sad and defeated. 'I'm sorry. I was upset. It's not easy seeing the man you love with someone else.'

'Jess!' Declan snaps.

She rounds on him. 'What? I'm just being honest.'

'It wasn't what we agreed.'

'Oh, fuck that for a game of soldiers,' she says. 'I'm exhausted, Dec. I just want to go home. I'm sorry for taking things out on your, your *girlfriend*,' she spits it out like it's a dirty word. 'I'm sorry for upsetting Rachel. I'm sorry for everything. I'm a horrible, bad person. OK, is that good enough for you?' Her lower lip starts to wobble. 'Can I go now, please?'

Declan softens. 'Don't get upset again, love. I'm sure Pandora accepts your apology, don't you?' He looks at me, his own eyes flat and weary. It's clearly been an exhausting afternoon for both of them, but at least they're managing to be civil to each other.

'Yes,' I say. 'And Rachel and I had a lovely afternoon in Shoestring. There are two dresses put aside for her there, in fact. Maybe you'd like to buy them for her together? I can give you a big discount. Say twenty euro a dress?' I was going to give Rachel one as a present, but in the circumstances I think it's best not to. It might put Jessica's nose further out of joint.

Declan rummages in his pocket and pulls out a twenty-euro note. 'That will cover my one.'

'Thanks, Dad,' Rachel says, taking the note off him. 'Can we get them now, Mum? Shoestring's really near, do you know where it is?'

Jessica's nose twitches. 'The secondhand place on Monks-town Crescent?'

Rachel nods eagerly. 'Yeah, Pandora and her sister, Jules, run it. It's really cool.'

Jessica sighs. 'OK, we'll go and pick them up, love. You get into the car, Rach. I'll just say goodbye to your father.'

As soon as Rachel's out of earshot, Jessica lowers her voice.

'I'm doing this for our daughter, understand?' she tells Declan. 'Not for you. We haven't finished our discussion, not by a long stretch.' Then she turns to me, the flint of earlier back again. 'And you can stop being so palsy-walsy with her, get it? She's my daughter, not yours. I say what she wears, not you.'

'I understand that,' I say, completely fed up with the woman and determined to stand my ground. 'But I intend to treat her with the same respect and consideration as I would my own daughter. So you're going to have to deal with that. She adores you both, but she's serious about that boarding school threat. So I suggest you have a good hard think about what's best for her before either of you open your mouths in future. Right now, I'm going home too. Nice to finally meet you, Jessica, no doubt we'll bump into each other again. Hopefully the next time you'll keep your shoes on.'

Jessica's mouth opens and closes wordlessly, completely flab-bergasted, but before she gets the chance to say anything, I turn on my heels and walk briskly back to the car, smiling to myself. There's no way Declan's ex is going to get the better of me. No way in hell.

Chapter 15

'I spotted a few questions from customers on the Shoestring Facebook page earlier, Pandora,' Jules says, walking into the Shoestring office on Friday afternoon. I've been working on the accounts and my eyes are boggled with numbers so I'm extremely pleased to see her.

She continues, 'I answered the easy ones – people looking for directions to the shop, and a couple of people looking for sell-in appointments. But there was one about what we'd offer for vintage Chanel that I wasn't sure about.'

'Thanks,' I say. 'I'll check it out.'

She looks over my shoulder at the computer screen and wrinkles up her nose. 'Spreadsheets – nasty. How are you feeling today, any better?'

I discussed the whole Declan/Jessica/Rachel thing with Jules at length on Sunday night. I desperately needed to get it off my chest and she was happy to listen, even if her advice was a little harsh. Shooting Jessica with Bird's air rifle isn't really an option.

I shrug. 'Almost human again,' I say honestly. 'Thanks for, well, for listening this week. I know I've been boring you to tears with the whole Declan saga.'

'Not at all, that's what I'm here for. Heard from him this week?'

I shake my head. 'Not yet. He's due back today, though, so I'm sure he'll ring later.' I asked Declan to give me some space, which, as he's been in both Birmingham and London for work this week, suited him just fine. Apart from the blood test worry that slopes out of its cave every now and then, I'm actually pretty OK, all things considered. And I haven't thought of Olivier for at least an hour now, which is definitely progress.

'I'd better get back to the floor,' she says.

'Is it busy? Do you want me to come out?'

'No, you stay here. Bird's happy to stay until close, we'll be grand.'

'Thanks.'

She squeezes my shoulder then leaves me to it. I save the spreadsheet I was working on, then click into the Shoestring website to check that it's all running properly. I immediately spot the first few lines of a brand-new post by Alex on the home page. Curious, I click into the blog and start to read.

The Shoestring Club Blog

Alex's Handover Dinner

We all met at my house last night (Saturday) for the last Farenze handover dinner. It's sad to see our first dress go, but the girls didn't come empty-handed. But first to the dinner itself, because I know a lot of our readers like the full details!

Menu:

Baked Pear and Stilton to start

Guinness and Beef Hot Pot (yes, I know it's summer, but it's my husband's favourite) with potatoes and salad from the garden

Arietty had Red Onion and Goat's Cheese Tart – I should have guessed she'd be a vegetarian

Eton Mess (with our own strawberries) – yum!

After dinner we all tried on our new Shoestring Club dress and paraded around the house like movie stars – readers, you should see it (in fact, look below for the pic – our brand-new Shoestring Club dress modelled by Arietty, doesn't she look stunning!) – it's heavenly. A dark red Maisie Hersh number, with a full, layered skirt that sits beautifully on everyone, even hippy old me. It's dressy, but with a jacket or cardigan you could just about get away with it at a posh lunch. I can't wait to wear it (with my slippers, probably!). Now that everyone has worn the first dress, Pandora and Jules are going to sell it in Shoestring and that will easily cover the cost of the Maisie Hersh – which is even better as I'm totally broke. Aren't they clever?

As I was last with the Farenze, I get the new dress first. It's currently hanging on the back of my bedroom door, its cheeky red material practically winking at me every time I walk past – fabulous! I'll hand it over to the next Shoestringer soon, but until then it's all mine – bliss!

The other Shoestring girls were so kind to me over dinner. It was the first time I'd met them in person, and I was horribly nervous. They're all so sophisticated and gorgeous. Pandora's a lot taller than I thought she'd be and Jules has the most amazingly beautiful curly auburn hair. And Arietty – she could be a model, seriously!

They were all terribly nice about the boys (my dogs), and the house, and even Markham (my husband). One of them (I won't out you, Jules, don't worry! Oops!) even said he was dreamy, like an Irish Johnny Depp.

Things are a bit difficult for us at the moment (like a lot of people in Ireland I know) but after last night I feel a lot more positive and even a tiny bit optimistic.

> I'd like to thank the Shoestring Girls for being so kind
> to me and for including me in their very special club. I
> feel most privileged to be part of the gang and I can't
> wait till the next handover dinner at my house.
> Blessings,
>   Alex XXX

I smile to myself. It's such a lovely post and I'm so glad Alex
enjoyed herself. I print it off for Jules to read later. Then I open
the Shoestring Facebook page. There are a couple of new messages, including one from Rowie, and I open it first.

Hi Babes,
  Guess what? Mega news! Olaf's been promoted and he's
moving back to Norway. He begged me to come with him
and I said I'd only consider it if he proposed first. So he did
– right then and there. Said he was happy to tie the knot
asap. Ha! Talk about U-turns.
  Anyway I'm thrilled, as you can imagine. I kind of fancy
a Norwegian wedding so we're going to have a tiny do in
Stavanger – his home town – just close family. Hope you
understand.
  My sister's offered to take over the lease on the shop –
she's delighted in fact, was dying to get out of Dell finally
– so it's all set.
  I know it's all very sudden!!! But I wanted to let you
know I'll be moving to Bergen as soon as we can get
everything sorted. Hopefully within the month. Exciting, eh?
  Hope to catch up with you before I leave, but it's all dash-
dash-dash at the mo.
  Talk soon,
    Rowie XXXXX

I sit back in my seat, reeling. Sudden isn't the word. I know Rowie's never been the most reliable of friends, in fact she can be rather self-obsessed to say the least, but we've known each other for years. She could at least have rung to tell me the news in person.

Jules pops her head back into the office. Before she gets the chance to say anything, I say, 'Hey, Jules, Rowie's getting married.'

'What? No way! I thought she said Olaf was anti-marriage.'

'He's obviously changed his mind. They're getting hitched in Norway. Place called Stavanger. And get this – she's moving over there with him in a few weeks' time.'

'Wow! That was quick. Bang goes the neighbourhood.' She studies my face. 'You OK, sis? You'll miss her, right?'

'I guess.'

'Look, Declan's just appeared outside. I lied, told him I thought you were out with a client but that I'd double check.'

I smile gratefully. 'You seem to be always covering my back these days.'

'I'm your sister, it's my job. Want me to tell him you're rummaging in other people's wardrobes or what?'

'No, tell him I'll be out in a second. I'll just finish up in here.'

'No problem.'

I type a short congrats message to Rowie, then quickly reply to the Facebook comments and questions, including the Chanel one Jules had spotted, and then log out again.

I walk onto the floor, and when I see Declan, his broad back leaning against the cash desk, I plaster a smile on my face that I'm sure doesn't reach my eyes. When he sees me, he beams instantly, steps forwards and swoops me into his arms.

'God, I've missed you this week,' he says.

I pat him on the back, hoping he'll let go of me soon, a little overwhelmed by his public display of affection. It's not like him to hug me on the shop floor, in front of everyone.

When he finally lets me go, I straighten my shirt. 'I'd kill for a coffee,' I say. 'Will you join me?'

'Love to. I'm just off the airport bus, hence the bag.' He gestures down at the neat black businessman's Samsonite which is sitting at his feet like a little dog. For some reason I hate seeing men pulling along wheely bags, don't ask me why. I try not to frown. An image of the battered brown leather hold-all Olivier used to fling over his shoulder flits across my eyes and I try to brush the thought away.

'Pandora?' Declan is looking at me crookedly. 'Are you all right?'

'Yes, yes, of course. Why?'

'I asked you how your week had been.'

'Sorry, just thinking about a . . . um . . . client. Let's grab a table.' He puts his hand under my elbow and swivels me towards the café. I pull my arm away, pretending I need it to flatten down my hair, but I don't think he's fooled. I follow him and his wheely bag towards the café area. My favourite booth is taken so we're at a table by the window instead, looking out on the small courtyard. I sit down opposite him and stare at the table, rearranging the salt and pepper pots so that they sit exactly side by side.

'Pandora, are you sure everything's OK?' he asks gently.

'I'm sorry; I just have things on my mind.'

'What kind of things? Last weekend?' He tilts up my chin with one finger, and then looks at me, his brown eyes open and sincere. I feel like swatting his hand away and, sensing this, he removes it.

For a second I consider saying, 'Yes, that too,' but also telling him about Olivier and how he rejected Iris; about the test; about how terrified I am about the result; about how it's stirring up all kinds of emotions that I thought I'd long suppressed. How much I miss my mum, how angry I am that what happened to her might also happen to me, and to Jules. But instead I just sit there, staring at him.

'That among other things,' I say finally.

He leans in towards me. 'Pandora, I know the whole Jess and Rachel thing got to you but it can't be just that. You're being very distant. Is there someone else? Is that it?'

I give a dry laugh. Honestly, is that the best he can come up with? Just because I can't deal with him today.

'No,' I say firmly. 'Nothing like that. I'm completely fine about the Jessica thing, honestly. I've moved on. I've just had an ultra-busy week, I've been up to my tonsils in shop accounts all day and I'm just letting work stress get to me, you know how it is.'

'Don't I just.' He slumps back in his seat. 'Well, that's a relief. I was starting to think the worst. Want anything to eat? I'm starving.'

He waves at Klaudia, who runs the café with her sister Lenka's help. She scowls at him.

'I see you,' she says sharply. 'I'm not blind. I'll take your order in a minute.'

'What's wrong with Klaudia?' he asks. I'm impressed. I've only introduced them once but Declan seems to be quick with names.

'She's usually in the kitchen. Lenka's on a day off and she is not happy about it. Klaudia's not all that fond of customers.'

'No kidding.' He picks up a packet of sugar from the bowl and starts flicking it through his fingers. Usually his restless hands wouldn't bother me, but today I find it incredibly irritating. Can't he just stay still?

'So, want to tell me about work?' he says.

I shake my head. 'Not really. How was your week?'

He blows out his breath. 'Pretty intense. You know the stadium project in Birmingham—'

He's interrupted by Klaudia. 'You ready to order?'

'Yes, thanks,' I say. 'Just an Americano for me. And some chocolate fudge cake. With cream.'

'Good. And you?' she looks at Declan. 'Let me guess. Americano and ham sandwich, yes? Irish men and their ham sandwiches.' She rolls her eyes.

He smiles. 'You're good. But I'd like it toasted, if that's OK.'

She gives a shrug. 'Fine.' Then marches off.

'Charming staff you have in here,' he says, staring after her.

I frown at him. OK, Klaudia can be a little sharp, but only I'm allowed to say that, not him.

'She's very efficient,' I say instead.

'She'd want to be, with that attitude. Anyway, let's not discuss your staffing issues. What are you up to on Sunday? I'd love to see you if you're free.'

'Is tomorrow night off then? I thought we were going to try out that new Italian in Sandycove that's getting all the rave reviews, Apollo's. You booked it weeks ago.'

He shifts a little in his seat. 'Ah, slight change of plan. If it's OK with you, I'm going to take Rachel and Jessica out. It was Rachel's idea. She wants to have a family dinner.'

'On a Saturday night?'

'It was the only night that suited Jess.'

I think evil thoughts about her, but keep them to myself. 'I see. Where?'

'Where what?' He looks at me in confusion.

'Where are you taking them?'

'To Apollo's. I'm sure they can squeeze Rachel in too.'

I stare at him. 'Let me get this straight – you're blowing me out to take your ex-wife to dinner using *our* reservation?'

'It's not like that.'

I fold my arms. 'What is it like, then?'

'It's what I said, a family night out.'

'But you're not a family any more, are you?' I point out.

His face drops. 'I thought you'd understand. You were the one trying to get me and Jess to communicate properly.'

I sigh. He's got me there. 'It's great you guys are talking and everything, but I haven't seen you all week and I was looking forward to stuffing my face with pasta, that's all. I've had one hell of a week and I could have done with a few drinks.'

Declan starts to smile.

'What?' I snap. 'Why are you grinning at me like that?'

'So you did miss me.'

'Yes, of course I did.'

He leans forward and looks me in the eye. 'You're not jealous, are you, Pandora?'

'Of Malibu Barbie with the hair extensions? Are you kidding me?'

He winces.

'Sorry,' I say quickly, 'that wasn't nice. No, I'm not jealous of your ex-wife. But I am fed up that you're taking her out to dinner, using *our* reservation. Especially when said ex wife—'

Klaudia cuts me off mid-sentence. She swings a cup of coffee across Declan's face and plonks it in front of him without spilling a drop. Then she takes a plate off her upper arm and whisks it onto the table too.

'One toasted ham special for the gentleman,' she says. 'Death by chocolate for Pandora. Your Americano is just coming too.' She takes another plate off her lower arm and places it in front of me. Then she hands me a small dessert fork. Seconds later she's back with my coffee.

'That is everything, yes?' she asks.

I smile at her. 'Yes, thanks, Klaudia. That was really quick.'

She doesn't smile back. I'm not sure I've ever seen her smile, in fact, but she doesn't look unhappy, just stern, as if she's doing everyone an immense favour by simply breathing the same air as they are.

'I aim to please,' she says. 'But God, I don't know how Lenka copes. Customers, *pah*!' She bustles off.

Declan's chuckling away to himself. 'She's certainly speedy. Scary, though. But back to the weekend. If you're really bothered by the dinner I can cancel. I'm sure Rachel will understand.'

I sigh. 'Best not to. Rachel seems fragile at the moment, and I wouldn't do that to her. No, it's fine. Just think of me as you're tucking into your *pasta al salmone affumicato*.' I sigh again theatrically. Declan knows it's my favourite.

He grins. 'I will. And Sunday?'

'Iris has been bugging me all week to take her to the pier. We'll have to stop her going over the side on her scooter.'

'I'd love a good walk down the pier. *Perfecto*.' He kisses the end of his fingers and blows them at me. Now if he was Italian it wouldn't irritate me, but . . .

What is wrong with me? I wonder as he launches into an update on his stadium project. I'm sitting here, smiling and nodding as if I'm listening, like a good little girlfriend, but I don't feel any connection to the man whatsoever. Not today. It's the blood test, I tell myself, the stress of waiting for the news has put me completely out of whack.

My eyes move over Declan's face, taking in the five o'clock shadow creeping over his chin and cheeks, his firm, dark red lips, his kind eyes, and I don't feel the tingle that I used to. There was a time when even the mere thought of Declan would send a squirm of desire though my system, but not now, not today. But maybe that's what happens after eight months. The flame dies down; the raging fire becomes a flicker.

Declan's a good man, I tell myself sternly. Snap out of it.

'I know there's something on your mind, Pandora,' he says out of the blue. I look at him, slightly startled. I thought he was still talking about his beloved stadium.

'When you're ready, I'm a good listener,' he adds.

I nod at him and smile gently, grateful that he's not pushing me. He reaches over and squeezes one of my hands under his. This time I don't feel like pulling it away.

'I'm here for you, Pandora. Remember that. We're a team. When you're ready and my divorce has come through, we should talk about taking this to the next level, maybe moving in together. You don't have to say anything right now, but just think about it, OK?'

Don't wince, I order myself. Do not wince. Relax those shoulders and smile, for God's sake. Moving in together is supposed to be a nice thing, a positive thing, not an imposition. It's normal, adult behaviour. It's progress.

I manage to squeeze out an 'OK'.

Declan seems satisfied with this. 'That's my girl. I can't wait to set up house. As soon as possible, yeah?' He lifts up his coffee cup. 'Here's to showing Jess how serious we are, eh?'

I clink my own cup against his. But his words have set my stomach churning, my nerves jangling – not another inner meltdown. No! I tell myself. Stay calm. You are thirty years old, Pandora Schuster. Time to grow up. Moving in with Declan would be a good start.

Chapter 16

It's Saturday evening and I should be at Apollo's with Declan (I'm still feeling a bit miffed about it), but instead I'm watching *Charlotte's Web* with Iris, the two of us curled up on the sofa with a rug over our legs. Halfway through the story I realize that it's probably not the best film to have chosen in the circumstances – it's about a pig who is fighting for his life with the help of a clever spider – but Iris's other suggestion was a *Pokémon* medley, which I just couldn't face. I'm in floods of tears during the final scene when Charlotte dies, and Iris can't understand why I'm so upset.

'Charlotte's a spider,' she says, looking at me crookedly. 'They don't live very long, Mum.' Iris is a bit of an expert; she reads every animal book she can get her hands on and, pre-Fluffy, used to keep woodlice and ant farms in the shed.

'But she's leaving her babies all alone in the world,' I sob.

'They're not alone, they have Wilbur, silly,' she points out. 'There's snot coming out your nose, Mum. It's disgusting.'

'Sorry.' I fetch a tissue from the box in the hall and, after mopping up my tears (and snot), stay out there for a few minutes, trying to compose myself. I hate Iris seeing me upset, but at least she's used to seeing me bawl during sad movie scenes, so it's hardly a first. The mere mention of *The Notebook* or *Steel Magnolias* is enough to set me off.

I go back in and watch the last few minutes with Iris, trying to stifle my sniffs, and then pack her off to bed. It's only nine and I don't feel like watching anything else so I decide to go up myself and read.

I pop my head around the door of the kitchen to say good-night to Bird. Jules is out with Jamie, and Dad's at a new all-female version of *Glengarry Glen Ross* with his theatre club. Bird's sitting on the sofa in the corner of the room, beside the Aga, working away on her *Irish Times* crossword.

'I'm heading up to bed, Bird,' I tell her. 'See you in the morning.'

She looks up and smiles. 'You look tired, poppet. An early night will do you good. Try not to worry so much about moving in with Declan. Give yourself time to think things through. It's a big step for you and for Iris.'

Jules! I'll kill her. I told her about Declan and his 'taking things to the next level' announcement earlier. But of course old big mouth couldn't keep it to herself now, could she? I can feel my back stiffen.

Bird reads me like a book. 'Now, don't be cross with your sister. She cares about you, Pandora. We all do. She's worried about you. We all just want you to be happy, darling. Your dad and I don't expect either of you to live here forever, although it has been lovely to have you around, don't get me wrong. I know I've been encouraging your relationship with Declan – such a lovely chap – but you've been a little quiet all day, which concerns me. You should be thrilled at this new development. Which does make me wonder.' She pauses for a moment before coming out with, 'Do you love him, darling? Really love him? Does he infuriate you and delight you all on the same day?'

I give a dry laugh. 'Infuriate, definitely. But honestly? I don't really know. How do you know if you're really in love? Proper love, I mean, not just romantic fairy-tale love.' I shrug. 'Anyway, other things are important too, right?'

She looks at me carefully. 'I'm not so sure, Pandora. Love is when the thought of living without a person makes you physically sick. Oh, I know, people say companionship is the important thing, kindness and consideration, yadda, yadda, yadda.' She swats the air and makes a tushing noise. 'Poppy-cock. Never underestimate passion. Your grandfather caused me more heartache than most, believe me, but every time I looked at him I still saw the handsome twenty-four year old that I married.'

I sigh. 'That was different. I'm thirty, Bird, and I have Iris to think about. I'd really like her to have a father figure. Eligible men are an endangered species and I can't afford to be choosy.'

Bird's eyes flare up. 'I did not bring you up to settle, Pandora Schuster. What are you talking about? You're a beautiful, vibrant, smart young woman.' She puts her newspaper down on the sofa, stands up and puts her hands on my arm. 'I know you've felt love, Pandora. When you came home from Paris, the pain and longing in your eyes . . .' She breaks off and shakes her head. 'Unless you feel the same way about Declan you must think about what you're doing very seriously. Relationships are hard enough, you know that. It's not fair on you, or Declan, or Iris to continue seeing him if your heart is not one hundred per cent in it. Do you understand what I'm saying?'

I nod wordlessly.

'So you'll think about it, yes?' she asks. 'And you won't make any snap decisions about moving in with him?'

I nod again. I yearn to tell her what else is on my mind, Olivier and the family's cancer gene, but I just can't. It's all too much.

'Yes,' I say instead. 'I do understand, Bird, honestly. I promise I won't rush into anything. Now I'm off to bed.'

She kisses my cheek. 'It will all seem brighter in the morning, darling.'

I can't seem to concentrate on my book. I read the words but they mean nothing. After a few minutes I give up and just lie in bed, staring at the ceiling. The spidery crack just under the cornicing to the right has got bigger and I wonder absently how the green and blue rubbery-looking scuff marks got up there beside it; probably Iris throwing one of her bouncy balls around again.

I switch off my bedside light and try to sleep, but it's no use, my mind is hopping all over the place and I can't stop thinking about what Bird said: 'I know you've felt love, Pandora.'

Then I have a thought. Iris's memory box. If I can't sleep I may as well do something useful. I switch my bedside light back on, throw a cardigan over my pyjamas, open the wardrobe door and find the Louboutin box, stacked innocuously with all the other shoeboxes. I pull out the Au Printemps bag and tip the contents out onto the floor. In among the museum maps and metro tickets I spot an old Chanel lipstick, black with a gold band, and the memories come flooding back, thick and fast. I sift through the photographs until I find the one I'm looking for and place it on my bed. I grab my pen and sketchpad from my bedside table and sit down and start to write.

Dear Iris,

Your Dad is a huge Oscar Wilde fan. Do you remember the story I used to read to you — The Happy Prince — about the statue who asked a little bird to pick off all the gold leaf covering him to give to the poor? And finally his jewel-stone eyes? That was written by Oscar Wilde. He was Irish, but he lived the end of his life in Paris.

One day your Dad asked would I like to visit Oscar Wilde's grave. He's buried in a famous cemetery in Paris called Père Lachaise, which is on a hill overlooking the city. As you know, I have a thing about cemeteries, so I said yes immediately.

It's the most beautiful place, Iris, huge, with stony

pathways lined by trees, and all these mad wild cats that fly out of tombs and scamper over your feet.

When we reached Wilde's grave – a big stone monument with a strange Egyptian-looking flying man on it – I realized the surface was covered in red marks. Your dad explained that the marks were kisses – people travel from all over the world to kiss Oscar Wilde's grave.

Then he took a lipstick out of his pocket, and smeared it over his lips. He looked so funny, Iris, with this serious face on him and the lipstick. I couldn't stop giggling.

'Stop laughing,' he told me. 'It's a very grave business.' That really set me off. Then he stood beside the monument, leaned forward, closed his eyes and gave it a big kiss. I took a photo of him doing it. I was laughing so much it came out a bit blurry but I hope you like it.

Your dad always made me smile, Iris, just like you.

Love always and for ever,

Mum xxx

I pick up the photo. Olivier is wearing a Panama hat, cocked back, while he's kissing the stone. His eyes are shut and it's blurry, so Iris won't be able to make out the detail of his face (which is what I want), but it will give her a good idea of his olive skin tone and the dark hair curling from underneath the hat. At some stage I guess I'll have to get rid of the rest of the photographs in case she finds them and uses them to try and track him down in the future, but I can't face destroying them, not yet.

Seconds after I'd taken the picture, he'd flung himself at me and kissed me, digging the camera into my chest. Luckily it was strung around my neck or I might have dropped it.

'Kisses for my two favourite people,' he'd said. 'Oscar and

Dora. You sound good together, no? Oscar and Dora. Like an old married couple. We will name our first son Oscar, yes?'

Son? My stomach had almost leapt out of my mouth. I was such a romantic then, and the thought of having a child with Olivier some time in the distant future thrilled me. Unfortunately when the daydream became a reality, I felt very, very differently.

I pick up the lipstick and open it. It's an old, almost used-up one of Bibi's, her signature bold poppy red, and I twist it up and peer at the stump, trying to make out Olivier's lip grooves, but the surface is smooth. He gave it to me that day in the graveyard, said the colour would suit me, but I've never used it. I was sentimental in those days, and I kept it as a souvenir.

Looking back now, his suggestion that I emulate his mother's make-up style seems a little strange, almost Oedipal, but at the time I thought it was sweet. From that day on poppy red became my signature lipstick colour too. Until I met Olivier I'd never considered standing out a good thing. But he changed me, made me realize that blending in, following the crowd, isn't half as much fun. My eyes well up a little and I blink them back and take a few deep breaths. Then, without looking at it again, I attach the photograph to the letter and place them both in Iris's box, along with the lipstick, and close the lid.

Chapter 17

'Where are you off to, darling?' Bird asks as I bustle into the staff room at midday the following Wednesday to grab my coat and bag. Darn, after the conversation on Saturday evening I've been trying to avoid talking to her one-on-one.

'A client in Greystones,' I say. 'I'm running a bit late and if the traffic's bad I'll be at least a couple of hours. Jules says she'll cover the floor.'

Bird's eyes rest on mine. 'Have you made a decision yet? About moving in with Declan?'

'No. I need to consider it carefully and things have been so busy, what with the shop and everything . . .' I tail off and shrug, but I can see that she's not overly convinced.

'Pandora, I really do think you're—'

My mobile rings and I whip it out of my pocket gratefully and check the screen. I don't recognize the number, but I say, 'Sorry, Bird, have to take this. See you later,' then I click on answer. 'Can you hold for just a second, please?'

I walk onto the shop floor and make a beeline for the front door, hoping Bird won't follow me. Luckily she gets the message and stays put. I know it's a little rude to cut Bird off like that, but needs must.

'Hello?' I say again into my mobile once I'm outside. 'Sorry about that. I was just moving off the shop floor.'

'Hi, Pandora. It's Markham. Is this is a bad time? I can ring back later.'

'Not at all. I'm just on my way down to Greystones, in fact.'

'I don't suppose there's any way you could call into Pet Planet? I'd love a second opinion on the posters and the invite for our event.'

'No problem at all. I don't think my appointment will take long.' And the added drive to Wicklow will keep Bird out of my hair for another while. 'See you at two-ish?'

'Excellent, thanks, Pandora.' He gives me directions and afterwards I punch a text message to Jules into my iPhone, telling her that I might be back a little later than I expected as Markham needs me. Then I climb into my Golf and pull away from Shoestring, thinking about Markham and Alex for a change instead of my own worries.

From what I've been reading on the Internet about agoraphobia, it stems from a fear of having a panic attack in a public place. Rowie's attack in Paris was frightening enough and she was with friends. I can't imagine what it must be like having an attack like that in public. No wonder Alex is anxious about leaving the house.

The client visit doesn't take long and I pull up outside the pet shop bang on time. It was worth the trip; however, there are now three pairs of designer sandals on the back seat of my car, still nestled in their shoeboxes – always a sign that they've been well taken care of – plus a Louise Kennedy heavy silk evening dress in gunmetal grey with a matching bag and stole, and a simple and elegant cream Jil Sander linen shift dress and swing frock coat which will make some lucky customer a perfect mother-of-the-bride outfit.

Pet Planet is a delightfully old-fashioned pet shop, with a large empty wooden pen just in front of the window, the bottom littered with fresh straw and sawdust, which must be for rabbits or guinea pigs.

I smile to myself at the wooden sign over the door, complete with the cute Pet Planet logo – a cartoon dog, cat and rabbit all sitting proudly on a globe. I hate plastic shop signs, they look so tacky. Yes, they are cheap and don't have any upkeep, but it's the one thing I insisted on for Shoestring – an old-fashioned wooden sign sitting proudly above the door, plus two smaller swinging signs. Luckily Dad, being a wood fanatic, was all for it. He crafted the signs himself and found a sign painter and blacksmith to add the finishing touches.

There's a white banner running across Pet Planet's front window – the red lettering reads:

Labs Who Lunch: Don't Miss our Dog Owners' Lunch this Saturday from 12 to 2. All dogs and their owners welcome.

There's a bubble of excitement in my stomach, or is it anxiety? I just hope Alex is well enough to make it to the pet shop and see all Markham's hard work for herself.

The red paintwork around the door and windows looks fresh and glossy, and peering inside, I spot cheery red gingham bunting that Markham has slung across the ceiling. A piece of paper stuck to the inside of the glass door panel gives more information on the lunch and how to book and at the end reads: 'Thanks for all the enquiries, unfortunately apart from the lunch, Pet Planet will remain closed for the foreseeable future. Please continue to order your pet supplies from our website.' It's tragic that such an obviously cared for and much-loved shop remains closed, but hopefully in time that will change. From what I've read about the condition so far, many doctors recommend exposure treatment for agoraphobia – a gradual introduction to the outside world. If we can get Alex to the shop, that will be a valuable first step.

I ring the doorbell and seconds later Markham answers and smiles at me.

'Pandora, thanks a mill for coming. I really appreciate it. What do you think of the banner? Is it OK? Alex usually does things like that. I'm a bit at sea about marketing the event. I don't want her to find out, obviously, so I'm avoiding placing an ad in a newspaper or anything like that, but I'm wondering about a flyer or maybe—'

'Hi, Markham.' I kiss him on the cheek. 'Slow down there. First of all, the banner looks great. I'm sure Alex will love it. Why don't you show me the event space and then we can talk business?'

He runs his hands over his head. 'Good idea. Sorry, I'm just a bit freaked out about the whole lunch thing. What if no one turns up?'

'It's all under control,' I say firmly. 'I'll be there, and Arietty has promised to come along too, and Jules. Arietty has even borrowed a dog for the occasion. Even if only a few owners and dogs turn up, it will still be fun. So stop fretting. That's the last thing Alex needs, you being stressed.'

'You're right.' He blows out his breath in a whoosh.

'The place looks lovely.'

'Thanks. Bit empty without any animals, though.' He looks around the large empty wooden compartments that must have once held the pets for sale.

'Do you miss working here?' I ask gently, suspecting the answer.

He nods vigorously. 'Every day. We had the best customers, Pandora. All types – teenage boys buying pigeon feed, young mums with toddlers who'd just drop in to have a look at the rabbits and have a bit of a stroke, older people buying treats or toys for their dogs or cats – half the time I think those customers only called by to have a chat with Alex. She remembered all their names, their pets' names too. She used to be a right chatterbox when she got going.'

'How is she this week?'

'No change really. Every day I suggest a little outing, a walk with the boys or a trip to the local shop, but she just says, "Some other time." I don't like to put pressure on her but we got a letter from the adoption agency on Monday. We've finally been put on the official adoption list.'

'That's great news.'

He winces. 'It is and it isn't. There's a meeting in their offices in town next month. We both need to be there. If Alex doesn't attend I'll have to explain our situation and we'll probably be taken off the list. If Alex loses her chance to have a child, I really don't know what she'll do. It frightens me, to be honest.' He gulps and I can see he's distressed. My heart goes out to him.

'Sorry,' he murmurs. 'I shouldn't be landing all this on you.'

'It's fine,' I say gently. 'A lot can happen in a month, Markham.'

'I hope so.' He pauses, then says, 'I'll show you the event room,' walking towards a door at the back of the shop. I think he's a little embarrassed at his outburst and wants to move the conversation forward.

I follow him through the door into a large rectangular conservatory.

'I bought the tables and chairs for next to nothing from a café that was closing down, but it's still a bit bare.'

I study the tile-topped tables with metal legs – they look old but solid. The curved wooden backs of the chairs are beautiful, even if the rattan seats are a bit worn-looking.

'It's ideal for what we want it for, though, isn't it?' I say. 'Tiled floor, lots of light and acres of space around each table for the dogs. All we need are some nice waxed tablecloths, cushions on the chairs and flowers on each table.'

I take my notebook out of my bag and start to make a list.

'And lots of water bowls for the dogs, I guess,' I add. 'Did you find someone to do the catering?'

'Yes. One of my sister's friends would love the job. She's just retrained as a cook after years in the bank. She's giving us a brilliant deal too, practically at cost. And a rep from one of the pet-food companies has already given me twenty free water bowls, they're heavily branded but I don't think anyone will mind. He's also promised me a box of doggie treats and some samples and vouchers to give out on the day.'

I smile. 'Excellent, we can do goodie bags. Like at a proper Ladies' Lunch. I have lots of contacts in Brown Thomas and I'm sure they'll give us some cosmetic and perfume samples. I can pick up some gift bags dirt cheap in the pound shop.' I add everything to my list. 'Now, you wanted to show me the invites?'

I follow him back into the shop and towards the desk, picking up a packet of rabbit treats off the shelves on the way for Fluffy. I rummage in my bag to find my wallet but Markham puts his hand in the air.

'Don't even attempt to pay for those,' he says. 'I'd be highly insulted. After everything you've done for me and Alex. I'm so grateful . . . it's . . .' He stops for a second, then sighs. 'It was all a bit difficult after Addie died. Alex's friends didn't really know what to say. They dropped into the house, but most of them have babies or toddlers themselves and I know Alex found that hard. When she asked one of them not to call around again with their newborn, I don't think she explained herself very well and the girl got a bit offended. The visits pretty much stopped after that. Alex became a bit of a recluse, to be honest, and a lot of our friends were joint friends so I've felt a bit isolated too, I guess. It's such a shame, Alex is such a lovely person and she adores company. I just feel so sad for her. It's no life, alone like that for large chunks of the day.' His eyes well up and his cheeks flush bright red. 'Ah, Jesus, I'm sorry. Ignore me.'

'Markham, you're under a huge amount of stress and of course you're worried about Alex, it's only natural. Do you mind me asking, is she on any medication or anything? I was reading up on agoraphobia and some doctors seem to recommend tranquillizers as well as exposure treatment. I'm sure you know a lot more about all this than I do . . .' I break off, not wanting to overstep the mark.

'She won't take anything,' he says. 'Refuses point blank. She's the same about antibiotics and painkillers. She's a big yoga head and she says the breathing helps with her panic attacks. I don't know, Pandora. For such a bright woman, she's away with the fairies sometimes. She thinks that her body will heal itself, that one day she'll wake up and be able to leave the house again. But that's nonsense; she's getting worse, not better.'

I think about this for a second. 'She does seem pretty strong willed.'

He laughs. 'That's an understatement.'

'A lot of phobias are in the mind. Once the stress lifts a little, the phobia becomes less overpowering.' I shrug. 'Maybe Alex *can* heal herself if she wants to badly enough. But she may need some help. I had this hand-washing thing when I was a teenager, after my mum died. Lasted nearly a year. I had to talk to someone about it, but in the end it was mostly willpower that stopped it. I can still get a bit OCD at times but I've learned how to recognize and control it.'

Markham looks surprised. 'You don't seem the OCD type, Pandora. You seem so together.'

'Overly together sometimes. I'm still a bit of a control freak. But it's not the worst tendency for us shopkeepers.'

'No kidding. There's a lot to keep on top of, all right. That must have been tough, losing your mum like that I mean. What age were you?

'Fourteen. She had breast cancer. She was carrying a cancer

175

gene. I've just been tested for the same gene and if I have it, I have an 85 per cent chance of getting breast cancer.' It's all out before I can stop it.

Markham looks at me, his eyes gentle. 'I'm sorry to hear that, Pandora. When will you get the results?'

'Some time in mid-June. It takes about six to eight weeks apparently.'

He sucks in his breath. 'That long? Must be a killer waiting around like that. I'd say it's doing your head in. Ah, listen, I'm so sorry, I've been waffling on about my stuff and the lunch and everything when you have that to contend with, talk about self-ish.'

'Not at all, it's good to have something else to think about – honestly. Maybe I won't have the gene. There's a fifty–fifty chance. Look, I haven't told my family about any of this yet, so please don't say anything to Jules. You're the only person I've told.'

For a moment he looks taken aback but he recovers well. 'Of course not. I guess it's easier to talk to someone who has a little distance from it all.'

'Exactly. I knew you'd understand.'

He looks at me, as if weighing this up. He has such a kind gaze I have to look away for fear that I'll start crying. 'It's a lot to keep to yourself, Pandora, but I do get it. But you may be surprised, it might not be as hard to tell people close to you as you think, and you know what they say, a problem shared and all that. If you want to talk about it, either now or when you get the results, I'm a good listener.'

'Thanks, Markham,' I say, genuinely touched. He's right, he is a good listener. Alex is a lucky girl. 'Now, let's have a look at this invitation.'

Chapter 18

That evening I'm just climbing out of the car outside Sorrento House when Declan ambushes me.

'Are you avoiding me?' he asks as soon as I've swung open my door, his face stern.

'Declan,' I hiss, nodding at Iris, who is sitting directly behind me.

'We need to talk, Pandora,' he says, unperturbed.

'Can you let me get out of the car first?' I say, feeling irritated. I saw him for a walk on Sunday, but Iris was cranky and it started raining so we had to cut it short. Since then he's called me several times, and yes, I should have rung him back, but I just haven't had a chance. OK, that's a lie. I haven't wanted to. I hate being backed into a corner, which is how I've started to feel. I need time to think about where our relationship is going. Bird's right – unless I'm absolutely sure, then it's not fair on Declan or on Iris to keep stringing him along.

'Hi, Iris.' He looks around my seat, his tone softer. 'How was school today?'

'Rubbish,' she says, as she unclicks her seat belt and kicks open the door. She's been in a right mood the whole way home. 'Dan Fisher spat at me at little break and then he stole our skipping rope, and when I told teacher on him, he kicked me on the leg for being a telltale. It was really sore.'

'The little f—' Declan stops himself. 'You tell that Dan Fisher from me that if he does it again I'm going to go straight into that school to have words with him.'

Iris looks up at him curiously. 'But you're not my dad. Only dads can do stuff like that.'

Declan's face falls. He opens his mouth to say something, then decides against it and looks at me, as if he expects *me* to interject.

Instead I climb quickly out of my own seat, close the door behind me, take hold of Iris's shoulders and spin her towards the front door.

'OK, let's get you inside, pet,' I say. 'You can start your homework with Bird while I talk to Declan. Don't forget your school bag.'

'Are you two having a fight?' she asks with interest.

I give a high-pitched laugh. 'Of course not. Whatever gave you that idea?'

'You both look all cross and frowny.'

'We're just tired from work,' I say. 'Now inside, please. Chop, chop.'

Once I've deposited Iris with Bird – who looks at me inquisitively when I explain that I need to talk to Declan, but, sensing that I'm not in the humour, doesn't interrogate me for once, for which I'm grateful – I go back outside.

'Can we walk?' I ask him. 'I have a thumper of a headache and I could do with some fresh air.'

'Sure.' He moves towards me to take my hand, but I pretend I didn't notice and thrust them both in the pockets of my cotton coat.

'Which way?' he asks.

'Vico Road?' I suggest. We walk silently to the end of the laneway, and then swing a left.

Half way up Sorrento Road, Declan says, 'Are you ready to talk to me yet? What's up, Pandora? Ever since I mentioned moving in together, you've been acting very strangely. If you're not keen I'd prefer you just came out and said so.'

There's no running away from it now. I think for a second before saying, 'Iris didn't mean anything by it, you know, the whole dad thing. She's very fond of you, Declan. She just doesn't see you as a father figure. Not yet. It'll take time.'

He stops walking, turns on his heels and looks at me. 'But do you *want* her to see me as a father figure? That's the question.'

'I want Iris to have someone in her life as well as me of course, but—'

'So it's a yes, then? To you both moving in with me?' His features loosen and he looks at me hopefully.

Yikes, that wasn't what I meant at all.

'I need time to talk to Iris, explain things,' I say. 'And you need to talk to Rachel and Jessica. It will mean big changes all round. Rachel may not be happy about sharing her room with Iris so we may need to look at getting a place with three bedrooms first.'

His eyes darken a little. 'Pandora, are you stalling?'

'No, I'm just being practical. Living together may not be a big deal for you, Declan, but it is for me. I've never lived with anyone before, and neither has Iris.'

'Would you feel happier if we were engaged? Or married even?' He studies my face. 'Pandora, are you OK? You look a little pale.'

'Fine,' I manage to squeeze out. After I heard the word engaged all the blood rushed into my ears, where it's still swirling around, making it hard to take in the rest of what I think is a proposal. Is it a *proposal*?

He stops, frowns. 'I'm sorry, I'm doing this all wrong, I should have a ring, but I'll just come out and say it regardless. Pandora Schuster—'

'What? No!' Now my heart is hammering in my chest and my cheeks are so hot they must be scarlet. All this wedding stuff is just too much, I have to stop him. But when I see Declan's hurt face, the guilt is crushing.

'I'm sorry, Declan, but this is all so . . . so fast,' I stammer. 'Living together is big, but getting married is . . . is enormous.'

'I'm fed up with all the uncertainty, Pandora. I want us all to be together. I want to wake up next to you and go to sleep beside you for the rest of my life. And I'm hoping you feel the same way too. I'm sick of being on my own, to be honest. The apartment is far too quiet and I think it will make things easier for Jess too. Force her into making a fresh start. The way things are at the moment, it's all a bit up in the air. It's hard on her; I'm sure you understand. Pandora, are you all right? You're not going to faint or anything, are you? You look like you're in shock.'

I stare at him, completely overwhelmed and flummoxed. And, yes, shocked. Does he really have to bring Jessica into every single bloody thing? Even his marriage proposal, if that's what this is. As to how I feel, I'm still not all that sure; but I don't feel faint, I feel anxious, horribly anxious, and slightly nauseous. I'm sure it's just my nerves. I've never been proposed to before; I have no idea how it's supposed to feel.

Actually, that's a lie. Olivier did mention marriage – once – completely out of the blue one late afternoon, sitting outside a café; he even drew a quick sketch of a dress on a napkin.

'When we marry, Dora, this is what you will wear.'

Back then, I felt like my heart was floating out of my chest and for a few seconds I swear I could hear bluebirds singing, like something out of a Disney movie, but we'd been drinking all afternoon and I knew he wasn't serious.

This is real life, and a proper, serious, adult proposal. A proper proposal. Declan is proposing. Suddenly it all comes rushing towards me – Olivier, the gene test, and now Declan's proposal – and I feel like my head's about to explode and before I know what's happening I completely panic and say, 'Declan, I need some space to think about all this. A break. I can't . . . I don't . . . It's all too sudden . . . too much . . . I'm sorry . . .' I can't seem to explain myself properly so I stop trying and just stand there, staring down at the pavement.

'A break? But I love you, Pandora.' He sounds distraught but I dare not look up.

'I should never have mentioned the marriage thing,' he continues in a rush. 'I just thought maybe that was why you weren't all that excited about moving in together, that underneath it all you were old fashioned, like Jessica, wanted to do things properly. I've messed everything up, haven't I?'

Now I do meet his gaze and he looks bewildered and upset.

'No, you haven't,' I say. 'It's me. I'm just not ready for all this.' I know I owe him a proper explanation. 'There's a lot going on at the moment, Declan. It's nothing to do with you, with us, honestly.' Markham's words flash into my brain, that it might not be as difficult as I think to tell Declan about the test. I take a deep breath. 'There's something else, something I haven't told anyone, even my family. Can we find somewhere to sit down?'

He nods, looking serious, sensing that it's something important. 'Of course.'

We walk on a little, in silence, until we find a low wall looking out onto Killiney Bay. We sit down and I stare at my hands in my lap. After a few moments I say, 'You know my mum died of breast cancer? I told you that when we first met.'

'Yes,' he says gently. 'She sounded like a wonderful woman.'

'She was. Well, before she died she left instructions with a friend of hers, Dr Oxenbury, that I was to be contacted around my thirtieth birthday. She was a friend of Mum's in college and now she does research into cancer genes. She wrote to me, asked did I want to get tested for the gene Mum carried, a hereditary breast cancer gene. So I had the blood test at the end of April and now I'm waiting for the results.'

'What happens if you have the gene?' he asks, cutting straight to the chase.

'I have an 85 per cent chance of getting breast cancer, and a 50 per cent chance of getting ovarian cancer.'

'Christ.' He says nothing else for a second, then takes one of my hands and squeezes it. 'I'm so sorry, Pandora. You should have told me. I would have taken you to the hospital, been there for you. Why didn't you say something? I don't understand.'

'It was all too much to take in. I may not even be gene positive. It's fifty–fifty.'

He latches on to that, his face brightening. 'That's good news, right? You have to think positive. If you have this gene thing, we can deal with it. Until then, there's no point worrying about it.'

Easy for him to say. But it's impossible to sweep something like that under the carpet; of course I'm worrying about it, every single day.

'When do you find out?' he asks.

'Around the end of June, maybe earlier, I hope.'

He whistles. 'Horrible having to wait so long.' He shakes his head. 'I knew there was something else on your mind.' He sounds almost pleased that he's been proven right. 'I knew it wasn't just the whole moving in thing. We won't dwell on it any more until you have your test results, OK? I promise. I'm here for you, Pandora. No matter what.' He lifts my hand to his lips and kisses it gently. 'We'll get through this. I know you probably don't want to talk about it any more, but thank you for telling me.'

He's spot on; I want to stop talking, just *be* for a change. I feel lighter for telling him. Markham was right; it wasn't as difficult as I thought it would be. Declan knows not to press me for details until I'm ready. In fact, so far he's been perfect.

We sit there for a long time, gazing out to sea, Declan's arm firm and solid around my shoulders, and for the first time in weeks, I allow myself to feel calm and even a tiny bit optimistic. It feels like old times, when we were just boyfriend and girl-friend, before I'd met Rachel or Jessica and things started to get complicated, before Ruth's letter, when everything was easy and I had my whole life ahead of me.

That evening, lying in bed, going over the day, I wonder if I told Declan about the blood test because I want him to know, or because it got me out of a sticky situation and deflected the attention away from his proposal. But surely it was the former, because otherwise wouldn't that make me a bad person?

If I get the all-clear, I tell myself, if I'm handed my life back, then I'm going to make damn sure I live it properly. Iris deserves a proper family and I deserve a good, kind, decent man. A man who understands me, who gives me space when I need it; a man who will support me. A solid man like Declan. I try to picture our wedding day: Iris in a pale yellow organza dress with a green sash – with her olive skin, yellow is stunning on her; Declan in a smart morning suit, with a buttercup-coloured silk cravat; Jules looking ravishing in emerald green, her auburn curls cascading down her back; and me . . . that's where the difficulty lies. What am I wearing? A classic ivory sheath? A Grace Kelly/Princess Kate-inspired lace-and-satin number? A frothy ballerina skirt with a sweetheart bodice? As I start to drift off, Olivier's napkin dress wafts into my half-conscious mind, and I go to sleep dreaming about the most heavenly wedding gown of them all.

Chapter 19

'Are you sure this is going to work?' Jules asks as we judder up Alex and Markham's laneway in my Golf.

'I hope so,' I say, gripping the steering wheel tightly, praying the ruts don't damage my chassis. 'You both know what you're doing, right?'

'I'm on dog duty with Markham,' Jules says. 'Arietty is on panic attack alert. Do you have the Valium and the paper bag, Arietty?' As Rowie is now in Norway organizing her nuptials, Arietty managed to find some herself. Presumably they're her mum's, but you never know with Arietty.

'Yep, all safely stowed in my rucksack. Along with this mutt's treats. My friend said he was an angel. What a liar! He's got a dicky bladder, sprays urine all over the place when he gets excited. I've already been weed on twice.' Arietty has borrowed a springer spaniel from one of the reptile keepers at the zoo for the lunch, but there's a reason he's called Tigger, and although he seems to have calmed down a bit since we collected them both in Monkstown, Arietty's still holding him firmly by the collar to stop him bouncing around the car.

'Gross!' Jules says.

I wrinkle up my nose. 'Please tell me he hasn't weed on my seats already.'

'I medicated him just before we got in the car,' Arietty says. 'He'll be fine for a couple of hours.'

I glance in my rear-view mirror. There's something about

the way she said the last sentence, overly flippantly, and the way she's gazing out the window that's making me a little suspicious.

'Medicated him with what?' I ask.

She looks blasé. 'Just a mild tranquillizer.'

I give a rather shocked laugh. 'Arietty! You gave him some of the Valium, didn't you? We might need those pills. And surely they're meant for humans? The poor mutt.'

'Poor mutt, my ass,' she says, nonplussed. 'That's good-quality stuff he's after getting, Pandora. And my silk dress will probably never recover from his pee fountain.'

Jules is chuckling away to herself. 'I have a funny feeling about this afternoon. And I don't mean funny ha, ha.'

'I know what you mean,' I say. 'Right, Markham's left the gate open; good man, Markham. Action stations, everyone.'

I press down on the accelerator to help the Golf lurch up the sloped drive and then turn a little too quickly, sending small stones flying, and pull up beside Markham's Land Rover. As arranged, the dogs are outside the house. Markham appears at the side door and waves at us, a nervous look on his face. He walks towards the car and Jules buzzes down her window.

'Hi, girls,' he says, putting his hands on the bottom of the frame. 'Look, I'm sorry, but I'm having second thoughts about taking Alex out. I told her about the lunch ten minutes ago, like you suggested, Pandora. To give her enough time to change but not enough time to worry about everything, but she's sitting on the bed – she won't budge. I've tried talking to her but it's no use. I think we'll have to go ahead without her.'

'How's her breathing?' Arietty asks, popping her head between the two front seats.

He seems surprised at the question and a little unsure. 'OK, I think. But I did notice her hands shaking.'

'What did she say exactly?' I ask him.

'That it's a lovely idea and it's a shame that she can't go.'

But I'm not giving up that easily, not after all our hard work. 'Can I try talking to her?'

He shrugs. 'You can give it a go. But I warn you, she's pretty stubborn.'

As I step out of the car, Jules asks me, 'Will we go ahead with getting the dogs organized?'

'Yes,' I say. 'If she really won't come, you and Jules can go on with Markham, give him a hand, and I can follow on later. The lunch has to go ahead regardless, it's booked out.' I already had a long chat with Markham this morning about the plans, and he was so excited about the prospect of getting Alex out of the house, so psyched about the lunch and possibly reopening the shop again in the near future, it's horrible seeing him so down-cast and flat now. The poor man looks worn out.

'Markham?' I say gently.

He's bending down, rubbing one of the dogs' backs vigor-ously, his arms wrapped around its big old belly, his face pressed against its coat, as if rubbing away his frustration and grief for a life he's lost, a future life he wants but can't have. It's heartbreaking to watch.

'Markham?' I say again, a little louder.

He looks up, his eyes glistening. 'I'm not expecting anything, Pandora, but do your best, please.'

'I will.' I make my way inside, through the doggy-smelling porch, into the warmth of the kitchen and up the stairs. Alex gave us a tour of the house at the Shoestring dinner, so I know she is behind the closed door with the pale blue wooden heart hanging on it. I knock gently. There's no answer, so after a few seconds I press the old-fashioned black iron catch open and walk inside. Alex is sitting on the bed, staring out the window, stroking the Maisie Hersh dress, which is sitting in a red puddle over her legs.

'Hi, Alex.' I sit down beside her. 'How are you feeling?'

She looks at me in confusion. 'What are *you* doing here?' She pauses for a second. 'Sorry, I didn't mean that to come out the way it did. I just had a bit of a row with Markham. I hate arguing with him, it really upsets me. We've been fighting quite a lot recently. Do you fight with your boyfriend, Pandora? Is it normal? I really don't know what's normal and what's not any more.' She breaks off and stares down at the dress. 'The material's amazing, isn't it? So soft. I've tried it on a couple of times. But you may as well have it back now. I cooked a special dinner for Markham last night. He seemed tired this week so I thought it would be a nice thing to do. I got all dressed up, heels, make-up, the works. I was sitting in the kitchen when he walked in from his mum's place and his eyes lit up when he saw me. "We're going out?" he said, all smiling and happy. But then he saw the table set for dinner behind me and his face dropped. I think he's had enough of me.' She looks up at me, her eyes wide and sad. 'I think he's going to leave me.'

'Alex, he's devoted to you. He's just tired and worried about everything. He's spent the last two weeks working his butt off to get Pet Planet ready for the lunch. You should see it, it looks amazing. Can't you just try and go? Your boys will be with you, plus me and Jules and Arietty, and Markham of course – and some of your old customers too. Markham said Mrs Hilton-Slazenger is dying for you to meet her latest rescue dog.'

Alex nods. 'Her previous fellow, Rex, died last year. She was devoted to him. Lovely woman, a bit scary, but her heart's in the right place. I'm so delighted she decided to go again, she's brilliant with animals.'

'Can't you just attempt to make it out of the house? I'm sure once you're in the car—'

Her eyes glitter dangerously. 'Pandora, you don't get it, do you? No one does. My heart's racing just thinking about it.'

And sure enough, she is starting to look agitated, her eyes flitting around the room, her hands balled tensely.

'What's worrying you the most?' I ask, genuinely interested. 'Is it having to talk to people?'

Her face darkens. 'How about getting sick in public for a start? Blacking out? Feeling like I'm having a heart attack; not being able to breathe? The pain, like someone's sticking needles into my organs and squeezing my lungs out like a sponge. Do I need to continue? Look, I can't just stop feeling the way I do because you've arranged this lunch. It was a very kind thing to do and I know Markie was hoping it would give me a real incentive to snap out of all of this,' she waves her hands around the room, 'but I can't. Don't you see? It's bigger than I am. And it's getting worse. I used to be able to walk to the end of the laneway with the boys, no problem. But now even stepping out of the house makes me nervous. Every day I try. I give myself pep talks, gear myself up to take the boys for a walk, but I just can't do it. I'm terrified.'

'Of what?'

'Of everything. Of leaving the house. Of not leaving the house. In the early days I was afraid of people asking me about . . . about Addie, OK? But now, most of all, I'm scared that Markham will leave me, that my family will break down. Markie and my boys, they're my family. I know it's not much, but it's enough for me. For us, I thought. But if I can't give Markie a real family, I know he's going to leave me eventually. He's obsessed. All this adoption stuff, it's not what I want. I want to live a quiet, simple life with Markie and the boys, and if we can't have our own children, then so be it. It means every-thing to Markham, having a son or a daughter, but I'm not sure I want someone else's child – does that sound awful to you? God, even saying it out loud like that sounds horrible, I know it does. But I can't help how I feel. I don't think I could love another child the way I loved Addie or the other babies I lost. That's the truth.'

'It doesn't sound awful at all,' I assure her. 'I know plenty of people feel the same way. But Alex, you have to talk to Markham about all of this. Promise me you will.' I want to tell her what he said to me, about only going through with the adoption to make her happy, but it's not my place. She needs to hear it from him.

'I can't,' she says. 'We just end up arguing all the time. I think he's at the end of his tether with me and with the whole situation with his mum and the shop. I've never seen him so down, he's always been the strong one. I want to support him, help him, but there's nothing I can do.'

'But there is,' I say gently. 'You can put the dress on, walk downstairs and get in the jeep with the boys.'

'I can't.' She starts crying. 'Haven't you been listening?'

'I have, and it's your turn to listen to me now, Alex,' I say, making my voice a little stern. She needs to hear this from someone and it may as well be me. 'I said *try*. You have to show Markham that you love him enough to try. He's worked so hard on this lunch and yes, OK, it was naïve of us to think you'd be able to attend, just like that; you're clearly not ready. But you have to show him how much you love him. *Show* him, understand? Not just tell him. You have to start thinking about treatment. I know you don't want to take tranquillizers or anything—'

'I'm not putting any of that poison in my system,' she says sharply. 'I'm sorry, but it's something I feel very strongly about.'

'Even if it might help you? Even to save your marriage?' It sounds cruel even to my ears, but I know I'll only reach her if I'm honest and direct.

She starts crying again, huge wracking sobs. 'You think I don't know that I'm ruining my life?' she demands through her tears. 'I'm not stupid, of course I know. But you don't understand. I can't go out!'

'Maybe not. Maybe you're right. But you'll never know unless you really try. Take one small step, Alex. Put on the dress. Get in the car. You may not make it to the end of the lane-way, but at least you'll have given it a shot. Surely Markham is worth that?'

She takes a few deep breaths, blowing the air out of her mouth noisily. Then she shifts the dress off her knee and onto the duvet beside her and slowly stands up.

'OK, OK, I'll do it,' she says. 'Tell Markie I'll be down in five minutes.'

'I can help you get ready if you like.'

She shakes her head. 'No, I need to do this alone.' She gives me a small smile. 'Pandora, you'd make an excellent dog trainer.'

I smile back. 'Thanks, I think. Jules would agree with you, she thinks I'm a right bossy boots. Call me if you need anything. I'll be just downstairs in the hall.'

As I walk back down the stairs, I think about what Alex has just said. Dog trainer? Not much of a compliment, but in the circumstances, probably justified. Alex is mad about dogs, so I'm sure she meant it positively. I linger in the hallway, worrying. What if I was too hard on Alex? Maybe she'll do herself an injury. Can anxiety attacks damage a person? Put strain on their heart? I don't think so. I wish I could remember, and I wish I'd done more reading, talked to a doctor, someone professional. What am I thinking, forcing Alex to do something that makes her feel physically sick? Why do I always think I know better than everyone else? Why do I have to try and control every single bloody part of the day? Suddenly I feel all at sea.

'Everything all right?' Arietty is standing in the doorway to the kitchen. 'You look as if you're about to take an exam or something.'

'Where are Jules and Markham?' I ask, trying to deflect her attention. I'm not sure I can explain myself to Arietty without sounding completely mad and neurotic.

'Outside with the boys. Ryle won't get into the jeep. I think he senses something's up. He keeps looking around for Alex.' She pauses, looks at me. 'She is coming, right?'

'She's putting on the Maisie Hersh as we speak,' I say.

Arietty lifts her eyebrows, clearly impressed. 'So you managed to talk her around; good for you. I always said that girl needs a firm hand, just like her boys. Are you OK, Pandora, you still look kinda funny?'

I shake my head and laugh a little manically at the same time. 'I'm all over the place, to be honest. I think I may have forced Alex into doing something before she's ready and—'

'I'm ready. Is it cold outside? Do I need a coat?' Alex is standing at the top of the stairs, smiling down at us bravely, the red dress swishing around her legs, a delicate, cobwebby cream cashmere shrug over her shoulders. The smile doesn't reach her eyes, which are still flickering with anxiety, but she's holding a green clutch bag in the shape of an apple against her waist determinedly. She wobbles a little, and puts a hand on the banister to steady herself. I'm not sure if it's nerves or the green high-heeled sandals.

'No, it's pretty warm. I'm loving the bag, Alex,' I add, trying to distract her. 'Is it Lulu Guinness?'

'No, I made it myself. Do you really like it?' She holds it up and the glittery surface catches the light.

'It's amazing. You can tell me how you made it in the jeep.'

'Jeep.' Alex's face pales and her breathing quickens.

I move towards the stairs, ready to offer her my hand, but she waves it away. 'I'm fine, really. Just give me a few seconds.' She closes her eyes and takes a few deep breaths. Then she opens them again and asks, 'My boys are in the jeep, right?'

'Yes,' I say, hoping Ryle has co-operated by this stage. 'With Markham.'

She nods silently and walks slowly down the stairs, step by painful step. At the bottom her heels click on the slate floor and she follows Arietty and me through the kitchen and outside.

Now and again I look behind me to check she's still there, but she is, and gives me a tiny firm nod as if to say, 'I'm doing this.'

We reach the front door without incident. Markham is sitting behind the wheel of the jeep. The front passenger door is ajar and he waves at us through the opening. Jules is in the driver's seat of my car, trying not to get bounced on by Tigger judging from the way she's swatting her hands at him.

'Alex!' Markham says, his face lighting up. I nearly cry when I see the sheer joy in his eyes. 'You look beautiful.'

'Thanks,' she says, giving him a good attempt at a smile.

The dogs (including Ryle, I'm relieved to see) bark at Alex and put their paws on the side window of the boot as if to say, 'Come on, Mummy, come with us.'

She looks at them, back at Markham, then closes the front door firmly behind her, and stands still for a second before picking her way over the dog toys and shiny metal water bowls towards the jeep. Arietty and I flank her just in case. But apart from her chest, which is heaving up and down with every breath, she seems to be hanging in there. She stops beside the jeep, places her bag on the dashboard, grips the roof bars and swings herself in like a pro. Then she leans forward, her eyes closed, and starts to take several long, noisy breaths.

Markham is watching her carefully. 'That's it, Alex,' he says, placing a hand on her back. She arches towards it, as if sucking in his strength. After a few more seconds, she sits up.

'I want to see the shop,' she says. 'I don't know if I can go inside, Markie, or even get out of the jeep, but I want to see what you've done to the place. Pandora says it looks amazing. I know I'm a pain to live with, I know I make everything so hard . . .' She starts crying again. 'I don't want to be like this. I want to get better . . .' she breaks off, unable to continue.

'I know you do, love,' he says. 'Please don't cry.'

She presses her fingers under her eyes to stem the tears. 'I'm so sorry about everything. I know you're under a lot of stress and I never meant to push you away. I just find it hard to talk about, you know . . .'

'Addie,' he says, willing her with his eyes to say her name.

'Addie,' Alex says in a tiny voice that's almost a whisper. 'My little Addie. She's gone and it still hurts so much. But she's still with me, in my heart, every single day.'

'There's nothing wrong with that,' he says. 'She'll be in our hearts for ever. But you can't let it ruin the rest of your life. Of *our* life. I know it hurts, believe me. But hiding away like this isn't going to solve anything, pet. Do you understand that?'

'Yes.' It comes out a little breathless but she sounds like she means it.

'I just want you to be happy, Alex,' he adds. 'I can't be happy unless you're happy, and that's the truth.'

Arietty nudges against me.

'Aah,' she says softly. 'That's the sweetest thing I've ever heard. He's a doll.'

'I know,' I whisper back.

They seem to have stopped talking, so I say, 'Arietty, would you mind travelling with Jules? It might stop Tigger from causing a crash. I'll go in the jeep with Alex and Markham just in case. Jules knows the way.'

'Sure,' she says. 'Good luck.' She gives me a warm pat on the arm.

I climb into the back seat of the jeep and pull the door behind me, slamming it a bit harder than I'd meant to.

'Sorry about that,' I say to Markham. 'Heavy door.'

'Built like a tank, this old girl.' Markham slaps the dashboard with the heel of his hand. 'Alex loves Landies, don't you, love?' He turns the key in the ignition and the engine starts with a splutter, then a noisy put-put-put.

Alex nods wordlessly. She's clutching the handle on the side of the door, her knuckles white.

'Ready, Alex?' Markham says, his voice raised a little over the engine.

She nods again, and he swings the jeep around and then follows Jules down the drive and onto the laneway. I put my hand on Alex's shoulder.

'OK?' I ask her.

She twists in her seat and I can see that she's not. Her eyes are full of tears and her breath is starting to sound ragged and caught.

I lean in towards her and ask, 'Do you want to go back?'

'No. I can do this.'

'You sure? Last chance.'

'Positive.'

'All right then.' I put my arm through the gap between the front seats and take her hand in mine. Her palm is sweaty and I'm sure I can feel her pulse palpitating wildly against my skin.

'You're doing brilliantly,' I tell her. 'That's it. Lots of deep breaths.'

We get to the end of the laneway and Markham slows to a stop and turns to her. 'Alex, as always, you amaze me, do you know that?' he says, with genuine wonder in his eyes. 'I know how difficult this is for you, but you're giving it a go. That's all I can ask. If you want to go home now, I'll understand completely.'

'I want to see the shop,' she manages to get out, her voice tight.

Markham leans over and kisses her gently on the cheek. Then he looks both ways and pulls out into the traffic. It's only a ten-minute drive, but I think we all feel every minute of it. By the time we get to Wicklow Town, I can tell that Alex is struggling. She's slumped in her seat, and seems almost fearful of looking out the window at the passing shops, cars and pedestrians. I can't work out what's she's afraid of seeing, but I figure her clearly deep-seated anxiety is probably not logical, and I doubt she could express it even if I asked her, so I stay quiet.

As we approach Pet Planet, she sits up a little.

'The woodwork's red,' she says, brightening. 'I like it. Much warmer than the blue. Oh, and the banner. Markie, it looks fantastic. Labs who Lunch. Ha! Was that your idea, Pandora?'

I smile. 'Guilty.'

'Hear that, boys?' she says. 'It's especially for you.' Mo, Digby and Ryle give appreciative barks from the back.

Markham finds parking just down the road from the shop. I have no idea how he reverses into the neat space, but he does it in one.

Noticing the impressed look on my face, Alex says, 'He's a great driver. One of his many skills.' She seems almost chipper.

Markham hops out and goes to open the door for Alex. I let myself out and stand beside him, for moral support and to check for passing traffic. He's watching Alex so intently I don't think he'd notice an articulated lorry, let alone a car.

'Take your time, Alex,' he says. 'There's no rush. Look, there's Mrs Hilton-Slazenger and her new dog, Paulina. I don't think she's seen us. She must be on her way up to the shop.'

'The lunch,' Alex says, suddenly sounding panicked. 'All those people.'

Then she sits quite still, staring out the windscreen as if in a trance, her chest rising and falling in rapid succession. Too rapid. Suddenly her face crumples and she starts crying again.

She says nothing, just looks at Markham and shakes her head. Then she collapses forward, her whole body shaking, her breath out-of-control fast.

Markham puts an arm around her back and moves his head close to hers. 'Alex, can you hear me? Alex? It's OK. I'm here. Pandora's right beside me. You're going to be all right. Breathe, pet. Do you hear me, breathe! Deep breaths, in, out, in, out. Slow as you can, love.'

'Here.' Arietty appears beside us and hands Markham a paper bag. He looks a little surprised but takes it off her gratefully.

'Breathe into this, pet,' he tells Alex. 'Everything's going to be all right, I promise.'

Chapter 20

'I'm so sorry you had to take me home, Pandora,' Alex says for the umpteenth time. 'After all your hard work, you're missing all the fun.' We're sitting at the kitchen table in Summer Cottage, Alex and I, both drinking mugs of hot, sugary tea and munching chocolate biscuits. She's wearing a navy fleece of Markham's over the Maisie Hersh, which looks a little odd, but she was shivering so much I grabbed the first thing I could find on the coat hooks in the porch. I'm completely rattled after having to drive the jeep back to Summer Cottage, and Alex is still very shaky after her panic attack.

I offered to take over, attempt to run the lunch in Markham's place so that he could take Alex home himself, but he refused.

'It's kind of you, Pandora,' he'd said. 'But the customers will expect either Alex or me to be here. I can't let them down, not after they've all been so loyal and supportive. I'm sure Alex will be fine once she knows she's homeward bound. No, I think it's best if you take her back to Summer Cottage. If it's OK with them, I'll keep Jules and Arietty here. I'll need a hand getting the dogs fed and watered and keeping everyone happy.'

At first, we'd tried to transfer Alex into my car, Markham lifting her out of the jeep and carrying her slowly towards my Golf, but Ryle started barking and pawing at the window, which distressed Alex so much that he had to turn around and put her back in the jeep.

'The dog senses how upset she is,' Arietty said. 'They often pick up things that humans can't. I wouldn't separate them, not right now.'

'But I can't drive that thing,' I said, pointing at the jeep. 'It's huge.'

'It's just a car, sis,' Jules said, patting my shoulder. 'OK, a pretty big one, but the mechanics are just the same. Take it handy. You'll be grand.' It was all right for her to say, she's like a man when it comes to cars – she can hop behind any wheel and drive like a pro within seconds. Which is kind of ironic seeing as she doesn't even own a car.

In the end I didn't have much choice. Markham's face was ashen and he looked so stressed, running his hands over his head again and again, that I had to acquiesce, and I gingerly climbed into the driver's seat. The window was open and Markham talked me through the gears – 'they stick a bit, you have to be quite firm with them'; the brakes – 'kind of strong, so don't brake suddenly'; and the loud whirring sound that the engine made – 'don't worry about the noise, it doesn't mean anything sinister'.

I managed to get us back safely, after a few rude beeps and flashing lights from boy racers who wanted me to speed up. But with the noise and the air coming in the scarily loose window frames, anything over sixty felt like rally driving, so I just ignored the speed merchants and kept to the left so that they could overtake me.

The jeep bounced happily up Alex and Markham's lane – one benefit of the Land Rover, I thought reluctantly, my hands still shaking as I pressed the accelerator and it roared up the drive. It screeched to a sudden halt as I punched the foot brake a little too hard. I was dizzy with relief to have made it in one piece. I turned off the engine, my ears still ringing from the noise. I'd said a few what I hope were comforting words to Alex during the journey, but I had no idea if she'd heard me over the engine.

Once inside, Alex walked through shakily and sat down at the kitchen table, Ryle lying over her feet, her other boys nudging me with their noses, while I put on the kettle.

Now we're sitting at the table, both our nerves somewhat restored.

'I was happy to bring you home,' I say. 'Honestly. It was . . .' I pause, searching for the right word. 'An adventure. That Land Rover is something else. The racket. How do you hear each other speak?'

She gives a laugh. 'We shout. You get used to it. Markie keeps promising to soundproof the exhaust, but he's busy and I don't like to nag.' She stops for a moment, stares down at the table and rolls a biscuit crumb under her finger. 'I let him down today, didn't I? I hope he isn't too upset.'

I smiled at her. 'No, you didn't, not at all. He was thrilled you managed to get that far. It's something to build on, Alex. You should see it as a positive.'

'I guess.' Her shoulders are slumped and from the way she's pressing her lips together, I think she's trying not to cry.

'You should be really proud of yourself,' I continue. 'Maybe you can visit the shop another day, when it's quiet.'

'I think I could do that. I could visit his mum too. I haven't seen her for ages. She's not great these days, poor woman. She can't come here because of her health. It's got to a stage where she doesn't really recognize anyone either, even Markie.' She gives a deep sigh. 'I need to talk to him about all that. He and his sister have done an amazing job, but I think it's time to let the professionals take over.'

'Do you mean a home?' I ask gently.

She nods, her lower lip wobbling. 'It's not an easy decision to make; she's had a really happy year at home with them nursing her, but from what I understand from Markie, she's not there any more. She wouldn't want them to put their own lives on hold for her; she was devoted to them, only ever wanted the best for them both.' She leans down and tickles Mo behind his ears. 'Life's tough sometimes, isn't it? Markham's so tired all the time and it makes everything a bit difficult.' Her cheeks flare a little. 'You know, spending time together, as a couple. Pandora, do you mind if I ask you something? I don't really have anyone else to talk to about all this.'

'Of course. Ask away.'

'How often do you and your boyfriend, you know,' her cheeks go even redder. 'Have sex. Every day? Twice a week? Once a month? What's normal? I read so many different things online, it's hard to figure out who's telling the truth.'

'Wow, OK, um.' I stall for a second, a bit taken aback by the direct question and the about-turn in the conversation. I know she's worried about their relationship, but it's all getting a bit personal.

She looks mortified. 'Sorry, I shouldn't have said anything. How embarrassing. Just ignore me. I'm always asking inappropriate questions. No filter, Markie says.'

'No, it's fine, really,' I say, trying to get over myself. It's obviously something she's concerned about and if she's relying on the Internet for answers, that's worrying in itself. 'I guess once you've been together for a while things change, don't they? Life gets in the way and, as you say, people get tired and bed starts to take on a whole new meaning. It becomes less about ripping each other's clothes off, and more about getting a decent night's sleep. Not very romantic, though, is it?'

She shakes her head wordlessly. I realize I haven't answered her question. 'I guess about once a week is normal or once a fortnight, if that's what you're asking. But so's once a month for a lot of couples, or every day for others. Honestly, I think everyone's very different and it's not something you should worry about.'

'We haven't, you know, had sex, since Addie died,' she says, her voice going up a notch. 'For a while I couldn't cope with even the thought of it and I pushed him away. Now Markie doesn't seem interested any more, and I've never been the one to instigate things in that department.'

'Maybe he still thinks you're not ready,' I say gently. 'Unless you've told him otherwise, he thinks you'd push him away again. I think you need to talk to him, Alex. About a lot of things.'

'I want to try for another baby,' she blurts out. 'Do you think I'm crazy?'

'Not at all. It'll give you a great incentive to get better. I'm sure Markham would be thrilled. But are you sure you're strong enough?'

'I want a baby more than anything, but I also want to do it for him. He's the most amazing dad, Pandora, you should have seen him with Addie. They were inseparable. She used to potter along behind him like a puppy. The way she used to look at him, like he was a god, it would break your heart. I know what you're saying, Pandora, but I'm stronger than I look despite all this panic attack stuff. After today, I really do believe that I can beat it, get back to some sort of normal, whatever that is. I could even cope with another miscarriage. If that's what it takes to have another baby, I'll do it. Sometimes we have to fight for other people, as well as ourselves – don't we? People we love, I mean. Otherwise why bother living? What's the point if we don't care enough for those we love to fight for them?'

Before I know what's happening tears spring to my eyes. I blink them away and stand up.

'Sorry, hayfever,' I mumble. 'Just get a tissue.'

Once in the bathroom, I sit down on the closed toilet seat and lean forward, my head in my hands. Alex is completely right. Unless we fight for those we love, what *is* the point? If Alex, brittle as she is at the moment, can summon up the courage to try and move forwards, to throw herself at life, with all its sorrow and messiness, why can't I?

Right that second, I know what I have to do. I have to contact Olivier again; not for me, but for Iris. She deserves to know her birth father. Unless I do everything in my power to make that happen, what kind of mother am I? And if he still refuses to acknowledge her, then at least I'll know that I've done my very best.

That evening, inspired by Alex's bravery, I sit down to write Iris another letter.

Dear Iris,

I know even after reading these letters you will still have questions. I have tried to tell you a little about what your dad was like, and to reassure you that we loved each other very much. But it just wasn't to be. Olivier is Paris through and through; and I'm Dublin. I love living near all my friends, love seeing Jules and Bird and Dad every day; love living by the sea; love walking the pier with you (and your scooter); love having coffee in Mugs Café; love browsing in Dubray Books. I've never wanted to live anywhere else. I couldn't live in Paris full time and Olivier's whole life is there.

Sometimes life is difficult, Iris, I'm sorry to say. Sometimes adults have to make tough decisions which they hope are for the best. I am sorry that you do not know Olivier; I am even more sorry that Olivier does not know you. My beautiful, clever, funny, incredible daughter.

But I want you to know this: your father was and I'm sure still is an incredible man. I have never met anyone like him; I think he's one of a kind. Strong and brave and funny and smart and sensitive and so gifted. His drawings used to make me catch my breath; he was able to capture something so perfectly in just a few strokes — astoundingly talented.

I have never once regretted meeting him or having you, my darling girl. Never.

The exquisite dress drawn on the napkin, that's one of Olivier's designs. He drew it for me on one of our final afternoons together. It is my last gift to you.

I treasure his memory, Iris, because he was a truly extraordinary man, but also because he gave me the most precious gift of all: he gave me you.

Love always and forever,

Mum xxx

I trace my fingers over the napkin, waves of emotion threatening to overpower me. The detail he managed to get into such a small sketch – the plain, elegant bodice, the delicate lace on the fluttering, butterfly-wing sleeves, the sweeping skirt with lace overlay; even now, nearly ten years on, the dress still looks as fresh as the day he drew it. I attach it carefully to the front of the letter with a paperclip and place it in the box. I take one last look at the contents and, with bleary eyes, close the lid.

Then I pick up my notebook and take a few deep, calming breaths before writing the most important letter of my life:

Dear Olivier . . .

Chapter 21

'Mum? Are you ready? Declan's here.' Iris is standing in the doorway of my bedroom, clutching her cycling helmet, her favourite sequined bag slung across her chest.

I jump and look up, hoping that I don't appear too guilty. I was about to rip up the letter I'd written to Olivier – which had arrived back slightly crumpled but unopened with Not known at this address, return to sender scrawled across the front. Jules had handed it to me on Friday morning. I'd only DHL-ed it to Olivier first thing Monday morning so he must have posted it back almost the instant it reached him.

'Post for you,' she'd said. 'Who's this Olivier Huppert you were trying to contact?'

I'd looked down at the envelope and immediately realized that the 'return to sender' message was in Olivier's hand-writing, his statement clear and concise: leave me alone. I felt like I'd been stabbed in the heart and for a second I didn't know where I was.

'Pandora? Are you all right?' Jules was staring at me.

I nodded, trying to compose myself. 'Just this French designer I wanted for the shop.'

'Any good?'

I shrugged. 'I guess it's irrelevant now. Must have moved. I'd better get back to the office.' I turned on my heels and walked away quickly. Once the door was closed behind me, I sat down at the desk, put my head in my hands and wept.

'Mum?' Iris is still standing there, waiting for me.

I put my hand over the letter and smile at her. 'I'll be down in a second.'

But I can't bring myself to rip it up. It just seems so final. So I walk towards the wardrobe and hide it in the Louboutin box for the moment.

'Mum!' Iris bellows up the stairs. 'Hurry up!'

I linger on the landing for a second, looking down into the hall. Iris is jumping from foot to foot impatiently, Rachel is already wearing her rollerblades and seems equally keen to get going, and Declan is standing in the middle of the two of them, carrying Iris's folded-up scooter, chatting away easily to the girls.

'There you are.' He looks up and smiles, his eyes twinkling. He looks genuinely thrilled to see me. 'Ready?'

I take a deep breath. 'Yes,' I say, smiling back. 'Yes, I think I am.'

'The girls seem to be getting on well.' Declan waves at Iris and Rachel, who have set up camp in the crow's nest of the pirate ship in the park on Dun Laoghaire seafront. We even had to pass their lunch up to them.

'Rachel seems to have taken Iris under her wing today,' I say. 'She can be very sweet when she wants to be.' After a minor sulk earlier when Declan wouldn't buy her a cotton beanie at the Farmers' Market in the park, and a few scowls about Declan making her wear her helmet on the pier, Rachel has allowed her sunny side to come out and is now trying to attract pigeons to her hand with bits of her bagel, which Iris is finding hilarious.

'She's starting to get used to her new big-sister role,' he says.

I think about this for a second, before realizing, no, the thought of Rachel being Iris's stepsister doesn't cause me any sort of anxiety at all. Interesting. I smile back at him. 'I guess she is.'

We sit there for a minute, watching the girls.

'Have you thought any more about getting engaged?' he says gently, catching me out with a very direct question.

I look at him. His eyes are hopeful.

'Yes. I mean I've been thinking about it,' I add quickly, not wanting him to get the wrong impression. 'Give me a few more weeks and then ask me again.'

He looks delighted but he knows not to push me, so he just says, 'I will, and this time, be warned, I'll come prepared. Jess is seeing someone, by the way. A guy she knows from the tennis club. He's a good bit older than her.'

Not again. For a second I boggle about men's minds. Don't they realize that talking about an engagement and an ex-wife in practically the same breath is bad form? Clearly not.

'Are you OK about that?' I ask carefully, already suspecting from his tone that Jessica's new beau is bothering him more than he'd like to let on.

He gives a snort. 'Not really any of my business, is it? He sounds all right and Rachel seems to like him.'

'She's met him already?'

'I know, I wasn't impressed. It's all a bit quick, don't you think? They've only been together a wet weekend. He brought her loads of CDs from new bands. He's some sort of bigwig in Sony Music. Jess seems to like him. A lot. She wouldn't stop talking about the bloody man.'

'It's good that's she's moving on. Isn't that what you wanted?'

'I suppose,' he says a little grudgingly. 'I guess it does make things easier. For us, I mean. It's very quick, though, don't you think? So much for still being in love with me.'

'Declan, you're making a new life for yourself, why shouldn't she? And you're right, it probably will make things easier. At least she won't throw her shoes at me again, eh?'

I nudge him with my shoulder but he doesn't seem to find it funny.

'That's what I don't understand,' he says. 'One minute she's distraught, saying she can't live without me, the next minute she's seeing some music honcho. It doesn't make sense. Do you think she's trying to make me jealous?'

'I doubt it, Declan. Look, as you said, she's just trying to move on. Don't try to overanalyse it, OK? Jessica sounds happy for once and Rachel seems a lot happier too, so maybe it's good news all round.'

'Yeah.'

'You don't sound all that convinced. Surely you just want her to be happy?'

'Rachel?'

'No, Jessica.'

'Course I do.' He looks down and starts rubbing at a knot on the wooden picnic table.

He really shouldn't be as bothered by Jessica's new boyfriend as he sounds. I study him.

Feeling my gaze, he lifts his head. 'Sorry, I'll shut up about Jess. I only found out this morning and . . .' he breaks off. 'Let's talk about something else.'

I look him in the eye. 'Declan, do you still have feelings for Jessica?'

I'm taken aback when his back stiffens and his eyes flare up. It's not like Declan to get riled. 'Of course I do. We've known each other for ever. We have a lot of shared memories, and Rachel of course. Jess was my first love, you always fall the hardest for your first love. And for a long time things were great. Until, you know . . .' He stops himself but I know he's referring to Jessica's affair. 'Anyway,' he continues, his tone lighter, 'I'm looking forward to a lot less drama this time around. We're good together, Pandora. Jess is too flighty, she drives me crazy with her mood swings and her outbursts. It's like living with a mad woman.' He pauses for a beat. 'Was, I mean. You're different; you're sensible and practical. I can depend on you. I know you're not going to go off the rails, or throw your shoes at me.'

Sensible and practical? I guess I am, but when he says it out loud like that, it makes me sound boring and predictable. 'Declan, I'm not always like that. I can do crazy with the best of them; you just haven't seen that side of me yet.'

He smiles at me. 'I don't believe that for a second. Private, yes; complicated, maybe. But not crazy. You're always looking after people, Pandora, that's who you are. It's what I love about you; you care about everyone so much, not just Iris, but Bird and your dad and your sister too. And me, I hope. My life's much calmer since you came along. Yes, we have the odd disagreement, but nothing like I used to have with Jess. Man, she could fight for Ireland.'

'Christ almighty, could you please stop talking about bloody Jessica all the time?'

Declan stares at me. 'Pandora, calm down. I'm sorry, I didn't realize it bothered you so much.'

'It does bother me, OK? I don't go on about my ex-boyfriends all the time.'

'We were married, it's a bit different. But if it makes you feel better, I'll stop, all right? I promise.'

He looks so genuine that it's hard to say anything other than 'Fine.'

'And about that sensible thing,' I say. 'I'm only sensible because I have to be, Declan. I'd love to go wild sometimes, be more spontaneous, but chance would be a fine thing.'

From the half smile on Declan's face he thinks what I'm saying is funny in some way, but I carry on regardless, trying to explain myself better. 'Half the time I'm too damn tired. Working full time and being a single mum is like having permanent low-level concussion. I'd kill to have the energy to be a full-on drama queen from time to time.'

'That's unfair; Jess isn't a drama queen. She just finds things difficult sometimes.'

'Declan, would you stop defending her? Please.'

'Sorry, sorry. But you brought it up.'

I'm about to protest, but Declan's mobile rings. He looks at the screen. 'It's Mum, do you mind if I take it?'

I nod silently, gritting my teeth. Now he's talking to his mother in the middle of a conversation. Great! And is that really how he sees me? As a calm, sensible nurturer? I don't see myself that way at all. I'd like to think that I *am* passionate at times, and hell, artistic even. I know he didn't mean to insult me, but the more I think about it, the more it irritates me. Why does Jessica get to be the 'fiery' one? And if I stay with Declan will I have to be 'sensible' for the rest of my life, always put other people first? Is that my destiny?

Declan waves his hand in front of my face, cutting into my thoughts. 'Sorry about that. I've finished talking to Mum now. She sends her love.'

'Is everything all right?'

'Yeah, yeah. She was ringing about this charity dinner dance thing in aid of Dad's hospital – she's putting together a table for it on Saturday week. It's a pop-up restaurant in a secret location in Dalkey. Black-tie dinner, live band, all in a marquee. What do you think? Will we give it a bash? You could give that nice pink frock you wore at the last ball another outing.'

'Declan! You can't wear the same dress to two events running. Especially not if it's for the same charity. Are you mad?' I'm still a bit irritated with him. In fact I'm not all that sure I want to go to his mother's bloody dinner dance. 'And I think I might have something on that night.'

'Please, Pandora. I'm sorry about mentioning Jess, really I am. It was stupid. And I swear it won't happen again. And I know you have a passionate side. In fact, I wouldn't mind seeing more of that passionate side later.' He gives me a knowing smile and takes my hand, his palm warm against mine. 'Please. It would mean a lot to me.'

I know he really is trying hard to make this work, and maybe I'm just being over-sensitive about the whole Jessica thing. So I put my irritation aside and say, 'It just so happens that I have another dress which might do the trick. So yes, it's a date.' At least I'll finally get the chance to wear the Maisie Hersh at something appropriate. I'm still not sure how I feel about Declan's assessment of me, or his disgust at Jessica's new man, but maybe I'm overthinking everything again. Maybe I should try to be more Zen-ish, like Jules, and live for the moment. And if he wants to eat in a tent with his mum and her friends, why not?

'Good woman. It's going to be a really special evening.' Declan takes my hand in his and kisses it soundly. 'I can always rely on you. You're fantastic, Pandora. Have I ever told you that?'

'Thank you, Declan.' I smile back at him. OK, I really do need to get over myself. Nothing wrong with being called sensible as long as it also comes with fantastic. Nothing wrong at all. And knowing Declan, he has plans for the night that might just involve a ring. I take a deep breath. Time to jump in with both feet. Time to finally grow up. 'Let's have dinner out tonight,' I suggest. 'My treat.'

'With the girls?'

'No, just the two of us. To celebrate, oh, I don't know, being together. I'm sure Jules will mind Iris. What do you think?'

'There's nothing I'd like more, Pandora. Thank you. For being perfect.' He leans over and gives me a kiss on the cheek.

Sensible, fantastic *and* perfect. OK, that I can live with.

Chapter 22

On Monday afternoon Klaudia from the café interrupts me in the office, shouldering open the door and scowling at me.

'There's a man at the desk delivering flowers,' she says. 'He's demanding to speak to you.'

I smile. It must be Declan. I stayed over at his place after dinner last night. I was determined to make it a fun, easy evening. When he grumbled (again) about Jessica's new man and how he was weaselling himself into Rachel's affections, I just plastered a concerned look on my face and nodded, agreeing with him until he changed the subject. When he suggested that Iris's manners were slipping a little – and to be fair she had been a bit cheeky that afternoon, even saying the dreaded 'whatever' complete with teenage eye-rolling when I asked her to move away from the edge of the pier – I didn't point out that it was Rachel's influence and that she was the one in need of being pulled up at times, I just agreed with him.

When I follow Klaudia out of the office and on to the shop floor, I recognize the 'delivery man' instantly and it's not Declan at all.

'Markham.' I give him a warm smile.

'For you,' he says, thrusting an enormous and slightly wild bunch of flowers towards me, the stems bound with thick red ribbon. 'They're from the garden.'

I run my fingers over the friendly daisies, the spiky purple allium heads and the floppy red petals of the poppies. 'Markham, they're beautiful. Thank you.'

'No, thank you. What you did for Alex last Saturday.' He shakes his head. 'It meant so much to her, to both of us. We went for a walk yesterday, just to the end of the lane with the boys, but it was a start. Alex is determined to go out every day now and she's talking about going back to work in the shop again as soon as she's able. Things are starting to look up, all thanks to you. I have the dress in the car too. Alex asked me to drop it in to you.'

'I did very little, Markham, honestly, and Jules and Arietty helped. You've just missed Jules in fact, she popped out to post something to a client down the country. You're very good to bring the dress, but I was thinking of organizing a Shoestring Club lunch this weekend – the official handing over of the dress, we like to do it on the day; it's kind of like a tradition at this stage. This Saturday if it suits everyone. Do you think Alex would be up to it? We're thinking of having it here, after the lunchtime rush. It shouldn't be too crowded then and I can get one of the girls from the café to cover for Jules. I have the weekend off, and hopefully Arietty can come along too.'

He considers this for a second. 'I'll mention it to her but I think it's a bit soon. Maybe next time. It will give her something to aim for. Or how about coming down to our place again? I know she'd love to see you all and I'm happy to cook.'

I smile at him. He really is the sweetest man. 'That would be fantastic. Are you sure?'

'Positive. About three suit you? Or is that too late?'

'No, three's perfect.'

He leans over and kisses me on the cheek, the flowers getting somewhat in the way. 'It's a date. And thanks again, Pandora.'

The following Saturday, I'm sitting at Alex and Markham's kitchen table, along with Jules and Arietty, who has swapped shifts at the zoo to be here. It's ten past three and we're all starting to get worried.

'I'm starving,' Jules says in a low voice. 'Do you think she'll be down soon?' So far there's been no sign of Alex. Markham has just gone back upstairs to see if she's all right. There are cooking smells in the kitchen, fresh bread and garlic, and the table is beautifully set with a blue gingham tablecloth and matching napkins. Alex has even placed a tiny glass vase with a daisy in it at every setting.

'Maybe she's having another panic attack,' Arietty says.

'Arietty!' I say. 'That's not very helpful.'

'Then where is she?' she says.

'And I wish you'd just tell us your bloody news.' Jules is starting to sound a bit grumpy. 'You're being very annoying, you know. It had better be interesting, sis, after making me wait ages.'

I ignore her, looking down and adjusting my knife and fork to make them sit perfectly parallel to each other.

Alex bustles into the kitchen, Markham following closely behind her. 'Sorry, sorry,' she says. 'I couldn't decide what to wear. You know how it is sometimes.' She leans down and kisses me on the cheek, followed by Jules and Arietty. She smells warm and homely, of rose perfume and baking, and she's made a huge effort to look nice, in a blue Liberty print summer dress, her hair in curly waves down her back and natural-looking make-up, including a touch of blusher highlighting her apple cheeks.

'Thanks so much for coming down to the wilds of Wicklow again,' she adds. 'It's so good to see you all.'

'I'll leave you Shoestring girls to it,' Markham says. 'Take the boys out for a walk.'

As soon as he's gone, Jules jumps straight in. 'Out with it, Pandora, spill,' she demands. 'We're all here now. What's this monumental news, then?'

'Ooh, yes, do share,' Arietty says.

All eyes are on me, so I say as nonchalantly as I can, 'Declan asked me to marry him.'

'No!' Jules stares at me. 'Seriously?'

'Yes.'

'What did you say?' Arietty asks.

'I said I'd think about it,' I say. 'But I'm coming around to the idea. I told him to ask me again in a few weeks.'

'When Markie proposed I thought I was hearing things,' Alex says, leaning her back against one of the kitchen counters. 'I was as sick as a dog you see, food poisoning, and there he was, sitting on the side of the bed, holding a basin in front of my head. I told him how much I loved him for looking after me and he said he wanted to look after me for the rest of my life and then asked me to marry him, just like that. When I realized he was serious, I was so happy I started crying and I couldn't stop. Then I puked again, so violently he had to hold my hair back. Which was very romantic, as you can imagine. I must have looked a state.'

I try not to laugh, but I can't help it. Jules and Arietty join in.

'I'm sorry,' I say through my giggles. 'But that's terrible. Poor you. But it *is* romantic in its own way. At least you knew he meant it, you know, the in sickness and in health bit.'

Alex grins. 'I suppose so.'

'Why are you making Declan wait if you like the idea?' Arietty says. 'Why didn't you say yes straight away?'

You can always count on Arietty to be direct, I think, trying to find the right words to explain. From the hush around the table and the way everyone's looking at me intently, especially Jules, it's the burning question on all their lips.

'I guess it's because I have Iris to consider as well as myself,' I say eventually. 'It's a big step. We're going to a black-tie thing in a secret location next Saturday night, and I have a feeling that he'll ask me again then.'

'That's so romantic,' Alex says. 'You'll have a much better proposal story than mine.'

'I think your story is perfect, Alex,' Arietty says. 'Wish I could find a man who'd hold a bucket for me while I puked. You're quite clearly made for each other. It's not the proposal that matters; it's the life afterwards, isn't it? If Pandora and Declan are half as devoted to each other are you guys are, they'll be just fine.'

'Thanks, Arietty.' Alex looks genuinely touched. 'I do love my Markie. I'd rather die than be without him.' She pauses and gives a short laugh. 'Sorry, I sound like a character from a Brontë novel.'

I look at Jules who is being strangely quiet. She's not smiling either. I catch her eye.

'Jules?' I say. 'Everything all right?'

'Sure,' she says. 'I'm happy for you sis, really. It's just a bit of a surprise, that's all. Declan's a nice guy and everything, but I didn't think you'd end up marrying him.'

'Why not? We've been together for eight months now. It's time to make a proper commitment.'

'I've been with Jamie for almost as long, and we're not running off to get married now, are we? Marriage is a big step.'

'That's different.'

'Why is it different?'

'Is just is. You're a lot younger than me for a start.'

At that second Jules's stomach rumbles loudly and she winces and laughs. 'Sorry, that was my stomach. It's clearly liking the cooking aromas.'

'Alex, what's on the menu? It does smell delicious.' I'm keen to move the attention away from my possible future engagement. For some reason, Jules seems to have a problem with it.

Alex smiles. 'Chicken cooked with garlic and cheese. A lot of garlic, knowing Markie. We grow it ourselves. And a vegetarian lasagne for Arietty. And let's eat right away.' As she busies

215

herself serving everyone, I remember what Alex said about Markham – 'I'd rather die than be without him.' They're such a passionate couple, and Declan and I just aren't like that. Maybe that's why Jules has reservations. Maybe she's right . . . Stop it! I say to myself. You love Declan, you're good together; it's proper, grown-up, responsible love. Alex and Markham are childhood sweethearts and their relationship is one in a million; and Jules and Jamie are like teenagers, can't keep their hands off each other. There's no use comparing other people's relationships with ours. Besides, it's normal to have doubts about getting married, I tell myself sternly. Everyone has them.

'So who's next with the dress?' Arietty asks once we're all tucking into our food.

'I was hoping to wear it at the dinner next weekend if that's all right with everyone,' I say.

'Of course,' Alex says. 'It's the perfect dress for a wedding proposal. That OK with everyone? And please tell me that there will be another dress after it. The Shoestring Club has been so much fun.'

Arietty nods. 'Absolutely. We definitely need another dress after this beauty. And I'm all for Pandora wearing the current one next.'

'Jules?' I say.

She shrugs. 'Sure.'

'Thanks, Jules.' I look at her and finally after a few seconds she smiles.

'I know you've been dying to get your hands on that dress,' she says. 'You've always looked amazing in red, sis.'

Chapter 23

Jules is right, I've been dreaming about wearing the Maisie Hersh ever since I first set eyes on it and I can't resist trying it on that very evening. It was just Iris, Jules and me for dinner, as Bird's singing at a choral festival and Dad's gone to support her. Bird invited me along, but I couldn't bear sitting in the audience, watching them singing their hearts out, wishing I was up there. I should never have left the choir; I was fogged by love and made the decision far too hastily. I really miss singing and I miss my choral friends, even if most of them are closer to Bird's age than my own. And now that Rowie's Norway bound I'm feeling a little friendless. Hopefully they'll take me back next season, in September. Maybe Declan would join too; he has an excellent voice. It could be something we do together, as a couple.

Right now, Declan is at Rachel's modern dance show. He asked me if I'd like to go, but as Jessica will be there I opted out. Iris is already in bed. Her door must be open as I can hear her CD player – she's listening to a Jacqueline Wilson audio book called *The Lottie Project* that she borrowed from the library – but I don't mind, it's not that late and she loves her stories. Jules is downstairs in the kitchen, clearing up by herself. She kindly let me off the hook.

'I know you're itching to give the dress a test run,' she'd said. 'Throw it on and come back down to show me.'

I've teamed it with black strappy Gucci sandals, a soft black leather jacket by Rick Owens that I 'borrowed' from the shop, a plain silver choker and a large silver dress ring. I think it works, but I walk carefully down the stairs and into the kitchen looking for a second opinion from Jules. When it comes to fashion, I trust Jules completely.

'Ta-da! What do you think?' I flounce the edge of the skirt like a flamenco dancer.

Jules looks up from the sink and smiles at me. She's up to her arms in bubbles, scrubbing what looks like the lasagne dish from dinner. 'Stunning. Love the jacket.'

The doorbell rings.

'That's probably Jamie,' she says. 'Would you mind getting it while I finish up here?'

'Sure.' I walk into the hall, my heels clacking on the tiles, and swing open the door.

'Hi, Jamie—'

I stop dead. It's not Jamie at all. There, standing on the doorstep, is Olivier Huppert. I'm frozen to the spot, staring at him, unable to say a thing or *feel* a thing. It's as if the whole world has stopped dead.

'What?' is all I can manage to squeeze out.

'Hello, Dora. Nice dress.' Olivier is staring at me, his face stony. 'Can I come in? I want to see my daughter. I want to see Iris.'

I don't move a muscle. Did he just say Iris? And *daughter*? I don't understand. My letter was returned unopened and he refused to listen to me in Paris. How the hell does he know Iris's name? What's going on? Suddenly ice rushes through my veins, and my head starts to spin and—

'Dora! Dora!' I hear Olivier, somewhere far away, calling my name.

And the next thing, nothing.

*

'Pandora?'

I open my eyes, slowly. Jules is crouched over me, looking concerned. I'm lying on my bed in the Maisie Hersh dress. In a flash it all comes back to me – Olivier! Olivier is here – in Dublin. And he wants to see Iris. But he can't. Iris knows nothing about him. Her dad appearing out of the blue like that will be too much for her, she won't understand. My heart starts to race.

'Take it easy,' Jules says, stroking my head. 'You fainted.'

'How did I get up here?'

'Olivier. He carried you. He's downstairs waiting to speak to you.'

'Tell him I'm sick,' I blurt out. 'Please, Jules. I don't want to talk to him. Take his mobile number; promise him I'll ring in the morning.'

'Pandora, he's come the whole way from Paris to see you. You should at least speak to him yourself. Explain.' She looks nervous for some reason.

'Where is he exactly?' I ask.

'Sitting in the hall. Shall I tell him to come on up?' Her eyes flit away from mine and she stares towards the doorway as if she's dying to escape. Something's not quite right here. She goes to get up but I grab her arm.

'Jules, why aren't you asking me who Olivier is, how I know him?'

'He told me already. He's an old friend of yours from Paris.' Her cheeks are turning bright crimson.

I stare at her. 'Jules, where's the interrogation? A complete stranger appears, out of the blue, a very attractive French one at that, and you have no questions for me at all.' I narrow my eyes. 'You know, don't you? You know who he is. What has he said?'

'Nothing! I don't know what you're talking about.'

'Why won't you look at me, then? What's going on?' I sit

219

up and swing my legs over the side of the bed and sit there thinking for a moment. Pandora Schuster is an unusual name, especially in Ireland; maybe Olivier Googled me, just as I'd Googled him.

I look at Jules again. 'I know you're hiding something and you'd better come clean, right now, because if I find out from Olivier that you have anything to do with this, I swear to God I'll never speak to you again. He knows Iris's name. Did he call in here earlier, is that it? Or ring here or something? Did you tell him about her?'

After a long pause she begins in a tiny voice, 'No, nothing like that. Please don't be angry with me. Sometimes I let Iris try on your shoes when I'm babysitting, and last weekend she opened one of the shoeboxes and found an old postcard with a ballerina on it. She brought it to me, asked could she cut out the dancer for a collage.'

My blood goes cold. 'Did she read the back of the card? Or anything else in that box?'

'No. At least she said she didn't.'

'But *you* couldn't help yourself, could you? I bet you read everything. Did you open the letter I wrote to Olivier?'

'No! I wouldn't do that. But the ones you wrote to Iris, they weren't even in an envelope or anything so I didn't think—' She stops abruptly, noticing my horrified expression.

I'm so flabbergasted that I can't even speak. I just stare at her. 'And Iris?' I manage to force out eventually. 'How does he know about Iris?'

She looks utterly shamefaced. Even before she utters the words, I know what she's about to say.

'I wrote to him,' she admits. 'Sent him some photos of her, along with photocopies of the letters. I think that's why he's here.'

'*You what?*' My heart threatens to jump out of my chest again and my cheeks burn with humiliation. Olivier was *never* supposed to read those letters. Tears prick the back of my eyes but I'm damned if I'm going to cry in front of this creature, this . . . this turncoat.

I'm so angry I feel like punching her. 'How dare you? Those letters were for Iris and only Iris. That's low, Jules, really low. Now get out! You can tell Olivier to get the hell back to France. I don't want to speak to either of you ever again.'

'He's Iris's dad, Pandora. You can't do that. It doesn't make sense. He sent your letter back unopened, so I know you were trying to contact him. And from the letters, you obviously loved—'

'None of that is any of your business. Go!' I begin to push her towards the door, not caring how roughly.

'Pandora! Look, I'm sorry.'

'I don't want to hear it,' I snap. 'Out!'

'Mummy, why are you shouting at Auntie Jules?' Iris appears at the doorway.

'Back into your room, Iris, please,' I say frantically. 'Now!'

'Who's that man?' She's staring straight at Olivier, who is by now halfway up the stairs.

'No one,' I say, shutting my eyes for a second and willing all this to go away.

When I open them again, he's joined us on the landing. He looks at Iris and then back at me.

'I am a friend of your mother's,' he tells her. 'Olivier.'

Olivier and I exchange a long look. I give a tiny shake of my head; implore him not to say anything else.

'We met in Paris a long time ago, before you were born,' he adds. 'Now I've come back to visit.'

'Cool,' Iris says easily. 'Mum brought me a present from Paris. A snow globe of the Eiffel Tower.'

'I like snow globes too,' he says, his eyes still fixed on mine. He doesn't look happy with me. I can't bear this. Seeing Olivier here, looking so damn good, smiling at Iris like that, glaring at me, it's all too much. I know that I wanted him to acknowledge Iris, but I've changed my mind. I was wrong. Utterly, completely wrong. It's too complicated, too painful.

'Olivier will be leaving tomorrow,' I say. 'So say goodbye now, Iris.'

I can feel Olivier's eyes boring into me, as I stride towards Iris, bustling her into her room. 'Come on now, bedtime.'

Please don't say anything, I will him inwardly. Please.

'Olivier is your dad, Iris,' I hear Jules say loudly behind my back.

I swing around and stare at her, open-mouthed. 'Julia! Shut up!'

'Why?' Jules's jaw is set but her voice wavers nervously. 'Iris deserves to know her dad. Olivier is clearly far too decent to force things against your wishes. I know you'll probably never speak to me again, but I love Iris with all my heart. She has rights too, Pandora. I know things weren't easy in the past, but can't you—'

'Stop.' I put both my hands up and spit out the words. 'Just stop.' She's gone too far this time. Poor Iris. It's not fair to burden her with all of this, not at nine. Jules has probably scarred her for life, blurting out the identity of her father like that. I can't bear to look at my daughter, although I know I have to. But Iris doesn't look anxious or even confused. She looks joyful; she's gazing at Olivier in pure wonder.

'Are you really my dad?' she asks him.

'Yes,' he says, his eyes twinkling. 'Which makes me a very lucky man. I could not have a more beautiful daughter.'

My eyes go blurry. Damn Olivier, he always did know the perfect thing to say.

Iris is studying his face.

'I look like you,' she says. 'We have the same eyes.'

'Yes, we do.' He nods, smiling still.

Then, quick as a flash, she runs past me and throws her arms around his waist, her head only reaching his stomach. For a second he looks completely taken aback, but recovers quickly, lifting her up in his strong arms and holding her close.

'Hello, Iris. I am very pleased to meet you.' He kisses the top of her head.

'I've always wanted a daddy, a proper one, I mean. My very own. Not like Declan. He's Rachel's daddy.'

'Who's Declan?' Olivier asks her.

'Mummy's fiancé.'

Olivier blinks a couple of times, but says nothing, just looks at me for confirmation.

I stare at her. 'Iris, what are you talking about? Declan's my boyfriend, not my fiancé.'

'Auntie Jules said you and Declan are getting married, didn't you, Auntie Jules? It's a big secret.' Her cheeks flush pink. 'Oops, sorry, Auntie Jules.'

Jules opens her mouth to say something, and then closes it again. I think she realizes that there's not much she can do to fix things at this stage. She just shrugs at me and murmurs, 'Sorry.'

'We have loads of secrets, don't we, Auntie Jules?' Iris says, giggling a little.

'Clearly,' I cut in. Jules is so out of line I can't fathom how she even dares to stand there, still breathing the same air as me. How could she? What if I'd changed my mind? Playing with Iris's feelings like that just isn't right. My hands ball in anger and if it wasn't for Iris's presence, I swear I'd knock my sister's stupid block off right this second.

The doorbell rings again.

'Must be Jamie,' Jules says, looking highly relieved to escape. She runs down the stairs and into the outer hallway. Seconds later she reappears.

'Pandora, it's Declan,' Jules hisses up at me from the bottom of the stairs. 'What will I tell him? I can't leave him on the doorstep.'

Oh – dear – God. This cannot be happening.

'There have been enough secrets, Dora,' Olivier says sternly. 'Go and talk to your fiancé.'

I wish everyone would stop referring to Declan as my fiancé. It's starting to seriously annoy me. 'He's not my fiancé,' I insist. 'Technically I haven't said yes yet.'

The edges of Olivier's mouth lift but he doesn't allow himself to smile. 'OK then, boyfriend. I will wait. I would like to spend some time with Iris.'

'It's late; she supposed to be in bed.'

He looks at me, his eyes flat and unreadable. It's obvious that he's furious with me but at least he's managing to control himself in front of Iris.

'Do you like stories?' he asks her. 'I could read to you if Dora says it's all right.'

Iris's face lights up. 'Please, Mummy?'

'Go on, but just for a few minutes, Iris, understand?'

I think for a second. Olivier's right, this is something that I can't keep from Declan; it's too huge, and frankly my system is already in shock, so I may as well completely overload it. 'Ask Declan to come in,' I tell Jules. 'Let's all go downstairs. I could do with a strong coffee. What about you, Olivier? Would you like anything?'

'No,' he says simply, his eyes still steely.

'I'll have a coffee if you're making it,' Jules pipes up.

She has such a nerve. 'Jules, I asked you to leave, please,' I say. 'You've done enough.'

She looks distraught. 'But what about . . .'

I pull her to one side. 'I don't want to shout at you in front of Iris,' I say in a low voice, trying to keep my anger under control. 'So I suggest you get out of here before I completely lose my rag with you. Understand? Go stay at Jamie's or something.'

'But I did it for Iris, Pandora. And for you.'

'For *me*? Are you completely mad? I'm having a nervous

breakdown here. I don't know how Declan's going to take Olivier's sudden appearance. I hope to God you haven't ruined everything. Just go, please.'

'Fine!' She grabs her jacket from the end of the stairs, throws it on and then rubs the top of Iris's head. 'Night, Iris. And good to meet you, Olivier. I don't regret writing to you, by the way.'

'Out!' I point at the doorway.

She stomps past me and swings open the front door, startling Declan, who is still standing there.

'I've been banished,' she tells him, before marching down the path.

'What was all that about?' Declan says, walking inside and closing the door behind me. 'Why did Jules make me wait on the doorstep? Rachel's show finished early so I thought I'd call in but if it's a bad time . . . should I just go?'

I open my mouth to try and explain, but Iris gets in first.

'Declan, this is my daddy,' she says, pointing at Olivier. 'He's from Paris. He's just arrived.'

Declan's face is a picture. He looks from Iris, to Olivier; and then his eyes rest on mine. 'Really?'

I nod. 'Jules wrote to him and Olivier decided to visit out of the blue. We're all still in shock.'

'That's great,' Declan says, clearly rather taken aback and confused but doing his best to hide it. 'I'm very pleased to meet you.' He shakes Olivier's hand a little stiffly. 'That's really something. You must be thrilled, Iris.'

Iris beams. 'We even look the same.'

Declan considers this, his eyes roaming Olivier's face. 'You certainly do. So . . .' he tails off, still staring at Olivier.

Olivier jumps in. 'Why don't I read Iris a story now? I know you wanted a coffee, Dora.'

I nod. 'Iris, show Olivier where your books are. Two stories in the living room and then straight to bed, understand?'

She nods. 'OK, Mum. This is the best day ever, isn't it? Can we go to the cinema next weekend?' she asks Olivier, hanging on to his arm. 'Please?'

'That depends on how long I am staying,' Olivier says. 'I will talk to your mother. But I will definitely see you tomorrow, yes?'

Iris beams. 'Cool! I know, we can read *Madeline*. She lives in Paris, doesn't she?'

He smiles. 'Yes. Bibi, your grandmother in Paris, she loves *Madeline*.'

Bibi! Yikes. How much does she know? Luckily I haven't got time to worry about that right this second.

Iris drags Olivier off by the arm and I take a deep breath before turning towards Declan.

'I'm so sorry, Declan,' I say in a rush. 'He just appeared on the doorstep. I had no idea he was coming and Jules let him in and—'

He grabs both my hands. 'Slow down, Pandora. You look awful. Must be the shock. Maybe you should sit.'

'I fainted a few minutes ago,' I admit.

'Right, let's get some sweet tea into you.' He leads me into the kitchen, sits me down at the kitchen table and flicks on the kettle, then folds his arms across his chest and parks his back against the counter, waiting for it to boil. For a second my mind is with Olivier and Iris. I wish I was there, listening to him read aloud, his silky voice describing the old house in Paris, covered in vines.

'Pandora, you look a bit dazed. You're not going to faint again, are you?'

'No,' I say, coming back into the room. 'I really am so sorry about all this. Declan, there's something I have to tell you, and please don't make any judgement, just listen. I went to find Olivier when I was in Paris for my birthday, to tell him about Iris.'

'He didn't know he had a daughter?'

226

I shake my head and stare down at the table. 'No. It was only a holiday romance and it would have ruined his life. He had exams you see, important ones . . .' I tail off, realizing now how lame it sounds.

'Go on,' Declan says. But his voice sounds stern.

'I wrote to him but it was returned unopened. But Jules found the letter and used the address to contact him again and then told Iris that Olivier was her father this evening when he appeared, just like that. I could have killed her.'

Declan shrugs. 'Iris seems OK with it. In fact she seems thrilled.'

'Yes, luckily she is, but she might not have been. Olivier seems happy to have been outed like that too, but what if he'd rejected her or something? Jules is such a loose cannon sometimes. And as to how long he's staying or what his intentions are, I just don't know. I haven't had a chance to talk to him properly about it yet.'

'I see.' Declan blows out his breath. 'Pandora, what am I going to do with you? I don't know where to start. With you, it's always so complicated.'

'That's hardly fair. You're the one with the insane ex-wife.'

He sighs again. 'I know. We're a right pair. I knew something had happened in Paris. You came back a different person.' He rubs his face with both his hands and makes a pained noise. 'Pandora, I think we need to do a lot of talking. But not right now. I have a lot of thinking to do first. Can we meet up tomorrow?'

My stomach lurches. What does he mean, 'a lot of thinking to do'? Maybe he doesn't want to be with me any more, not after what I've done, keeping Iris's existence from Olivier for all those years. I wouldn't blame him. I may not even be alive in a few years' time. No, I'm a bad bet, it's no wonder he wants rid of me. And before I can stop myself, I start to cry.

'I'm so sorry,' I say through my tears. 'I'm a mess. You'd be better off without me. I understand if you want to break up with me, honestly. But please don't do it tonight. I couldn't bear it.'

He reaches out and takes both my hands in his and looks at me earnestly.

'Pandora, what are you talking about? I love you. We can work this all out, understand? But I need you to be completely honest with me, tell me everything. Can you do that? I'll call in tomorrow after work, OK?'

I give a silent nod.

He leans down to kiss me and I twist my face a little so it lands on the side of my lips. I can't deal with anything else, not tonight. My emotions are all over the place, swirling dangerously. Then, feeling bad for trying to pull away, I hug him towards me and whisper, 'Thanks for being so good about all of this.'

After Declan has seen himself out, I sit there, alone for a few minutes, finishing the mug of tea he made me before he left. This all feels so surreal. Olivier's *here*, in the living room, with Iris. And he seems utterly taken with her, wants to be in her life. My lips curl into a tiny smile. Life is just so strange sometimes. I'm an emotional wreck, but when I think of Iris, of the way her eyes shone when she realized she was the mirror image of her French dad, it makes everything seem a whole lot brighter.

Chapter 24

I'm still sitting in the kitchen, thinking, when I feel someone's eyes on me. I look over and find Olivier standing in the doorway and for a split second I'm back in Paris, watching Olivier walk into our café, my heart filled with pure joy, but then I remember why he is here and my happiness melts away.

'*Ça va*, Dora?'

I shrug and blow out my breath noisily. 'I have no idea.'

He gives a short laugh, pulls out a chair and sits on the edge of it, leaning forward, the table between us. Even sitting, he has all the taut energy of a panther about to pounce.

'Iris is in bed now,' he says. 'She is a tyrant for stories. I ended up reading her three.'

'She loves her books.'

'Takes after us both, then. She showed me some of her drawings too. She has talent, yes?'

I nod silently, waiting for the storm which, from the look in his eyes, I know is about to hit.

He sits up a little. 'So I put the cat among the pigeons tonight, showing up unannounced, yes?'

'No kidding. Why didn't you tell me you were coming?'

He runs his finger over a scratch in the table, shakes his head and gives an incredulous snort. 'Why didn't you tell me that you were pregnant, Dora? Answer that. All these years I had a daughter. And you kept her from me. Do you think that is fair?'

'No, of course not, but you were only seventeen. You had exams. I thought it was for the best.'

His eyes flash. 'Fuck the exams, Dora. You think exams are more important than a baby?'

I recoil from the hurt and anger in his eyes. 'I wasn't thinking. I was scared, confused. I wanted to protect you.'

'From my own baby? Are you crazy? Or maybe you wanted to protect yourself, Dora? Was that it? Maybe you did not want to be stuck for good with a guy you did not love.'

I pause, blinking back tears. 'That's not true. I did love you, you know that. You must have read the letters that Jules sent you. The ones meant for Iris.' My cheeks burn as I remember the contents. 'I made a mistake, I see that now. And I did try to tell you about Iris in Paris.'

'Ten years later. I have missed nine precious years of her life, Dora. Nine years I can never get back.'

'I'm sorry. I'm so, so sorry.' Tears flow down my cheeks and I wipe at them with my fingers.

He sighs. 'Dora, stop. Please.' He gets up and for a second I think he's going to put his arms around me, but he doesn't, he stands behind me, back against the kitchen counter, so close that I can smell his familiar orange scent and my heart constricts again. God, even now I want him so much that it hurts.

'So what happens now?' he asks after a moment. 'With Iris, I mean.'

I swing around on my chair to look at him, my heart racing. What does he mean exactly? Now that he's seen her, knows what she looks like, is that it? I ask the question that I know have to ask: 'Do you want to see her again? After this weekend, I mean.'

He draws back a little, stares at me. 'What? You think that I would disappear back to Paris, never see her again, and break her tiny heart? I am not like you, Dora.'

I wince, his words cutting me, but I know I deserve it. 'Sorry,'

I murmur, my cheeks burning. Of course he wouldn't do that. Not Olivier.

'How often can I see her, Dora?'

'Whenever you like. And she can visit you too, in Paris.'

'Thank you. We can talk about the details later but I will visit as often as I can. And between visits I will email and phone. Jules was correct when she said that Iris deserves to know her father. And we have nine years to catch up on, both of us.'

I nod silently, feeling small and horribly guilty. 'Yes.'

'Dora, I must ask you, why now? Is it because Iris was asking questions about me?'

I look down at my left hand, still wearing the large silver dress ring, and rub its smooth surface. 'Yes, yes, that's it.'

'You are lying. What it is? What is wrong?'

Within seconds I'm crying again. 'I'm sorry.' I brush the tears away again. 'I think I'm still in shock. Everything's fine.'

He folds his arms across his chest. 'I'm not leaving until you talk to me, Dora.'

'I know we have a lot of catching up to do, but not tonight, please. I'm exhausted. It's been a stressful evening as you can imagine.'

But Olivier won't budge. He leans towards me. 'You are not in love with this man, Declan, but he wants to marry you. Is that it?'

'What? No! I do love Declan. This has nothing to do with Declan.'

'So tell me about him. What does he do?'

'He's an architect.'

'And?'

'Olivier!' I glare at him.

'What?'

'Can you please just go? I'm asking you nicely, but I'm a bit on edge here so I can't be responsible for my actions if you're still here in two minutes.'

The edges of his mouth twitch. 'Is that a threat?'

'Yes, it is. Now go.'

'Why don't you say yes to the man if you love him? Set a wedding date.'

'It's not that simple. There's Iris to think about, and his daughter too. I don't know why I'm telling you this anyway. It's none of your bloody business.'

He's blatantly smiling at me now, rather sardonically. 'But I am family, Dora, remember? It is my business. I am part Schuster now.'

'Oh, you're so fecking annoying. Just get out.' I slap him on the arm, my palm making a wet fish noise on his leather jacket.

He snorts. 'Temper, temper. You'll need to do better than that.'

'Stop being such a child. There are things going on that I don't want to talk about, OK? Private things.'

'I know this, Dora. Which is why I'm still here.'

'Please, Olivier. You have to leave. Right now. Bird and Dad will be home soon and I really don't have the energy to . . .' I tail off. The mere thought of explaining who Olivier is to Bird makes me jittery with nerves.

'I have always liked the sound of Bird. I would like to meet her. And now is as good a time as any.'

'Olivier!' I stand up, grab his arm and start trying to drag him towards the door. But it's no use, he's holding on to the edge of the kitchen counter with a vice-like grip.

I let go, put my hands over my face and give a moan. 'For the love of God, Olivier, would you please just go? I swear I'll talk to you tomorrow, but right now I'm so tired I practically can't see straight, let alone think straight.'

'Five minutes,' he says. 'We will talk for five minutes and then I will go.'

'Do you promise?'

'I promise.'

I sigh, and then sit back down again. Olivier is the most obstinate person I have ever met, and I know it's the only way that I'll get rid of him. I take out my iPhone and set the timer. 'OK, five minutes, starting now.' I press the start button and place it on the table in front of me.

He rolls his eyes. 'A stopwatch, Dora? Is that really necessary?'

'Four minutes, fifty seconds left.'

'Oh, come on, Dora.'

'Four minutes, forty-seven seconds.'

He sits there, shaking his head.

'What?' I demand.

'You haven't changed a bit.'

I give a laugh and tap the edges of my eyes. 'Really? Check out the wrinkles.'

'Wrinkles are good, Dora. The more you have, the more you have lived. May we all live to have many, many wrinkles. That's what Bibi always says.'

She's right, I think. So right. 'How is your mum?' I ask, genuinely interested.

'Good now. She had a lump removed from her breast two years ago. Frightened me more than her I think.'

I try not to respond, but I can feel my face blanch.

Of course Olivier, being Olivier, notices. 'I am sorry. Your mother . . . that was stupid. Forgive me.'

I stare down at the table but I can feel his eyes on me. I look up and there's a strange expression on his face.

After what seems like an eternity he finds the words that I was hoping he wouldn't find. 'You are sick, Dora. Is that it?' he says, his voice tender and kind.

And that's when the waterworks really start: huge, wracking wails.

'I'm sorry,' I say, wiping at my eyes with the heels of my hands, mortified for the umpteenth time this evening. 'I just . . .

Oh, God. Olivier.' And before I know what I'm doing I'm on my feet, throwing my arms around his neck and clinging to him tightly, bawling uncontrollably.

'It's OK, Dora. You cry. That's right, let it all out.' He holds me tight, his strong arms across my back. It's so familiar, so damn good, which makes me cry even harder.

I cry until I'm a snotty, soggy mess.

'I'm so sorry,' I say again after a few minutes, when I'm all cried out. My breath is a little ragged and I must look a fright. I pull away from Olivier, grab some kitchen roll from the counter, blow my nose and then dab at my still-watering eyes.

'I'm sorry, I must look a state.'

'You always look beautiful, Dora. It was my undoing.' His eyes are soft and I start crying again, overwhelmed.

This time he doesn't hold me. His arms are crossed and he looks uncomfortable. I take several deep breaths, steeling myself. I know he only hugged me because he didn't have the heart to push a crying woman away, but for a few seconds I was in his arms; and now, out of his arms, I feel bereft. But I have to tell him some time, so why not now. I sit down again and try to calm my breathing.

'Mum had a hereditary cancer gene,' I begin, taking it slowly. 'If I have it there's an 85 per cent chance that I'll get breast cancer too. I was tested for it and the results are due back any day now. I'm so worried about it. What if I'm positive? What if something happens to me? I don't want Iris to go through what I went through with Mum. It's not fair. She's only nine. Why did it have to happen to me? Or Mum. She hadn't done any-thing wrong—'

Olivier puts his hands up the in air. 'Woah, there, Dora. Start at the beginning. Explain about this gene and the test.'

While I go back to the beginning, Ruth's original letter, Mum's gene, the blood test, Olivier listens to me silently, giving the odd nod to show he's with me. When I've finished I look him squarely in the eye.

'That is why I had to find you,' I say. 'I want Iris to have at least one parent who is alive.'

Olivier frowns so deeply his hair covers his eyes a little. 'Dora, you must not say such things. There is a very strong chance you do not have this gene, and if you do there must be treatment, things you can do. Knowledge is power, yes? There is no point worrying about it until then. You will make yourself ill.'

'That's what Declan says.'

'You have told him everything? All your worries?'

'Yes, of course.' I hesitate. 'Some of it. I don't like to burden him with it.'

'Some of it.'

'We talked about it once, OK? Look, I think about it all the time, but I can't tell him that, he'll think I'm some sort of obsessive lunatic. I worry about having to have my ovaries cut out, not being able to have another baby. I know Declan wants more kids.'

'Dora, if he loves you it won't matter. You wouldn't be much use to a baby dead.'

I'm so shocked I give a half laugh, half snort. 'Olivier! You can't say things like that.'

'Why not? You already have Iris, and Declan has a child too, yes? You are both lucky.'

'Yes, yes, we are.'

'That is enough for any man, a child and the love of a woman like you. That would certainly be more than enough for me.'

My eyes well up and I wave my hand at him. 'Stop, you're setting me off again.'

'I am sorry; I should not have said that. But it is true. He is blessed.' His expression darkens. 'What about Iris? Does she know about the gene?

'No, absolutely not. I haven't even told Jules.'

He tilts his head. 'Just Declan?'

'Yes. And one other friend.'

'Why are you carrying this practically alone, Dora? You must let people in. You were always terrible that way; trying to deal with everything yourself. No more secrets, understand? You must talk to your sister and to Declan. He seems like a decent man. I'm sure he'll listen to your concerns, support you.'

I nod. 'He is decent. Too decent. I don't know if it's fair landing all this on him, he has enough problems of his own. His ex-wife is a complete bitch and his daughter, Rachel, can be quite difficult.'

He gives a very French shrug, his hands at shoulder level. 'Life is difficult for most people. But it is how we deal with the speed bumps that matters. Do we go slowly and timidly, creep over them, or accelerate and roar over them?'

'Damaging our car, you mean?'

He laughs. 'It's only a metaphor. A bad one at that. You know what I'm saying. You must give your relationship a chance. Do not run when things get difficult. Stick with it. Talk to the man. Stop pushing him away.'

I jut my jaw out. 'I'm not pushing him away.'

Olivier just smiles at me in an annoying, smug way. 'Let Declan in. Let him surprise you.'

I sniff into my kitchen roll, wondering why I suddenly feel so flat. Then it hits me. Olivier is stating quite clearly that he's happy for me to be with Declan, that he has no feelings for me. I think at the back of my mind since the minute that Olivier appeared on the doorstep I've been in fairy-tale land, spinning myself a yarn – that Olivier will realize how much he still loves me and we'll ride off into the sunset together on one of those huge Disney white chargers, Iris on the horse behind us, little arms wrapped around my waist. But life's not like that. Olivier's giving me permission to let go of the dream and to move on with my life. At least his anger towards me seems to have dissipated.

'You all right, Dora?' he asks gently.

I nod, wiping my tears away with my hands.

'I will be,' I murmur. 'You're right, I need to talk to—' I was about to say Jules, but after what she's just done, there's no way I'm telling her anything.

'Bird,' I say instead. 'And Declan too. I'm sorry for being such an emotional car crash, Olivier.'

'It's OK. I'm used to it. You were always very emotional, Dora.'

'Was I?'

'Yes, of course. Are you crazy? You cried all the time. And laughed too. Now I will go and we can talk about Iris tomorrow, yes?' He moves towards the door. 'There is something I must do in the morning but may I take Iris out for lunch? At one? Would that suit?'

'She'd love that. Thank you for being here, Olivier. I can't begin to tell you how much it means to me. To both of us.' My eyes start to well up again.

'I should be here,' he says simply. 'It is both my duty and my joy. Iris is beautiful, I am lucky to have such a perfect daughter. Now I will go; *à demain*.'

After seeing him out the door I walk wearily up the stairs to bed. Lying there, thinking about the evening, I start to feel horribly guilty. I never asked Olivier about his life – his work, his shop, was there anyone special. It was all about me. How rude.

Seeing him has brought back all kinds of feelings that I've tried to suppress over the years. And he's right – I was emotional in Paris, I was passionate. I felt deeply, I loved deeply. With Olivier I was a different person. But all that is gone now, buried in the past, and I have to move on with my life, forget about him, which is going to be difficult if he's going to be a part of Iris's life. Why is life so damn complicated?

A little later I'm still lying there, wide awake, my mind churning, when I hear someone come in downstairs. Seconds later I hear my door open.

'Pandora? Are you awake? Can we talk?' It's Jules.

I prickle all over with irritation. Is she out of her tiny little mind? I pretend to be asleep and eventually she goes away, shutting the door gently behind her. But there's no way I'm going to sleep tonight.

Chapter 25

'Pandora? Are you awake?'

I open my eyes. In the gloom I can just about make out Bird, sitting on the edge of my bed.

'What time is it?' I mumble.

'Nearly twelve, darling.'

I push myself to sitting, yawning so hard that my jaw cracks, and switch on my bedside light.

'I haven't slept so late in years.' I rub my eyes with my knuckles. I slept very badly last night, taking ages to drop off and waking several times in the night. Even after the lie-in I feel like I've been run over by a bus.

'I know, darling. Which is why I didn't wake you earlier. I figured you'd had a rough night, what with Iris's dad appearing on the doorstep like that.'

So she knows. My cheeks burn furiously. I look at her, expecting anger or at the very least confusion, but her gaze is steady, calm even.

'How . . . ?' I splutter.

'Jules told us this morning while Iris was outside playing with Fluffy. She thought it might take some of the pressure off you. She also explained about writing to Olivier. She really is very sorry, Pandora, she never meant to hurt you.'

I'm suddenly wide awake. 'She had no right! Those letters belong to Iris. Olivier was never meant to read them.'

'Well he has, and that's why he's here. So in the end

everything has worked out for the best, hasn't it, darling? I believe he's calling over later to see Iris. I'm so looking forward to meeting him. Your father too.'

I bow my head, rub my hands over my face and give a tiny moan. 'Poor Dad, is he OK? He must be in shock.'

Bird nods. 'He's surprisingly calm in fact. It takes a lot to shake Greg after all he's been through over the years. After Jules broke the Olivier news to us both after breakfast, Iris came skipping in, asked Jules had she told us about him yet. When Jules said yes, Iris babbled on and on about "her new dad", as she called him – *Olivier Huppert*.' She pronounces it perfectly; I'd forgotten that Bird has excellent French.

'Lovely name isn't it, *Olivier*?' she continues. 'So French. Anyway, Iris thinks he's wonderful, and very handsome. She really is rather taken with him and he does sound most interesting. I can't wait to see him in the flesh.'

I stare at her suspiciously. 'That's it? After nine years Iris's dad appears and that's all you have to say? That he sounds interesting. No questions? No interrogation?'

She shrugs, lifting her pink jacket off her shoulders. She's looking elegant and poised in the full Chanel suit today, her hair swished back off her face in her customary up-style. 'All in good time, darling. From what Jules has said, Olivier isn't going anywhere. I'm just so delighted for Iris. Her face is positively glowing this morning. I've never seen it so lit up. She's usually such a serious little thing.'

Irritation ripples up my spine. 'Are you implying that she's been unhappy all this time? That I'm not enough for her? That Olivier is some sort of Prince Charming, sweeping in to rescue the serious princess and make her smile? Is that it?'

'Not at all, darling.' She pats my hand. 'Stop being so prickly. You've done an amazing job; Iris is a credit to you, everyone says so. But Olivier is an added bonus, you must see that. The more people who love that child, the better, don't you think?'

'I guess so,' I say, still feeling out of sorts.

'You get dressed, my love. And put on something nice. French women are awfully well put together.'

'Excuse me? What has that got to do with anything?'

'We don't want to let the side down, do we? I've put Iris in her darling little sailor dress. It's a little short, but I've popped leggings on under it, and her sparkly party shoes. She insisted. Wanted to look nice for her dad.'

'Did she now?' I glare at Bird. Even though I'm sure she's telling the truth, it does sound like Iris all right; I blame Bird for encouraging Iris to dress up. I did wonder why Bird is looking so smart on a Sunday. But as for me, I'll wear what I damn well like!

Bird gets to her feet and starts making towards the door. 'Oh, do stop scowling at me, darling. Try to snap out of your moody blues before Olivier arrives. For Iris's sake. I know this is all very unsettling for you and I understand that you feel a little usurped, but you have no reason to. Iris adores you. That will never change. Even if she does want to visit him in Paris, it will only be for holidays, nothing permanent.'

She obviously spots my face falling because she swiftly adds, 'Surely you've considered the possibilities? Oh, my darling, you haven't, have you?' She walks back and sits down beside me again, stroking my head. 'I'm a silly old fool. Pay no attention. Forget I said anything.'

I sniff, trying desperately not to cry. 'What if she does want to live with him? Paris is so much more glamorous than Dublin.'

'She won't. Her roots are here. With you. With all of us.'

'But what if something happens to me?' I blurt out. 'I want her to grow up here, in Ireland.'

Bird holds my gaze for a long moment. Something flickers behind her eyes, but I can't quite make it out. Anxiety? Empathy?

'And so she will,' she says firmly. 'Your father is her legal guardian, remember?'

I nod. I'd drawn up a will years back with a lawyer friend of Mum's called Tish Sadler. She'd visited the house one day, soon after Iris was born, offered to do it for free. It had seemed odd in the circumstances but she'd insisted.

'It will give you peace of mind, Pandora,' Tish had said. 'Kirsten asked me to help her girls in any way I could. Please, let me do it, for her. If you ever need any legal advice in the future, you only have to ask, understand?' Mum had such amazing friends, like Tish and Ruth Oxenbury.

'Pandora?'

'Sorry, yes, I remember. But Olivier is her dad. Maybe French law is different? Maybe he has the right to take her away from me?'

'That's just tosh, Pandora, please,' Bird says rather sternly. 'Stop worrying yourself over nothing. Olivier sounds like a decent man. He's not going to do anything of the sort. I don't know what's got into you today. It's not just Iris, is it, darling? What's wrong? You haven't been yourself for weeks now.'

Just then Jules bustles into my room. 'Olivier's here.'

'What?' I snap at her. 'He's not due till one. Tell him to come back later. I'm not even dressed.'

'Said he couldn't keep away.' Jules gives me a tentative smile. 'How are you feeling this morning?'

'Fine! No thanks to you, however. If you think I've forgiven you, you're sorely mistaken.'

Bird puts her hands in the air. 'Girls, please. Not while we have a guest. A very special one at that.' Her eyes dance. 'Where is he?' she asks Jules.

'Bird!' I say. 'Will you please wait so that I can introduce you and Dad to Olivier properly?'

'Too late,' Jules says. 'He's already in the garden helping the old man build a bigger run for Fluffy. Tell him I said goodbye, will you? I have to run to work now. Lenka will be doing her nut by this stage, I'm already late. Hopefully I'll catch him this evening before he goes back to France. Dad's talking about having a barbecue and he's already invited him over.'

At this, Bird stands up. 'I'll see you in the garden, Pandora. And do put on something decent.' With that she walks out.

'What are you staring at?' I snap at Jules, who is still lingering near the door. 'Traitor!' I yell at her, full blast.

She splutters with laughter. 'Pandora, I'm supposed to be the melodramatic one in this family.'

I throw my pillow at her. 'Out!'

Why does no one in this family take me seriously any more? It's most irritating.

When I finally walk outside, Bird is lying on a wooden sun lounger, watching Iris, Olivier and Dad who are all on their hunkers, tinkering with chicken wire and pieces of wood, Fluffy in his small run beside them, watching with interest.

'We were wondering where you'd got to, darling,' Bird says. 'Olivier was just telling us about his shop. It sounds wonderful.'

Olivier smiles up at me, one hand shading his eyes from the surprisingly bright sun. 'Good morning, Dora,' he says. 'You look nice.'

Despite my best intentions, I've made an effort in a cream, brown and yellow Missoni dress with a flattering ruffled skirt, teamed with simple sandals. It took me ages to find the right don't-care-what-I'm-wearing outfit and put 'natural' make-up on.

'Afternoon,' I point out. 'And you're very early.'

'Couldn't keep away,' he says easily. 'Iris is fantastic with a hammer. Must have inherited that from Greg.'

Greg? So we're on first name terms now, are we? I try to scowl at Olivier, and then turn my attention to Iris.

'Iris!' I say sharply. 'Your dress. What is that?' There are earth-coloured streaks down the front.

'Wood stain,' Dad says. 'It'll probably wash out.'

I sigh and put my hand out to her. 'Come on, let's get you changed.'

'I'll only get dirty again, Mum. Can't I just stay here, please?' She presses her hands together, like she's praying, and a silver charm bracelet falls down her slim wrist.

'Where did you get that?' I ask, staring at it. The chain looks chunky and expensive.

'From Dad,' she says. 'Look, nine charms. One for every birthday he's missed, isn't that right, Dad?'

Olivier smiles at her warmly. 'That's right, *ma chérie*.'

She shows me her wrist proudly. 'This one's the Eiffel Tower. Dad's going to show me that when I visit Paris, aren't you?'

Olivier smiles at her again. 'Yes, certainly.'

Of course he wants to show her Paris, he adores his city. Bird was right. My heart tightens.

Iris continues brightly, 'Then there's a baby crib, an abacus, that's for counting on. And when you spin this little disc it says "I love you". A ballet shoe, a hat, a pair of lips, a tiny book, a rabbit for Fluffy, and what's this one again, Dad?'

'A tiny church.' Olivier's cheeks colour a little. He's not religious, but Bibi is. 'To keep you safe.'

I look at Olivier. How could I possibly be angry with this sweet, thoughtful man? 'It's beautiful,' I say quietly. 'Did you say thank you, Iris?'

'She did,' he puts in. 'She's going to draw me a special picture too, aren't you, Iris?'

Iris nods. 'And one for my granny in Paris. Did you know I have another granny, Mum? She's called Bibi.'

I take a deep breath. So much for Iris to take in, for all of us to take in, but she seems to be taking it in her stride.

Olivier catches my eye. He has the good grace to look a little apologetic. 'Dora, can I speak to you for a moment? Inside maybe?'

'Sure. Iris, you'll need to change before you go out to lunch with your dad.'

'You're coming with us of course, Dora.' Olivier smiles at me, his brown eyes twinkling, and I'm ashamed to say my heart lifts a little. 'Please say you will.'

'I have to work this afternoon,' I say.

'Jules and Lenka will be perfectly fine on their own,' Bird says. 'You go, have fun, *Dora*.' Her lips quiver in amusement as she uses Olivier's nickname for me, and I give her a look.

In the living room, cooler than outside, Olivier sits down beside me on the sofa and it makes me nervous so I move away from him a little, towards the arm. If I strain my neck I can see Iris and Dad working away on the run, Bird lying back on the sun lounger reading a hardback history book.

'I am sorry, Dora,' he opens. 'I know I am very early but I could not sleep last night. I kept thinking of all the time I have lost, all the years of Iris growing up I have missed. Worrying about what kind of father I will make.'

'You're already a big hit,' I say, hoping I kept the slightly sour note out of my voice. I feel guilty at keeping him from her for so long, as well as a little jealous of all the attention Iris is giving him, which is combining to make me defensive and ratty, but I can't seem to help myself.

He stares down at the rug and straightens some of the tassels with the tip of his boot. 'I didn't mean to tell Iris about Bibi, you know. I wanted to talk it over with you first. But Bird was asking me about Paris and my family and it just came out. Iris must have overheard us. She started asking about her new granny and I didn't want to lie to her.'

I smile wryly. 'Bird has a way of getting information out of people, all right. Does Bibi know about Iris?'

He lifts his head, looks at me. 'Yes. I had to talk to someone.'

'What about the woman in the shop? With the Coco Chanel

hair cut. Why didn't you talk to her? She's your girlfriend, isn't she?'

He snorts with laughter. 'Mimi? God, no! You'd be more her type.' He smiles at me broadly. 'I must tell her that you thought we were a couple, she will find that amusing.' He tilts his head, looking at me intently, his eyes soft. 'And you? Everything is all right with Declan after last night, yes?'

'I hope so.'

'*Bien*. I am happy for you. And for Iris. The more people who love her the better, yes?'

'That's what Bird always says.' I wasn't going to bring it up, not yet, but now seems as good a time as any. I steel myself, and then say, 'How is this going to work, Olivier? Seeing Iris, I mean. She's very settled here and I'd prefer if she didn't miss any school.'

'Of course not, school is important. To be honest I have no idea. But if it's all right with you, Bibi would like to meet her granddaughter as soon as possible. Like me, she just can't wait. The weekend after next if it suits. What do you think?'

I worry at my lip for a second. I'm sure Bibi isn't exactly thrilled with me, keeping Iris a secret for all these years.

'Bibi, she has mellowed,' Olivier says, reading my mind. 'I swear.' He crosses his heart with his finger. 'She promises no drama.'

I laugh. Bibi and no drama don't belong in the same sentence. The woman was born theatrical.

'OK,' I say, remembering what Bird and Olivier both said. They're right – the more people who love Iris, the better. 'Please tell Bibi that she'd be most welcome.'

Sitting in the car on the drive of Sorrento House, I toy with where to take Olivier for lunch, suggesting one of the Dun Laoghaire seafront restaurants or Dublin city, before Iris makes a suggestion.

'Can we go to the Shoestring Café, Mum? Please? We can show Dad the shop and everything. And they have pancakes.'

'I'm sure Olivier wouldn't be interested—' I begin.

But I'm wrong. 'That sounds perfect,' he says with a grin. 'I'd love to see your shop, Dora.'

Iris gives Olivier the grand tour while I mind our booth and wait for the food to arrive. It gives me the chance to be a bystander, to watch Iris drag Olivier across the shop floor by the hand, darting him from the bag and hat stand, where she makes him try on a wide-brimmed lilac wedding hat as she giggles delightedly, to the dress rails and the wall of shoes.

He listens to her prattle carefully, as if it's the most interesting thing he's ever heard, interrupting her to ask questions or to make comments, really engaging with her. It's a joy to watch and it makes my heart sing.

'Impressive,' Olivier says, sliding back into his seat beside Iris. 'Interesting stock – some very good labels. Where do you source it?'

'From our customers mainly. Irish women can be quite stylish, Olivier.' I give him a teasing smile.

He laughs. '*Bien sûr*. You are one of the most stylish women I know, Dora.'

I can feel my cheeks pink up. Iris is staring at me, her eyes bright, clearly delighted to see her 'parents' getting along so well. Luckily at that moment her pancakes and hot chocolate arrive. Over lunch she chats away happily, answering all Olivier's questions about school, her friends and Fluffy.

While we linger over coffee, Iris spots Jules walking across the shop floor juggling an armful of hats destined for the display boxes, and runs over to give her a hand, leaving Olivier and me at the table. I'm pleased that Jules didn't approach us, just gave Olivier a smile and a 'See you later.' I'm not in the humour for an argument.

As we sit watching Iris pottering along behind Jules, her

arms loaded down with wedding headgear, Olivier picks up a paper tube of sugar and starts weaving it through his fingers.

'*Ça va*, Dora?' he asks in a low voice. 'You seemed quiet over lunch.'

'I'm just a little tired.'

He gives me a soft smile. 'I couldn't sleep last night either. Finding a daughter like this is incredible. Like a miracle.'

Guilt dances in my solar plexus again. 'I know you feel you've missed her early years and I'm so sorry—'

Olivier lifts both hands. 'Dora, stop. No more sorries. There is no point looking backwards; we move on from here, yes? I must go back to Paris first thing tomorrow morning, but I will ring Iris during the week. Maybe on Wednesday evening? And I will be back very soon with Bibi, remember?'

My stomach twists a little at the mention of Bibi's name, but I nod. 'Thanks for being so decent about all this.'

He shrugs. 'I was angry with you yesterday I admit, but what's done is done. You have a lot on your mind; there is no point in me adding to that burden. I know I have asked before, but things with Declan, they are all right, yes? You intend to marry him, to make things permanent?'

'I think so, yes.'

'*Bien*. Iris needs a proper father figure. With the shop and my design work, I cannot be in Dublin as much as I would wish. I am glad you both have someone. It is important to me. I want you both to be happy.'

I feel a little overwhelmed again so I say nothing. Why does he have to be so bloody charming? Every time he says something sweet it's like someone is driving a nail into my heart – knowing that this amazing man was once mine and that I ruined everything by running away from him. But how was I to know that he'd accept a daughter into his world with such seeming ease? I try to console myself with the thought that maybe ten years ago things would have been very different. At seventeen surely he would have run a mile at the thought of being a father? I try to tell myself that it has all worked out for the best – Iris now has Olivier in her life, and that's the only thing that matters.

'Will you ring me if you get your test results in the meantime?' he asks.

I start a little. It's been over six weeks now and I could get the results any day, a stark fact that I've been trying to put out of my mind.

'OK.' I stare down at the table, unwilling to meet his compassionate gaze. I know in my current hyper-emotional state that it will set me off again.

'I am glad that you are getting married, Dora. I think that it will make you happy. You deserve someone to take care of you for a change. It will give you stability.'

Now I really am on the verge of tears. I keep my head bowed. Stability? I know he's right, but it makes it all sound so final, so *sensible*, that word again.

He slides his hand over and touches his fingers to mine. 'I read your letters, Dora. What we had was special, we both know that, but it is in the past. But know that I will always carry that time in my heart.'

I give a nod, the lump in my throat so big that I'm unable to say a word. Then I stand up suddenly, murmur, 'Sorry,' and make a dash for the bathroom. Once inside I dissolve into floods of tears.

That evening Jules is poking away at the barbecue a little distance away while Bird, Dad and I sit around the large round garden table, drinking rosé wine and munching Pringles. The bowl of olives – Bird insisted, said Olivier would think us very uncouth with our usual 'salty snacks' – remains largely untouched. Iris is on her hunkers in the new, improved rabbit run with Fluffy, trying to teach him tricks with a small red ball, and being surprisingly successful. Rabbits are a lot smarter than anyone gives them credit for. Declan and Olivier have yet to arrive.

'Excuse me for just one second,' Bird says. 'Either of you want anything from the kitchen while I'm in there?'

'No thanks, Bird,' I say and Dad shakes his head.

As soon as she's disappeared Dad turns to me. 'Pandora?'

I think I can guess what he's about to say. Dad's always been the peacemaker in our family, and he hates when Jules and I argue.

'Jules is really sorry for writing to Olivier. But he's here now and everything has worked out fine in the end. Iris is thrilled. Can't you just forgive her, move on? Not talking to her is a little childish.'

'Childish?' I cross my arms huffily. 'It could have all gone horribly wrong.'

He's studying my face so I look away.

'But it didn't, did it?' he says.

'No, but it could have,' I insist. 'She just doesn't think before she does things or opens her mouth and I'm sick of it. She even told Iris that I'm marrying Declan.'

His eyebrows arch. 'Aren't you? Jules seems to think that it's a done deal.'

'That's not the point. I told her that in confidence. She should have kept her mouth shut. Especially to Iris.'

He twists his mouth, giving a half grimace, half smile. 'Your sister gets a bit carried away sometimes. She doesn't mean any harm, she worships you.'

I don't reply, just give a 'humph'. Out of the corner of my eye I see someone walking up the drive so I swivel around in my seat. It's Declan, and he isn't alone. Olivier is strolling along beside him, like an old buddy, so close they're practically bumping shoulders. They stop at the edge of the drive and Declan slaps Olivier's back; then Olivier, ever tactile, pulls him into a hug. Then Declan spots us, points us out to Olivier, and they both wave and start making their way towards us over the grass.

'Gosh, they look friendly,' Dad says. 'Isn't it great seeing them both get along so well. Lovely for Iris.'

I give a non-committal hum. Frankly, I'm not so sure I like this new bro-mance. I stare at Declan and Olivier, who are both smiling widely. What on earth were they talking about? Iris? Me? My heart sinks. I dread to think.

Chapter 26

Early on Wednesday morning my mobile rings, waking me up. I check my alarm clock: half past seven.

'Hello?' I answer groggily.

'Pandora, it's Ruth. Sorry, were you asleep?'

I instantly snap awake. Ruth wouldn't be ringing me at this hour for nothing.

'No, no, it's fine,' I say. 'Have you got them? The test results?'

'Yes. I'm so sorry you've had such a long wait. If you come into my rooms—'

Rooms? Shit! 'It's bad news, isn't it?'

There's a long pause and it's as if the world has stopped and my veins have been pumped full of freezing mercury. I screw my eyes shut.

'Just tell me,' I say. 'Please?'

'I really would prefer if you'd come in, but . . . well, OK . . . it's good news, Pandora. You're in the clear. The tests have all come back negative. You don't have your mum's BRCA1 gene.'

My eyes spring open and start welling up. 'Are you sure?'

'Positive. It's brilliant news, Pandora. I'm so pleased for you. Now, it will probably take a little while for it to sink in, so in the meantime please treat yourself gently today. Ring me if you have any questions, anything at all.'

'What about Jules? Does it mean she might not have the gene either?'

'No, she has the same odds as you had, fifty–fifty, I'm afraid.

Will you talk to her about having the test? In your own good time, of course.'

'Yes. I'll make sure she contacts you soon.'

'Please do feel free to come in and see me any time you like, Pandora. Oh, and I almost forgot, there's a courier on the way to your house with a letter for you. I asked for it to be delivered before nine. I know you probably have work today, but can you wait in for it? It's from your mum.'

'Mum?' Now the tears start flowing freely.

'She asked me to send it to you as soon as the test results came back.'

'I see. Ruth, thank you so much for everything. I'm sure Mum would . . . would—' I'm crying too much to continue.

'I know,' she says gently. 'And it was a privilege to be able to help you, Pandora, truly it was. I hope this is a weight off your mind. Make sure you have all the usual health checks, yes? Plus smears, breast checks and mole mapping.'

'I will,' I promise.

After clicking off the phone I realize I've been practically holding my breath during the whole conversation. I inhale deeply and blow it out slowly. I feel as light as a feather, free. But I still can't stop crying. Huge tears of relief and sheer joy. Olivier! I have to ring Olivier and tell him the news. I promised. I stop in my tracks, realizing I instantly thought of Olivier and not Declan. Of course I should ring Declan first. I wipe away my tears with the back of my hand, give a few big sniffs and then scroll to his number.

'Pandora?'

'Declan. The tests came back clear. I'm OK. I don't have the cancer gene.'

He gives a delighted whoop. 'That's amazing news, love. I'm so happy for you. For us. I knew it would all turn out just fine. After all that worrying, eh? We must celebrate. What are you doing later? Can I take you out for dinner or something? Oh, actually it's family dinner night, but I could call in afterwards, bring some champagne. Say nine-ish?'

'That would be lovely.'

We make arrangements and as I put the phone down Iris comes bounding into the room, all ready for summer camp in her sky-blue tracksuit. She's fixed her own hair and the pony-tail is a little skew-whiff, which makes her look even more adorable.

'Mum, it's Wednesday. Dad's going to ring tonight, isn't he?'

'That's right. Come here, you.' I stand up, pull her into my arms and give her a big hug. 'Tell me how much you love me.'

Iris giggles. 'Stop being such a weirdo.' She wiggles out of my embrace and runs towards the door. 'I'll see you in the kitchen. Your nose looks a bit snotty, Mum. Maybe you should get a tissue.'

'Cheeky minx, out you get.'

She runs away laughing and I blow my nose, then sit back down, playing with the phone, wondering if I should ring Olivier before deciding against it. It's only just after six thirty in Paris and I don't want to bother him so early, so I text him instead, hoping it doesn't wake him.

Test results back. Good news. All clear. Pandora XXX

I look at the three kisses for a moment, and then decide to delete them before sending it. Olivier's arriving with Bibi at lunchtime the Saturday after next, and although I'm nervous at the prospect of seeing her again, Iris can't wait to meet her 'new' granny.

During breakfast there's a knock on the door.

'Must be the postman,' Bird says, standing up. 'I'll get it.'

It's only once she's left the room that I realize it's probably

Ruth's courier. I walk into the hall just in time to see Bird close the door to a man in black lycra.

She hands me a brown padded envelope. 'It's for you.'

I rip it open and pull out the letter inside, instantly recognizing Mum's curly handwriting.

Bird spots the writing too, and staggers to the right a little, resting her hand on the banister to steady herself. She looks at me and whispers, 'Kirsten?'

I nod. 'I have so much to tell you I don't know where to start. You'd better sit down.' I lead her into the living room and we sit on the sofa together. I carefully place Mum's letter on the cushion beside me.

'Mum had this hereditary cancer gene . . .' I begin.

As I tell her all about Ruth and the test and Mum's letters, Bird's eyes well up. When I've finished she nods. 'Such a clever girl, my Kirsten, tracking Ruth down like that; making sure her babies were properly looked after. Genius.' She takes both my hands in hers and squeezes tightly. 'I'm so glad you don't have the gene, Pandora. It must be such a relief. But why didn't you tell me about all this sooner? I can't believe you've been dealing with this on your own, my darling.' She stops for a second and smiles gently. 'And Olivier. That's why you wanted to contact him. Things are starting to fall into place.'

'I didn't want to worry you.'

She shakes her head. 'Oh, Pandora, that's my job. To worry about you, and your sister. I take it you didn't say anything to your dad about the test.'

'No. Not even Jules.'

'Did you tell anyone, my darling? Rowie?'

'Just Declan and Olivier.' I leave Markham out.

Her eyebrows lift. 'Olivier too.'

I can feel myself blushing so I quickly say, 'Olivier guessed that something was up. I wouldn't have told him otherwise.'

'You'll have to talk to your sister now. You can't let all this silliness get in the way. Did Ruth say anything about Jules's chances of being clear too?'

'She said it was fifty–fifty, like me.'

'I see. I guess we can talk about Jules later. Today is your day.' She strokes my cheek, her fingers cool against my hot skin. 'My darling girl. I'll leave you to read your mum's letter now. Take your time, I'll drop Iris to camp. Jules and I will cover for you in work until you get there.'

There's a voice behind us. 'Will we now?'

We both whip around. Jules is standing in the doorway, hands on her hips, glaring at me as if I've just slapped her.

'And why should I cover for her, exactly, Bird?' she demands. 'I spend my life helping her out and what thanks do I get? Sweet FA.' She shakes her head and gives a breathy laugh. 'You're unbelievable, Pandora.'

'What are you talking about?' I ask her.

Bird waves a hand in the air. 'Girls, please keep it down, little pitchers, big ears and all that. I'll be in the kitchen with Iris when you've quite finished. But do remember how much you love each other.'

'Love?' Jules sneers. 'You don't keep huge, monumental secrets from people you love. Like bloody cancer tests.'

'Talk!' Bird says, jumping to her feet. 'Get it all out in the open.' Then she scuttles away, closing the living-room door firmly behind her.

I try to walk away but Jules grabs my arm. 'When were you going to tell me?'

'Tell you what?'

'About Mum's cancer gene. I was in the hall, I heard everything. I can't believe you kept it from me.'

'That was a private conversation, Julia. How dare you?'

She sets her chin defiantly. 'She was my mum too! The minute I found out something like that I would have told you. Why didn't you tell me? Why? I'm your sister.'

'I was trying to protect you.'

'From what? The truth? Jesus, Pandora, you always do this.'

'Do what?'

'Try to control everything. Take everything on your own shoulders, push people away.'

'I do not!'

'Yes, you do. I bet you were all like,' she puts on a whiney voice, '"Jules won't be able to cope with this, so I won't bother telling her, I'll just keep it all to myself 'cos I'm such a big martyr."'

'It wasn't like that.'

'Really? What was it like then? From what you were saying to Bird you obviously didn't tell her or Dad. What about poor Declan?'

'What do you mean poor Declan?'

'Come on. I know you think you're doing the right thing, that he'll make a good stepdad for Iris and all that, but he's not right for you. He's a lovely guy but he's as boring as hell.'

'Jules! That's a terrible thing to say.'

'Sorry, but it's the truth. He's so predictable.'

'You've said enough. Stop! This isn't about Declan.'

She has the grace to look contrite. 'Sorry, you're right. Look, what I really want to know is does getting negative in this test thing mean that you're not going to get Mum's cancer?'

'That's exactly what it means.'

'And I need to get tested too, right?'

'Yes. I'll go with you, help you through it. Waiting for the result is the worst bit.'

'See!' Her eyes spark.

'What?'

'You never gave *me* the chance to support *you*. That's why I'm so bloody angry with you, Pandora, you never let me help you. I understand now why you wanted Olivier to meet Iris. But you've never once said thank you for getting him to Dublin.

OK, I understand it was a bit underhand and devious, but it worked.'

'I don't want to talk about it right now. Any of this. Especially Olivier.' I start to walk towards the door.

'You have to stop trying to control everything,' she says to my back. 'Life's messy, Mum used to say that, remember? Stop trying to do the right thing the whole time. Sometimes the wrong thing *is* the right thing.'

I swing around and stare at her. 'Jules, that doesn't make any sense.'

She looks exasperated. 'Does everything have to make sense?'

'Yes! Yes, of course it does.' With that I stride out the door, up the stairs, across the landing and slam my bedroom door behind me. Once I'm alone I sit down on my bed and start to read Mum's letter.

Dearest Pandora,

I promised you another letter after you got your result – well, ta-da! And I can't tell you how happy I am that you don't have my blasted gene. It is truly a day to celebrate.

I know the past few weeks (months maybe?) have probably been a nightmare, trying not to worry, but failing miserably. You were always a bit of a worry wart, even as a little girl. But now you've been given a gift, Pandora – you've been granted your life back – and I want you to treasure it.

You don't have to do anything dramatic like climb Mount Everest (unless you like mountain climbing, darling – then go right ahead!), or swim the Irish Channel, but I want you to savour every day, Pandora, even the bad ones. Wake up happy to be alive.

Find work that you love and throw yourself at it. If you do so, the money will come in time. Even if it doesn't, as long as you can pay the bills you will still be happy.

Cherish your family. I hope Bird is still around; listen to her; she may be a little direct sometimes, but she has the wisdom of Solomon and a heart of gold. Look after your father for me, my beloved husband, my soulmate. I hope he has found love again, but I fear he probably hasn't. I understand that. He's the only man I've ever truly loved and I know he feels the same way about me.

I know I said it in my last letter, but I want to say it again: I was doubly blessed to have not one, but two remarkable daughters. You and your sister make my heart sing. Promise me that you'll take care of each other. When the time is right, encourage your sister to have the test and support her journey. You will have the benefit of hindsight, but don't be too surprised if she is upset with you for not telling her earlier, not letting her support your journey. With love comes anger and hurt and sometimes regret, that is life I'm afraid. Life should be celebrated in all its messy glory. Because it is glorious.

Finally, find a man that you love with all your heart, Pandora. A good man, yes; a kind man, maybe like your father, a practical man. But above all, find a man who makes your heart sing when he walks into a room, who makes you feel, who sets your soul on fire. Do not settle for anything less.

Oscar Wilde once said, 'We are all in the gutter, but some of us are looking at the stars.' Reach for the stars, my darling, in all things, most especially in love.

Finally, be happy. Savour every day on this wonderful earth, now more than ever. And know that I carry you and Boolie with me, always. I love you now and I will love you forever. Remember that.

All my love,

Mum xxx

When I walk back downstairs after reading Mum's letter several times, my eyes still blurred with tears, Jules is in the hallway, putting on her cycling helmet.

'You've just missed Bird and Iris,' she says, her voice tight, then looks at me carefully. 'They've headed off in the car. You OK?'

'Not really. I just miss her so goddamn much, Boolie. It's not fair.'

Jules looks a little confused. 'Iris?'

'No, Mum.' I start crying again.

'Come here, sis.' She pulls me into her arms and hugs me tight, rubbing my back with both her hands. 'Look, I'm sorry for sending Olivier those letters. You're right, I shouldn't have interfered.'

'No! I'm the one who should be sorry. Olivier wouldn't be back in Iris's life if it wasn't for you.' I pull away and look at her, wiping my eyes and taking a few deep breaths before saying, 'I should have told you about the test. Mum wrote me letters, you know, to help me through everything. They're amazing.' I explain a little about Ruth and their friendship. 'Would you like to read them?'

Jules's eyes light up. 'Are you sure?'

I nod. 'No more secrets. I don't think she'd mind.'

'Not much she can do about it now if she does.'

'Jules!'

'Sorry, sorry. Bad joke. Are they very sad?'

'No, not really. But it does make me miss her all over again. She was pretty special, wasn't she?'

Jules nods. She blinks rapidly and I can tell that, like me, she still misses Mum deeply.

'Hey, at least we have each other,' I say. 'And let's not fight again, it's too exhausting.' I smile at her gently and bump her with my shoulder. 'Friends?'

'Forever.' She throws her arms around me and we give each other an almighty hug.

Chapter 27

'What do you think, Bird? These shoes or another pair?' I stare at my reflection in the full-length mirror. There's something not quite right. The red Maisie Hersh dress looks perfect, I'm happy with the black leather jacket, and my silver and grey 70s clutch bag, but the slate-grey satin peep-toes are causing me grief. I think they may be throwing my outfit off, but I can't figure out which shoes to wear instead, classic black Prada courts or red satin kitten heels. The black sandals I'd intended to wear have a heel tip missing and I only noticed it this evening; most annoying.

She frowns. 'The Prada courts, my darling.' I try them and she's absolutely right, they're perfect.

The doorbell rings in the hall. It must be Declan – bang on time as usual.

'Have a lovely time, darling.' Bird kisses her fingers and blows them at me. 'You look beautiful.'

'Thanks for babysitting,' I say, popping my powder and lipstick into my bag.

'Jules will be doing the bedtime stories. She's much better at voices than I am, has Iris spoiled with her amateur dramatics.'

I laugh and as soon as she's gone, I rush downstairs, swing open the door and smile apologetically at Declan, who is checking his emails on his iPhone.

'Sorry, sorry,' I say. 'I got caught up for a second.'

Declan smiles at me and slides his phone into the pocket of

his dinner jacket. 'Don't worry, I'm used to hanging around on the doorstep. It always takes you Schusters ages to open the door. You always seem to bump into someone or get distracted on the way; it's like Dublin Airport in your house. You ready?'

'I'm all yours.'

He leans down and kisses me on the cheek. 'I'm very glad to hear it. You look amazing, by the way. I've never seen you in red before. Suits you.'

At that second I'm reminded of Olivier's 'I love you in red', but I push him out of my mind and beam at Declan. 'Thanks.'

'We could walk from here, but I'll save your feet,' he says, leading me towards his car.

As we pull out of the drive, I wonder about the venue. Declan has refused to tell me where the dinner is being held; he's very excited about the whole 'surprise' element. All I know is that it's a pop-up restaurant somewhere very unusual, which could mean anything – a graveyard, or the local Cuala GAA pitch, but realistically probably just someone's garden.

He was right, it's very near. After a three-minute drive he parks the car on Green Road and politely offers me his hand to help me step out. Then he takes a flowery silk scarf from his pocket. It smells of musky perfume.

'Yours?' I ask, archly.

'Mum's,' he says with a smile. Then he adds, 'Close your eyes.'

'Why?'

'I'm going to blindfold you.'

I chuckle. 'You kinky devil. Very *Fifty Shades of Grey*.'

His face is a picture. 'Pandora!'

I grin. 'I know, I know, you want the venue to be a surprise. OK, I'll play along, but if I trip in my heels I'll blame you.'

He locks the car, and then places the silk across my eyes.

'Ready?' he asks.

'Yes!'

He spins me round several times, making me feel very unsteady on my feet. 'Declan, is this strictly necessary?' I ask him, mid unsteady pirouette.

He just chuckles. He takes my arm firmly and starts to guide me along the pavement.

'Declan, I can tell we're going downhill, towards the sea, so that spinning lark was a complete waste of time.'

'Stop being such a spoilsport. Right, nearly here.'

The tang of sea salt hits my nostrils and I can hear waves lapping against the shoreline. We stop for a second and I hear the sound of a car passing – we're crossing Harbour Road.

'Careful now,' he says, 'this bit is steeper.'

The toe of my court shoe catches on an uneven piece of ground and I stumble a little. I grab at the scarf with my free hand.

'Can I take this off now, Declan? I'm going to break my ankle and I think I know where we are.'

'Almost there. Just a couple more steps.'

Suddenly I feel a fresh breeze on my face and hear conversation and hearty laughter.

Then a familiar voice booms, 'Declan, what on earth have you done to poor old Pandora? Do take off that silly headscarf. I would never have given it to you earlier if I'd known what you wanted it for. She's going to fall into the harbour if you're not careful.'

Declan just laughs and says, 'Hi, Mum, thanks for spoiling my surprise.' As soon as he unties the scarf I see Hester Bloomfield standing in front of me in a voluminous yellow jacket which must surely be her husband's and makes her look like Laa-Laa from the *Teletubbies*. There's a large green and white striped sailing bag at her feet. We're on the old stone pier at Dalkey Harbour, just in front of Dalkey Island. It's a beautiful evening and the sun's still shining down, making the waves glitter. There's a cluster of men and women behind Hester, all with red, yellow or navy sailing jackets over their finery, reminding me of the pictures I've seen of the *Titanic* in one of Iris's information books – women in ball dresses being lowered into lifeboats – which sends a faint shiver down my spine.

'I'm so delighted you could make it, Pandora,' Hester says, beaming at me. 'It's going to be such a fun evening. I hope you have good sea legs.'

She points down at a snake of open wooden boats. The first one is loading up at the steps, and, as I watch, a woman slips on some slimy green seaweed and has to be helped to her feet again. Luckily her dress is black and there are no seaweed stains when she's righted.

'Here you are.' Hester reaches into the bag, pulls out two more yellow jackets, and passes one to me and one to Declan. Mine smells a little musty, but I put it on regardless.

'Luckily it's a calm night, so we should stay quite dry,' Hester says. 'The plan is to have dinner on the island and then to finish the evening with dancing in the Cliff Castle just down the road. The boats aren't insured to cross Dalkey Sound after sunset, hence the early start to the evening. Dinner at seven, boats leave to drop us back to the mainland at nine sharp. All a bit of a rush but it'll be worth it to eat on the island, don't you think?'

'Where's Douglas?' I ask, looking around. Douglas is Declan's dad, a nice man, quiet and kind. I've only met him a couple of times, but he's always been very sweet to me.

Hester waves her hand airily. 'He went on ahead. One of the boats offered to take him dolphin-spotting before dropping him off. There's a pod that live just off the island, apparently they pop up all the time. You know Douglas, anything for a good story to tell over dinner.'

Declan gives a laugh. 'That would be Dad all right.' He turns to me. 'You all set for a boat trip?'

I nod a little nervously. Boats aren't really my thing, especially these tippy-looking, old-fashioned things, but I don't want to disappoint him.

The boat ride is just as nerve-wracking as I'd imagined, but I try not to think about the bobbing movement and the slight shudder from the wooden hull as the choppy waves hit it. Calm, Hester said? I'd hate to see the water on a stormy day. There's a large marquee on the crest of the island, with jaunty coloured lights strung along its walls – our pop-up restaurant, I presume – and I focus on this instead, and on the ant-sized people milling around outside it.

After what seems like forever, but is probably only about ten minutes, we arrive at the island's small whitewashed harbour and Declan insists on doing a He-Man act, carrying me out of the boat and onto dry land, which makes me giggle hysterically. I feel like kicking my legs and yelling 'Helll-ppp, hell-ppp, I'm being kidnapped,' like Penelope Pitstop, but I'm too afraid of losing a shoe. Besides, I'm not sure our fellow diners – mostly surgeons and doctors from the hospital – would appreciate my attempt at humour.

'You youngsters go on ahead,' Hester says, shooing us with her hands. 'I'll potter along behind you with the old folk.'

We smile at her, and then follow the crowd slowly up the rough steps and the grassy incline towards the tent, the strains of classical music getting louder and louder as we draw nearer.

Declan pats my hand, firmly clutching his upper arm. 'I'm so glad you're here, Pandora. It's going to be a very special evening.' He stops for a second, twists around and gives me an intense, loaded look.

I was right; Declan's going to propose again, tonight. My stomach squirms nervously. I was all set to accept only hours ago, but now I'm not so sure; the old doubts are back and my feelings on the whole wedding subject seem to be vacillating wildly by the minute. Olivier's sudden reappearance in my life isn't exactly helping matters. My mind is as clear as a muddy pond.

I wonder how Declan intends to pop the question. He's hardly Mr Spontaneous, so he's certainly got it all carefully planned out. Something suddenly occurs to me. Dear God, please tell me he's not going to do it in front of everyone, like you see in Hollywood movies? Some poor sap falling to his knees in a busy Italian restaurant – it always seems to be Italian for some reason – in front of his beloved, and when she says yes (and it's usually a yes) the fellow diners jumping to their feet and clapping and shouting, 'Champagne on me for the happy couple.' Do things like that happen in real life? I hope not! I'd be mortified. Surely Declan's not the type. He's far too traditional, for a start. Besides, his parents are here, and I don't think Hester would approve of a big public display of affection like that. No, I think I'm safe there.

Dinner is a rather sedate affair. I'm not sure what I expected – that one of the eminent male physicians (and they are largely male) would suddenly grab the microphone and start belting out a camp version of a Shirley Bassey song? The food is decent but nothing startling: a crab starter, followed by grilled salmon and strawberry roulade – all very safe. The after-dinner speeches are the usual 'Thanks for coming, please give all your money to the hospital' type thing, with a stern warning not to miss the last boat back, unless you want to be stranded.

Hester manages the table's conversation like an old pro, throwing out clever openers to suit every taste. Nothing too contentious to start with: themes that everyone at the table can get their teeth into – the wisdom of local planning decisions, what international authors we'd all like to see at the Monkstown Book Festival; and a little more contentious – plans for the future of the hospital, which is the current topic under debate. I'm afraid she's lost me on that one.

'Pandora?' Declan asks softly as his dad and one of the other doctors pontificate on the wisdom of moving the hospital out of Dublin city and into the suburbs.

'Yes.'

'How about a trip around the island?'

'Now? Don't we have to go back to the mainland soon?' I say, trying to put him off a little and cursing myself for not slipping my flat fold-up shoes into my handbag. I'm not keen on wrecking my Pradas tramping around on the scutty island grass. 'It's almost nine.'

He smiles at me. 'We won't get stranded, I promise. I have something arranged. Don't look so worried, it doesn't involve any extra walking.'

'In that case, absolutely.' I'll be glad to get away from the table, to be honest.

'Excuse us, everyone,' Declan says to the table, getting to his feet. 'We're just going to get some air. We'll see you all back at the Cliff Castle later.'

'Have fun, darlings.' Hester waves her fingers at both of us, her eyes sparkling. I was right; she does know something.

'I didn't know you could . . . um . . . drive a boat,' I say loudly over the growl of the engine. 'Or is there some sort of special word for it?'

I cling to Declan's back like a bushbaby as we power through the waves. I'm sitting behind him on a padded seat in an orange open-topped boat, and with the wind blowing in my hair it's a bit like being on a motorbike splashing through an enormous salty puddle. I have baggy yellow oilskins on my legs to match the sailing jacket and, underneath, my dress is ruched up around my waist like a giant nappy. I must look a sight but there's a nip in the air and I'm nice and toasty. I've told myself to stop worrying about the Maisie Hersh getting creased and to enjoy the ride; this boat seems to be designed for cutting through the waves.

Declan laughs. 'For a yacht or a dinghy it's helm. For this one, a RIB, it's drive.'

'A RIB?'

'Rigid Inflatable Boat. This one is Dad's baby.' He leans over and slaps the rubbery side of the boat affectionately.

'So he wasn't dolphin-spotting earlier?'

'No. He was collecting this from Dun Laoghaire and driving it over to the island's harbour.'

'That was decent of him. It must be quite a long way by sea.'

'Any excuse. He loves being out on the water. So, ready to hang on? We're going to the far side of the island to check out the seal colony before the light fades. We'll have to speed up a bit.'

'Go for it.' I wrap my arms tighter around Declan's wide back and give a little squeal as the boat accelerates. It's bouncy, the boat rising and falling over the waves like a rollercoaster, but I'm starting to enjoy myself. It's certainly different. We pass the end of the island and Declan points at the shoreline.

'There's the colony over there,' he says. 'You'll be able to smell them in a minute.'

He slows down a little and as we coast past I spot the sleek grey bodies lying on the rocks, some looking at us with interest. Their eyes are dark and broody, almost human, and I instantly think of the Selkie stories that Mum used to tell us, of women who are half human, half seal. My nose twitches, bringing me back to the present. Declan's right, the air reeks of fishy sea-animal musk.

We potter along for a few minutes until Declan stalls the engine and twists around. 'I'm just going to drop the anchor.'

'Do you need help?'

'Stay where you are. You might break a nail.' He chuckles away to himself. He has a point; I wouldn't have a clue what to do, but his sexist comment riles me a little. I'm not a 'nail' kind of girl, he knows that.

Oblivious, he throws his leg over the seat with the ease of someone who's grown up in boats, makes his way towards the pointy front, picks up an anchor and drops it over the side. The heavy metal chain whooshes over the rubber and when it finally stops Declan manoeuvres the boat backwards and forwards a little to make sure that the anchor has taken, then rejoins me on the seat, this time facing me.

He has that intense look in his eyes again, so I try to lighten the atmosphere by waving my hand at the water. 'The dolphins must be asleep.'

'Give them time.' Then he stares at me once more. I hold his gaze for a second, and then look away. I can still feel his eyes on me, but he's not saying a word.

'It's a lovely evening,' I say, eager to break the silence and to stop him staring at me like that; it's unnerving. 'They were lucky with the weather. With Irish summers the way they are, it could have been a washout.'

'True. And you wouldn't have had the chance to wear that lovely red dress, then. Have I told you how beautiful you look tonight?'

'Yes. Several times.'

'Pandora, can I ask you something?'

My stomach fills with butterflies and I can feel blood rush to my cheeks. I flash him a smile. 'Of course.'

'How do you feel now? About the test, I mean. Has it sunk in yet?' he asks, catching me out.

'Relieved. Also a bit worried about Jules, I suppose. But for some reason I have a good feeling about it. I know this might sound stupid, but I think Mum's watching out for both of us, wherever she is. Like our very own guardian angel.'

'That's nice. And I'm sure you're right. OK, I have another

question.' He pulls himself up and I sit up a little myself, bracing myself for his proposal, trying to concentrate on looking happy and pleased.

'Are you still in love with Olivier?' he asks.

'Olivier?' I repeat, stalling for time. Just hearing his name makes the hairs stand up on the back of my neck. Even if I do have feelings for Olivier, he certainly isn't interested in me, not that way. He made that very clear when he encouraged me to say yes to Declan.

And last weekend, just after Olivier had left for the airport, I'd asked Declan what the two of them were talking about all afternoon.

'Work,' Declan had said simply. 'And what a great mother you were. And Iris. He's a really interesting guy to talk to. I guess in a strange sort of way he was giving me his blessing to be Iris's stepdad.'

'Is that what he said?' I'd demanded, desperate to know everything.

'In so many words, yes. He said Iris was lucky to have me in her life and that he hoped we'd invite him to our wedding.'

For some reason this had irritated me and upset me in equal measures. Olivier had only been in Dublin a wet weekend and already he had everyone twisted around his little finger, even Bird and Declan. How dare Olivier mention a wedding and how dare Declan presume that I was going to say yes? I'd been out of sorts for hours over it, until Iris had managed to distract me with a mammoth movie-and-popcorn session.

'Pandora? Say something.' Declan's face is very earnest.

'I will always love Olivier,' I say honestly, coming back into the moment. 'He's Iris's dad. The same way you will always love Jessica, I guess. But we've both moved on, we both have new lives.'

'Yes, we do.' Declan pats my hand. Funnily enough I wasn't

talking about *us*; I was talking about Olivier and me. But I know it would be churlish, not to mention unkind, to correct him. Anyway, he seems satisfied with my answer.

He takes my hand in his. 'Pandora, I want to spend the rest of my life with you.' He reaches into the pocket of his sailing jacket with his other hand and pulls out a small midnight-blue velvet box.

As I stare at the box my stomach turns somersaults.

He takes away his hand and carefully opens the lid.

'It's beautiful,' I whisper. A fabulous antique diamond ring twinkles at me, a simple setting – white gold with one large stone surrounded by about a dozen smaller ones.

'Told you I'd do it properly this time.' He swings his leg over the seat again, slowly this time, taking care not to drop the ring, crouches down on one knee and then, finally, says the words that I've been expecting all night: 'Pandora Schuster, will you marry me?'

My breath quickens and for a moment I can't say a thing. He looks up at me expectantly, his face full of hope. Right then in the corner of my eye I spot something moving in the waves. It's a dolphin, its back arching in the water. For a second I'm distracted, and then I concentrate on Declan again. I know what I *should* say, but it feels all wrong for some reason. Maybe I still need time.

His face falls, then starts to cloud over. I can't stand disappointing him, not after he's been so patient already and planned such a romantic proposal. I just can't.

'Declan, yes,' I hear myself say. 'Yes, of course I'll marry you.' But my voice sounds flat even to my ears.

He's quiet for a long moment, and then finally he sits back on his hunkers and zips the ring back into his pocket. 'This isn't right, Pandora. And I'm not going to accept your answer.'

'What?'

'I love you, with all my heart, I'd do anything for you, but I just don't think you feel the same way about me.'

'I do!' I protest, but he's not done yet.

'Pandora, I know you love me. But I don't think you love me enough. I think you're with me for the wrong reasons.'

'What are you talking about? That's not true.'

'I saw the way you looked at Olivier, Pandora. And you've never looked at me like that, not once.'

I open my mouth to protest but he gets in first. 'But this isn't about Olivier,' he says. 'This is about you, Pandora. You can't marry me because you think it's the right thing to do. It's not fair on either of us. I don't want you to wake up in five or ten years' time and decide that you've made a mistake. Or even worse, spend the rest of your life wondering if there is someone else out there for you, someone you might look at the way you look at Olivier, but sticking with me because you feel you should. We're a good fit, Pandora, we both know that, but it's not enough. Look at me.'

I've been staring down at the grey floor of the boat, so I lift my eyes.

'I love you,' he says earnestly. 'With all my heart. But I can't spend the rest of my life worrying that you're going to leave me. Do you understand?'

Words from Mum's letter ring in my ears – *find a man who sets your soul on fire* – and it's like a box has been opened. I look at this man, this good, kind, decent man, and I know that he's right. I love Declan but I can't marry him. As I give him a small nod I feel a rush of relief tinged with terror surge through my body. What am I doing? I don't want to be alone for the rest of my life.

As if sensing my thoughts, Declan holds both my hands in his. 'You'll be OK, Pandora, we both will. Trust me. And I'm not going anywhere. If you need me, I'll be there. I promise.'

I nod again, unable to talk because of the huge lump in my throat. I'd mapped out everything so carefully – I'd marry Declan and we'd live a happy, contented life together. What now?

Chapter 28

'Mum, Mum, I think I see Dad.' Iris grabs my arm and pulls me to my feet. We've been sitting on the hard plastic airport seats for so long that my bum is almost asleep. Olivier and Bibi's flight was delayed for over an hour and Iris is now completely wired, from excitement and the after-effects of a giant Mars bar that we devoured between the two of us, mainly out of boredom on my part. It's late, almost nine, but she's still hopping around like a Duracell bunny.

We walk quickly towards the metal barrier, Iris unfurling the paper banner she's been clutching in her hand. It reads 'Fáilte go Baile Átha Cliath' (Welcome to Dublin), with lots of Irish and French symbols surrounding the lettering – the Eiffel Tower, the Arc de Triomphe, the Ha'penny Bridge, the James Joyce Tower. It took her all week to make and she's very proud of her work. She makes me hold one end of it and she grips the other.

'Up higher, Mum,' she instructs, hoisting her own side towards her head.

'They won't be able to see your face, pet,' I say.

She lowers it a little, her eyes still fixed on the sliding Arrivals door.

Then she squeals and jumps up and down on the spot, waving with her free hand. 'It's Dad! Daddy, Daddy! Over here.'

Spotting her, Olivier gives Iris a side-splitting grin and

marches towards us, the brown leather bag flung over his shoulder bouncing with every step. He smiles warmly and winks at me, making my insides turn over.

'Hello, Dora. Good to see you.' Is it my imagination or does his gaze linger just a little too long on the red dress I'm wearing? It's not the Maisie Hersh, which is still at the dry cleaner's after last weekend's wrinkle-inducing boat trip and, besides, would be far too much for collecting anyone at the airport, even a stunningly handsome ex-boyfriend and his terrifying mother. It's another dress, a simple crimson wrap-around, teamed with my black leather jacket and zebra-print ballet pumps.

Olivier turns his attention to Iris. 'What a beautiful banner, Iris.' He rubs her head affectionately. 'You are so clever. A true artiste. Look, Bibi.'

And there she is, pulling a huge scarlet suitcase behind her, Bibi Huppert, looking almost exactly as I remember her – tiny, not even five foot, her hair still a rich dark brown and swept up in an Audrey Hepburn chignon, impossibly stylish white-framed sunglasses over her eyes. She's wearing a flowing sea-blue silk dress, a jaunty pink-checked cotton scarf wound around her neck. As always, I can't keep my eyes off her. She has this aura that sucks you in. We started out wary of each other all those years ago in Paris, but after a while became not quite friends, but friendly at least. Goodness knows what she thinks of me now.

She lifts her sunglasses and rests them on top of her head. 'Dora. So we meet again.' Her green eyes spark with fury. I gulp, withering a little inside. She is still utterly formidable.

'Bibi,' Olivier says, his voice sharp. 'Play nice.'

'For you, Olivier. Only for you.' Bibi walks around the barrier towards me, presses her hands down on my shoulders and kisses me almost violently on both cheeks. She smells citrusy and annoyingly fresh for someone who's just stepped off a plane.

'Bibi,' I say, a noticeable quiver in my voice. 'Thanks for coming over.'

She ignores me and looks at Iris instead, who's almost the same height as her. Then she smiles, the clouds lifting from her face.

'This must be my darling grandchild,' she says. 'Olivier's right, you look just like him. Uncanny.'

She cups Iris's chin in one of her hands for a second. 'Beautiful. Like a wild flower.'

Tears spring to her eyes and she sighs dramatically and waves her hand in front of her face.

'You must excuse me, Iris,' she says. 'I'm still getting used to the idea of being a grandmother. But it is wonderful. I am very, very happy to meet you, my dear. Now you must tell me about all the things you like. Drawing, yes? And Olivier tells me that you have a little rabbit?'

'Yes, Fluffy.'

'You can tell your grandmother as we walk to the car, Iris,' I say, anxious to start moving as the steady flow of passengers into the Arrivals hall is making it rather crowded and noisy. Besides, the sooner I drop this harridan at the hotel the better. Be civil, I tell myself. She *is* Iris's granny.

'Or would you prefer Bibi?' I ask the woman, anxious not to annoy her further.

She considers this for a moment, then looks at Iris. 'You can decide, Iris. What would you like to call me?'

'You don't really look like a granny,' Iris says, making Bibi chuckle with delight. 'And I call my other granny Bird, even though she's actually my great-granny. My granny's dead. Isn't that right, Mum?'

I nod. Bibi's eyes linger on mine for a second, before she pulls them away. I'm sure I spotted sympathy in them, but maybe it's just wishful thinking.

'Bibi it is, then.' Bibi squeezes Iris's hand. 'I was hoping you would say that. I don't feel old enough to be a grandmother.'

Olivier grins and looks at me. I give him my best attempt at an amused smile, and then I lead the way towards the exit. Olivier walks beside me, and Bibi and Iris follow us, the wheels on Bibi's case making a low rumbling noise behind her. As Iris chatters away happily about Fluffy and her summer camp to Bibi, I'm stuck for words. Olivier doesn't seem to have noticed his mum's icy stares at Arrivals, but maybe he's just being very male and trying to keep out of it. Now and then I glance at him, and he just smiles back at me easily, melting my heart every single time.

Up ahead, there's a queue to pay the parking fee and we join it. Iris, still holding Bibi's hand, jumps around a little, finding it hard to keep still.

'This is boring,' Iris says. 'Can we go on ahead, Mum? I know where the car is.'

'OK,' I say, but I must sound a little unsure because Bibi sniffs.

'I'll make sure my granddaughter gets there safely,' she says.

'Thanks,' I say. 'You go on too if you like, Olivier.'

'No, I will stay here. Keep you company.'

As soon as they are out of earshot Olivier says, 'I was so pleased to get your news, Dora, about the test. I didn't want to say anything in front of Iris. Thank you for texting me.' Am I imagining it or is there a slight edge to his voice? 'You must be very relieved, yes?' he adds. Now he sounds kinder, back to his old self.

'No kidding,' I say. 'I feel like someone's lifted a giant black cloud off my back. I only realized how stressed and worried I'd been afterwards.'

'It is a lot to carry alone.' He looks at me and for a moment our eyes lock until I glance away. 'And everything else? OK, yes?'

I presume he means Declan and I'm about to update him when there's a loud cough; it's my turn to pay and the man behind us in the queue is clearly impatient. I take out my ticket and feed it into the slot.

Walking away from the machine after I've paid, Olivier asks again, 'So, everything else is good?'

The moment has passed, and instead of giving him the full update I say, 'Everything's fine, thanks.' I'm tired and I know it's the lazy option but I don't really want to talk about Declan. I still feel guilty about the whole proposal thing and discussing it with Olivier of all people seems wrong. I've only spoken to Declan once since last weekend – I rang him to see if he was all right – and the conversation was a little stilted.

Olivier takes a second to say, 'Good,' but thankfully he leaves it at that.

'How was your flight?' I ask, guiding the conversation towards safer water.

He shrugs. 'Late but fine. It gave me and Bibi a chance to catch up. She was very nervous about meeting Iris. She spent all week trying on different outfits to make herself look more like a grandmother.'

I stare at him. 'Really?' I'm surprised. It's not like Bibi to be nervous about anything.

'Yes. In the end she decided just to be herself. As you can probably tell from her outfit.'

I smile at this. 'It's usually best, I find.'

He catches my eye. 'Yes. Hiding things from the people you love can hurt.'

I can feel my cheeks flare up.

'That was unkind,' he murmurs. 'Forgive me.'

'No, I deserve it. You've been very understanding about the whole thing.' I pause for a beat. 'I guess that's why Bibi isn't exactly thrilled to see me.'

He shakes his head, his lips doing that very French *pah* thing.

'It was a surprise, a big surprise, but she is happy to be here, Dora. Happy to have a grandchild.'

I look at him. 'Olivier! She practically ate me back there. I'm clearly not exactly her favourite person.'

'OK, I admit, she was angry for a few days. But she has calmed down. Now she just wants to get to know Iris. As I do.'

Calmed down? I'd hate to have seen her in full anger mode. It's only for a few days, I tell myself, and she's clearly besotted with Iris already.

'Thanks for being so decent about all this,' I say, feeling small and wishing with all my heart that I hadn't simply fled, that I'd had the strength to tell Olivier and Bibi the truth ten years ago.

'Do not worry about the past, Dora,' Olivier says, reading my mind. 'We will have a good weekend together, all four of us. Yes?'

My heart sinks. 'I'm really sorry, Olivier, but I have to work tomorrow afternoon. Bird and Lenka will manage in the morning, but Jules is away for the weekend with Jamie, and Saturday afternoons are always mad busy.'

He looks a little disappointed but it may just be wishful thinking. After all, why should he care, he's over to see Iris, not me.

'I understand,' he says. 'Having a shop is a bind, yes? Perhaps we could visit Sorrento House in the morning and then go for lunch in Shoestring? I know Bibi would like to see your house and also where you work.'

'That sounds perfect.' Bibi obviously hasn't changed a bit. Still as nosy as ever. Strangely I find this reassuring. At least she's consistent.

As we approach the road, Olivier puts his arm out in front of me, as if I were a child. 'Careful, Dora.'

I get this overpowering urge to grab it, pull him towards me, throw my arms around his neck . . .

'Dora?' His curious gaze breaks me out of my reverie. 'You all right? We can cross now.'

I follow him across the road wordlessly, not trusting myself to speak, telling myself firmly to snap out of it.

Chapter 29

The following morning Olivier and Bibi arrive a little later than planned, at eleven. I'd taken them straight back to their hotel last night as Bibi looked tired and Iris was having trouble keeping her eyes open.

'Till tomorrow,' Olivier had said in the reception, kissing me on both cheeks. Again I had that urge to leap into his arms, but I just said, 'Yes. *À demain*,' and made myself leave, quickly, before I did something that I'd regret.

'Sorry we're late,' Olivier says, climbing out of the passenger seat of the taxi. 'I couldn't get Bibi out of bed this morning. We nearly missed breakfast.' He gives Bibi a hand out of the back of the car.

Bibi brushes down her floaty silver-grey silk dress and snorts. 'It was you who insisted on breakfast, Olivier. I would have been happy with a coffee. I know you love the Irish breakfast but not everyone can eat half a cow before lunch, darling boy. Now where is my beautiful grandchild?' She spots Iris running down the path. 'I have more presents for you, Iris. From Paris.' She lifts a Petit Bateau carrier bag in either hand.

'Bibi!' Iris dashes towards her, gives her a hug and then whips one of the bags out of Bibi's hands and starts rummaging in it.

'Iris!' I tell her. 'That's very rude. Wait until we get into the house,' but my darling daughter has already pulled out a pair of soft white cotton pyjamas with tiny pink flowers all over them. Bibi is just laughing.

Iris squeals, holds them against her and says, 'Thanks, Bibi!'

'You will look adorable in them,' Bibi says. 'And do you like make-up?'

Iris's eyes light up. 'Oh, yes!'

'Good,' Bibi says. 'Actually skincare, to be accurate, rather than make-up. Never too young to look after your complexion, little one. But your father is right. Let's go inside and you can empty out all the bags, yes?'

I'm about to protest that it was my suggestion, not Olivier's, but it sounds petty so I say nothing. Olivier catches my eye and gives me a gentle smile.

Iris grabs Bibi's hand and drags her into the house.

'Bird said to say sorry she missed you this morning,' I say to Bibi's back. 'She's covering the shop for me and I'm afraid Dad's also at work, but you'll meet her later and Dad tonight. He's offered to cook. I hope you'll both come over for dinner? Around seven?'

'Thank you,' Olivier says. 'If that's OK with Bibi, we'd love to. Bibi, are you listening? Dora has invited us over for dinner this evening.'

Bibi swings round and smiles at him. 'That sounds lovely. The more time I get to spend with Iris the better.'

'You're welcome,' I say, looking at her pointedly. She just ignores me and turns back to Iris.

Olivier has the good grace to wince this time. 'Sorry,' he says in a low voice. 'It's early, she'll snap out of it.'

'Don't worry,' I tell him magnanimously. 'I know she's not a morning person. I'll make a strong pot of coffee, might put her in a mellower mood.'

'Good idea.' He smiles at me, his eyes so warm, so tender, and once again my heart turns to mush. Oh, just stop it, I tell myself. He's only here for one more day. He has no interest in you, don't kid yourself.

I'm a little nervous about Bird and Bibi's first meeting, but it goes surprisingly smoothly. When we walk into Shoestring, Bird's at the desk, pricing stock. As we walk towards her, she lifts her head.

'Olivier, how lovely to see you again,' she trills. 'And this must be Bibi.'

'Yes,' Olivier says. 'Bibi, this is Bird, Iris's great-grandmother.'

'Bibi is tiny, just like you, Bird,' Iris pipes up.

'Perfectly formed, you mean?' Bird gives Iris a mock frown.

Iris giggles.

'Delighted to meet you, Bird,' Bibi says, stepping forward and kissing Bird on both cheeks. 'What a wonderful name. Iris has told me all about you, of course. And is that Chanel? It's beautiful.' Bibi puts her palms out in admiration at Bird's favourite jacket.

Bird smiles. 'Yes. Vintage. We're thrilled to have you both here. Iris has been so excited all week.' Bird says something quickly in French that I can't quite make out. Then she adds, 'I must show you a fabulous hat that's just come in. It's rather dramatic, but I think you could pull it off.' She takes Bibi's arm and leads her away. The women lean towards each other, chatting away in French like old friends.

I watch them a little wistfully, wishing things between Bibi and me were as simple. I'd always thought she hated me, but according to Olivier, I was wrong. Even though I was terrified of her in Paris all those years ago, I admired her so much, still admire her, I suppose, despite her current frosty behaviour towards me. But Olivier has always been her life, so I don't blame her. If the shoe was on the other foot, and someone had betrayed Iris's trust, I know all my she-lion instincts would come fully into play.

Olivier smiles at me. 'That was easy. Kindred spirits, I think.'

I smile back. He's right. Bird and Bibi make the perfect match.

After lunch – which is quite rightly focused on Bibi getting to know Iris a little better, and Bibi telling Iris all about Olivier as a little boy (unsurprisingly, he was dreamy and artistic and full of mischief), leaving Olivier and me to chat about Shoestring, his shop in Paris and fashion in general – Bird offers to give Olivier and Bibi a guided walking tour of Monkstown and Dun Laoghaire. She's something of a local history expert and Bibi is all for it. Iris isn't keen until Bird promises her a Teddy's ice cream.

Before they all leave, Olivier pulls me aside for a moment. 'I must talk to you, Dora, alone. Can we find some time this evening perhaps?'

My pulse quickens and my cheeks feel hot. Does he mean . . .? Surely not . . . I stare at him.

He must see the light in my eyes, the sheer longing, because he instantly stamps it out. 'About Iris and the future,' he says simply.

'Of course,' I murmur, feeling deflated and utterly stupid. 'Iris. Yes, I see.'

He looks at me quizzically for a second before I quickly add, 'Have a lovely afternoon. I'd better get back to work. You know how it is. Busy, busy.' I turn away from him, walk swiftly back towards the till and bury my head in the drawer underneath the desk.

Which is where I once again find myself half an hour later, this time pinned there by Sissy Arbuckle, her orange breasts hanging out of a staggeringly low-cut top. How she manages to front a glossy television show looking like a lap dancer, I'll never know. She reeks of chemicals too – she must have just stepped out of a fake tanning booth.

'You can't possibly sell my Gucci belt for fifty euro,' she's squealing at me. 'It's scandalous.'

I don't have the energy for this. I've been decent enough to look through her latest sell-in items, even though we have a policy of not taking in clients' stock at the weekends as it's too busy.

'Sissy, very few of our customers have a size six waist,' I say patiently. 'And I thought you said you got it free at a fashion show.'

She pulls herself up huffily. 'Yes, well, I did. But if I'll only get fifty euro for it I think I'll take it back. Give it to someone as a birthday present or something.' She grabs it out of my hands.

'You do that,' I murmur.

'Pandora?' I hear a voice to my left. I look over.

'Alex!' I come out from behind the till and give her a warm hug, delighted to see her. 'What are you doing here? Where's Markham?' I look around.

'He's outside in the jeep, reading the paper. I'm on my own.' She smiles, clearly thrilled with herself.

Sissy gives a loud cough. 'I don't think we've quite finished, Pandora.'

'Sissy,' I say. 'This is a dear friend of mind, Alex. She doesn't get up to Dublin very often and I'd really like to catch up with her, I'm sure you understand. Would you like to call back later?'

At first Sissy looks appalled. She's clearly not used to being usurped by fresh-faced women wearing flip-flops, faded denims and simple white T-shirts. But then she surprises me.

'Friends *are* important,' Sissy says. 'Very important. Besides, I'm already late for a nail appointment. I'll be back in an hour.'

'Was that the girl from *Red Carpet*?' Alex asks as we watch Sissy totter out the door in her kitten heels.

'Yep,' I say.

'She seems nice.'

I smile at Alex. 'You know something, she's not the worst.

286

And she's pretty loyal to us. Do you have time to join me for a coffee?' I wave my hand at the café. 'I can get Lenka to mind the floor. Only if it suits. Markham too, if he likes.'

'I'd love that. But if it's OK, I'll leave him where he is. I need to start doing things on my own.'

'I understand.' A few minutes later we're settled at a table in the café. I reach over and gently nudge Alex's hand with one of mine.

'It's so good to see you,' I say. 'And you look fantastic.' And she does – her hair is falling down her back in a blonde cascade, her skin is pink and slightly flushed, and her eyes are twinkling.

'I feel great.' She beams at me. 'Things are so much better now. Thanks to you.'

'I did nothing, honestly.'

'You gave me the kick start I needed to get my life in order. That's not nothing. Markie's back running the pet shop and one of our old part-timers is helping out at the weekends. I'm doing two mornings a week, starting slowly, and I'm loving it. Some days are harder than others, but I'm managing. My new counsellor says I'm coping really well. She's really helping too.'

'That's brilliant. I'm so happy for you, Alex, truly.'

Alex smiles again. 'Thanks. Is Jules here? I wanted to thank her too.'

'She's actually away. Jamie whisked her off for the weekend to the Merrion Hotel.'

'Very swish.'

'No kidding. She wanted to surprise him at dinner so she's taken the Maisie Hersh with her. I hope it's OK with everyone. It was a last-minute decision and we didn't have time to tell you and Arietty or to have a handover dinner or anything.'

'Of course it's OK. And I'm sure Arietty won't mind. But once everyone has worn it, there will be another dress, won't there? I love our Shoestring dinners. And maybe I'll have something to wear the new dress to very soon. Markie has been talking about having another dinner party, a bigger one this time, for friends and family. To celebrate, well, everything really. You'll all be invited.'

'Sounds fun. And I know Jules has her eye on another dress, so yes, the Shoestring Club will definitely live on. It came in only last week and it's stunning – peacock blue with gold embroidery . . .'

Chapter 30

That evening, my stomach lurches when I pull into the drive and spot who's sitting on a rug under the oak tree, reading. Bibi. As I lock the car I wonder can I legitimately sneak past her and dash into the house, and if she asks about it later, claim that I didn't see her? But too late, her head is up and she's beckoning me over. 'Dora! Come here.'

I swear under my breath, but force myself to smile as I walk towards her. She pats the rug beside her and I sit down. My body is tense, waiting for her finally to have a proper, private go at me.

'Don't look so frightened, Dora,' she says, smiling archly. 'I don't bite.'

'Since when?'

She just laughs. 'Let us get a few things straight. You are the mother of my grandchild. Yes, the news was rather unexpected, but she is a charming girl and a real credit to you.'

'Thank you,' I say a little tersely.

'So, we must learn to get on, yes? For Iris's sake and Olivier's sake.' Her eyes narrow. 'But don't think that I haven't noticed.'

'Noticed what?'

'You always had this way of looking at him, with those pretty big eyes of yours, and it is still there. You still have feelings for him, am I right?'

My cheeks burn with humiliation. It is that obvious? Bibi has always been direct, but why did she have to ask me that? I wish the ground would just swallow me up. I open my mouth to protest but she cuts me off. 'Dora, when you ran away from Paris you almost destroyed him. He didn't know what to think. Had he done something wrong, had you met someone else? Was your whole relationship a great big lie, were you stringing him along the whole time?' She shakes her head and *pah*s.

I open my mouth to protest again but she puts her hand in the air.

'Let me finish,' she says. 'You also left without a word to me. I considered us friends. I enjoyed our conversations, Dora. You are a smart girl and you are not afraid to speak your mind.'

I press my lips together, tight, trying not to cry. Bibi Huppert, the wonderful, charismatic Bibi, considered me her friend. How had I not seen that?

'I understand that you were trying to protect Olivier,' she continues. 'That you considered him too young to be a father, but you were a coward. Your actions were an insult to my son and also an insult to me. I cannot seem to get over that. I believe I will in the future, but it will take time.'

Now I am crying. She's right, totally right. I underestimated Olivier dreadfully.

I gulp. 'I'm so sorry. I *was* a coward and I behaved appallingly. I know that. But please—'

She puts her hand up again. 'In the meantime you have raised Iris impeccably. She is a joy to be around. And strong, like you. This is good. I understand you came to Paris to find Olivier, to tell him about Iris, but he turned you away. Then your sister sent him the beautiful letters written for Iris, telling her all about her wonderful father. That touched me, deeply.' She pauses, raising her chin a little. 'That at least we agree on. I also believe Olivier to be exceptional, as you know.'

I have never met anyone as genuinely devoted to another human being as Bibi Huppert is to her son. I give a small laugh. 'Only too well.'

She has the good grace to smile. 'Olivier would not allow me to read any of the contents, but he says they were heartfelt and chronicled your time in Paris together and your love for him.'

I nod. 'Yes. Please believe me, I did love him, with all my heart. I was afraid, I didn't know what to do, I didn't want to ruin his future. So, yes, I ran.'

'I believe you did love him and I understand why you left. But I want you to make a promise to me. That you will never meddle with my son's affections again. I believe you are engaged now, yes?'

'Actually,' I stall for a second. Bibi is staring at me, imperiously. It would be easier to say yes, to buy myself some time. But there have been enough lies, enough secrets.

'No,' I say instead. 'I broke up with Declan last weekend.'

Despite a small gasp she manages to hide her obvious surprise well. After a weighty pause she says, 'May I ask why?'

'No, you may not,' I say sharply.

She gives a tiny smile. 'Ha! Very good. I have always liked *you*, Dora. I do not like what you did to my son, but we all make mistakes. But if you hurt him again I will kill you, do you understand?' Her steely eyes bore into mine.

'It's not like that. He doesn't have any feelings for me, Bibi. Believe me.'

She gives a loud *pah*. 'Dora Schuster, for a smart girl you are very stupid at times. Tell him. Tell him about Declan. See what happens.'

'I don't think I can.'

'Then you are not the girl I thought you were.' She picks up her book again and opens it in her lap. 'Go! You will find him in the kitchen. He is showing your father how to prepare Chicken with Forty Cloves of Garlic.' She waves her hands at me. 'Oh, don't just stand there, girl, life is short. Go!'

*

As I walk inside Sorrento House I shiver. Yes, it's cooler inside than out today, as it often is in the summer, but it's not just that. I try to think about what to say to Olivier, how to explain how I feel, but my mind is going blank. After speaking to Bibi there's a bubble of hope in my stomach, but I'm also terrified. What if he rejects me?

Then I think of Mum. Of my beautiful, kind, smart mum and how disappointed she'd be if I didn't swallow down my nerves and reach for the stars.

Be brave, Pandora, I tell myself. I take a deep breath and walk into the kitchen.

There he is, Olivier Huppert. Perched on the edge of the kitchen table, chatting away companionably to Dad, who's stirring a saucepan on the Aga. Iris is crouched over the table, drawing dresses. I just stand there, watching the simple family scene, allowing myself to feel happy for a second.

As if feeling my gaze, Olivier looks over and for a long second our eyes lock. My heart pounds in my chest and I know I'm the colour of a tomato but I don't care.

He smiles. 'Dora! At last.'

'How was work, love?' Dad asks me.

'Fine,' I answer, my eyes still locked on Olivier's face. There's something in the air, anticipation, and I'm not surprised when Olivier says, 'Would you excuse us for just one minute, Greg? There is something that I must give Dora,' and then bustles towards me, in a waft of garlic and orange aftershave.

Once I've followed Olivier into the hall, he rummages through his bag and pulls out a very large brown padded envelope.

He hands it over. 'These letters belong to you, Dora. Or, strictly speaking, Iris. I hope you don't mind but I added something.'

I nod silently, too overwhelmed to say anything. I sit down on the bottom of the stairs, and pull out the contents, remembering the story of Pandora's box once again and wishing with all my heart for Hope to flutter out.

No Hope; instead there are my letters, tied together with a plain white ribbon, and also a pale blue envelope sitting on a nest of white tissue paper. I pull out the letter inside, my heart racing.

Dear Iris,

I made this for your mum to celebrate our five-month anniversary, but she left Paris before I had the chance to give it to her. Your mum is very special to me and always will be.

I am so happy to have you as my daughter, Iris, but I am not so good with words, instead I have made you something. I hope you like it.

All my love,
Dad

Feeling rather emotional, I place the letter on the step beside me and carefully peel back the tissue paper. Inside there's a bag made from Olivier's favourite fabric, the light blue cotton with the tiny abstract flowers. He's embroidered hundreds of tiny red silk hearts all over the surface, bursting from the bottom corner of the bag and moving upwards like an exploding firework. I run my fingers over the hearts, so lost in my own little world that I've almost forgotten Olivier is right beside me, leaning over the banisters, watching.

He startles me when he says, 'It's the shirt I was wearing when I first met you, Dora. The bag is for Iris. Your present is underneath.'

'She'll love it,' I say, desperately trying not to break into tears. 'It's exquisite.'

'Thank you.' He's still looking at me intently.

I lift out the bag and stare at the hand-painted silk scarf

underneath. The pattern looks familiar, splashes of red poppies against a lush green background. I remove it from the tissue carefully and shake it out. It's not a scarf; it's a dress – the most stunning yet simple dress I've ever seen, with a low round neck, tiny round buttons running down the front covered in the same silk, perfectly executed cap sleeves, and clever waist darts. It looks blissfully easy to wear, yet luxurious at the same time. I look for the label but there isn't one, instead there's a small hand-stitched heart with the number five inside it. Five for our five precious months together.

'Oh, Olivier,' I whisper, completely overcome, my eyes bleary. I rub them with my knuckles. 'The pattern, it looks so familiar . . .'

'It's one of Bibi's paintings.'

'Of course! The one that used to hang above the fireplace. I loved that painting.'

He smiles. 'It's still there. Maybe you can visit, see it again some time.'

'I'd love that. I'll keep the dress safe for Iris when she's older.'

'I made it for you, Dora,' he says. 'Take it, please.'

'OK, but I'll show it to her when I give her the letters. Our story won't be complete without the dress. At some stage I will have to explain to Iris why I left Paris, left you. But not now.'

He tilts his head. 'When will you give her the letters?'

'Maybe on her eighteenth birthday. If that's all right with you. Along with all my other mementos of our time in Paris. As well as the letters there are old photos, postcards you sent me, all kinds of things. I'm keeping it all safe in a shoebox.'

He smiles. 'It sounds like a wonderful gift. A box of special memories, yes? But you must promise me to wear the dress, Dora, I made it especially for *you*. And we do need to talk about Iris, and about what's going to happen.' He nods down at the stairs. 'May I join you?'

'We can go into the living room,' I suggest.

'No, I like the stairs.'

I shift up a few steps and he sits down so close to me that I swear I can feel his body heat radiating off him.

'So, the future,' he says, twisting and leaning his back against the wall. 'I would like to spend a weekend in Dublin every month if that is all right with you.'

'Yes,' I say. 'Absolutely.' Come on, Pandora, I will myself. Tell him about Declan. Have courage.

'Down the line, if I can persuade some of the Dublin shops to stock my menswear, maybe longer.' He shrugs. 'Who knows? Perhaps Iris could come to Paris and work in my shop when she is in college, yes? Like you did, Dora. It would be excellent for her French and I would love to have her. Bibi too.'

A tiny knot of jealousy twists in my stomach. I'd give anything to be that girl again, young, carefree, in love . . .

Olivier is staring at me. 'Are you all right, Dora? You look upset.'

'I was thinking about Paris,' I say truthfully. 'How much I miss it, the city and—' I swallow down the lump forming in my throat. 'And the time we spent together. And about what a bloody mess I've made of everything since then.' My eyes well up again and I wave my hand in front of my face, mortified. 'I'm sorry, ignore me. It was just so perfect – Paris, I mean – and you, I guess. I loved you so much, Olivier. I should never have run away like that, I should have known you wouldn't abandon me. I should have trusted you, what was I thinking—' I'm sobbing so much now that I have to break off. 'I'm so sorry,' I manage finally, before dropping my head to my knees and winding my arms around them, trying to shut out the world.

I can feel Olivier's hand resting on my back. 'Don't cry, Dora. It is all in the past. And what are you talking about? You have a wonderful shop, a fantastic daughter; you're getting married soon—'

I lift my head, tears splattering from my eyes. 'No, I'm not!'

Olivier looks confused. 'What about Declan?'

'We broke up last weekend.'

He snorts and shakes his head. 'When were you thinking of telling me exactly?'

'I didn't think you'd be interested.' I sniff and wipe my eyes with my knuckles, trying to compose myself a little.

'Really?' He's staring at me with such intensity that it's scary. 'First you *text* me your test results, now this. It's not like you to be so . . . so thoughtless. Dora, why did you break up with Declan? What's going on? Is there someone else?'

'Yes. There is someone else.'

He stares down at the hall tiles. 'Oh, Dora. Poor Declan, such a nice man. But I understand. Marriage is a big step. You must be sure . . .' He tails off and sighs. 'Chicken, I must get back to the chicken. ' He goes to get up but I put my hand on his knee.

It's now or never, I tell myself. 'It's *you*, Olivier,' I say urgently. 'I can't get you out of my mind, and it's driving me crazy. That's why I can't be with Declan. I'm still in love with you. Are you satisfied now?'

'Dora?' He looks at me, his eyes full of hope yet slightly wary. 'Do you understand what you are saying?'

'Yes! I love you. The truth is I've never stopped loving you. You make me feel alive, Olivier, and you make me laugh and oh, I don't know . . . I think we're supposed to be together. I know I've hurt you terribly but if you could find it in your heart to forgive me—'

'I have always carried you in my heart, Dora, always,' he says simply. 'You ruined me for other women, you and that smile of yours. When I heard about the test, about how I might lose you for a second time, it was almost too much to bear. But are you sure, Dora? This isn't just a whim?'

He wants me. After everything that has happened, after all the mistakes I've made, Olivier still wants me. In a heady rush, all the pain and heartache of the past ten years melt away. 'I've never been more sure of anything in my whole entire life,' I say. 'The moment I saw you on the doorstep I wanted you so badly that my heart almost leapt out of my chest. You set my soul on fire, Olivier. You're the one. The only one.'

He smiles, his eyes twinkling. 'You used to accuse me of being too flowery, Dora, remember? But you are a poet now, yes?'

I laugh and punch him on the arm. 'Stop teasing me.'

He puts both his fists up. 'You want a fight, Dora. Go on, I give you first punch.'

I slap them away. 'Be serious for a minute, Olivier. I'm trying to tell you how I feel about you. You're ruining our serious moment.'

He smiles again, his eyes warm and calm. 'But this is no surprise to me. I knew, Dora, I knew you still loved me. Underneath that serious new exterior I could see the old Dora simmering away, just waiting to jump out. It was in your eyes. I just hoped you'd have the courage to find yourself again and to come back to me. We are meant to be together, it is simple. But this time, no running away, understand? And no secrets. Swear to me?'

'I swear. And you're not running away either.' With that I throw my arms around him and pin him against the wall, our faces inches away from each other.

He laughs delightedly. 'Welcome back, crazy Dora. I've missed you.'

'There is one slight problem,' I say. 'You live in Paris, I live in Dublin.'

'So I will move. It is not a big deal. Or we can all split our time between the two cities – you, me and Iris. The travelling Hupperts.'

'Huppert-Schusters,' I put in.

He grins. 'The Huppert-Schusters. God love us. We sound

like characters from a children's book. But, you know, anything is possible, Dora, if you really want it to work.'

I think about this for a second. It's more than I dared dream of – me and Olivier, together, forever. Iris having her real dad around. A proper family. I feel so lucky, so blessed, so happy. Without any hesitation, I say, 'I do,' and then I kiss him.

Notes on BRCG1

The gene that is mentioned in the book, BRCG1, stands for Breast Cancer Gene 1. It's a human caretaker gene that produces a protein that repairs DNA. If this gene mutates or is damaged, DNA is not repaired properly and this can increase risk for cancers.

If this is the case, there is an 85% chance of breast cancer developing and a 50% chance of ovarian cancer.

The gene was discovered in 1995, and in the book, Kirsten Schuster died in 1998. However, for the sake of the plot, I have played with the dates somewhat. Also, in 'real life' Pandora would have been offered genetic counselling before being tested for the gene; however, the circumstances in this book are rather unusual.

For more information see www.cancer.ie or
www.breastcancercare.org.uk

If you are interested in finding out more about the BRCG1 gene, Emma Hannigan's memoir of her experience 'Battling and Slaying Cancer Six Times', *Talk to the Headscarf* (Hachette, 2011), is highly recommended.

Acknowledgements

My grateful thanks to the wonderful Ms Sarah Rastall, Consultant Surgeon (Breast Cancer) at the Shrewsbury and Telford Hospital. She kindly took time out of her busy schedule to read this book for accuracy. Any mistakes are entirely my own.

Thanks also to my agent, Peta Nightingale, for all her hard work on this book and to Natasha Harding and Trish Jackson at Pan Macmillan for their support.

Thanks must also go to my family: Mum, Dad, Kate, Emma, Richard. And my own gang at home – Ben, Sam, Amy and Jago.

To my dear friends Tanya, Nicky, Andrew, Liz and Carolyn; Noelita, the Wyvern gang, Frances, Nikki and Fiona; and to my wonderful pals in writing Martina Devlin, Clare Dowling, Martina Reilly, Marita Conlon McKenna, Judi Curtin, Niamh Greene, Sinead Moriarty, Monica McInerney and Vanessa O'Loughlin. My kiddie-lit friends also keep me sane – the gang in CBI, David Maybury, Tom Donegan and Oisin McGann.

David Adamson and Cormac Kinsella, my Pan Macmillan team in Ireland, work tirelessly to sell and promote my books; and huge thanks to all the booksellers who continue to support my books, especially the gang in Eason and Dubray.

Finally to you, the reader. This is book eleven and many of you have been loyal readers for over ten years now. I thank you – for allowing me to live a writing life.

Yours in books,
Sarah XXX

PS Do write to me – sarah@sarahwebb.ie – I love hearing from readers.

Or you can catch me on Facebook – www.facebook.com/sarahwebbwriter or Twitter @sarahwebbishere

If you have young teens or tweens in the house, check out my Ask Amy Green series – see www.askamygreen.com for details.

If you enjoyed *The Memory Box* then you can continue to read more about the Schuster sisters in *The Shoestring Club*. And find out what happened to Julia when the love of her life turned her down . . .

The Shoestring Club

Join The Shoestring Club

Wanted: Two girls to time-share a one-of-a-kind dark-pink silk chiffon dress.

Guaranteed to make you look and feel drop-dead gorgeous.

When the love of her life, Ed, announces his surprise engagement to her best friend, Julia Schuster is distraught but determined not to let them see how much she's hurting. She spies a remarkable dress in Shoestring, her sister's vintage clothes shop, and knows she'll only be able to stagger through the wedding day, showing everyone how over Ed she is, if her body is wrapped in its soft silk chiffon. Unfortunately it costs mega bucks and she's barely hanging on to her job as it is.

Arietty Pilgrim can't and won't attend her fiercely competitive school reunion unless she can arrive wearing exactly the same dress. But working as an elephant keeper in Dublin Zoo does not a millionaire make.

However, fate has a funny way of bringing people together. Just as Julia starts to flounder amidst family troubles, problem drinking and a broken heart, she meets Arietty and the two of them set up The Shoestring Club – time-sharing one extraordinary dress and beginning a life-altering friendship.

Prologue

In June I screamed for two days solid.

It all started on a quiet Sunday morning. I was standing behind the till at Shoestring, my sister Pandora's designer swap shop, flicking through a copy of i-D magazine and minding my own business, when Pandora handed me a cream envelope.

'This was in the postbox outside,' she said. 'Must have been delivered last night.'

I looked at the envelope suspiciously. Plush, expensive-looking, my name – *Julia Schuster* – carefully handwritten in sky-blue ink across the middle.

I relaxed a little. A final warning from my credit card company was unlikely to come in such smart packaging. Then I peered at it closely. The script looked familiar but I couldn't quite place it. Wish I had. I would have thrown the whole wretched thing in the bin unopened. Or burned it.

'Take it.' Pandora thrust the envelope into my hands. 'Some of us have work to do,' she added with a sniff and then walked off. I rolled my eyes behind her back. Pandora was in one of her moods and I'd spent most of the morning trying to avoid her.

Curious, I ripped open the envelope and pulled out the letter, which had been wrapped around an invitation card. I unfolded it and read the Dear Jules at the top. Only then did it come to me – of course – it was Lainey's neat, prissy handwriting. Bloody nerve. My stomach clenched at the mere thought of Lainey Anderson. But being terminally nosey, I had to read on.

Dear Jules,

I know we haven't spoken since the morning after the party and I'm still SO sorry about all that. I hope your head is OK. Those stitches must have hurt.

You're totally right, I should have told you about me and Ed beforehand. The night of his birthday-do was a rubbish time to announce it. But when you got back from New Zealand, Ed made me promise to keep quiet for a few weeks, said you needed time to process everything. I guess after that the right opportunity never came along and, to be honest, I was a bit scared of what you'd say. And the longer I left it, the harder it got.

I hated sneaking around behind your back, Jules, believe me. And I feel even worse now that you're so upset. But at least there was no one in the toilet to hear you screaming at me that night. I genuinely had no idea you'd take it so badly. You told me you were completely over Ed, that you had no idea what you'd ever seen in him.

OK, I understand how you must have felt, being the last person to know, and I swear the proposal came as a complete shock to me too – I genuinely had no idea he was going to fall on his knee like that, in front of everyone! But you know Ed, he loves a bit of drama. At least Kia was there to catch you when you fainted and take you to the hospital.

Please answer your mobile, Jules, I really need to talk to you. I rang the shop but Bird went all funny and refused to put you on the line, said you were distraught and that she'd shoot me with her air rifle if I went near the shop or ever tried contacting you again. (Does she actually own one by the way? Or any sort of gun? I wouldn't put it past her!)

I rang back loads of times and eventually managed to get Pandora who said you were shaken but as well as could be expected in the circumstances; that the scar on your head would

heal even if the scar on your heart would be there for all eternity.
(Everyone in your family's so melodramatic, Jules, but I do love
them for it!)

Look, I know you and Ed have oceans of history – I was the
one who picked up the pieces every time you guys argued. But
that was a long time ago, things change, people move on.

Anyway, I guess you need some space right now, but we've
been best friends for ever and I really want you there at the
wedding. And Ed feels the same way too. I know you're unlikely
to want to be a bridesmaid after everything that's happened, but
if you change your mind the offer's still there.

Please, please, please say you'll come! It won't be the same
without you. I'll try calling in to the shop again. I'm not giving
up, we've been friends for too long and I don't want to lose you.
Besides, who's going to help me find the perfect wedding dress?
My sisters will probably put me in some sort of hideous meringue.

Please forgive me! I miss you, Jules.
Love always,
Lainey XXX

There was a smiley face over the 'i' of her name and I stared at
it, practically growling. I pulled the thick cream invitation and
RSVP card out of the envelope and ran my fingers over the em-
bossed gold writing. Classy.

MR AND MRS NIGEL ANDERSON
REQUEST THE PLEASURE OF THE COMPANY OF

Julia Schuster + guest

AT THE MARRIAGE OF THEIR DAUGHTER
ELAINE MILDRED ANDERSON TO
EDMUND PATRICK POWERS

AT ST JUDE'S CHURCH, DALKEY

ON SATURDAY 27TH OCTOBER AT 2.00 P.M.

AND AFTERWARDS AT
THE ROYAL ST GEORGE YACHT CLUB,
DUN LAOGHAIRE

RSVP SEA VIEW, VICO ROAD, DALKEY

My eyes started to well up and I blinked the tears back furiously, grabbed a pen and scribbled across the RSVP card:

Never! I'd rather die. You have got to be kidding me, Lainey!

Then I ripped the invitation in half, which wasn't easy as the card was ultra thick, threw it on the floor and stamped on it. Lainey and Ed. My best friend and the love of my life – together, for ever. It was really happening.

And that's when I started screaming.